D0840025

6.00

CASINO SARATOGA

CASINO SARATOGA

A MIKE FLINT MURDER MYSTERY

BY R. AUSTIN HEALY

MARSHALL JONES COMPANY
Publishers Since 1902
Prescott, Arizona

Marshall Jones Company
Prescott, Arizona

© 2000, R. Austin Healy. All rights reserved
Library of Congress Card Catalog Number
00-104978
I.S.B.N. 0-8338-0239-9

PRINTED IN THE
UNITED STATES OF AMERICA

*This is a work of fiction. While the places are
generally real, any resemblance to actual people
or events is purely coincidental.*

Other Books In The Mike Flint Series
By R. Austin Healy

The Ninth Race, 1994
Sweetfeed, 1996

For my wife, Joan.
With love.

ABOUT THE AUTHOR:

R. AUSTIN HEALY *lives in Clifton Park, New York, with his wife, Joan. They have six grown children. Healy's two previous books in the Mike Flint detective series,* The Ninth Race *and* Sweetfeed, *are best-selling regional thrillers. He is currently at work on a movie script, based on all three Flint tales, as well as a fourth book in the series.*

CONTENTS

CASINO SARATOGA

PROLOGUE

It was the preacher, Walter T. Grant, who first raised his voice in opposition to gambling in Saratoga in 1951. A short, balding, thin, anxious man with owl-sized eyes that peered down at his congregation from behind thick, bifocal glasses, Grant felt he was coming to grips with a problem too long overlooked by politicians and law enforcement officials alike. Grant deemed gambling the worst sin of its kind because it stole money from those who could least afford it.

The stifling hot interior of Saratoga's All Assembly Church on this August Sunday morning was proving unbearable for the two hundred or so faithful parishioners. They sat uncomfortably to hear the sermon that Grant had picked to address the moral issue of gambling and what he called "its adverse effect on the principles of all Christianity."

Grant let go with both barrels, first pointing a wrinkled and bent arthritic forefinger at an imaginary church object. He followed that by the slow, soft, whispered voice that gradually built into a thundering monologue of patented phrases that sounded to some listeners like an overplayed record – one that had been spun once too often. The congregation listened, without showing a sign of irreverence, while Rev. Grant rambled on.

In a rear pew, seated with his two teenage sons, Tom, thirteen, and Leo, fourteen, local hotel owner Larry Wilson fought off a yawn and leaned forward, resting his elbows on the pew in front of him.

What was Grant really getting to, Wilson wondered. Hadn't he stood behind the ranting reverend at the pari-mutuel windows last August while Grant placed a twenty dollar bet on a nag that ran dead last? And later, wasn't he privy to Grant's tongue-lashing of the horse's owner, jockey, and trainer for such a poor performance? Could this be the same man of the cloth who personally conducted church raffles and Monte Carlo night, now telling everyone that gambling in Saratoga was a hardened vice taking the old town to rack 'n ruin?

"Christ said to give to the poor, not the track or the gaming houses," Grant admonished his sweltering audience. "Families come first, not horses and bookmakers. Can our city survive long in this atmosphere? Is your soul worth losing? The bloodsuckers at the gaming parlors don't care if the kids get fed, as long as they get theirs. Who lets them get away with it? You know who. Your elected officials. It's depraved power working against the good of the people. And I ask you, who's worse, the officials who let it happen, or the racketeers and gamblers who promote it?"

Grant glanced down at Tom Clare, his aging, yet quite active, Saratoga district attorney uncle, a man who was spearheading the fight against gambling. Clare looked up approvingly at his nephew.

The afternoon sun made its presence known on the church's south facing stained-glass windows, so that now the stone structure's interior was heating up to an unbearable degree. A few parishioners made a move toward the center aisle, to which Grant, pounding his fist on the podium, demanded that no one leave until his sermon was over. Grant's tirade might have gone on for another hour had it not been for the sudden and unmistakable thud of someone's head striking a pew which, for the first time since he started his tirade, forced Grant to pause to investigate the interruption.

One man stood up. "It's your Uncle Tom, Reverend Grant. He's passed out from the heat. Must have cut his head. Why, he's bleeding!"

Still muttering his sermon, Grant moved swiftly from the pulpit to his uncle's side and lifted his head in his shaking hands. "You'll be fine, Tom. All you need is some fresh air." Three men assisted Grant and they lifted Clare's two hundred pound, slumping body into their arms. Struggling to hold him, they sped him toward the large oak entrance doors. Once outside, they laid him on the church lawn, and Grant placed a pillow someone had handed him under his uncle's pale and lifeless-appearing head and neck. A steady line of parishioners squeezed their way out of the church, taking advantage of this incident to vacate the premises before Grant could call them back. Services for the day, as far as they were concerned, were over.

One lady came over and sprinkled water on Clare's forehead. Another fanned him with a church bulletin. Fortunately, the sun had dipped behind the church's west wall, and a long shadow covered the spot where he lay. After about five minutes, Grant thought he saw his aging uncle stir. A smile crossed Grant's ashen face, and with a relieved twinkle in his eyes, he looked up at those still standing around. But then Grant felt the soft neck he was supporting suddenly go cold against his right hand. Uncle Tom's head fell to one side. His eyes opened ever so slightly, then shut tight. Clare let out a long breath and then stopped breathing altogether.

"My God," screamed Grant. "I think Tom is dead."

At that very moment, a man slipped out of the Methodist Church's back door, entered a waiting limousine and watched the crowd on the church's front lawn from the window as the car crossed over Washington Street and headed south. It had been the first time in twenty years that mob hit man Jake Palermo had set foot inside a house of worship. This day he didn't come to pray. Palermo carefully rubbed the blood of Tom Clare off a shiny steel blade with a large white handkerchief and placed it back in its sheath next to his left breast.

"So how did it go?" asked the car's driver.

"The heat was deadly in there," said Palermo.

1. LAKE LONELY

A bone-chilling March wind made its way south out of Canada, riding high in the northern jet streams on a black, starless night. It crossed over the Adirondack Mountains of New York State where, with a sudden fierce velocity, it fell a few thousand feet until it virtually hugged the frozen high peaks of Mt. Marcy and Whiteface Mountain near Lake Placid. It eventually swept southeast and then directly south, so that its arctic cold grip froze everything in its path, curling around each bend and cove of Lake George, whose ice was already seven inches thick.

It blew further still through the quaint hamlet of Glens Falls, whipping and whistling around and about the great, stately white clapboard houses of the northern residential area. It continued along the slick, ice-covered Hudson River just west of town, frosting the ancient, tall, wide-paned windows of the ghostly, aged red-brick former mill buildings and then howling directly down Route 87 to

Saratoga. There, seasoned Saratogians, anticipating the coming frigid onslaught, were wisely
dug in for this annual inconvenience.

The cold was so numbing and penetrating
that John Stark of Saratoga's Whitehurst Thoroughbred Farm near Saratoga Lake found it
necessary to place small electric heaters near
the horse stalls where five thoroughbreds were
boarded. This measure was taken after Stark
had already covered each horse with a wool
blanket. It had been the third year in a row that
March had produced such maddening, sub-zero
temperatures. The icy wind, coupled with a full
snow cover over the region, added to the feeling of foreboding that accompanied the cold
siege. Roads, sidewalks, driveways, bike paths,
jogging trails, cross-country and alpine ski terrain were covered in the ice-encrusted crystal
blanket.

No one in Saratoga with an ounce of sense
would dare venture out in this colossal weather,
save for the most needed services. No one, that
is, except Albert Sacca, who was on a padded
wooden rocking chair in the confines of his ice
hut in the middle of Lake Lonely, ice fishing,
defying the elements. Let others less daring
remain within their heated dwellings. Not
Sacca. He was content to fish, in his thermal
underwear, two pairs of tight, woven wool pants,

a warm Pendleton shirt, a lambskin vest, triple-layered hooded coat, double insulated rubber boots and down-filled gloves with liners.

Sacca could brave anything winter could throw at him. He was quite content, dressed as warm as he was. The wind and the cold could whip around him all they wanted. Inside his small six-by-six wooden shanty on the lake, he was protected. The aches and pains of a man in his eighties, suffering from mild arthritic attacks, kidney problems and poor circulation, plagued Sacca, but even these afflictions could not keep him from ice fishing Lake Lonely, not even on the worst days or nights.

On this occasion, Sacca was using a new maneuver to catch fish he'd never tried before. He had tied three hooks to three lines and low-ered them ten or so feet through the small hole in the ice to the lake's murky, dark depths. Each hook had a different bait on it. One fish hook was covered with a small, round ball of hard-ened Vaseline; another with live bait, and the third, the one he figured would draw the lake's evasive pike and bass, with a combination of meat, tightly packed and wrapped with a strip of rotten bacon.

This done, Sacca rocked back on his chair and took a long sip of red wine from one of three bottles he had brought along for the long night's vigil. A burning oil lantern on a small wooden box by his side, gave off just enough light and heat to further add to Albert's relative comfort. Inside his coat pocket he had stuffed two salami on rye sandwiches, smothered with mustard. He could feel two Garcia Vega cigars touching his chest in another front coat pocket. These would be lit in celebration once he landed the evening's first fish. The second cigar, or "see-gar" as he pronounced it, was to be smoked when he tripled that number. It was a rewards game that he played with himself, and it subconsciously made him focus on the task at hand. Fishing, as far as Albert Sacca was concerned, was a sport with a serious side.

His vigil on Lake Lonely had few equals. Most other ice fishers were on Saratoga Lake proper, waiting, as most fishermen did, to land the elusive large pike. Albert wasn't just interested in pike. If he caught one, fine. If he didn't, fine,too. Lake Lonely was just that for Sacca, lonely and deserted at this time of year. And, that suited him fine.

On this bitter, unforgiving evening, about one hour into the wait, Sacca felt a slight tug on his line. "They're nibbling, just teasing me," he said. "Go on, I'm very patient. Do your nibbling. Sneak up on the bait and chew as you will. When I think you're ready to really bite,

I'll set the hooks and I'll catch you whether you are a bass, perch or pike."

Time was on Sacca side. His mind could drift like the winter's blowing snow to other things while he waited to land his fish. And of late, Sacca was prone to remembrances. Had he not come to this area in the 1930s when things were very different? Had he not seen the high life of Saratoga and the glittering, sparkling majesty of it all when the bustling casinos were going full tilt? Yes. Yes.

His was a checkered past. Recruited as a very young man into Don Tony Cira's crime family, unquestionably the criminal power base of the lower and upper Hudson Valley region, Sacca rose quickly within the ranks. He adapted to every task Cira gave him. Loan sharking. Numbers. Collecting from the bookies. Then, finally, larger assignments, eventually killing. When it looked most promising for Sacca, things suddenly took a turn for the worse.

He was busted three times in two years by special federal strike forces, served four years in Comstock, and later was indicted for racketeering, a charge on which he was acquitted because of a hung jury. Sacca was dropped from Cira's family by the mid-1940s, not physically fit for service. Yet he remained loyal to the Don, and loyal in his heart to the family that had supported him. In time, this devotion was again recognized and the Don reinstated Sacca, though not at full family status. It was a financial and ego-deflating blow, far less remuneration than he had become accustomed to, but he accepted it as a necessary evil.

When Don Cira died and Carmine Bocca succeeded him, Sacca, for reasons he never understood, fell out of favor with Bocca. He was still paid by the family, but his duties were reduced to minimal, worthless tasks. It was Bocca's way of saying that he was no longer needed. Then, just when he was at his lowest point within the family's ranks, a further damaging and absurd charge was planted on him resulting from a 1940s Saratoga summer jewelry heist. A prominent family was robbed of its ageless gems, including a particular diamond pendant set on a thin gold chain, which was valued in the thousands, but which carried an intrinsic value that could not be measured in dollars.

The robbery, one of the most brazen of its kind to take place in that Saratoga era, happened late one August evening at a Lake Lonely mansion, rented by the MacEntyre family from Connecticut. Ironically, during the big heist, the MacEntyre's were dining at Casino Saratoga. Sacca was not even in Saratoga at the time. He was in Canada. He remembered it well, because it was his first-ever visit north of the border. Had he been in Saratoga, things might have been different on that fateful night. There would have been no bungling, and the MacEntyre jewel heist would have been a smooth caper.

Sacca's hands shook as he recalled the incident, related to him days later by one of Don Cira's soldiers who was there. Sacca clearly remembered the trembling voice of Ron Belmonte from that distant day, sobbing the details of a robbery gone awry. How on that August evening he and two other family soldiers, Peter Gaspary and Tony "Fats" Santori, stole across Lake Lonely in a small guide boat to the dock of the MacEntyres' rented summer mansion. The lake was very dark and calm, except for the outer amber lights of Riley's Casino reflecting off of its glass-smooth surface.

Belmonte related how Santori had carried a key to the mansion's side door, a key he had acquired from a butler who was heavy in debt and in need of cash. It was the way they had entered many homes in Saratoga over the years during racing season, and always when the dwellers were out dining, hobnobbing, or partying at one of the casinos. These robberies were sometimes a year or two in the planning.

Diamonds were the loot of choice, because they could be fenced in any number of secondary markets, especially diamonds with a special history.

There was a ready supply of takers for these precious stones. The MacEntyre diamond collection had always been a much sought after prize among jewel thieves.

Belmonte told Sacca that he went directly from the boat to the darkened mansion and opened the door. Once inside, the others followed. The mansion had been cased over a dozen times prior to the heist. The whole operation was planned to take no more than fifteen minutes. Belmonte said they entered the upstairs master bedroom in the front of the house where, as he had been told, the jewels were hidden in a secret wall compartment near the bed. He told Sacca when he turned on a small flashlight to see the wall, his two accomplices came into the room at the same time and waited until the compartment had been penetrated.

The contents were dumped quickly into a canvas bag, and the three started back down the carpeted staircase. Suddenly, the house lights went on and a girl in a silver evening dress came into view at the foot of the stairs. Belmonte said they caught sight of one another

other at the same moment. The surprise of it left all four momentarily shocked until the girl, apparently sensing the gravity of the situation, bolted to the dining room, screeching as she went. Belmonte couldn't remember exactly what went down in those panicky seconds that followed the girl's flight. The group went running down the stairs after her, banging into furniture and knocking over lamps and assorted household objects.

Belmonte recalled that the girl left through the double dining room door to the east verandah, which faced the lake, and somewhere between the darkened lawn and the mansion, Gaspary caught a glimpse of silver dress moving toward the water. He shouted, "Stop, stop!" But as the figure moved farther away, the moon broke through a dark blanket of low-hanging clouds. In that instant, the girl hesitated and turned toward them, the diamond at her neckline sparkling like the North Star, though none of the intruders realized what it was that was shining.

It was also a fateful moment, for Santori, moving with the swiftness he was known for in mob circles, pulled a stiletto from inside his jacket pocket and flung it at the small, glittering object. Belmonte, in telling Sacca about the incident, described how he could actually hear the stiletto's wired, metallic ringing as it flew through the pitch darkness, ten or so yards to its intended victim.

Belmonte, choking back more sobs as he continued his gruesome story, said the sound that followed was like none he had ever heard before, nor would ever want to hear again in his lifetime. "A soft, moaning sigh," he told Sacca. "I could hear the steel blade piercing her throat where it split her trachea. She let out a sucking sound, followed by a rush of air." Then the dark night was filled with the eerie stillness of death echoing across Lake Lonely. "I will never forget that awful sucking sound. It haunts me each and every day," Belmonte said. "When I finally reached the spot where she had fallen, I shined the light on her face. Her eyes were still wide open, as if she were about to scream. But she was very dead."

Belmonte said he saw only the stiletto's pearl handle protruding from the girl's neck, its six-inch, razor-sharp blade clearly embedded in her silky-white throat.

Further panic ensued when the group had to decide what to do with her body. As Belmonte told Sacca, they had no idea who this girl could be. The MacEntyres had no daughter, only a son. In laying out the heist, everyone's whereabouts were accounted for in the MacEntyre family that night. The parents were dining at Casino Saratoga, and the son was supposedly at a bachelor party for the night. So who was this girl in the silver dress with two dark lines of newly flushed blood from her veins making a cross on her neck where the stiletto rested? This lovely, beautiful girl, who unexpectedly had upset their night's work? And why would she go to the mansion unescorted? All very imposing questions, but certainly ir-relevant at the time, Belmonte told Sacca, be-cause of the stupid, uncalled-for aggression of Santori's dagger tossing. Belmonte further re-lated that in the madness of the moment, Gaspary was tempted to pull the dagger from the girl's throat and drive it into Santori's heart for his wild mistake.

Belmonte said that the second he put the light on her, he got a weird, gut feeling that everything after the incident would go wrong – and it did. He recalled how the three, carry-ing her lifeless body, thrashed their way through the brush of the outer mansion prop-erty, then ran along the shoreline to the small guide boat. Belmonte had hung onto the loot bag for fear of dropping it in his haste to leave the premises. He described how he, Santori, and Gaspary had dragged their victim, all trying to get into the boat at once, and the craft rocking

17

as they entered it. Gaspary had knocked one oar into the lake with his right foot and then jumped into the shallow water to retrieve it. Then, dripping wet, he complained he was chilled, even though it was a warm summer evening with no breeze. Santori had jabbered away to Gaspary, telling him how babyish it was of him to complain.

There was a senseless series of wrong moves in the boat as it moved out onto the lake, just to the right of Riley's lights, out of sight on the rippling, black surface. Belmonte recalled how he had looked back at the MacEntyre place only once during all of this confusion, and that he could plainly see the large house silhouetted against the eerie, swaying, hanging branches of the weeping willow trees that surrounded the mansion. He remembered the lifeless body of the young girl, stretched over the boat's bow, one arm touching the lake's surface as the group rowed away.

Yet that wasn't the worst thing that happened that ill-fated night, he told Sacca. Halfway across Lake Lonely, Gaspary shifted his position and the boat started rocking side to side. Santori tried to steady it, but Gaspary, admittedly not a strong swimmer, and knowing they were at mid-lake in the darkness, panicked. Before anyone could calm him down, he shifted once more and the guide boat flipped over. Belmonte told Sacca how, in that dreadful instant, he clung to the loot bag as he entered the water, first being driven beneath the overturned craft and struggling desperately to get some air at the surface without losing the loot. Then he told of how the girl's body, twisted beneath the guide boat, touched his own body and then sank. And how Gaspary, gasping for breath and swinging his arms wildly, had grabbed his neck and squeezed tightly, almost taking the two of them down.

There had been no sign of Santori, only Belmonte and Gaspary fighting to stay afloat and clinging to the guide boat, which they found nearly impossible because of the boat's slippery bottom. However, Gaspary did manage to grab the remaining ore and to hold on. Belmonte related how his right arm had been numb from holding onto the loot bag, which was doubly weighed down by the water. His left hand and arm cramped, his fingers and forearms weakened with each movement. Worst of all, neither man had been willing to shout for help, even if anyone was within listening range.

"We were victims of our own mad doing." Belmonte said he could just make out Gaspary's head as it went under, with the shimmering, faint glow from Riley's reflecting on the lake around him. Belmonte said he held the loot for several minutes more until, with a pain and soreness he'd never before experienced, he had to let go. He could only think of saving himself. Of staying alive. As the boat moved ever so slowly, he pumped his feet with water-logged shoes. Belmonte told Sacca he was half crazy with fear of recrimination due to the worthlessness of the entire evening's work, the girl's needless killing, and the loss of Santori and Gaspary, not to mention the loot.

Sacca remembered Belmonte describing how he managed to survive drowning and finally made it to the far shore, and how he staggered through the thick forest around Lake Lonely until he came to a road that eventually led to town. He said he walked the entire distance, which he estimated to be eight miles.

The following day, Don Cira, with the help of a high-ranking state trooper he'd had on the mob's payroll for years, sent divers to Lake Lonely to retrieve the bodies of Gaspary, Santori, and the girl. The divers were also instructed to find the loot, but only came up with a torn heist bag and remnants of what Belmonte reportedly said was taken that night. It was all over before the media got involved. The girl's body was disposed of in a lime pit near Stillwater. Belmonte, not sure what Cira had done with Gaspary's and Santori's remains, thought they were burned in a steel mill blast furnace in Watervliet, near Troy. Or was it Cohoes? Not a trace of any of the bodies was ever found. It was a classic mob cover-up.

Sacca also recalled that Belmonte saw the newspaper headlines two days later, which reported the girl as missing. Strange as it may have seemed, there was no mention of the robbery itself – not one word. Had Cira, with all of his great power, squashed that too? Belmonte said he never did find out why. His standing in the Cira family hit rock bottom following the Lake Lonely debacle.

He told Sacca he was personally reduced to menial mob work in Hudson and Catskill, running numbers for a time. Two years later, the family dropped him altogether. He was relegated to a life of silence and worthlessness, for fear of his own life being taken by Cira. As Belmonte later told Sacca, "To be spared death, was a triumph in itself."

2. THE VOTE

Harrison Cole was busy swirling his large, wet mop along the vinyl tile floor of Saratoga City Hall's main corridor, sweating profusely in his wool shirt, as he mopped toward the meeting room doors, which were tightly shut on this March Thursday. Nevertheless, Cole could see the silhouettes of the five council members through the ancient, smoked glass panels, and he also could hear them shouting at one another. Although he really couldn't make out a word they were saying, he knew it was a heated debate, no doubt exacerbated by the evening's agenda. Still, it was uncommon for the five members to argue inside the chamber. They rarely raised their voices while meeting, at least not in Cole's memory.

Cole had been the custodian of City Hall for over half a century, having come to the job in his mid twenties. During his watch, many council members (mostly men) had come and gone. This year, however, there was one woman on the council. Many of the former council members Cole had known were now dead. Same for several Saratoga mayors. Still, Cole was here, doing what he knew best, keeping the old edifice sparkling for current and future generations. Meetings were always, in Cole's recollection, conducted with the utmost civility. But, on this night, Cole was cognizant, as was all of Saratoga, that the council would be voting yea or nay on the return of gambling to Saratoga, gambling other than that which was conducted each summer at the famous race course on Union Avenue.

Pressure had been building for months from assorted pro-gambling groups, with equal weight from the other side coming from staunch opponents to the return of gambling, whether it was slot machines in local stores or the full-fledged return of casinos.

Cole's mop swished along the tiles, leaving a gleaming sheen under the glow of the corridor's overhead lights. In his normal routine, Cole, when finished mopping the floors, would spread a light paste wax over the tiles, then buff them down. When buffed and dry, you could see your face in the tiles. Cole took great pride in his work. His last floor for the evening would be in the council chambers, though he wasn't sure by the tone of things

when he'd get to it. It was already well past
8 P.M. and there was no sign that the five were
about to break up their meeting.

So Cole found other things to occupy his
time while the argument raged on inside the
chamber. Shortly after 9:30 P.M., he was aware
of a sudden silence in the chamber. The silhouettes were still there, but the voices had
ceased. Cole knew it was decision time. They
were probably voting by secret ballot. No, they
were counting hands. He wasn't at all certain
what they were doing, but he had a gut feeling
that the council was making its choice. It had
been like that back in the fifties, when the five
men on the council made the decision to oust
gambling from Saratoga. It was a similar March
night, and he recalled how other council members had agonized over the decision then, as it
apparently was doing now. Cole could well
sympathize with their dilemma.

At the very moment the Saratoga City
Council members were casting their votes, men
of other persuasions were gathered in a great,
gray stone gothic Hudson River mansion near
Catskill, New York, waiting out the vote. If fa-
vorable, there would be a celebration of sorts,
topped off with a bottle of vintage red wine. If
a "no" vote were to emerge from the council
chamber, these men in Catskill would postpone

25

any celebration and address the matter based on their own values and vested interests.

As it turned out, the city council narrowly turned thumbs down on the highly charged issue of casino gambling in its revered and historic Spa City. There were two yes votes and three no votes. Within minutes of the meeting's adjournment, the men in Catskill made their decision.

Carmine "The Shark" Bocca, the much-feared and ruthless godfather of the middle and upper Hudson Valley region's former Don Tony Cira crime family, gave orders to have three of Saratoga's councilmen killed. Slightly hunched at the shoulders these days, Bocca was once a straight, muscular six-footer who had gained a reputation in mob circles as one who was not only tough, but also smart. His brain, not his brawn, was the reason Don Cira had hand-picked Bocca as his successor. Bocca's decision this evening was a simple deduction. If the councilmen found it necessary to kill the return of gambling to Saratoga, Bocca would kill the councilmen. A fair enough exchange, he reasoned, for their unreasonable behavior and obstinate attitude throughout the previous months of debate on the gambling issue.

Bocca, working through key associates behind the scenes, thought he'd bought enough votes in the council to ensure passage of the heated proposal. He had indirectly made it known that he was willing to phase in gambling over a fifteen year time frame. The three opposing members were adamant that gambling would not return to Saratoga. Bocca considered much of their opposition riddled with hypocrisy. After all, wasn't the race course a haven for gambling? Didn't people come and lose money at the windows? Why, then, were these same people not allowed the pleasure of casino gambling?

The contract to kill the three councilmen was not delivered in Bocca's normal, vicious, rough-toned voice, but rather in more of a faint whisper to Jake Palermo, his trusted chief lieutenant, who would, as Bocca knew from past assignments, carry out his Don's wish with the utmost dispatch. The elder Bocca, just days away from his eighty-eighth birthday, had sworn to bring back gambling to Saratoga, and no damn little bunch of snobby gentlemen, whether councilmen, councilwomen, or the mayor himself, were going to stand in the way of his resolve.

As in all family matters, it was purely a business decision, done to bolster the family's prestige while securing its foothold on what Don Bocca deemed would one day reap fortunes for all of his two hundred man army. He did not discount the fact that he was upholding the honor of the late Don Cira himself.

The Don had lost a fortune in the 1950s when Saratoga slammed the doors on its thriving casinos: Newman's Lake House, Smith's Interlaken, Mother Kelly's, Piping Rock, Riley's Lake House, and his favorite among all gambling emporiums, Casino Saratoga, that glittering consortium of gaming parlors east of town. All were gone now because of the ambitions of a few politicians. What did they know of human nature? How, in Bocca's reasoning, could these small-minded bureaucrats deprive society of one of its most deep-rooted social cravings, casino gambling?

Bocca understood the psychological makeup of gamblers. After all, he'd been one all his life. Rather than gamble in back rooms or running numbers, the dyed-in-the-wool gamblers wanted casino gambling. It was not for politicians to destroy those dreams. Don Bocca considered it a personal mandate from Don Cira's grave, and he intended to enforce his will and raw power, no matter how many lives had to be snuffed out, to avenge Don Cira's death.

Besides, the family was fuming at the loss of revenues to the Indian tribe that had reclaimed lands in Connecticut and on the St.

Regis reservation in northern New York and had opened up multi-million dollar casinos, which had affected the mob's stability in both states. The Indian casinos had such an effect that no less than three secret meetings were called by seven mob families during the past five years. The legitimacy of the Indian gambling locations, coupled with the inability of the mob to do anything to stop it, were both frustrating and costly. All the political greasing in the world was getting the family nowhere. The politicians were rolling over and playing dead on the entire gambling issue. It was high time the family took matters into its own hands.

All of these were current happenings in the ongoing saga to regain the family's grip on proposed legalized gambling in Saratoga. Bocca knew he'd leave the return to gambling in the hands of Lamar Tocco and Al Guido, his two nephews, both respected lawyers in the tiny resort village of Lake Luzerne, a thirty five minute drive northwest of Saratoga on Route 9N. This long, carefully planned step back into Saratoga was over four decades in the making.

The former Don Cira had laid out every facet of the plan, to the very day he uttered his final deathbed whisper. Following Cira's death, Bocca swore an oath that Saratoga would be reclaimed for the family, no matter the cost.

Months and years were dedicated to mapping out the strategy that would ultimately allow the family to achieve this goal, starting with the grand deception that the mob was no longer, or ever would be, interested in returning to Saratoga. It was a public relations ploy that was started in the late 1950s by Cira, who had leaked stories to key, news-hungry reporters in search of a hot scoop.

The press could always be manipulated, Cira had said. He was a master at arranging such stories on which the press would bite. Then there was the complete withdrawal of all family activities, including a hard-and-fast rule that no family member should be seen at the famed race course in August, a dictate that had family members grumbling from its inception.

"To be denied the pleasure of attending the track in August," as one loyal Don Cira street soldier put it, "was worse than having your right hand cut off." To which Cira, upon hearing of his soldier's remark, promptly had the man's right hand cut off, then had the man killed, stating emphatically, "Discipline must be maintained at all times," a reminder to all family members.

Oh, Cira withdrew from Saratoga all right. The two latter-day family lawyers had not yet been born, but old Cira knew that in time some productive female member of his family would be forthcoming with these bright, lawful siblings. And they would be pillars of their community, model citizens ready to put the family in the right spot at the right time.

There was no immediacy to Cira's plan. The crafty don was appreciative of time as both a healer and a great dissipater of public opinion. He was prone to telling close family members, "Five years and people begin to forget. Ten years and they've lost the will to remember. Twenty or thirty years and the family can reinvent itself. Remember that most of the men who prosecute you today will be out of office or dead in that time frame. We will still be around. The family never dies. The family goes on forever. Time is always on our side."

So it was that Bocca, remembering Cira's words, gave the order to move on the councilmen. It would all look accidental, no telltale signs of murder. Those days were gone. Bocca's men knew every councilman's daily routine. The family, Bocca often boasted, had a better surveillance network than the FBI.

There were four men and one woman on the Saratoga City Council. Bocca already had two of them in his hip pocket. The three do-gooders had to go. Unfortunately, one of them was female. Eliminating this one woman member, along with the two councilmen, was not an easy task. Killing women, especially political types, had been done in the past, but it was a delicate thing at best, and filled with many hidden dangers if not carried out properly. The public took considerably less kindly to women being murdered. Men, yes. Bocca knew one could kill a man with a good, or not so good reason, and get away with it. He personally had killed nine men, using different methods, though he had never killed a woman, or ordered one to be killed. It would be a first, and he felt uneasy when he thought about it, but not scared. Nothing on earth scared Bocca.

Perhaps, as was his nature, he honored family second to no other thing in life, and to him women represented the family core, the mainstay of a family. His feeling of apprehension with this order didn't last long, but it was bothersome. Once committed to the decision, Bocca held steady. His eyes were cold and penetrating as he looked at Palermo's round face with the crooked nose, a nose that had been broken several times over the years when Palermo was a champion prizefighter. Palermo's hands, now wrinkled with age, were thick as ham shanks, and what little was left of his once dark wavy hair was matted to his odd-shaped head, which sat on an eighteen-inch neck, bulging with rippling, purple-colored veins.

Bocca eyed Palermo for several moments, then whispered, "Do what you must do for me, Palermo. Remember, three very unwise people must not ever grace Saratoga again. I now put them in your hands." He lifted Palermo's right hand and studied it, as though he were studying a diamond. "Yes. I know you will do the right thing at the right time. Be careful. Make this a clean affair. No traces. Don Bocca dislikes traces."

In response, Palermo's two hands touched the warm hands of Don Bocca, in a respectful, departing gesture and nodded his head in acceptance to carry out his Don's wish.

"Let them sleep in the chilled lake water," Bocca further instructed him. Then, when Palemero had gone, Bocca walked over to his large, polished cherry desk, slid open its center drawer, and took out the list with the councilmen's names neatly written on it. He read it carefully, using thin-rimmed pincer glasses to do so.

> *John Stark*
> *Molly O'Neill*
> *Tom Bochard*

Bocca had a profile of each member. The wise Don, like his predecessor, knew each person's strengths and weaknesses. Like Stark's gambling habits and his eye for pretty women, married or single. This could be exploited, if necessary, to lure Stark into a trap. Palermo knew best how to make this all fit when the time came. Stark owned his own insurance agency. No doubt, without his clients' knowledge, he had spent premiums on his gambling habit. If so, Palermo would flush this out. Stark also was married with two children. At forty-two, a Union College graduate with three years of regular army service behind him, Stark had expressed a desire to further his political career.

Bocca first thought he could buy Stark off by indirectly priming his political pump. But this did not carry any weight. He found the man both cocky and unappreciative. He had to go.

Tom Bochard was his own man. At a spirited thirty-eight, he moved his way into Saratoga political circles by virtue of his Uncle Allen's money and the old-boy network. Allen Wentworth had made his money in shipbuilding during World War II, and later amassed millions more on Wall Street where, it was said, he did it all by insider trading deals that never were detected by the Federal Trade Commission. His nephew Tom had no sense of real wealth, nor of politics either, but that didn't seem to matter much to most Saratogians. With Bochard's good looks, his real estate agency was thriving and his political career appeared bright. Bocca had decided a long time ago to draw a dark curtain on Bochard.

As in all things, Bocca knew timing was everything. Bochard, a staunch Republican like all of the other members of the council, possessed a quiet charm and dressed the part, usually in single-breasted suits of dark gray or blue pin stripe. His dark hair always was combed back neatly, and his face, even in winter, was tanned as if he'd just sunned himself at Saratoga's Victoria Pool.

Single and very much a ladies' man, Bochard had only one weakness Bocca knew of – he was a lifelong diabetic. Bocca fantasized that Palermo might do Bochard in with sugar. The method didn't matter, as long as Bochard was removed.

Next came Molly O'Neill, all five feet, six inches of her, with her flaming red hair dripping off her shoulders and a penchant for dressing in smart-looking business suits and an ever-present array of Gucci handbags. A local woman of means who had gone to Yale on a scholarship at age seventeen, and later, upon returning to Saratoga, having decided on law school, finished three years later at the top of the Class of 1985 at Albany Law School. She then joined Ernst and Andrews, one of Saratoga's leading law firms. A terrible loss of legal talent would be realized when Palermo got hold of Molly O'Neill, Bocca mused. But there was no other alternative. O'Neill, along with the other two, had thwarted Bocca's wishes to the earth's end. So be it, Bocca told himself. If she insisted on voting against gambling, he had no choice.

Still, deep down in his bowels, the thought of rubbing her out greatly disturbed him. He couldn't exactly put his finger on it. With Palermo handling the assignment, it would go as routinely as parking one's car. He shifted to a nearby leather chair, sat down, and finished his glass of wine in silent, meditative thought.

What foolish people these are, Bocca again grumbled to himself. What very foolish people. Did they think we would sit still forever waiting for their "no" votes? Bocca lit a cigar, took a few puffs, and eventually lit the piece of paper that he held in his hand with it. Holding the burning object in his right hand until it almost reached his fingertips, dropping the smoldering remainder into a nearby ashtray, he let it slowly extinguish. When it had, he crushed the black paper with his thumb until there was nothing to distinguish it from the cigar's ashes.

Secrets of this kind were always confined to his memory.

There never was, nor ever would be, a paper trace, a point he often found very difficult to convey to his newer family members, especially the ones that were always trying to upgrade the family business through computers or cellular phones. Bocca was dead set against any of these modern electronic devices. Word of mouth was all the communication he needed.

As for Palermo, he could always be trusted to carry out his assignments. Like Bocca, Palermo was aging gracefully, near his age in Bocca's recollection, yet still spry enough to kill a man half his age with his bare hands, if necessary. Old prizefighters had that deadly talent. Their fists were lethal weapons. Bocca remembered Palermo's quick hands when he was battling middleweight contenders in New York's Madison Square Garden in the late 1940s. Bocca could still visualize the blood-stained canvases and flying teeth, the low blows to the groin, the grueling, post-fight recovery periods, the slow, painful comeback and long training hours preceding the next fight. The mob dictated the winners and losers of most of those fights - seven out of ten were pure setups - but not once did Bocca ever recall Cira asking Palermo to take a dive, like so many fighters had in those turbulent, dangerous days.

No, Palermo was a special talent, with classic fighter's instincts and an iron-clad will to stay in the fight, no matter how tough. The mob had great respect for Palermo. It was not ring battles that ended Palermo's career in his midtwenties, but rather a bizarre incident when he fell off of a delivery truck while working part time as a New Jersey dock worker. Palermo shattered both elbows, and splintered his forearm bones. His fighting days were over. So Cira, knowing he could use Palermo's talents, gave him a job. It was a relationship that became more solid as the years went by. Eventually, Palermo became a family member.

Bocca moved away from his desk to the large, opaque window on the second floor of his Hudson River mansion. He pulled back the drapes that had been shielding the moonlight. Bocca could see across the glimmering Hudson to the rolling, snow-covered hills that housed the ghostly sprits of Washington Irving and the mysterious characters he wrote about in *The Legend of Sleepy Hollow*. Bocca was an avid reader of Irving's tales, though no family member aside from his wife, Milla, knew about it. He smiled to himself as he recalled how Ichabod Crane, Irving's schoolteacher, disappeared, never to be seen again. His smile broadened, as he further thought, "A very appropriate ending for three unfortunate Saratoga council members."

How the times had changed, thought Bocca, withdrawing from the window and seating himself once more at the large desk. He was very upset and confused about the current ways the mob operated its business, tired of dodging the electronic eavesdropping of the state and federal agents, who made his life difficult and stressful. At times, Bocca suspected that the very walls of the mansion were recording his every word and innermost thoughts. Still he had to direct and guide his loyal family, for if he did not, then who would? After a time, Bocca picked up a nearby phone and called a special New York City number. He waited until it rang four times. Then he hung up. Seconds later, the phone rang and Bocca picked it up again. "What can I do for you?" asked a soft, deep male voice.

Bocca leaned forward in his chair and whispered into the receiver, "Your friend in Las Vegas. Tell him not to oil the roulette wheels just yet. Tell him we've run into a snag in 'Toga town. Tell him the family will be going home, but not yet. Tell him Palermo is on a mission, and when it is completed, I'll have new orders for him. Tell him Don Cira's favorite 'Toga haunt still awaits his services. But not until we're in a position to make our move. Tell him that for me."

"As you say, Don Bocca. I will convey your message."

In the stillness of the night, Bocca felt a sudden resurgence of energy in his weary bones. He sensed a renewed rush of blood to his fingertips and lower limbs. It was in that instant, much like it had been in earlier days, that he felt something exciting was about to happen. It was this elixir that had always sparked Bocca's creative genius and kindled his interest. He was taking command again of a delicate situation, and it was this challenge that gave him an indescribable joy.

Yes, he'd be directing the family's return to Saratoga in due time. Thinking about it, images of past, brighter days and nights in Saratoga danced in his head. Like the time he had first visited the famous Riley's Lake House on Lake Lonely as a young, budding capo in Cira's family.

He remembered the long, horse-drawn carriage ride from Saratoga's rail station on the far west side of town, rumbling past the grand dame of Saratoga hotels, the Grand Union on Broadway, then past Congress Park and Canfield's Casino, the granddaddy of all gaming halls. They rumbled along Union Avenue, past the stately mansions that served as mostly fraternity houses for Skidmore College.

He remembered his first glimpse of the race course itself, with its sweeping slate-roofed clubhouse, its grandstands a panoramic silhouette against the late-afternoon August sun amidst the magnificent elms and tall, leafy oaks. He recalled it all very well. He also recalled that it was a Friday and that the Travers Stakes was being run the next day. Mob operatives from everywhere were in Saratoga for the Travers.

Bocca considered himself fortunate to be chosen by Don Cira to attend the track that weekend though, as he recollected, he was not then a full-fledged family member. It was a unique time and place when a young mob inductee could appreciate the rewards of being associated with a successful family. Bocca could still hear the cautious words of Don Cira ringing in his head, "Go have a good time. Keep your nose clean. Act like a gentleman. Wear a tuxedo. Don't gamble too much, and certainly, don't drink too much." Bocca assured the Don he would do nothing to disgrace the family, as he kissed his ring and thanked him for letting him attend the Travers.

It was turning dark when the horses, their coats steaming in the night's sudden chilled air, came abruptly to a halt in front of the yellow stucco entrance to Riley's Lake House. Bocca soon found himself swept inside, walking with an assortment of arriving guests, all laughing and talking in excited tones. There was, he recalled, urgency on each one's part to get the first look at Riley's interior. The place had that kind of magnetic lure. Bocca was taken with Riley's, finding it quite luxurious to a young man of modest means.

He had come out of New York's Hell's Kitchen, in a time when "Hell" was a mild word for it. His father, Charles, dropped dead slinging around a heavy crate of shrimp at the Fulton Fish Market when Carmine was twelve. At first he thought he'd be forced to go out and work to support his mother and younger sister. Carmine's mother was devastated by her husband's death, and she further worried that Bocca's schoolwork would be affected. His academic record, to that point, had been above par, so she wanted Carmine to continue his schooling. The crisis was settled when Carmine's uncle Frankie "The Shadow" Bocca, a questionable mob figure, volunteered to take over his brother's financial obligations.

It was said much later, well after Carmine graduated from high school and Frankie was dead, that the family's real benefactor was Don

Cira, though he never acknowledged it. Nevertheless, there was a debt to pay on Carmine's part. When it was time to go to college, he was asked indirectly by Don Cira to join the family. Carmine first begged off, electing to enroll in New York University.

The summer following his first year of college, while working at the same market where his father had died, Carmine was accused of stealing. The dock foreman, Danny Stallone, a known Cira family member, made the charge. Carmine Bocca was booked and charged with grand theft. The incident brought about his dismissal from NYU. Don Cira intervened through his lawyers and Stallone dropped the charges against Bocca. But the trap was successful, and Don Cira got what he wanted, as he always did. The method didn't matter. Carmine Bocca had learned a bitter, yet useful, lesson from this. It would serve him well on his way to gaining the family throne. But for all of his power and money, he regretted never having finished NYU.

So, on this first visit to Riley's, as he stepped onto the mosaic tile floor and moved toward the octagonal-shaped dining and dancing room, admiring the art deco furniture and hand-painted murals, he was caught up in the atmosphere. He was also aware of the many hand-

43

some men and statuesque women. Women in full evening dress, their necks glittering with diamond and ruby jewelry, men offering cigarettes from solid gold cases, along with equally valuable gold or silver lighters. The kings and queens of society were all here at Riley's.

Bocca felt it almost theatrical, but he knew it was for real. He also was conscious that it was their money that kept the family business thriving. He went into another room, brushing past a voluptuous long-haired blonde in a rose-trimmed white dress who smiled at him and walked away. "Behave yourself at all times," he heard Don Cira's parting words ringing in his ears.

Finally he made his way to the main gaming room, but not before smelling the sweet aroma of broiled Maine lobster and crepe suzettes emanating from the dining room, as waiters scurried in near-military precision between tables, some pouring wine and champagne, others uncovering trays of squab, chicken or native frogs legs. And all the while, a full band played soft dinner music. In comparison, the nightclubs in New York appeared shabby.

Bocca was startled at the gaming entrance. A lump formed in his throat. He rubbed his eyes and looked again. He saw the unmistakable, hard and scarred face of Lucky Luciano standing near one of the room's several roulette tables. My God, he thought, this is real power.

There were four mob men in Luciano's company. Bocca could spot them a mile away, though it appeared that Luciano was standing alone. After all, hadn't Don Cira, in passing, let it be known that Luciano was part owner of Riley's, along with Frank Costello? Or had he heard it elsewhere within the organization? Then it dawned on him what Don Cira's real reason was for sending him to Saratoga and Riley's.

Bocca figured Cira wanted him to experience the power that comes with complete control, to feel the freedom by which powerful, well-heeled bosses could impose their will and dictates on others, how they could be accepted into the right circles, such as Saratoga's summer horse racing elite. Not carousing, but socializing, within the limits of society – the Whitneys, Mellons and Phipps. Later, after trying his hand at blackjack, Bocca went back to Riley's dining room and, much to his surprise, saw dapper Bing Crosby dining with a ravishing redhead. The same evening, having seen all he wanted to of Riley's, Bocca went to Piping Rock, just off Union Avenue.

He drank champagne in those days, and on this festive evening he consumed more than a few glasses of the bubbly, against Cira's best advice. At Piping Rock, Bocca met a startling, tall brunette named Catherine West. She had arrived with a date, a family friend, but somehow they had become separated. Bocca, brash and confident, took over. Catherine forgot all about her date. The two went from one gaming table to the other, then to the roulette tables where Bocca, like Luciano in Riley's, played it cool and low key. He won two thousand dollars in less than an hour. He could have won more, but he didn't want to be conspicuous.

Catherine was lucky too, winning eight hundred. It was a night of bliss with his newfound friend. By and by, Bocca and Catherine grew tired of gambling and decided to take a walk. They stepped outside of Piping Rock to a full moon, which beamed off the lake's surface. As they sat on a small, marble bench and peered across the lake, Bocca lit two cigarettes and handed one to Catherine.

Inside, the orchestra was playing a song Bocca liked, but he couldn't remember the name. Now it was time to talk. She was a blue-blooded beauty, with high cheekbones, piercing blue eyes, and creamy-white skin. Dressed in a full-length black and silver lace dress and a lavender knit shawl, she was all class.

It was very late, but Bocca insisted that

they have a nightcap of champagne before going their separate ways. "Your date will be very worried by now," Bocca told her. Catherine blushed and pushed the hair off the front of her face. "Oh, Frank. Poor Frank MacEntyre. He's always going off someplace. We make a habit of losing one another."

"Perhaps I can help you find him?" Bocca asked.

"No need for that," Catherine replied. "I'll just take a carriage back to town or go looking for him. They have a summer place nearby. Frank will show up eventually."

"Are you here for the races?" Bocca asked.

She laughed. "We're here every summer. My family has been coming to Saratoga for years."

"And your family is?"

She turned a full face to Bocca, her eyes burning into his. "Why, West. As in textiles. Ever been to Connecticut? My grandfather and his family practically own the state."

"Only once," he replied, now staring at the single, brilliant diamond laying softly around her neck. It appeared as though it was suspended there, however, he then noticed a very thin gold chain, so thin it was barely visible. So enthralled with her beauty at the casino, Bocca hadn't noticed the diamond until now, not even during their gaming room romp.

47

She felt his eyes on it. "You're admiring my diamond."

He came closer. "Yes. It is very beautiful. Don't tell me it's a West family heirloom?"

"Well, almost. My uncle gave it to me. Uncle Wilber, he's always surprising family members with expensive gifts. This was my graduation present when I finished Vassar. Do you like it?"

He immediately realized he was staring at the diamond. "Oh, yes. Very much. Quite distinctive. A unique setting, too."

"You'd like Uncle Wilber. He's a man's man. You look like a man's man."

Had it not been for Don Cira's words still fresh in his head, he would have taken her in his arms that very moment. Instead, he stood up and walked a few paces away. It was the only way to repress his need to hold this very attractive, intelligent, delicate woman.

They sat for a while longer and made small talk. Catherine directly asked Bocca once or twice what he did for a living and inquired about his family, but he skillfully avoided giving her a straightforward answer. All of her questions were answered with guarded, measured responses. In those minutes and in the brief hours they had spent together, Bocca seriously questioned his present existence with the Don Cira family, thinking how different this meeting would have been had he finished NYU and never joined the family.

* * *

When Bocca next looked up from his desk, the room was almost dark. He turned on another lamp and resumed reading the profiles he had started earlier. He then put them down. Why, after all these years, did he regress to that evening with Catherine West? Wasn't he happily married to Milla? Yet, as he sat calmly by himself in the quiet of the night, the image of Catherine West and that extraordinary night in Saratoga was clear in his mind. He pondered the question: Whatever had become of her?

3. MOLLY O'NEILL

Snowmobiling was Molly O'Neill's winter passion. A brisk nightly ride on her Honda 240 Cat was something she had dreamed about all day at work. This bitter March night would provide the perfect snow base. It would be fast traveling. At the far end of East Avenue, she eased her Honda out onto a familiar wilderness path and throttled her machine at one-quarter spin toward Union Avenue, hanging a left and making a turn due east in the direction of Saratoga Lake. The stiff night wind was at her back, the machine's runners snapped over the iced roadside surface, and sprays of fresh snow cut across her headlight beam. She relished this kind of night. She changed her mind halfway to Saratoga, and headed for Lake Lonely. It was less apt to have any fellow snowmobilers at this time, and more likely to have a thicker, more reliable ice cover. She had to unwind. The prior week's proceedings weighed heavily on her mind.

The turbulent council meeting and several

business deals had not gone well. She'd blow them all out of her head on this ride. She and her machine, acting as one, were all she con-centrated on now. *Faster. Faster.* Let it all hang out. She approached the deserted white oval at Lake Lonely's northern shoreline, at approxi-mately thirty miles per hour, throttling a notch higher as the machine leveled on the flat snow and pitched forward. Within fifteen seconds, she had it up to forty-five miles per hour and was gaining speed. It was wild. At fifty, with the machine swaying ever so slightly, she watched as long, high rooster tails of snow fell behind her, spreading out in the stiff wind like a comet's tail.

The cold air licked at her lips, virtually the only part of her body that was exposed, and she quickly buried her chin into her high snowsuit collar to avoid frostbite. Otherwise, she was warm and comfortable. Her gloves and boots were battery heated. She spun back and forth across the lake three times, then started a series of long, round turns that took her from one shoreline to the other. She streaked along the small inlets and then outward in linking "S" turns, a maneuver she had mastered and excelled at in local snowmobile competitions. Tonight, the lake was hers. The thrill and free-dom of it was exhilarating.

Albert Sacca, asleep in the rocking chair in his hut, suddenly awoke to the noise of Molly's machine vibrating the ice beneath him. He cracked open his door and peered out. He saw the bright beam and heard the whining of the engine again in the distance. The light then shone directly back across the lake at Sacca. He slammed the door and sat back in the rocker. It appeared as though the machine was about to tear through the hut. The noise was almost deafening. It veered off at the last second. He listened as the engine died away, now only a muffled sound, then nothing at all. Seconds, then minutes, ticked away and Sacca waited. "Thank God," he whispered. "That damn machine is gone."

At the moment he said it, he felt a stiff tug on his fishing line. One quick jerk, followed by another. It startled him. He moved his small lantern closer to the hole. The line drew slowly down, and he tightened it ever so slightly. Without warning, the line began slipping from his grip. He could feel the heat generated by the line as it slid between his gloved fingers. He braced one foot against the shed door and yanked hard. The line slackened momentarily then went straight again. Sacca grunted and pulled once more with both hands. It was a tug-of-war for the next five minutes, to the point of near exhaustion for the old fisherman. His arms and legs were tiring.

Then he got an idea. He flung open the shed door, and outside in the numbing cold, dragging what free fish line he had left, Sacca wrapped the line over one shoulder and leaned forward, using his entire body weight. His strategy worked. He felt resistance for a few seconds longer, then he could feel it let up. He gave one big tug and knew in that moment his catch of the evening had given up its fight. Gathering the wet, frozen line in his hands, he raced back inside the shed just in time to see a pike's nose come through the hole. Sacca knew he'd caught a granddaddy of a fish. He held the line tightly for fear it might go back under. With one hand, Sacca reached for the lantern. Now, in full light, he saw just how big his catch was.

The fish was so large Sacca couldn't get it through the hole. He quickly took his ice chopper and began enlarging the hole, carefully chipping about its edges so as not to chop away any of his catch in the process. He wanted no harm to come to this prize, for certainly he was holding one of the largest pike ever caught in Lake Lonely. It might even rival the prize pike of Saratoga Lake. No matter, he wasn't about to risk losing it now.

It was several minutes before Sacca finished

widening the hole sufficiently so he could ease his catch from the dark, cold lake water. He grabbed the fish by one gill and hoisted it upward, taking on a spray of freezing water in his face in doing so. He let out two loud yelps, holding the pike lengthwise across his lap. Its belly was round and plump, and its eyes seemed to glare at Sacca in defiance. Sacca figured it weighed over fifteen pounds, perhaps more. Its magnificent, silver-blue skin glistened in the lantern's glow. "You're a beauty," Sacca found himself addressing his fresh catch. Then, poking at the fish's belly, he wondered aloud, "might you be full of little pikes? Such a girth." The fish twisted to one side, almost falling from Sacca's lap, but Sacca held on tightly to the line and forced one arm down on his straining catch. "You'll not be returning to the lake tonight, big fellow."

Just then, Sacca thought he heard the machine returning. He pushed open the hut door and listened, all the while restraining his treasured pike, which wiggled from side to side. But with the door open, he could hear only the howling wind. He continued listening. If the noise he had heard had been the machine coming back to the lake, it must have gone elsewhere, he reckoned, or else he was hearing things in his old age that didn't exist. He knew this was a possibility. It had not been that way earlier in the evening, though. For then, he had seen the machine's light as well as heard its noisy, whining engine. It was not the first time these snow machines had disturbed his tranquility on Lake Lonely. In fact, these occurrences were becoming more common. Considering the times, he realized there weren't many places of solitude left around Saratoga, not like in the early days when he had enjoyed complete freedom from such careless, noisy interlopers.

He shut the door once more. Now he could concentrate on his fish. He took a sharp, five-inch boning knife, starting just behind the fish's gills and cutting a straight line down its soft belly to its tail, letting the blade sink in no more than an inch, as he slowly, surgically, relieved the fish of its insides. As Sacca spread open the pike's belly, a rush of red, black, and purple remains fell to the icy shed floor. Sacca looked down among the mass of innards and saw something shining back at him. He reached over and lifted the object up to the light.

"Saints in heaven," he gasped. "It's a diamond pendant, attached to a thin gold chain." He peered at it again. Then, turning it over, Sacca noticed that there was an inscription, though it was difficult to read in the lantern's light. He squinted and held it closer, but couldn't make it out. Sacca had no doubt this was a real diamond and the chain was solid gold. He'd heisted enough precious stones in his criminal career to know one on sight, bad light or not. He felt the blood rushing to his head. His hands trembled. "Could this be?" he thought. "Was this not near the very location on Lake Lonely that Ron Belmonte had talked about where, following the bungled robbery, the MacEntyre loot had been lost?"

Sacca sat down in the rocking chair in stunned disbelief. He reached over once again and inspected the gooey mess of fish guts. He discovered a second object, this time a small string of pearls, the size of early peas. This shocking discovery further shook his aging body, as the reality began to take hold. In the confines of his little, snowbound fishing shed, nearly isolated as it was, Sacca's subconscious began to recall Belmonte's very words. It all flashed through his mind, as clearly as though he had been a part of it. The killing of the pretty socialite girl, the desperate escape by Gaspary, Santori and Belmonte, and Belmonte's futile attempt to save his accomplices and the stolen booty. And now Sacca had not only resurrected part of the cursed loot, but possibly resurrected memories that were better left dead.

It was a lurid thought, one that bothered him immensely. He tucked the pendant and pearls into his inside jacket pocket and zipped it tightly. Composing himself, he sat back and lit a cigar. After a time, he continued gutting his fish. He then packed snow inside of his catch, wrapped it with a piece of canvas and tied it with string.

He decided to go home. It was still dark and cold outside. The wind had subsided, but the icy chill had a stinging bite and Sacca, hugging his fish tightly beneath one arm and pressing the pendant and pearls with the other, began his long walk off Lake Lonely toward his one-room shack in the thick woods near Yaddo, an artist retreat, exactly two miles away. Halfway across the lake, he came across some snowmobile tracks. His night vision was still good. He'd trained himself to adjust to the night light, no matter how dark, as it allowed him to move about undetected.

One hour later, in the warmth of his little shack, with the aid of a lamp and a magnifying glass, he took out the necklace and read the engraving, "To My Beloved Catherine from Uncle Wilber." He held it in the light for a minute. "Catherine." He felt a sudden pain in his stomach, followed by a chill up his back. He called out her name again. "Catherine." In reading the engraving, he realized only he, among the old mob members, knew her first name. The rest had all gone to their deaths not knowing who she was. It was a revelation that both surprised and disturbed him. The value of his find had not even been considered. A brilliant diamond pendant and a pearl necklace of undetermined worth, "stripped," as Belmonte had put it, "from the silky white throat of a dead, nameless beauty." Except that now, he, Sacca, knew her first name.

What could he do with these gems? Worse yet, to whom could he tell his story? Would old Don Bocca, still Godfather of the Hudson Valley, be interested in such a rare find? Might he try to retrieve more of the loot? Surely it was somewhere down in Lake Lonely's murky bottom. The possibilities of what he discovered this night were spinning through his head. Sacca looked at his fish, still wrapped in canvas on the nearby table. He then examined the gems once more. Inwardly, he laughed. Then, a more humorous thought occurred to him, "This is truly a fish story no one will believe."

At the intersection of Union and East avenues, just opposite the race course gates, Molly O'Neill eased off the throttle and slowed her machine down, making one wide turn and gunning it again to keep it from sliding around on

her. It was now past 11 o'clock and both avenues were deserted, save for one van that went
up East Avenue some twenty yards ahead of
her. Through the swirling snow she could barely
make out its taillights, though she knew she
was gaining on it.

At one point on East Avenue, she had an
opportunity to pass the van, and did so. She
was only a quarter of a mile from her home, but
the cold was stifling. Even her battery-heated
boots were cooling down, and she couldn't remember if she had put new batteries in. No, it
was time to go home. She'd enjoyed her
evening's ride, but enough was enough. A hot
cup of coffee, a warm bed, and a good book
were in her thoughts now. She blinked her
headlights as she went by. What followed was
a bizarre series of skidding, spinning and fighting desperately to stay on her snowmobile,
which suddenly was being forced to one side
of the street by the van. In the split second she
had to analyze the situation, her instincts told
her the van had lost control on an icy patch,
and hopefully, would straighten out. It wasn't
until the machine's beam was focused directly
on the Humphrey S. Finney Pavilion that she
realized it was a deliberate move on the driver's
part.

The enclosed glass and concrete pavilion,

where she had spent so many August nights watching the annual Saratoga Yearling Sales, now loomed in front of her. She envisioned herself shattering through the glass facade. The machine's high speed, the van pushing her snowmobile further and further over, and her inability to break in time, spelled certain doom. She could only remember swerving, in one last desperate move, to avoid hitting the glass head-on and being thrown from the machine, as it went crashing through the facade. She slid a long way on the snow-covered pavilion's circular driveway, flipped over completely at least twice, and bounced off the metal fence adjacent to the structure. Molly heard a bone crack as she recoiled off the fence.

She vaguely recalled the screeching pavilion alarm going off and being covered with a shower of splintered glass. Molly was certain her right shoulder was broken. Severe pain crippled her right side. She tried to sit up, but couldn't. She fell back, the chinstrap from her badly damaged helmet choking her. Her snowsuit was torn open in several places and she felt the bitter cold on her skin. She fought to maintain consciousness. Molly was aware that the van had pulled into the driveway and had its lights, directly on her. The van door opened and a figure, presumably a man, though she wasn't certain, came toward her.

"Had an accident little lady?" she heard him say. "Must be that you're not finished yet. I'll take care of that."

Molly's vision blurred. When she finally was able to see again, she could only make out a figure entering the van and the sound of the revving motor. Molly was sure he was going to run her over. She said a quick prayer, shut her eyes, and waited for the inevitable. The van started rolling toward her. With strength she didn't realize she had, Molly managed to roll over three times, just far enough to clear the driveway and put herself part way between a cement abutment and the van.

The driver came to a sudden stop, backed up and came at her from a more acute angle. She rolled further to the right of the abutment, thwarting the van's advance. Molly heard the unmistakable, metallic click of the van's door as it opened. Out of the corner of one eye, she watched in fear, as the mysterious figure came toward her. She was fighting severe pain, and penetrating cold. Besides, she was terrified. Molly felt aware of the stranger dragging her by her feet back onto the driveway. Unbearable pain now ripped through her body. It was most acute on her right side where, she knew, her arm was broken.

She knew,too, that this crazed person, for whatever reason, would not be denied. She said one last silent prayer and closed her eyes. The van's motor revved once more. The gruesome death she anticipated on the icy pavilion driveway was suddenly interrupted. A flashing light that passed over her head shone directly into the van's windshield. There were pounding sounds of a scuffle, and men's shouting voices. She couldn't make out how many. It was all too confusing. Molly raised her head just in time to see the van backing away from the pavilion, and turn down East Avenue.

Pain went up her back and centered at the nape of her neck. A soft male voice spoke. "We cannot stay with you. We must go. There will be help here soon. I'm covering you with a blanket. Lay still. Everything will be okay. Jake Palermo will bother you no more. His days of killing are over." With that, the soft-spoken good Samaritan stood up, paused over her for a moment, then disappeared as quickly as he had come.

Molly O'Neill was so perplexed at this juncture, so baffled, in so much pain, and so cold, it was like passing through a bad dream. Someone tried to kill her, and someone had gone out of his way to save her. What was going on? Could it be a case of mistaken identity, or was she really a target? Who the hell was Jake Palermo? Whose face was behind the soft, re-assuring voice? Where, on this bitter wintry night, had he come from? Molly was certain others were with him. If so, who were they? The pavilion alarm, which activated when her machine pierced and shattered the glass, was now silent. The blanket helped, but she was still very cold. Fear of freezing to death before help came was foremost on her mind. Momen-tarily, she heard sirens and saw flashing red lights streaming over East Avenue from Union.

Somewhere, between the nightmarish inci-dent on East Avenue, and the anxious ambu-lance ride to Saratoga Hospital, Molly fell into pain induced semi-consciousness, so much so, that the two EMT's caring for her called ahead to report she'd gone into shock. When they arrived, the doctors at the hospital rushed to her aid.

Molly was quite battered, but otherwise in fair condition. It would be several hours before she was well enough to convey what had hap-pened, or what she thought had happened. It was Chief Nealy who almost lost it when she mentioned Jake Palermo. Palermo, of the Don Bocca crime family.

"Bocca is back. God bless Saratoga this year," Nealy said.

The chief speculated that different crime families now had their sights set on Saratoga's potential future gaming. In the hours that followed, O'Neill was the most popular and most sought-after Saratoga City Council member. Nealy, expecting the worst, assigned round-the-clock police officers to protect her. All visitors were thoroughly screened. Nealy was fearful of the mob following through on taking Molly's life.

The press, in short order, took care of exposing the whole Don Bocca family and their historical tie to Saratoga's gambling days. They went to extremes, in Nealy's opinion, hypothesizing the mob's current designs on gaming.

"This frenzy of reports and articles are detrimental to Saratoga. Totally blown out of proportion," Nealy said. Beginning with the wire service accounts, overlapping to TV, and finally, in spite of all Frank Duffy could do to play it down, the *Saratoga Star* continued to carry articles. It was a story whose widespread implications carried a momentum of its own.

The gaming stories also broke, in all their startling detail, just when the *Star* was poised to publish a tangled, spider-web piece centering on impending blackmail within the city's revered Chamber of Commerce. Duffy said it was just more fuel for the fire in a town already smoldering in its own hot-bed of rumors. As he told his wife, Martha, "Hang on to your Travers bonnet. A stiff wind is blowing through this old town, the likes of which we haven't seen in some time."

On the green-colored sawdust pad, at the foot of the Humphrey S. Finney Pavilion's auctioneers' podium, where spirited thoroughbred yearlings were sold for millions, Molly O'Neill's mangled red and black snowmobile was piled like a twisted metal sculpture. Its padded, cushioned seat split open like a boiled lobster tail, its white-foam contents showing. The snowmobile had gone through the pavilion like a meteorite, managing to rip up several rows of plush, red seats in the process. The costs of repairing the glass, seats and assorted damage was estimated to be at least $40,000.

"I had quite an expensive ride," Molly would later joke with friends.

Three days after the crash, Jim Trimore, an insurance adjuster representing the World Global Insurance Group, came to Saratoga and began digging into the affair. On the surface, his appearance and investigation would have seemed routine. The pavilion was well insured. But Trimore's report was not so routine.

In fact, he tossed in the proverbial monkey-wrench by stating in his summary that "without the smoking gun – in this case the mysterious van and its nasty driver," all he could determine was that "Molly O'Neill had hit the throttle once too often during her winter joy ride." And had, he further theorized, lost control of her snowmobile and crashed, unassisted. Questioned as to who, then, had called for the ambulance, Trimore said it could have been any number of people. Probably a passerby who didn't want to get personally involved, but was good enough to dial "911." The existence of a van and driver had to be proven if Trimore were to recommend settlement of damages to his company, and that was that.

On hearing of Trimore's remarks, Frank Duffy, attending a hastily called meeting with Tom Nealy, Dr. Blake and his *Saratoga Star* sidekick, Billy Farrell, decided he'd have a stiff drink. "How much more salt can they throw on this?" Duffy asked. "There's Molly lucky to have her limbs attached after such an accident, and this Trimore is calling her a liar in public. I've known this girl all her life. I'd dare say, she's not capable of making up such a tale." He downed his drink and stared at the others.

"Has anyone here informed Trimore that Jake Palermo's body is lying on a slab in the Albany morgue? Might that change his report?"

"Wrong." Nealy interrupted. "We have a

very dead Jake Palermo, I agree. I don't think it means a thing to Trimore." Nealy turned to face Duffy.

"Frank, let's face it. You can't tie Palermo to the O'Neill incident, even if you tried. I'm not at all sure that his death and her accident are related. No one here can say it is. It might be. Anything is possible. Trimore's going to make a case for his company. If he can prove, or disprove her story, he may just recommend they sue Molly for the damages. I'm not ruling out any possibilities. I am saying we have two situations facing us. One dead Jake Palermo, and a young councilwoman who claims some-one tried to kill her. Coincidentally, both came about at the same time. That in itself looks fishy. But it proves nothing. We, like Trimore, have to find the van, and hopefully, the driver. At least the van.

"We're assuming at this point there is such a van. If so, who drove it and where is it now? We couldn't pick up tread marks at the pavil-ion because the ambulance and several EMTs who assisted in Molly's rescue obliterated them. So we're seeking a dark-colored van, blue or black, who knows? A van thinly described by a terrified Molly O'Neill as best she could make it out on that snowy night. Now do you see where I'm coming from? These insurance hawks will not give in easily. Trimore has a job to do. So do I. So do we all. And let's be honest here, it's in our best interest to keep a cap on this for now. Trimore will probably hear about Palermo soon enough. In the interim, I'm not about to march him down to Albany Medical Center for an introduction. Are we in sync on this?"

There was a collective nodding of heads.

"About Palermo's ghastly death," Dr. Blake said, "what's the final verdict?"

" Not a clue," replied Nealy scratching his head. "He was cut up unmercifully. Butchered is more like it. I'm passing the ball to your court, Doc. You have a better rapport with the pathology department at Albany Med than any of us. We're depending on you to keep us informed on its progress. Personally, I think someone was making a statement with the way they hacked him up. Perhaps an old mob vendetta being settled. I just don't know. Let's concentrate on finding that van. Then Trimore will be satisfied that Molly wasn't dreaming it up."

Nealy paced slowly back and forth across Blake's large living room, sinking his heels into the plush blue carpet as their eyes followed him. Then he abruptly halted, grabbed his forehead with his right hand, and sighed. "Let's suppose there was a van and that Jake was driving it. Let's go along with Molly's account of the whole thing. If this is so, who in hell interceded on her behalf? We haven't really thought this one out, have we? If Palermo was sent by Don Bocca to kill Molly, who sent someone to kill Palermo? If Molly was a target, why? The fact that she voted against gambling? Bocca might kill her for that. He's done worse in his day. And if that's true, aren't the remaining members of the council who voted that way also in grave danger? I'm doing all the talking here, but I need your input."

"Go on." said Farrell. "You're doing just great. I think you're on to something, Chief."

***

The phone at the main desk of the Royal Hawaiian Hotel gave two soft rings and was swiftly picked up by the alert desk clerk. He held the receiver away from his right ear because the male caller was shouting his words.

"I want to talk to Mike Flint. Is Mike Flint at your hotel?"

"No," said the clerk. "Mr. Flint is not here."

"Nonsense," said the caller. "He told me he was registering at your place."

"Oh, yes," replied the clerk. "He is registered. What I meant to say is that he is not here at this time."

"Well, where in hell is he?"

"I'm not exactly certain."

"That's not what I want to hear."

"Perhaps you can leave a message and Mr. Flint will get back to you?"

The voice became more irritated. "You don't seem to understand. I have to talk to him. Now!"

A little while prior to the call, Flint had strolled past the desk with that beauty, heading out to the pool. The clerk remembered his rather direct order, delivered with with a "don't screw up" smile, that under no circumstances was he to be bothered with phone calls or messages. "No way, no how."

"If you will kindly leave your name and number, I'll ask Mr. Flint to call you when he returns."

"Look, son, I know Flint better than anyone. I'd say he told you not to bother him, right?"

The clerk hesitated. "I'm having difficulty understanding you, sir."

"No you're not. You understand me very well. Now do me a big favor. Go get Flint. Tell him Harry Waite is calling. And don't come back to the phone unless he's with you. You get me?"

Even with the Royal Hawaiian's air conditioning working properly, the clerk could feel beads of sweat on his face. He had no idea who

Harry Waite was, but he sensed he was talking to a hot-tempered, rough character, and it upset him. Still, he didn't know what to do. Give in to the caller, and Flint, always a big tipper, would lose his cool. Not many guests, even at the plush Royal, tipped like Mike Flint.

So he told Harry: "I must take another call. Try back in an hour." Then he hung up.

No sooner did he walk away from the phone, than it rang again.

This time Harry Waite's voice sounded almost vicious. "Hang up again and I'll have your head," Waite threatened. "I'm telling you for the last time, get me Mike Flint!"

Fright now turned to panic. The clerk began to sweat profusely. His vocal cords suddenly contracted. He couldn't speak a word.

"Answer me!" Harry bellowed.

A barely audible sob was all Harry could hear.

"The cat got your tongue, son?"

The clerk gulped and hissed back. His attempted reply came out in an asthmatic-like wheezing rush. Harry listened and waited. More wheezing and gulping.

"For Christ's sake, say something."

Eventually the clerk's voice came forth. "My throat's too dry. I can't speak. You'll have to call at another time."

"Don't you dare hang up that phone." Harry fumed at him. "You don't have to say a thing. Just get me Mike Flint. I mean right now. This minute. This is urgent police business. Do you comprehend that?"

In the same instant Waite said that, the clerk looked up and Mike Flint, still in his swimming trunks, leather sandals and large, white towel with the RH monogram on it, was standing at the reception desk. The clerk, his eyes belying fear, flung the phone at Flint and made a dash for the back office. Flint leaned over and picked it up and listened.

"Son, you doing what I told you to do?"

My God, Flint smiled. It's old Harry.

"I'm growing very impatient, son. Now, for the last time, go get Flint. And don't hang up."

Flint held the phone for several playful moments, contemplating his options. Either whistle in Harry's ear, or speak to him. He decided to do both. One short bar of the Marine hymn. That should do it. Oh, the phone tag he had had with Harry over the years. Life wouldn't be worth living without it. In all the give-and-take, had either of them gained the upper hand? Did it really matter? Just more exercise in trivial, verbal pursuit. But Flint always enjoyed these rap sessions, so he whistled the hymn.

"You crazy bastard, Flint!" Harry, recognizing it, shot back. "You should have your lips worked on. You can't even carry a proper tune."

Flint's attempt at doing it again failed as he broke out laughing. "It's not my whistling, Harry, it's the wax in your ears preventing you from hearing a true note when it's delivered."

"Very comical, Flint. Very comical."

"You know me, Harry. I only speak the truth."

"Well here's a little truism you'll not like to hear. Ready?"

"Probably not," said Flint, looking back at the pool where Sandy was lounging. The pool reflected the sunlight off her gold, one-piece swim suit. Her long dark hair hung down to the deck as her tan legs and arms soaked up more Hawaiian bronze. He really wasn't anxious to talk to Harry. Not in this setting. He paused, then spoke.

"So now that you've scared the clerk half to death with your threats, what's up?"

Harry dropped his voice three octaves. "You got the death part right, Mike. The very worst kind. I got a call from Chief Nealy in Saratoga last night. He thinks the old town is ready to go to war over the return to gambling. In Nealy's opinion, the war might have started yesterday with the ugly death of one prominent mob member, Jake Palermo."

Flint interrupted. "Don Bocca's Palermo?"

"I'm afraid so, Mike. It was no ordinary gang hit. Palermo was mutilated almost beyond recognition. His eyes were scratched out and small chunks of limestone put into the sockets. The fingernails were pulled out and his tongue split apart. It was a savage killing. Whoever did him in was making a big statement. Though we haven't figured it out as yet. They burned some word into his forehead, but it's too messy to decipher."

"It's the strangest killing I've heard about in a long time," said Flint.

"Well," Harry continued, "now the ball's in Don Bocca's court. No one knows what Bocca will do about this. Nealy is dammed scared. The town fathers just rejected the reentry of gambling up there. That's not sitting well with Bocca or the mob. I can only guess that Palermo was sent to Saratoga to put the fear of God into the local officials. So, Mike, we come to you, like we always do. This is messy business and needs immediate attention. Can you cut that Hawaiian respite short?"

It suddenly seemed to Flint that the air-conditioned Royal Hawaiian foyer was getting cooler. He eyed Sandy again. She was still resting on her back, but now she had a wide-brimmed straw hat over her face. "Hell knows, this isn't going to set well with Sandy, Harry."

"I didn't think it would."

"No, you don't really know how she feels about me taking on assignments. That Sweetfeed thing almost ended our relationship. It's that serious. I'll have to pass on this one. Get out that black book of yours. I'm sure they're others that owe you one."

Harry couldn't help but take advantage of this remark. "Yeah, Mike. But no one who knows Saratoga like you."

"I've had my fill of Saratoga. I told you that when we wrapped up the Sweetfeed affair. Sandy refuses to go near the place. Said she gets bad vibes in 'Toga. Can't really blame her, can we?"

Harry's pleading continued. Flint let him go on, as he always did. Every conceivable reason to support his old friends in Saratoga was put forth by Harry. He was at his persuasive, nagging best, but Flint wasn't buying it. Not just yet. Flint had the phone at his side as Harry went on. He and Sandy had been in Hawaii just six days. It had all been spent here on Waikiki Beach, right in front of the Royal H. He liked the beach, she preferred the pool. Nevertheless, it was relaxing. The Royal H held some fond memories for Flint. Expensive, yes. He wasn't enamored with the five hundred fifty dollars a day room, but they had an ocean view and loved being pampered by the hotel's exquisite service.

Let the other tourists have Maui and the Big Island. Flint loved everything about this place. It was a beachfront oasis among the tall hotels, replete with bullet holes on its exterior from Dec. 7, 1941. Reminders that not all days on the famous golden beach were pleasant ones. Why was it that he felt any obligation to respond to Harry's wailing call? Flashes of his first two encounters in Saratoga reminded him that he was due to strike out. He knew he just didn't have the spunk left to tackle every dirty job that came along. Now in his mid-fifties, he detected slowness in most everything he did.

He'd even worried about it with Sandy. Would she discover one day that she had made a mistake by taking up with a slightly over-extended private investigator? One who wasn't always as sure of himself as he once had been? All the insecurities that had haunted him in recent years quickly passed through his mind. He also thought of Dr. Arnold Blake and Frank Duffy, the editor, his Saratoga friends.

How could he forget their warm reception and the way they took Sandy and him in, as if adopting them as family. Certainly there was reason to consider going to Saratoga. But then, had it not always been the way he chose to go or not to go? Duty was one thing. Friendship was something completely different. Duty had its limitation. Helping friends in time of need had no limits. It was, Flint knew, a weakness he'd never overcome, and no doubt Harry was aware of his soft side when it came to friends.

"Well, Flint, will you take the job?"

Flint's reply was slow in coming. "It's not solely my choice, Harry. I'm only fifty percent of the picture now. I need to talk with Sandy. I've already told you how she feels about any Saratoga ventures."

"True, true. I can fully sympathize with her." Harry's voice choked off while agreeing with Flint. "I didn't pick the spot. Circumstances dictate it. Unfortunately, Saratoga comes up heads again, but we don't have an alternative."

Flint took one more glance in Sandy's direction. She had moved from the lounge chair to poolside. He saw her dip one foot into the pool and slowly withdraw it. He admired her firm, tapered legs and the soft, rounded tan shoulders as she made ready to dive in. Selling her on this one would not be easy. It might even be impossible. Besides, they had eight days left on this visit in paradise. It was all paid for. Every expensive dollar's worth. If he were to accept, it would cost Harry a pretty penny in

Royal H's non-refundable recovery cost. Would discovering who knocked off Jake Palermo be worth that stiff bill? He wanted to express these sentiments to Harry, but decided not to until he'd had time to discuss it with Sandy.

"I'll have to call you back, Harry. No commitment at this time."

"Don't disappoint me Flint. I'm in a real bind."

The Royal Hawaiian reception room was oddly void of traffic as Flint set the phone down. Not even a bellcap was in sight. The desk clerk, frightened off, evidently wasn't about to come out again. Flint pondered how to handle this with Sandy. If, in fact, he was going to do anything at all. Why not let it go, he thought? After all, he'd paid his dues in Saratoga. Harry was perfectly capable of finding someone else to tackle this assignment. Besides, from what Harry told him of Jake Palermo's demise, it was a situation that could only get worse.

Flint was well aware that Don Bocca would not let the murder of his long-time trusted lieutenant, Palermo, go without being avenged. Knowing Bocca from past experiences, several unkindly deaths would most certainly be in the offing in coming days and weeks. Saratoga would soon be swimming in a blood bath. Flint felt a tightening in his stomach. Before going back outside to confront Sandy, he slipped over to the patio bar and ordered a scotch and water. Then, on second thought, he told the bartender to make it a double straight scotch on the rocks.

"You want it straight, sir?"

"Yes. Straight," said Flint. He checked his watch. It was four thirty. He then asked the bartender, "What day is this?"

The man gave him a quizzical stare. "Friday."

"Why, yes," said Flint. "I know it's Friday. We have a dinner date at the Barefoot Bar. How could I not know it's Friday?"

The bartender, without asking if Flint wanted a refill, topped off the glass with scotch.

"You're reading my mind," said Flint,

The bartender smiled. "You can get thirsty in the sun."

"Wrong," Flint corrected him. "This has nothing to do with thirst."

"Oh. I see. Something is troubling you?"

"Now you're closer." Flint agreed. "Trouble. That's the right word. It's an occupational hazard that has a way of following me no matter where I go. But you wouldn't really understand what I mean."

Flint realized that the bartender was busy washing the remainder of the glasses from a tray and wasn't tuned into his conversation. He laid down a twenty dollar bill, gulped the last ounce of scotch and walked slowly back to the pool area. He felt loose now.

The bright Hawaiian sun warmed his whole body within seconds. Sandy was just coming out of the pool. He paused to watch her. She spun around and tossed a dripping wet lock of dark hair back over her right shoulder. The moment their eyes met, Flint's face betrayed him. She could read the worry in it even from twenty feet away. She went back to her lounge and sat down, pulling a towel over her head, purposely trying to avoid looking at him. It was all body language between them for the next few minutes. She not wanting to hear him say it; he not able to say it. Nor daring to mention Harry.

Flint knew Sandy would go nuts at the very idea of Harry having called. It was what seemed now like an age-old dilemma. Tiptoeing the thin wire between sweet, romantic bliss with Sandy, or unforeseen danger. A tug-of-war he had neither won nor lost since meeting up with Sandy four years earlier in Saratoga. He agonized time and again over it. Give up crime busting altogether or risk losing Sandy to it. The all-too-painful memories of past loves and solid friendships lost because of his work. Yet, he prided himself on bringing cases to closure when others could not, and those rewards could not be ignored, either.

And the money. Money always counted, though he often found himself saying it didn't. A lifestyle had to be maintained. The Royal Hawaiian and a dozen other plush vacation spots like it don't come cheap. Perhaps, for the last time, he'd make the commitment. No. On second thought, he could not commit to it on his own. She'd have to be with him all the way, or he'd beg off. He had to get her more involved. That was the problem from the beginning. It haunted them when he was last in Saratoga to investigate the Sweetfeed thing. Sandy was left out. She not only resented his going off to face unknown hazards, she also felt completely left out of his life. He knew now, that if he were to commit this time, somehow she'd have to feel she wasn't being set adrift. Though to include Sandy meant exposing her to potential dangers. He found it difficult to reconcile this prospect.

The game of do or die that Flint was immersed in most of his adult life had, as he always rationalized, been one of give and take. He knew that to base any decision purely on his love for Sandy would be to thwart all objectivity of his chosen profession. It took a greater love on his part to keep her away from the lurking uncertainties of such work. He could not bring himself to tell her just yet. He decided he'd tell her later at the Barefoot Bar. Not that it would be any easier.

They swam for a time in the Royal Hawaiian pool and later took a short walk down Waikiki Beach to the Outrigger Club where Flint had one more scotch and Sandy sipped a gin and soda. Flint was watching some young surfers catching the breakers some 100 yards from shore. They crossed within inches of one another's boards, rode the rolling whitecaps for a time and then disappeared into the mixed blue and dark waters. He admired their agility and courage.

"Thinking of surfing, Flint?" Sandy poked him playfully.

"Why not, I've done everything else, haven't I?"

"Almost." She laughed. "It does look exciting."

He stood up and stretched his arms over his head. "Well, we probably won't surf, but we can do the next best thing."

"What's that?"

He directed her gaze to the beach where two local boys sat on an outrigger canoe.

"Are you game?"

She stood to join him. "Shove off, mate.

Let's do it."

In the lightness of the moment, Harry's phone call went out of Flint's head. They went down the beach and made arrangements to ride the outrigger. Within thirty minutes they were paddling, along with the two boys, out to meet the breaking surf off Waikiki. The Royal Hawaiian, its pink facade reflecting the afternoon sun, seemed much smaller from this distance, and the ocean seemed strangely ominous and much wilder. The beach boys, heads and shoulders bent forward, dug their paddles into the surf as each breaker went by, picking up more momentum as they moved the outrigger further out. The outrigger's bow cutting smoothly through the rolling, forceful waves, creaked as it pitched forward and backward in seesaw motion.

Sandy and Flint, not able to keep in sync with the beach boys paddling rhythm, gave up trying to assist. At a distance from shore of some three hundred yards, the boys turned the outrigger around, doing so in quick motions to avoid an oncoming roller. The lead paddler turned to face Sandy and Flint. He smiled and pointed one finger to a big roller aft of their rig, then shouted a command to his teammate in the rear. Sandy suddenly felt her stomach draw inward as the outrigger leaped forward, crested on the roller's tip, and jetted toward Waikiki Beach. Flint held Sandy by the waist while gripping his legs tight against the craft's sides to keep from tumbling overboard. All about them, darting in and out of the breakers, were boarders, some crossing their bow, others trailing off a short ways. Flint was surprised by the traffic. As they got nearer to shore, the boys resumed paddling at a fierce pace. Twenty yards off the beach, they spun the rig around and headed out again. It was a maneuver they would perform five times within the next hour, to a degree that Flint was getting pains in his legs. On their last run the boys went all the way to the beach, coming to an abrupt stop, jolting Flint and Sandy forward, nearly propelling Flint over Sandy's shoulders. He grabbed the gunwales to hold himself back.

"You like that ride?" asked the first paddler, his jet-black hair falling over large, round dark sunglasses.

Sandy, wobbling to her feet in the warm sand of Waikiki, holding Flint by one hand, drew a deep breath.

"It was different, I can tell you that."

"A real rush," added Flint.

The second paddler came up to them. "You come back tomorrow, earlier. We'll show you big rollers. Too calm this afternoon. Mid-day, come on outrigger mid-day. I'll show you."

Sandy shook her head. "No, thank you. Once was enough."

Before returning to the Royal H, Flint took Sandy to the Banyon Court at the Moana Hotel. They sat on the wide hotel verandah on white wicker furniture with large, pillowy cushions. Flint ordered two Singapore Slings.

"A bit early for those, isn't it?" Sandy said.

"It'll settle us from the outrigger. Besides, they serve the best slings in Hawaii right here."

She reached over, taking his hands into hers, and looked him directly in the eyes. "Flint, I think you're trying to soften me up for some bad news. Am I right?" She followed the quivering lines about his tan, unshaven face, and observed the hesitation in his eyes. "Tell me now. Tell me before we have those drinks. I don't what to be half stupored when you tell me. I might later regret agreeing to whatever it is you're about to tell me."

His head went backward and he stared at the cloudless sky.

"It's not fair. I know it's not fair." He gripped her shoulders and gently turned her around. "Harry called. It's deja vu all over again. Trouble in Saratoga."

Her eyes opened wide and Flint saw her face tighten at the mouth. Then, slowly, she fell back from his grip, her body slumping against the large backrest of the wicker chair. Finally, she spoke. "I thought we had an understanding about all this?"

He paused before answering. "We did. And, I've kept to it so far. I haven't committed to anything. All I said is that Harry called. He called on behalf of those mutual friends we have in Saratoga. Chief Nealy, on the official end, Frank Duffy, Dr. Blake and the rest."

The waiter brought their drinks. Flint took a long sip. Sandy fingered the rim of her glass and lowered her head. "What's it this time? More poisoned thoroughbreds and nasty killers?"

"Anybody's guess," Flint sighed. "A key mob operative was murdered. There's a push to reinstate gambling in Saratoga. The mob's been waiting in the wings since the fifties to get back in. The old mob boss, Don Bocca, has a personal stake in making it happen. Unfortunately for Bocca, the in crowd in Saratoga doesn't want gambling. I guess there's a few who do. One or two developers are voicing their approval for renewed gaming, but that's only because they own most of the prime real estate that would benefit from casino gambling. Some want to install slots at the track. Some want to separate the action and keep it on the fringe of

Saratoga. State and local politicians are perplexed on the issue. Tax revenue is being lost to the Native American tribes that now run gambling on their reservations in western New York and other states.

"After being stomped on for years, the Indians have rights of sovereignty granted to them by Congress and Supreme Court. They call it special privileges to make up for the past wrongs inflicted on their people. The mob wants to establish a foothold before too many more Indian operations get started."

"So why do you have to get involved?" Sandy glared at him.

"I don't. I told you that, unless, as I said, Blake and the rest can't find someone else to help them."

Sandy began sipping her drink. There was a long, strained, silence between them. Flint said nothing more. Sandy finished the Singapore Sling and motioned the waiter for another.

"Let's forget about it this evening," Flint insisted. "Pretend the subject never came up. We'll finish here, go to dinner at the Barefoot Bar and hit some hot music places later on. What do you say, love?"

"No. I want to discuss this right now. I want that second drink and I want to talk this out once and for all."

Flint was uneasy with her attitude. He knew it wouldn't get any easier after she had her second drink. A four-piece string band came into the Banyon Court and began playing soft, familiar Hawaii melodies. By the time Sandy's second drink was delivered, the mood and the setting had changed dramatically. So, Flint had another drink. He realized they'd be here longer than expected.

He tried once more to disengage her. " Can't we let this rest for now?"

She lifted her drink. "I'd rather talk."

An elderly couple passed by their table. The woman, dressed in a light, tan ankle-length dress had a string of sparkling diamonds around her neck. The man wore a dark silk suit. Flint figured they were in their late seventies. It was a common sight at this beach location. The rich and elderly, enjoying the fruits of their labors. He wondered if he'd ever be in that envious position? Better yet, would he ever reach that gilded age? He then fixed his gaze back on Sandy. The music had stopped.

"Gambling," he said quite suddenly, as if the conversation had never ceased. "Everyone thinks the answer to all their financial problems is gambling. That they'll all get rich by a stroke of gambling luck. Even the local and state politicians believe it. If you're inept at running a government, well, try gambling. It's a sure panacea, they believe. So that's what's going on in Saratoga. Those who wisely oppose it and those who insist on it. If we don't, someone else will, seems to be the rallying call. The facts and revenues are impressive, I'll agree. There's a little Oneida Nation group sitting on a small tract of land near Utica that opened up Turning Stone Casino a few years ago and now takes in millions. I heard they average eight thousand visitors a day. Bocca knows those figures."

Flint took a gulp of his drink and leaned his elbows on the table. "When you think about it, Saratoga is the perfect setting for gaming. Past history proves it. But when you weigh the consequence of casino gambling and its potential negative effect on the ballet, arts and related attractions in that small town, I believe the timing is not right. I'd say it's past peak for gambling at the Spa. With Palermo's death, though, the war has obviously begun. I don't want any part of it. If I go, it will only be out of obligation to our friends. We're a team now. This decision must be mutual. Unless you're with me on it, I'm turning Harry down."

Sandy was rolling the empty glass in her right hand. "Sorry, Flint, for my ingratitude. It's not Saratoga. It's not any particular place. It's all about you. About having you to myself. Not wanting to endanger you. How much can one man contribute? You've put yourself on the line too many times. Now they're begging again. If anything were to happen to you, I couldn't cope. I know myself. I'd wind up in a nut house. Though I also know how you feel." She lingered on her words, not able to express it properly. "I know one thing. I want to be with you on this. If you go, I'm going too. You'll have to put up with me, no matter how difficult it gets. Can we agree on this?"

He pulled her to his lap, her warmth and smell of perfume intoxicating his senses. He was oblivious to other guests sitting nearby.

"I'm afraid for both of us," he admitted softly. "More so for you. I need you every minute. My life is a hollow shell without you. I fear taking you on these assignments. Anything can happen. Yet I fear more leaving you behind. It tears me apart. If I give Harry the word, you're coming, we'll face this together. Is that a deal?"

She buried her head in his chest and cried gently. "Yes. Yes."

4. GET ME DR. BLAKE

It was Chief Nealy that Sergeant Galea heard, hollering down the wood-paneled hallway of City Hall, his voice sounding irritated and hoarse.

"Get me Dr. Blake on the phone," Nealy demanded.

Galea pushed his electronic Rolodex and watched it spin till Blake's number appeared. He dialed it. Betty Flood, Dr. Blake's receptionist, answered. "No, the doctor's out right now. Can I help you?"

"This is Galea. Chief Nealy wants the doctor."

"So does everybody in Saratoga. It's been one of those days. He's at the Y playing handball. He's got his beeper. I guess you can disturb him, though he won't like it. Handball's his only retreat from the pace."

"I can appreciate that," agreed Galea. "But you know Nealy. Thanks, Betty."

Nealy's thundering voice came up the hallway again. "Did you reach Blake?"

"I'm trying his beeper right now," Galea shouted back.

"Make it quick. I have to talk to him."

Galea entered his number in at the beep. A few moments later, Dr. Blake called.

"He's on," Galea notified Nealy.

Galea hung up when Nealy picked up his phone.

"Arnold," Nealy began in a resonant voice. "Any more on Palermo's autopsy? I'm concerned about this killing. Very concerned."

"Only what you originally were told," said Blake.

"No final report yet?"

"Well, Tom, it's pretty much what we said when he was first found. The mutilation was almost ritualistic in its severity. Whoever did it wasn't just trying to rub him out. They were making a statement of the worst kind. I'd say it was purely pathological. The poor devil was mutilated over his entire body. Scratch marks, pin holes and assorted torture marks. I don't have any idea how many men Palermo killed in his mob career. But I can tell you this, he paid for it dearly."

"That's what I've been saying. This spells big trouble. Hell, Arnold, I hope that damn fool St. Jacques isn't moving on Saratoga with his Canadian mob. It sounds very much like his calling card. I'm not saying it is St. Jacques, but he can't be completely ruled out. If he and Bocca are at war, we're in deep manure and Saratoga's in deeper manure."

"I agree with you, Tom, it looks very bad at this point. I never gave St. Jacques a thought. After Flint's last encounter with St. Jacques in Quebec, I was of the opinion he wasn't interested in any operations south of Crown Point. But, then, I could be wrong."

Nealy lifted his tired feet to the desktop and stretched his sore legs and back, cocking the receiver under his chin. At the same time, he reached in the desk and took out a pipe and examined its contents. It was filled with his favorite Captain Black tobacco. He remembered stuffing it full over two weeks ago and never once having smoked it. He decided now he needed a good smoke.

Blake, wondering about the silence, spoke again. "You still with me, Tom?"

"Why, yes," said Nealy, firing up his pipe. "Where were we?"

"St. Jacques." Blake reminded him.

"Yes. Well, St. Jacques and Bocca. Two of the worst you'll ever meet. Why do they have to live in this region of the country? And, why can't these mob types leave well enough alone? *If* St. Jacques had a hand in Palermo's murder."

"Maybe we will find out who's involved," Blake reassured him.

"How's that?"

"Flint."

"Is Flint in Saratoga?"

"Not yet, but he may soon be."

"How do you know?"

There was a sudden tone of excitement in Blake's normally controlled professional voice.

"Harry Waite called me an hour ago. He's been in touch with Flint. Waite thinks he's convinced Flint to come back again. He's still with Sandy, so no doubt she'll be coming with him. Waite said he'd know for certain by tomorrow. If it's a go, we had better figure out some place for them to stay. There wasn't any mention of Flint's fee, though somehow we'll have to come up with it. I hope your slush fund is a hefty one."

Nealy's feet slipped from the desk, hitting the tile floor with a loud thud.

"Money. Damn well knew we'd have to spring for something. The slush fund is dry. No matter. If we have to pass the tin cup up and down Broadway, we'll find a way to pay Flint's freight. If he can thwart this war before it gets out of hand, I'll give him a gold bar. Even if I have to rob Fort Knox. Tell Waite we want Flint here pronto."

"I'll do my best, Tom. By the way, do you really think the mobs are fighting among themselves? And if so, why such a gruesome type killing? It's been bothering me all week. Christ, they practically skinned that old mobster alive, from what I've been told by the pathologists."

Nealy took a deep breath. "You're not the only one trying to figure this out, Doc. As I told Galea yesterday, it's savage in nature. Not your average mob hit. They usually keep it simple and clean. Some real nasty killing took place in the old days, but not in recent years. The mob's been striving to keep a low profile. The press will have a field day with this once the truth is known. Which reminds me, have you talked to Duffy over at the *Star* yet?"

"No, I haven't. I expect he's got his investigative reporters working overtime."

"I better call him," said Nealy. "Better yet, why don't we meet for a drink and discuss this whole mess?"

"Fine by me."

"Noon tomorrow," Nealy offered. " If we can get Duffy out. How about the Saratoga Brew House on Phila Street?"

"Noon it is," agreed Blake.

When the conversation ended, Nealy strolled across the office and pulled a file from the gray metal filing cabinet. He went over to the window that looked down on Lake Avenue where it intersected with Broadway, and began reading the file's contents. It was not pleasant reading.

He pored over the details of Flint's first investigation in Saratoga three years earlier where Sara, the young girl informant, had been killed. He remembered all the trauma and unfavorable publicity the old Spa City had received over that affair. Of course, there was further embarrassment to Nealy because he didn't know Mike Flint, nor did he have any idea that Harry Waite's special New York City crime unit was operating in Saratoga.

Nealy viewed it then, and did so now, as unprofessional in both concept and implementation. In retrospect, knowing the complexity of the investigation, he knew it could not have been accomplished without Flint's help. Still, it gnawed at Nealy's professional pride. After all, wasn't he the Chief of Police? Wasn't he called forth by the Saratoga community to protect and defend the town? He read further.

The second embarrassing incident was even worse. Flint was summoned by Blake and Duffy to find out who killed the Spa's most famous former prima ballerina, Claire Valova, and Ann Bifford, her once-trusted thoroughbred veterinarian. Behind the insurance money plot was the backstretch's old sage, Sweetfeed, and his friend, Waterman.

When Nealy found out that Sweetfeed was part of the insurance scam, it almost destroyed his faith in mankind. It dug deep at the roots of his moral conscious. It was devastating in every sense of the word. Nealy recalled how it took him weeks to recover from it, though all the time he had to keep his daily appearance and attitude on a professional level. Others, but not the police chief, could wear the wailing and outward grief around town. Nealy knew that and he put on a remarkable front in public. Everyone noted how steady he was through it all.

They all died because someone wanted to make a quick, dishonest buck. Nealy's back fought off a shiver as he recalled how his old friend, Track Superintendent Joe Hennesy, died. He was found bound and gagged by the one person in town Nealy never would have expected to be involved in the insurance scheme, Todd Wilson, the landscaper. Nealy was ashamed it happened on his watch. A sordid mess of unimaginable consequence. Dead bodies all over town. It was a nightmarish experience, shredding the very fabric of Saratoga's society.

Then came the most humiliating and soul-searching aspect of the Sweetfeed affair, the decision by Blake, Duffy and the others to keep Valova's involvement in the horse killings secret. Of all the revered persons about town, Valova's implication shocked the hardened Nealy to the bone. Against all his intrinsic ethics and police code of conduct, Nealy had to swallow this bitter pill so the Spa's reputation could be preserved. A tightly woven, three-year string of murder and mystery not seen in the town in a century was more than enough to elicit thoughts of resignation from Nealy.

But he refused to give in and admit he'd been beaten on his own turf. Men like Flint may very well better address crime fighting on this scale, Nealy was thinking. Yes. Let the Flint's of the world deal with the sinister, methodical killers. Flint was, in Nealy's opinion, trained to filter them out. If it required killing in return to justify the means, then an expert devotee of the martial arts, with a killer's instinct like Flint, was probably the right choice. It was not Nealy's way, but sometimes it was the only way. Flint had proven this on his last two Saratoga assignments, legally approved by Nealy, or not.

Nealy came back to the most recent killing. " Why," he said aloud, "would anyone want to kill a man like this?" As the technician from

The Albany Medical Center morgue had so graphically described it, "The poor fellow looked like a plucked chicken, skinned twice over." Nealy knew that once Don Bocca became aware of the demise of Jake Palermo, his old lieutenant, in such a gruesome way, all hell would break loose. Bocca would suspect everyone, striking quickly and without impunity.

There would be thunder up and down the Hudson Valley from the old Don, and Nealy was afraid Bocca's wrath would extract a terrible toll before it was over. Nealy had been privy to these wild gang wars in past years. He'd actually conducted an investigation in the early fifties that thwarted a mob war between New Jersey and Boston crime families bidding for power in Springfield, Massachusetts, where he first entered law enforcement. He knew that once a war got started, very little could be done to stop it. He wasn't about to let it happen in Saratoga now.

He also knew he'd need Flint's help if he were to avoid an inner mob vendetta. He lit a cigar and let the smoke out slowly, watching it curl upward toward the high ceiling. Little ringlets of donut-size white smoke, one after the other, went up and disappeared. Then he remembered the previous year's devastating Ostrander Estate fire and the large, bellowing clouds of smoke that filled the sky that dreadful night of Meredith Ostrander's lawn party. It all came back to him in a heart-rending flash. The tragedy and the aftermath, including caretaker Carlos Mann's indictment for arson.

Meredith's heart attack that killed her a few days following the fire, the loss of so many horses, property and cars consumed on that night – each smoke ring reminded Nealy further of other incidents attached to the nightmarish fire. Why, wasn't it the aging insurance man from Kentucky, Stuart Clayborn Witt, who had sat at this very desk and prompted last year's unnerving investigation with his sudden disappearance? Nealy visualized the fellow's round, red smiling face, with the large-brimmed straw hat, that lead him to compare his looks to that of Colonel Sanders. When, in the final stages of the investigation, they found that Witt was brutally murdered at the hands of that old backstretch hand Sweetfeed himself, it was news even a hard-bitten cop like Nealy had difficulty swallowing.

It was all coming back to Nealy, leaping from his subconscious in a most unpleasant manner. One smoke ring went sideward, pushed, Nealy noticed, by a sudden draft of air within the semi-lit office. He spun around to face the door. Galea's mustached face appeared.

"Oh, for Christ sake, Sargeant, you've ruined my perfect donuts. Thus far I had thirty or so going skyward."

"I know," said Galea, now inside the office and standing at Nealy's' desk. "We smelled the cigar on the upper floor. Thought you had given them up." Nealy held the cigar up with two fingers. "A good smoke calms the nerves. You should try it sometime."

"Well," continued Galea, both hands now pressed on the desk top, "the mob hit is really getting interesting. Dr. Blake called a half hour ago to say he has to talk to you before closing. Wouldn't give me any details. Did say, however, that he's been in touch with a local man who may know something. You'd best call Blake."

Nealy planted the half-smoked cigar in a large, glass ashtray, twirling it once or twice till it was out. Galea, visibly displeased with its aroma, backed toward the door. "I'll get the Doc on the line from upstairs. I'll connect you." "Please do that," answered Nealy, still half absorbed in the reports he'd been scanning. He then put them back in the drawer.

A few minutes later the red light on Nealy's phone blinked. He picked up the receiver.

"That you, Doctor?"

"As sure as this is Friday," Blake replied.

"Galea says you may have a lead."

"Yes," said Blake. "But it's a strange one. Got a call yesterday from a professor at Union College in Schenectady. Thomas Halfmoon Hitchcock. He heads up Union's anthropology department. He's a full-blooded Iroquois, born and raised on the St. Regis Reservation upstate. Says he has more than a curious interest in Palermo's murder. I asked him why, and he said he didn't want to discuss it over the phone. I suggested we set up a meeting. I mentioned to him that you'd probably be included. He had no qualms about this. What do you think?"

"What am I to think?" asked Nealy. "Can't be your average nut if he's a professor at Union, can he? We're going nowhere with this investigation now. Anything's worth a try."

"That's what I was thinking," agreed Blake. "We also have Flint coming in, so he may want to get involved with this Halfmoon guy."

Nealy stretched his legs and propped his feet once more on the desk. "Flint will be in next week. Let's set the meeting for mid-week and let's do it on Halfmoon's turf. Call him back and select a Schenectady location. I'm sure Union has an appropriate spot where we can gather. Privacy is what we're looking for. Then Nealy, thinking about it, said "I'm not up on anthropology, Doc. I'll have to depend on your expertise in this category. They study apes, don't they?"

"That and many other beings," Blake said.

"Fine by me," Nealy added. "By the way, I haven't touched base with Frank Duffy on any of this yet. Will you call him and see if he wants to attend this meeting? He may still be working late at the *Star*. I have to give Frank credit for keeping the Palermo murder low key. Not easy with all those young, eager reporters baiting him to sensationalize every off-beat happening in town. He's a class act."

"I'll get to Duffy today," Blake said.

"See you soon," Nealy told him, setting the receiver down.

Nealy pondered his next move. He was still uneasy. He looked at the wall calendar. March 15. Less than five months to racing season. Why in hell did all of these unfortunate situations take place in or near springtime, he wondered. It was as if fate was putting him to the test each season. Pressuring him from all angles till he was ready to burst with frustration. He felt his pulse. Not good.

He figured his blood pressure was running high, too. He didn't even want to guess what it was. What bothered him most was the insecurity of not knowing when the next shoe in this Palermo murder case would drop. If only he could get inside the mind of Don Bocca. What was the sinister, diabolic, old mob boss thinking this very minute? It gnawed at Nealy's stomach.

Whatever Bocca was planning, it would not be nice. Nealy knew he'd be facing many sleepless nights ahead until this whole affair unraveled. He also knew he needed Mike Flint's help more than ever.

5. DUFFY

Frank Duffy told his wife, Martha, "Give me some peace. God knows this town needs it. What, with all these reports of murder going on in Saratoga, is anyone to do? We never had these problems, not even in the thirties when that old rascal, Albert Bartone was running bootleg whiskey down Lake Champlain to Ticonderoga and then to Lake George."

Bartone had boats that could outrun any motor craft on the lakes, including the big ones the cops had. An aircraft engine, Duffy remembered, powered Bartone's boat. It used to get so hot, its twin exhaust stacks blew flames into the night sky, roaring and spraying huge streams in its wake. And even when the cops saw it coming, they couldn't catch it. It was a brazen thing to behold.

Duffy remembered the time he actually witnessed a midnight chase on Lake George when Bartone's speedy craft out-raced three police boats, leaving one marooned on a dark island, where it crashed while pursuing Bartone's men.

"At the height of the booze flow from Canada, we had a few shootings here and there, but nothing of this magnitude. No, it was mostly done among the bootleggers. Now the shooting and killing include the innocent. The Wild West right in our own backyard. It's a travesty."

Martha poured Duffy a cup of coffee. "I must say, Frank, you're getting a little old to involve yourself in this stuff. I know that sounds harsh, but it's true. Let Nealy and the rest handle it. We're not up to this anymore."

Duffy tipped the hot liquid to his lips, blew on it for a second and eyed Martha with a look of bewilderment.

"Fine that you're able to trivialize our importance in all this, Martha. I'll beg you to speak for yourself. Aged or not, I have a responsibility to Saratoga that says I must be involved. As long as I'm living and breathing. True, I'm too damn old to chase and fight, but not so old that I can't use my mind and experience to assist Nealy and the others in any way I can. Besides, Mike Flint's on his way here. Whatever is going on, whatever forces are at work now in Saratoga, I can't say. I have all the faith in the world that Flint will find out." He pursed his lips once more and sipped. "Damned if this isn't the hottest coffee I ever had."

"No hotter than usual," Martha snorted back.

Duffy, his gold-rimmed pincer glasses resting on the tip of his nose, thumbed through Saturday's edition of *The Star*, an issue in which he had no hand. Duffy was now allowing junior editors to complete the Wednesday and Saturday papers without his assistance, an arrangement he had worked out with *The Star's* publishers, anxious to turn over the old editor's 60-year revered position in an orderly transition to younger, more progressive editors.

It was a gray day dawning on Duffy's horizon, and he dreaded it every waking moment. Martha, on the other hand, was silently welcoming his retirement – forced or voluntary – so they could enjoy their remaining days in peace and quiet. The past three years had been especially trying. Duffy's golden parachute could not come any too soon in Martha's opinion.

With all the recent upheaval in Saratoga of late, Martha wanted nothing better than for Duffy to get out. Call it quits once and for all. If the town was toying with the return to gambling and the prospects of being overrun by gangsters and low lifes, then so be it. But Martha would not be a party to it. No, she'd had enough.   And why Duffy insisted on keeping his nose in the middle of all this wrangling was beginning to disturb her even more. Wasn't it only sensible that people in their late seventies step aside? Hadn't she, hadn't Duffy, pulled the sled for too long? Thoughts of a beach house in Florida or the Caribbean were more to her liking now.

Duffy's beloved *Saratoga Star*, no matter how important in his life, was becoming a burden Martha could no longer tolerate. She felt it was high time to put her foot down. Today was as good as any day to start.

She was just about ready to blurt out her feelings when, with a startled turn of her head, the front door to the living room opened, and Billy Farrell, Duffy's lifelong buddy and newspaper crony, stepped inside unannounced.

"Damned if you didn't half scare me to death," Martha admonished him.

Farrell, smiling, replied, "Just Billy Boy, Martha. Just Billy Boy."

"We have a doorbell, Billy Boy. Use it."

Duffy was on his feet. "Pay no attention. Remember when no one in town shut a door? Never had to, right, Billy?"

"Yeah." Farrell agreed. "They swung both ways. You could come and go confidently."

Then he rubbed his forehead with one hand. "Christ, Frank. That was a long time ago."

"Well it hasn't changed among us," said Duffy, ushering Farrell to be seated. "Though Martha here is a bit touchy these days about unlocked doors, aren't you, Martha?"

"Better safe than sorry, I say." Martha called from the kitchen to which she had retreated.

"Guess Billy will have a cold beer while you're out there. If you'd be so kind."

"I suppose you want one too?"

"No, darling. I'll have a touch of scotch. A half jigger over the rocks."

Martha appeared again in the living room. "No scotch for you, Duffy. Doctor's orders. Settle for a beer, or nothing at all."

Duffy looked at Farrell with a blank stare. "Now they're telling us what to drink. Nothing is sacred in this world anymore."

Farrell winked back. "I get the same advice from Helen. Maybe they're trying to tell us something we don't know."

"Whatever it is, I don't want to hear it," said Duffy. "OK, Martha. Two beers."

Martha came back with two pilsner glasses foaming over at the brim. Duffy grabbed one with his pudgy, small round right hand and Farrell lifted his glass with two cigar-size fingers and half emptied his beer in one swallow.

111

"Don't tell me," said Farrell.,"it's the new North Country Amber? Wonderful taste."

"Not quite," Duffy said.

"But it is from a local brew house," insisted Farrell.

"Almost."

Farrell finished the rest of his beer. "I'm certain. It is North Country, isn't it?"

Duffy raised his glass and drank. "Try Phila Street. How about the Big Brew House? Pretty good stuff, eh?"

Farrell held out his glass to Martha for a refill. "I'll drink to the Big Brew House."

"If you're driving, I'm serving no more than two beers this evening, Billy. So enjoy it while it lasts."

Duffy knew that Farrell had not come over just to have a beer. No, Farrell was here to discuss the latest incident, as they had done over sixty years of hometown friendship. Duffy knew Farrell, like himself, was upset with the most recent killing of Palermo.

Farrell called Duffy earlier in the week to say how very grave he felt the situation was. And how ironic that this killing took place in winter. It almost had a familiar ring to it. After all, hadn't Robin's murder three years ago taken place in winter, casting a deep shadow over their little town? Likewise, Clare Valova and Ann

Bifford's murders and investigations began during the winter months.

It was, as Farrell had told Duffy, a bad omen. Almost as if a curse was placed on Saratoga in recent months. A curse to test their collective wills.

Duffy tried to assure his friend that it was nothing of the kind. Sure, Duffy was equally concerned. Who wouldn't be? Though he attributed it to dynamics at work that were well beyond their control. Even beyond Chief Nealy's control. Circumstances and big money were the real driving force behind most of it.

That, and the iron will of one determined mob boss to seek revenge for a long-dead mob boss that really had no relevance in today's world, save for money, control and a wishful hope to turn the clock back.

It was Duffy's conviction that Palermo's demise was the result of mob infighting. Vendettas of old being played out on a modern stage. Unfortunately, the stage was Saratoga. Why in March? Why in Saratoga? Anyone's guess. Only a man with Flint's experience was up to the task, Duffy assured Farrell as they finished their beers. If not Flint, then who?

Farrell agreed, telling Duffy that Nealy expected Flint within two days, and relating that Nealy had no idea where Flint and Sandy were

113

staying. Nor did Dr. Blake. He had not asked anyone to make lodging arrangements, though he presumed Flint would handle his own accommodations, locally or otherwise. With a little persuasion, they coaxed Martha into filling their drinks half way. When they were done, Duffy walked Farrell to his car.

"Keep in touch, Billy. I guess we'll all have to meet when Flint finally does arrive. Doc Blake will no doubt set this up."

"Fine by me," said Farrell. Then, hesitating a moment before entering his car, he added, "Frank, I never really asked you where you stand on this whole gambling issue."

"Knowing me as well as you do, I didn't think you'd have to ask," said Duffy.

"It's such a sticky thing," said Farrell. "It's got this whole town tugging at one another. Even the Chamber of Commerce is split right up the middle. Three years ago, no one on the Chamber wanted gambling. Why the change?" Duffy put his hand on Farrell's shoulder.

"Money. Damn greed and money. Pressure, fear. Lots of reasons for people changing their thinking. None of them good, or sound. But that's life. Or, as we all know, a haunting fear that the race course with all its troubles may not be around much longer. Gambling will kill this town surer than anything. Let them take it elsewhere. Keep it on the reservations. Keep it in Atlantic City. Not in Saratoga. Drive slow, friend. Pray that Flint can help us once more."

Duffy waited for Farrell to back out on the street, and watched till he drove off. Back inside, Martha was just shutting off the kitchen lights.

"Billy gone?" she called to Duffy.

"Yes. He's halfway home by now."

Martha came in and held her husband's arm.

"Billy looked worried tonight, more than I've seen him in recent months. Is he well?"

"Fit as a pup. Worried, yes. Aren't we all? Let's to go bed, mommy."

6. FLINT'S BACK

The phone in Dr. Arnold Blake's office rang on Monday night as Blake was arriving home from a late meeting at Saratoga Hospital. He checked his watch. It was 10:30 P.M.

"Doc?" He recognized Flint's familiar, baritone voice. "We're here in Saratoga. Sorry for calling you so late. I want a meeting as soon as possible. If not tomorrow, no later than Wednesday. You can set it up."

Blake rubbed his eyes. "Yes, Mike, anything you want. Where are you staying?"

"We're nearby. I'd rather not say at this time. Call Harry in New York when you've got the meeting lined up. He'll relay the message to me. The less we talk over local lines, the safer this operation will go. And no cell phone conversations. They're picking those conversations out of the air at random. I feel better channeling things through Harry for now. Once we've established a secure, local communications system, we won't have to use Harry. One thing more, Doc. I'd like to see every bit of news copy that's available since Palermo's death. You can start with the *Star's* coverage. I'm sure Duffy can supply all that's required. But I'd like to review the wire service stuff, also. The more I think about it, you can dump this whole request on Frank."

"You'll be reading for a month," interrupted Blake.

"I'm a speed reader, Doc. Besides, Sandy can help me go through it all. It's very important I get all the past news stuff I can. Bocca is a conservative man by nature. Dangerous and unpredictable, yes. But very conservative by mob standards. He pays strict attention to press accounts. Always has. The old Don won't take unnecessary chances. You can bet he'll be reading every printed word and basing his moves accordingly. He won't act suddenly if he feels the heat is on. The last thing he wants is a caravan of reporters circling Saratoga trying to scoop one another. Remember, he's been patient for over 40 years. The mob wants back in here, but not at the expense of their statewide operations."

"The cat's out of the bag, Mike. One very badly cut up, dead Palermo was all the press needed to arouse their suspicions."

"Not necessarily so," Flint tried to assure

him. "That's why I want all those news clippings. If the news types are treating this as an isolated hit, we may be all right. They'll hang around till they bore one another with stale jokes, then leave town. Or, as I figure it, until we devise a way to make it look like Palermo was killed by one of his own. There are ways to rig this, though it won't be easy."

Blake seated himself behind his big mahogany desk and pulled the phone closer. "Fine, Mike. But we have Molly O'Neill's account of the other night to deal with. How do you explain that away?"

Flint lowered his voice. "Can you come up with the mysterious van, Doc? It can be any van. As long as we produce one that fits Molly's description. Mind what I'm saying here. We don't come up with the reported fanatical driver, we simply produce the van. Naturally it has no plates. No fingerprints. No identifying marks. It's a van. Someone drove it recklessly at O'Neill. Perhaps a drunk. No one knows.

"This justifies her story, while proving nothing in the way of a deliberate attempt on her life. If we can confuse everybody, we'll have time to concentrate on what really took place on East Avenue. With Nealy's help, of course, we can stall the investigation for days, maybe weeks. We'll need all the time we can get so I

119

can sift out the mob connections, both Bocca's and whoever. If it's St. Jacque's Canadian mob trying to take control, I'll know that shortly.

"The pressure on Bocca could be coming from a number of mob mavericks. Saratoga is prime gambling ground. No pun intended, but the stakes are high. Keep the van option open. I may not have to use my bag of dirty tricks. If I do, it has to come off just right to be believable."

Blake drew a deep breath. "It's your call, Mike. Give me Harry's number. I'll take care of the details here. Nealy's been sweating this one out. He'll rest easier knowing you're finally in 'Toga." Then Blake added, "How's Sandy? Are you two engaged yet? No. Forget that. It's none of my business."

"Sandy is fine," said Flint. "She's not along for a joy ride. She wants to work with me all the way. I'm against it, of course, but she's insistent. I couldn't have taken this assignment unless she became a full partner. We fully share with each other, be it love or danger. Your former nurse is still as beautiful as ever and every bit as independent. I wouldn't have her any other way."

"Give her a kiss for me," said Blake.

"Will do, Doc. See you soon."

Though it was almost eleven, Blake decided

to call Duffy and Nealy at home to convey Flint's wishes. Blake reached Duffy in bed, but not before Martha had given him a piece of her mind on his age and the fact that he wasn't really geared these days to handle all the intrigue and pressure of recent months.

Wasn't Duffy's daily routine at *The Star* pressure enough for an aging editor? Must he bear the brunt of every dastardly deed perpetrated in Saratoga? No, younger men should face these problems. Duffy had more than paid his dues over the years. Then realizing she had gone too far, she regained her composure, lowered her voice to a more even tone, and said, "Forgive my nastiness, doctor. But as you well know in your profession, we all have our boiling points. I've reached mine."

"I understand, Martha. Your point is well taken. It's just that we've become so used to Duffy's wise counsel, we don't always stop to think of the consequences. And that goes for me, psychiatrist or not. I'll only be a minute with him, if he's still awake."

"One moment," she said.

When Duffy came on the phone, Blake knew he was talking to a man with one ear already solidly glued to his pillow. Duffy's voice was a mere whisper of its normal self. Blake was thinking that perhaps he had caught Duffy between consciousness and a dream. That fine crossover where, as he so often encountered with some patients, the mind's not quite sure if it's awake or asleep. In any event, he told Duffy of Nealy's desired meeting with Flint, with hopes that Duffy would remember it when he got up in the morning. It was the best Blake could do under the circumstances and owing to the late hour of his call.

"We're turning into a bunch of night owls," Blake mused.

Blake's phone call to Chief Nealy was next. Blake kept his call brief. Nealy, fending off a yawn, sounded pleased and relieved that Flint was finally in Saratoga, and also acknowledged that this first meeting would be of the utmost importance. When his call to Nealy was completed, Blake decided to retire for the evening. He checked in on his wife, Ellen, already asleep with the book she had been reading resting on her chest. He gently removed the book, pulled the covers up around her shoulders, undressed himself, save for his shorts, and slipped in next to her. He turned out the reading light, rolled to one side and soon fell into a deep sleep.

Somewhere in the depth of his subconscious, Blake drifted into a strange, disturbing dream. Black-hooded individuals were running down Saratoga's Broadway with torches in their hands shouting at one another, though he couldn't make out a word they were saying. Suddenly they turned east on Lake Avenue and abruptly halted in front of *The Star,* which was all lit up. At that moment, Duffy's face appeared in *The Star's* Lake Avenue window. The hooded devils tossed their torches at the building and one struck the window where Duffy was standing. There was a pause, then a spontaneous burst of flames that engulfed *The Star.* Blake then saw Duffy on the building's roof, flames dancing all about his little frame, his white hair blowing in the updraft caused by the roaring fire. Then, in a puff of white smoke, both Duffy and *The Star* were no longer. Only a vacant lot remained. The black-hooded strangers were also gone. Blake found himself in a cold sweat, sitting upright in bed.

The bedroom was silent except for Ellen's low, steady breathing. How weird, he thought, that such a dream should invade his subconscious. Blake had never been prone to dreams of any sort, as far as he could remember. He wiped the cold, dripping beads from his face.

As a psychiatrist, he thought he was above such things. Now, experiencing the dream's realism, with all its frightening aspects, he could appreciate the terror and anxiety of many of his frail patients who often came to him for help with their dreams, or night terrors, as they often called them.

He felt Ellen's hand on his right arm. "What is it?" she asked.

"Nothing, darling. Nothing."

"Arnold, your body is wet," she said.

"I know. I woke up in a cold sweat. Actually, I was dreaming. I had a bad dream. Don't ask me why I've taken to dreaming, but I did. I believe it was a psychosomatic reaction to the day's proceedings. Clinically speaking, of course. In truth, it was a damn scary dream."

"Well you'd best get into the shower," Ellen insisted. "Then I'll make you a cup of hot chocolate. You should take an aspirin while you're at it."

Early the following morning, shortly before the Blakes had their daily 7 A.M. coffee, the kitchen phone rang. Blake answered it.

"No, I don't believe it. God knows that is a coincidence. I'll be talking to Duffy later. Thanks for calling us."

Ellen could read the puzzlement in her husband's face. "More bad news, Arnold?" she inquired.

"Yes and no," He replied, setting the receiver down. "Seems they had a small fire at *The Star* last night. Nothing too serious. Started in the downstairs printing section. They apparently doused it before it got out of hand."

He looked out the kitchen window and smiled. "You know something, darling? We live in a strange world. It's getting stranger all the time in my estimation."

Ellen looked up at him. "What makes you say that?"

He was still staring out the window, at what she didn't know, and he failed to answer her. In his mind he was trying to replay his dream, but it did not come clear. The dream, and the reality of the actual newspaper fire, would bother him the rest of the day.

7. MEMORY LANE

Mike Flint and Sandy stepped outside the front door of Saratoga's Sheraton Hotel, their first exposure to the city since arriving earlier that morning in a shroud of secrecy that rivaled the best of Flint's past cloak and dagger missions. In retrospect, he knew he was being overly cautious for, after all, who, with the exception of Blake and his cronies, would recognize him anyway? His precautions were really for Sandy's sake.

Former hospital employees, or close Saratoga friends might well spot her, having worked with Blake prior to her sudden departure two years ago. Secrecy had to be maintained for all its apparent folly. Their hurried departure from Honolulu and the rush to Saratoga was taking its toll. Flint was irritable and tired. Sandy was still silently fuming that Harry Waite had interrupted their Waikiki Beach vacation. Not to mention leaving that beautiful oceanfront Royal Hawaiian Hotel room Flint paid a king's ransom to secure. And to come back east in March of all months. July or August, maybe. Not March. How could Harry pull such a stunt? She felt worse for Flint with his water-thin California blood. At least she had spent a few years in this unforgiving winter climate, a climate she admittedly never liked nor got used to, but rather endured. For Flint it was pure hell. No matter how warmly he dressed, cold was cold.

So now they were out on Broadway, just across the street from the former Firehouse Restaurant. Sandy pointed it out to Flint. " It seems strange to see the old Firehouse closed. What fond memories."

Flint grabbed her arm. "I guess we shouldn't be showing our faces on Broadway, but I don't care. Let's go for a walk."

"Fine," replied Sandy. "Like you're fond of saying, let's live dangerously."

Surprisingly enough, the bitter cold they had anticipated was nothing more than a mild, late-winter breeze suddenly sweeping through Saratoga. A seasonal thaw that normally came in January, but arrived very late this year. Thaws were both a curse and a blessing, depending on what you did for a living in Saratoga. Old Sacca hated winter thaws. It melted the ice on Lake Lonely and played havoc with his fishing. On the other hand, the city's street department loved thaws. Road crews had less snow plowing to do and the city saved money on road salt. About the only places not affected by winter thaws were the local bars. People ventured out to drink no matter what the weather.

So now, with their rubber-soled boots sloshing along, they walked slowly down Broadway, past City Hall, crossing over Lake Avenue where Flint could look eastward and see the *The Star* building and a bit further down, The Parting Glass, Frank Duffy and Billy Farrell's hangout. Then farther along Broadway, they crossed over Caroline Street with its variety of watering holes and eateries. There was one new jazz place neither had seen before, One Caroline Street, which was closed this night. Next in line was Lillians, and Flint squeezed Sandy's hand and smiled in recognition of the night three years earlier when he had met her for the first time.

The whirlwind happenings of those hectic days and nights flashed across both their memories. The bathtub murder of Sandy's friend Robin; Sandy's own close call with death. It was all coming back. Flint's equally chilling flirtation with death in Quebec from Maurice St Jacques, the Canadian mob king. In the faint lights of Lillian's, they looked into each other's eyes and without saying a word, embraced. Those memories were so vivid in their minds that he could feel Sandy trembling under her wool coat – the way she had trembled the night Flint had rescued her from certain death.

After a time, they continued walking. They paused at Phila Street and Broadway to gaze over at two relics of Saratoga's gilded age, The Rip Van Dam and Adelphi Hotels. There was activity within the Rip's lobby, but the Adelphi, except for one lighted window on the third floor, was closed and dark. Sandy remembered many exciting visits to the Adelphi when the New York City Ballet was in for its annual July soiree. The hotel now appeared bleak and forlorn.

A stream of water poured off Broadway and down Phila as they stepped gingerly through the slush to the far curb. Sandy squeezed Flint's hand tightly and her pace slowed. It was a moment of fear and surprise, for she realized she was standing outside her former apartment building, the building in which Flint killed her would-be assassin. It was a revelation she wasn't particularly happy to remember. Flint sensed her apprehension.

"Do you want to go back?" he asked.

"No. It's fine. It's just that it caught me off guard. How could I have forgotten so quickly that I lived here?"

Flint held her arms. "Easy," he said. "We've been living a whirlwind life since that first night. You've absorbed so much in the interim. Just think about it. And I haven't made it any easier on you. I should have told Harry no thanks on this assignment."

"You know you couldn't," she insisted. "We're here because we made the commitment to friends to be here, no matter the outcome. I went along with it, too. It wasn't a solitary decision." She walked away a few paces, then stopped and turned to face him. "You know something, Flint? Think how different it all would have been if you hadn't interceded that night. I'd be just another headstone in the family's plot in Boston. It's really profound when I look back on it.

"Worst of all, Saratoga, the world for that matter, might never have known why I was killed. Oh, they'd talk about the poor murdered nurse for a time, but it would all be forgotten and, the more I think of it, so would I. But you changed all that, didn't you? She threw her arms over her head and spun around three times, the soft, melting snow beneath her feet becoming a small puddle of water. "Oh, if anyone has a knight in armor, I do."

She was then in his arms again, crying and

131

laughing softly on his whiskered cheek.

"Destiny. It was destiny," Flint told her. "No more talk of what might have happened. Let's continue on." Forty steps later they were in front of Madeline's Coffee Shop, a trendy new Saratoga spot that Sandy recalled was a vacant storefront when she lived nearby. They peered in the window.

"You may not believe this," Flint said. "In the fifties this place was a bar. I recall it now. The D'Andrea family ran it. The same family owned the Firehouse." He took her by the arm and, backing away from the window, looked upward. "Yeah, this is it. Right next door was the Colonial Restaurant."

"Be my leader," she laughed.

"Two things I'll never forget."

"What's that?"

"A pretty face like yours, and the bars I have visited in my time." She tugged him along.

He looked up again. "What have we here?" In the semi-light they passed a new brick building with display windows. Flint read the sign in front: Eddie Bauer. "Let's see. Number 340 Broadway. That's a Saratoga address I do remember."

"I know this one, too," she blared. "A stiff drink says this is where The Colonial was located."

"They should have erected a shrine on this lot," said Flint, leaning forward to get a better look at the structure. "You are right. It was The Colonial. Bob Quinn's place. That is to say until the sixties when some sick character torched it, along with several other vintage buildings in town."

Flint wrapped his arm about her waist. "I was in Nam when I learned of the fire. Imagine, being half a world away, lonely and frightened out of my wits, yet affected by word that an old bar-restaurant had burned down? It was like losing a close friend. The Colonial had such class, such uniqueness."

Sandy clung to him. "My grandfather often talked of The Colonial. Famous people hung out here, didn't they?"

"Well, I was a faithful patron."

"Yes. That's why it was so popular. They came from miles around to see Mike Flint. I can here the thunderous applause now."

"Not quite. But I was privileged to be in there when The Man Who Came to Dinner was present. And more than once."

She let out a soft giggle. "The Man who?"

"Monty Woolley. The actor, Monty Woolley. At your young age, you may have to dig a bit to discover who he was. Let me tell you. From the early twenties to almost the fif-

133

ties, Woolley was a genuine celebrity – stage and screen star. He was a Union College professor before the theatrical bug bit him. A local boy, at that. Yes, he was a Colonial regular, along with writer Frank Sullivan. I even remember the bartender's name. Pat Cruise. Mixed the best Rob Roy I ever had."

"I was still sipping sodas," Sandy said. "No, let me think. I wasn't old enough for sodas."

He held her gloved hand tightly. "I robbed the cradle."

She kissed him again. "Good. Rob it all you want."

They lingered a while longer, then slowly moved on. Flint checked the time. It was almost midnight. The soft, warm breeze was now giving way to a cooler, stiff wind. The sidewalks became slippery once more.

"We're losing our Hawaii-like temperature," Flint said. "Shall we go back?"

"Must we?"

"It's up to you."

"I want to walk in Congress Park," She informed him. "Late as it is, I want to walk the park."

He led her across Spring Street and they walked several yards till they came to the main gate of Historic Congress Park on Broadway. Two vintage street lamps lit up the drive and

Flint, holding Sandy's right arm, guided her through the gate. Inside, the grounds were dark.

One hundred paces further, the ghostly, brick hulk of the Canfield Casino, now an historical Saratoga icon, loomed before them. Tiny candle-size lights illuminated some of its large opaque windows. To their right was the outline of the park's gazebo, perched on the edge of a small pond.

"My word," Flint whispered. " Wouldn't Don Bocca give his right arm to take this place over?"

"Don Bocca?" she inquired.

"He's not worth knowing," Flint assured her.

"But you know him!"

"I know of him. Many people know of him. Few have ever seen him. Fewer yet want to see him. He's a man of death and destruction. Much like the little man that came to do you that fateful night we met. The difference is Don Bocca signs the death warrants. Others carry them out." Flint walked up near the Casino.

"What a plum this would be for the mob." Sandy was becoming confused with Flint's talk. "Why would this Bocca want to take over the old casino?"

Flint touched her cheek. "Ego. Nothing more than ego. Unless we want to toss in raw power, too. This building, this icon, represents the pinnacle of early American gambling halls. All the modern-day gaming joints in Las Vegas and Atlantic City are mere impostors compared to Canfield's. Not a prayer it will ever happen, but I can imagine they've entertained the thought. Bocca and his crowd are hell-bent on reestablishing gambling in Saratoga. They've got the money and muscle to do it. The timing is right. New York's legislators all have soft bellies and willing pockets these days. Bocca knows it.

"All the mob families know it. Bocca's main obstacle lays right here in Saratoga with some local politicians and do-gooders who don't want gambling.

"My...I mean our...mission, is to find out what's going down and when. We have to thwart Bocca's plans. No easy task. Maybe even impossible. Bocca's made the first move. Jake Palermo, one of his most trusted henchmen, tried to murder a councilwoman, Molly O'Neill. Someone, or some persons, intercepted Palermo. He showed up dead.

"Who killed Palermo? Why did they kill him? Who's next in line? Logic would tell us Bocca will strike again. Question: Will the mysterious Palermo murderer block Bocca's next move? I'd say Saratoga is in for a tough spring and maybe even a long, hot summer. I say we've walked enough for one night. We have the meeting with Blake and the boys tomorrow. Let's get back to the Sheraton and sleep on it."

"You can carry me," she kidded him. "Your speech tired me out."

He turned around and bent down. "Hop on, we're on our way."

The walk back up Broadway was fought against an even stiffer headwind, with the cold cutting into their faces and penetrating their jackets. By the time they reached their hotel, both were shivering, and Flint was complaining that his feet were wet, cold and bordering on numbness.

"We'll get you into a hot bath, then I'll rub them for you," Sandy promised him.

"No," said Flint. "I'll go to the bar and have a stiff drink. Maybe two or three."

Inside the lobby, she tugged him in the direction of the elevators, hugged him tight until it came, steered him through the elevator doors, pressed the third floor button and hauled him to their suite, pushing him into the deep-carpeted room ahead of her. She then went directly to the bathroom with its over-size, sunken oval tub.

"You know something," Flint observed in a condescending voice. "I think I'm being led around by the nose."

She was in the midst of drawing his bath, and called back, "What's that you say?"

"Nothing. Nothing important, anyway. How's my bath?" She came to the door, motioned him to come in, and smiled. "It's just like you, love. It's hot. Very hot."

8. GIBSON...ON THE ROCKS

In the late afternoon hours of the day preceding Flint's and Sandy's arrival in Saratoga, Dr. Blake received a phone call of an odd and strange nature from Eileen Gibson of Circular Street, near Congress Park.

Her voice was raspy and difficult to hear, so Blake, sitting in his office, turned up the volume on his speaker phone. At first the name Gibson meant nothing to him, but as the faint, wispy voice continued, Blake suddenly recalled who she was, or who he thought she was: Judge Gibson's wife.

A genuine relic of Saratoga's past and corrupt political dynasty. He was labeled the "Dirty Judge" following the grand gambling investigations of the fifties. In fact, Blake had somehow thought both Gibsons were long deceased. This sudden revelation both amused and puzzled him.

"I'm calling on behalf of my husband, Louis," she explained to Blake. "He's not well. I mean, not mentally well. He's been ranting and raving for the past three days of past happenings, and I've reached the breaking point. I'm old and my health is going. Do you understand?"

Blake hesitated before answering. Then finally he replied, "I believe I do understand, Mrs. Gibson. If not the cause and effect, at least your frame of mind as we speak. Please tell me more." In the background Blake could barely hear her husband's voice, though he couldn't make out what he was saying. Then there came a loud banging sound, followed by an even louder scream. Blake felt his blood pressure rise, thinking in that instant that Mr. Gibson had assaulted his wife. There was silence for a moment, then, to Blake's relief, Mrs. Gibson's soft, quivering voice came back on line.

"Excuse me, Doctor. I dropped the phone." She apologized. "Now let's see, as I was saying, Mr. Gibson —I mean the judge – can't seem to sleep properly. He's not eating his meals, little as they've been of late. What few hours he spends sleeping is mostly a mixture of tossing and turning from one side to the other, so that the bed's blankets get tangled in knots, often wrapping around him like a straight jacket. It's impossible to keep him still. My God, he turned eighty-eight last week. Where does a man of his age get the energy to toss around so much?

And the nightmarish tirade I have to listen to day and night. The insistent, repetitive stories of all those hearings of 1951 and 1952. He just repeats and repeats them over and over again. Citing this case, that witness, this and that defendant and the endless attorneys he had to deal with. There's no end to it."

She stopped to catch her breath. "Why, just last night he was demanding to see Governor Dewey, insisting that the investigation was a sham, that the grand jury in Saratoga never would convict anyone, and that he, Gov. Dewey, was on a witch hunt. I told him to stop. I told him the governor's been dead forty-odd years now. It didn't register. He kept on. I told him that most of the people he was talking about were dead. That it all happened forty-six years ago. Still, he went on, saying the investigations were still in progress and further insisting he'd do everything in his judicial power to thwart them. Can you see my concern for the judge, Doctor? He's living in yesteryears. It's engulfed him. He can't separate the present from the past. What am I going to do?"

"We all have our moments," Blake tried to reassure her. "The judge may just be going through a temporary relapse. Is he running a fever? Has he recently had a cold, or virus? Any number of things can trigger this unusual behavior. Though, from what you say, I think I had better have a look at him. I have other appointments that will take up the balance of this day. If you'd like, I'll come by tomorrow." Blake checked his desk calendar. "I can make it in the afternoon. Say around two. How does that sit with you?"

She let out a sigh. "Another night of his ranting. I don't know if I can stand it. But if it has to be at two, two it will be. I'll be waiting on the porch for you. You know our home? If not, it's number 56. The big, white house with the pillars. You can park under the portico. If it's raining, be careful of the steps. They can get slippery. On second thought, park under the portico and come up the front steps. We've installed slip-proof runners on them. Had to, ever since I fell and broke my right hip five years ago. Age has its downside, doesn't it?"

"Depends," replied Blake. "It has its golden side, too. It's all a matter of perspective. I'll be there at two."

There was a reluctance on Mrs. Gibson's part to end the conversation, so Blake let her talk a few minutes more before finally begging off, feigning he had another call. Before she hung up, Blake heard the Judge call out, "There won't be any convictions in my court. The damn governor better understand that. Let them impanel all the jury they like. Let the Governor's Extraordinary Grand Jury spin its wheels. And if he brings on board Justice Tom Garrity of the Supreme Court of the Eighth Judicial District, I'll stymie *his* efforts, too. Tell him that for me."

Yes, Blake realized, the old judge was hallucinating in pretty good fashion. Blake was amused by the irony of the call, smack in the middle of a new period when there were those in Saratoga trying to resurrect gambling. He couldn't wait to visit with the "Dirty Judge." Perhaps, in the judge's retroactive hallucinating, Blake reasoned, he might find bits and pieces of Saratoga's gambling history that may foreshadow things to come.

It also dawned on Blake that Flint may well enjoy sitting in on the call with the judge. Though Blake's recollection of the investigations was vague, Blake did recall hearing of Judge Gibson's involvement at the time. Actually it was Timothy Harris Gibson, the judge's half brother, who Blake better remembered hearing about. Taking an empty briar pipe and sticking it between his lips, Blake bit down on the stem. He'd given up lighting his favorite pipe five years earlier, but out of habit, pretended to smoke it on occasion. In his outer office, Blake listened to the hiss of a radiator and the stiff wind lashing against the large opaque window panes of his circa 1840 upper Broadway Victorian home.

"The Bag Man," Blake said aloud. "Yes. The Bag Man." Every kid in Saratoga knew the story. Harris Gibson trucked sacks of payola money to local officials when gambling was at its peak. He did so while his stiff-collared, sanctimonious judge brother sat on the County Court handing out jail sentences to those with lesser offenses. Blake recalled Gibson's little black Ford pickup truck was as familiar a sight coming and going from the likes of Arrowhead, Piping Rock, Smith's Interlaken, Newman's, Riley's Lake House and The Brook, as Astor's limo.

It was right after the war. With the fighting in Europe and the Pacific ended, gambling was again flourishing in Saratoga. And, not just in Saratoga. Illegal gambling was thriving farther southeast in Mechanicville.

He suddenly thought of his old uncle, Mark Blake, who caused a minor scandal in the family about that time when he got drunk and wound up in Mechanicville where he lost a week's pay at the tables. Blake took another imaginary puff on his pipe. It was like a good movie to the kids of his time, he recalled. Cops and robbers. Good guys and bad guys. Though as kids, neither he nor any of his cohorts saw or participated in any of it. Certainly though, like his Uncle Mark, many of the parents did. Wasn't it fashionable? Wasn't it harmless? Wasn't it all a big entertaining game?

The old judge, now raging about Dewey, was doing exactly what most Saratogians of that time did. Wasn't Dewey, and later Senator Estes Kefauver, chided for muddling in the lives of Saratoga citizens? As young as he was in 1946, the vividness of it all clearly came back to Blake. Could this new surge toward casino gambling be history reincarnated? If so, how many Uncle Marks and Judge Gibsons would it create?

But for now, there were more pressing issues at hand. The dark and sinister forces down in the Hudson Valley were no doubt planning their next moves in Saratoga. Very likely, Blake reasoned, to reap revenge for Jake Palermo.

* * *

From far across town, Albert Sacca let out a screech of joy, as he held the diamond necklace once again up to a light, and observed its brilliance. The light's reflection off the exquisitely cut stone almost blinded him. Sacca cried in viewing his rare Lake Lonely catch. Tears of joy ran down his wrinkled face. It was, however, a mixed feeling. Inwardly, Sacca knew this prize carried a curse of its own. Nevertheless, it was too beautiful, too precious to let go of. He'd take his chances, he concluded. Return of the necklace to Don Bocca would be his redemption. Or, as a dark thought suddenly occurred to Sacca, his death.

* * *

Dr. Blake set his pipe down and sat back in his desk chair. He then picked up the phone and began dialing Frank Duffy. Halfway through dialing, he stopped and placed the receiver down.

Silently he gave himself some of his own professional advice. "Call it a night, Doc. Get some sleep and start fresh in the morning." With that he got up and went to his bedroom. The streets of Saratoga at this hour were deserted. Blake went to sleep thinking of Mike Flint.

* * *

Albert Sacca dozed off clutching the diamond necklace and dreaming of his welcomed return to the Don Bocca family.

* * *

Don Bocca could not sleep. The deep-seated hatred he felt for certain people in Saratoga on this night was all he could concentrate on. He had been informed of Palermo's death. That in itself had enraged Bocca, though no one in his powerful family had the nerve to tell him just how horrible old Jake's death had been. His trusted lieutenants felt that certain details were better left unsaid.

9. THE SARATOGA SAVIORS

The anxiously awaited meeting between Flint and the group, which now humorously referred to itself as "The Saratoga Saviors," was, at Nealy's insistence, moved to the Saratoga Music Hall, located on the third floor of City Hall on Broadway. It was readily accessible to all and very close to Nealy's office. Nealy picked it because of its privacy during mid-week when the hall was seldom used. They were to meet at 11, have a short strategy session, and Nealy had asked Sgt. Galea to bring over sandwiches and hot drinks at noon.

Nealy instructed each one to come alone and further stationed one of his men at the bottom floor entrance to make doubly certain only members of his group entered the building. Nealy had escorted Flint from the Sheraton Hotel just up the street from the Music Hall and they were the first to arrive. They went straight into the building and took the elevator to the third floor. At intervals of two to three minutes, the others appeared. First Duffy, with his full-length wool coat pulled tightly about his body, and his gray fedora slightly tilted over his glasses. The second he stepped into the warm elevator from the chilled Saratoga air, his glasses fogged up. When he reached the third floor and the door slid open, all he could make out were two blurred figures. He wiped his glasses, and put them back on.

"Oh, my God. It is you, Mike Flint!" he exclaimed.

"Here in the cold flesh," Flint said. "Just as cold as you."

Duffy reached out with a damp leather glove and shook Flint's hand while nodding to Nealy. "I can put up with this inconvenient cold now that I know you're with us."

The hum of the elevator making its way up with another passenger drew their attention. This time Billy Farrell stepped off, brushing some wet slush off his camel hair coat.

"Glad to see you again, Farrell," Flint said.

"Not as glad as I am to see you," Farrell assured Flint.

Dr. Blake arrived next, followed by Galea, who assured Nealy that no one had followed them. At that, Nealy turned a key in the elevator lock, so that it would be inoperative during the meeting.

"It's unlikely we'll be disturbed up here,"

Nealy said. " Unless, of course, they have a sky hook."

Flint smiled. "Anything's possible in Saratoga."

Save for the barren Music Hall stage and its tied-back velvet curtains, the room was empty. Nealy invited them to a smaller room where a table and chairs were in place. He motioned for them to sit.

"It's not exactly the Gideon Putnam lounge, fellows, but it will do for now," he sniggered. "I guess we can officially welcome Mike Flint. Though knowing your dislike for our winters, it embarrasses me asking you here this time of year."

Flint turned to face all four. "I came for two reasons: Sandy gave me permission. Then I got to thinking of you all and decided I owed you one." He eyed each one. "Perhaps it's my last debt to society, I don't know. You can count on me to give it my best shot. That's all I can promise."

Dr. Blake jumped in. "Mike, we know this was a difficult call on your part. On Sandy's part, for that matter. You don't owe us anything. If anything, we've imposed on your good nature and, needless to say, your sense of duty. I'll apologize for the whole group right here and now. But I'll qualify that apology by saying we'd be dead in the water without your help." Blake looked at the others. "I think my sentiments are shared equally among us."

"Aptly said," Duffy agreed.

Nealy dropped a small leather briefcase on the table and opened it. He took out some papers and handed them around. "These are photo copies of some notes I made last week," he told the gathering. "Mike hasn't the slightest idea what's happened here the last two weeks, other than he's aware that Palermo was killed by unknown sources. Maybe we can go over the notes and piece a few things together. I've outlined five points that I feel best describe the situation, if not in chronological order, at least in importance to the murder itself. Not to discount the reported murder attempt on Molly O'Neill by Palermo. Or the bogus attempt by Palermo, if you choose to believe that sleazy insurance adjuster Trimore and his hypothesis."

Nealy moved over to Flint's side. "I'm getting ahead of myself. For Mike's sake, let me take it from the top. Point one: Palermo was brutally murdered. So who did it? Point two: Molly O'Neill was a target that snowy night. Who targeted her? Point three. Molly was saved from certain death. Commendable. Question: Who saved her? Point four: Is this all tied into the gambling issue? Point five: Palermo's death

tells us Don Bocca is involved. But, who's trying to thwart Don Bocca's efforts? There's a lot
going on here. I could add one more: Is Don
Bocca's rival our notorious mob acquaintance
from Canada, Maurice St. Jacques? Come to
think of it, St. Jacques' men are very capable of
mutilation the likes of which Palermo received.
But logic tells me that St. Jacques knows that
Bocca is capable of similar retaliation. Why
would St. Jacques risk it? I'm stumped at this
juncture. Anybody got any ideas?"

They looked at one another with blank ex-
pressions. All except Flint, who now had moved
over to the large Lake Avenue side windows
where he peered down at a car that was having
trouble making the grade upward to Broadway
on the slick pavement.

Flint, with his back to the group, asked,
"Who besides St. Jacques and Bocca might have
designs on Saratoga's possible return to gaming? Has anyone really addressed this angle?"

"Not a clue," replied Nealy. "Unless, of
course, NYRA, the New York Racing Associa-
tion."

"Forget them," said Flint. "I'm trying to filter out realistic culprits."

Nealy's face reddened.

Flint moved in front of the stage. "We've
got a real drama here, haven't we? Plots and

subplots galore. Mysterious killers and good Samaritans. Do-gooders and bad guys. In their midst, as I see it, there's a third player. Someone or some party that feels it's got an equal claim to Saratoga's gambling future. Perhaps someone or some party that doesn't even want gambling in Saratoga. Someone on a crusade. Someone out to protect the town from past abuses."

Flint came over and pressed his hands on the tabletop in front of them. "Let's not rule out St. Jacques. But let's not fail to explore other possibilities. Do you get my train of thought? In short, who besides St. Jacques and Bocca have the most to gain, or lose, for that matter, if gambling does come back?"

Blake spoke up. "Flint poses a good question here," he told the others. "If we have overlooked anyone, I can't think of who it might be. But that still doesn't say that other parties aren't interested in Saratoga's gambling future. This should be our focus as we go forward. Don't you agree, Mike?"

"Yes," said Flint.

As planned, Galea was sent to fetch lunch. Several areas of the investigation, as laid out by Nealy, were discussed, including an update on Palermo's death. Nealy actually had lab photos from Palermo's autopsy, courtesy of Albany

Medical Center Hospital. Billy Farrell, upon viewing them, remarked, "Why for God's sake, they butchered the bastard."

The reasoning behind Palermo's slaughter was discussed, with no one in the room able to guess who might have stripped the old mafioso's body and left it in such a disgusting state.

Galea returned shortly with lunch. But after seeing Palermo's photos, there was a sudden lack of appetites.

With the meeting concluded, Nealy, in his normal precautionary manner, had each one leave as they had come, singly. Blake and Flint, however, departed together, for Blake wanted to talk further with Flint.

Blake returned with Flint to the Sheraton where they went to meet Sandy. Blake hugged her on entering Flint's third-floor hotel suite. Then, holding her at arm's length, told her, "You haven't changed a bit. More beautiful than ever. Could it be Mike Flint's influence?"

"No," Flint said. "She's a natural beauty, my presence notwithstanding."

Flint suggested drinks. Blake begged off, but settled for a Coke. They then seated themselves in soft, comfortable lounges in the suite's outer room, Sandy sitting close to Flint with one arm draped over his shoulder. Blake, admiring both, told them how pleased he was that they had discovered each other.

"You're too kind, Doctor," Sandy said. "But it's the truth, isn't it Mike?"

Flint gripped her hand, and leaned his head on her shoulder. "Who would have thought?" he said to Blake.

They chatted for almost an hour before Blake left. On his way out, Blake, remembering Eileen Gibson's frantic phone call, explained it to Flint and asked if he'd like to tag along on his official Gibson visit?

"Certainly," Flint said. "When is it?"

Blake looked at his watch. "In about an hour. I'll pick you up near the rear parking lot in fifty minutes. It's only a six-block drive." He smiled at them. "I can assure you, it will be interesting. Not likely you'll ever meet anyone to equal Judge Gibson, from all I've heard about him over the years. Perhaps Sandy would like to come?"

Blake turned to her. "We're partners, aren't we?"

"No," said Sandy. "I'll beg off this one. The judge will feel he's outnumbered."

Flint walked Blake to the elevator.

"How serious is it?" Sandy asked Flint when he returned.

Flint kissed her lightly on the right cheek. "As serious as murder can be, my love."

10. 'IT'S THE DON'

Two weeks from the time Don Bocca had learned of Palermo's death, he made a phone call to his nephew Lamar Tocco, a lawyer in Lake Luzerne. Bocca phoned late at night as was his habit, so that Tocco was awakened from a sound sleep by his excited wife, Marie. She handed her husband the phone with trembling hands.

"It's the Don," she told him, her eyes betraying her fright.

Tocco, fumbling with the receiver, answered with a deep yawn. "Yes, Uncle. What can I do for you?"

"How are things in Lake Luzerne?" asked Bocca. Tocco knew that small talk was not why Don Bocca had called at this ungodly hour, but he listened. "Very cold. Nasty, nasty weather they tell me. I prefer the valley. Oh, the Hudson Valley gets cold at times, but never gets as cold as your neck of the woods. Of course, Florida would be even better. But busy men like us can't afford such luxury, can we?"

Tocco winked at his wife. "I suppose not, uncle."

"Well," Bocca continued, " we will be very busy in the next few days. That's the reason for my call. We ran into a snag in 'Toga three weeks ago. I view it as a temporary setback. Perhaps I was asking too much of Jake at his age. As they say, Jake's spirit was willing, but his flesh was not up to the task. He served me well over the years. He will be missed dearly. Nevertheless, the family business must go on. Do you agree?"

"Most certainly," Tocco assured him, wondering, as he said it, where the Don was leading.

Bocca coughed, hesitated a moment, then went on. "There is more than one way to skin a cat. Molly O'Neill survived. So much for her. We can't go after her again this quickly. So we'll let her wait till a more opportune time. I do, however, intend to take out one of the two remaining councilmen. And, I want to do it soon. Of course, nephew, they'll be expecting me to send someone just like Jake to do the job. If I were Nealy, or the state police, I'd think the same way. Wouldn't you?"

"No. I mean, yes. Yes, uncle. I'd think along those lines, too," Tocco said, trying to stay awake.

"Good, good that you think like me. Someone must. My days are growing short. The long arm of the family reaches far and wide. It takes brains as well as brawn to run this family. Though you'd never know it, surrounded by the fools I must deal with. You and Guido are the only ones I can entrust anything to. That's why we produced two smart lawyers."

Tocco eyed Marie as Bocca spoke. My God, Tocco was thinking. The old man's giving himself credit for Guido and me finishing law school. The next thing I know, he'll be claiming he created us.

Tocco bit his lip replying to Bocca. "We'll never forget how much you did for us, Uncle. We'd be street rats without you."

"No, no. Not you smart boys," Bocca bragged. "You are my human computers. My legal eagles. With you, we will retake Saratoga. Remember, it is our destiny."

Marie, sitting on the edge of the bed, looked at her husband with the face of a frightened schoolgirl. Bocca's very name had sent shivers up her back ever since she and Tocco first met. It was the reason she had faked illnesses and dreamed up dozens of other excuses not to visit Bocca in his Hudson Valley estate when invitations came. It was her opinion that her lawyer husband didn't have to accept the invitations either.

After all, she told Tocco more than once,

"Just because your uncle is a high-up mob figure doesn't mean he can fraternize with you and ruin your reputation."

This was an oft-repeated phrase that Tocco wished she wouldn't express, fearing that one day she may say it aloud in the wrong company, which could be both embarrassing and harmful all around.

He and Guido knew what their sole purpose in Lake Luzerne was, even if their wives were ignorant of their plans. Nevertheless, the chilling reality of his and Gambino's predicament gave Tocco a wrenching pain in his stomach. And all because of one old man's dream of past glory. A dream, Tocco realized, that had little chance of materializing in this present age. If only Don Bocca could see it that way.

"Nephew, nephew," Bocca said, startling Tocco from his thoughts. "I woke up early this morning. Long before the first rays of light were seen on the Hudson. It was both a premonition and a dream wrapped into one. It was at a reception. A political reception at the Saratoga Polo Club. John Stark was greeting guests at the grand entrance, taking time to shake each person's hand as they entered. It was early evening and a cocktail party followed on the enclosed patio. You and Guido and your wives were attending. Somehow, during cocktails, while there was a flurry of activity in the room, someone manages to slip a little pill into Stark's champagne glass. He always drinks champagne. Dinner is served within the hour. Following dinner, Stark gives a fine speech. He receives a standing ovation. His bid for re-election appears ironclad.

"Stark goes home that evening, elated with his presentation and his acceptance by all. He suffers a diabetic seizure sometime between midnight and sunrise. He rushes to the bathroom in search of his insulin, but there's none to be found. He staggers from the bathroom and goes for the phone. It doesn't work. Stark's wife, Patty, who sleeps in another room down the hall, doesn't hear him. He can't get any help. Stark dies the miserable death he deserves. It was a clear, beautiful dream, nephew. It ended as I wanted it to end, almost."

"Why is that?" Tocco asked.

"I'm not sure. Perhaps in my subconscious another voice was telling me there was a reluctance on someone's part to slip Stark the pill in the first place. That the total commitment for this kind of thing was not to certain people's liking. A lack of courage to carry out a request from the Don."

There was a long hesitation and Tocco had to listen to Bocca's heavy breathing in his ear.

Then Bocca went on. "Why this shadow came across my mind in the middle of a totally fulfilling dream, I can't say. A fluke, perhaps. A deep doubt with no merit. Yet still very real in my dream. So many doubts lurk in the background these days. So, nephew, in the dark of my room, fully awake, I re-ran the dream over and over. Finally I realized there was no need to worry who would place the pill in Stark's drink. It came to me in a flash. I'll have you do it."

Tocco glanced at Marie again. This time his hand was trembling. Bocca's request came like an electric shock, burning in his ear, as he tried to devise an appropriate response. This was, as Tocco had heard all too often from other family members, the moment of truth. The time when one was called upon to pay his dues. It was a debt he didn't want any part of, nor would Guido, if asked do to the same. He was certain of that. Bocca, in Tocco's estimation, was going mad in his old age. Driven, as Tocco saw it, by revenge, not objectivity. A fatal mistake made by those men of the old guard. Striking out blindly at those opposed to their plans, no matter how inappropriate and ill-advised.

He waited just long enough for his hand to stop shaking before replying.

He calmed his voice and delivered what he

hoped would be a wise and timely diplomatic alternative to Bocca's plan. Namely, that killing Stark so close to the attempt on O'Neill would, if picked up by the press, be counterproductive to all the years of planning and scheming so carefully implemented to this point.

"It is my professional advice as an attorney not to pursue such action at this time," he strongly urged Bocca, quickly adding, "Uncle, please don't misconstrue this as a cowardly way out. Take it at face value, as a smart, prudent maneuver. Time is on our side. We've waited over forty years for our reward. Molly O'Neill escaped Palermo's grasp. Nevertheless, you effectively made your statement. I beg you to give this more time. Time must always be considered in our overall strategic objective. Besides, your nephews can be of more value to you in legal ways."

Bocca's breathing became more labored. When he again spoke, his voice was resonating with detectable irritation. A voice and personality Tocco secretly detested. An abominable monster. A man who had, in his time, produced more widows and orphans than some minor wars. Tocco knew you had to deal with Bocca with the utmost caution. The wrong word said, an idea misconstrued, wrong signals – any number of things – could, and often did, provoke Bocca's wrath. Tocco weighed his thoughts and responses accordingly. One had to persuade Bocca with logic and reason. Frontal approaches were useless. He had to be made to believe it was his idea coming through in any confrontation. Tocco, still nervous, waited for his uncle's answer.

"They never reward weakness, nephew. No. I say Stark must go. Still, you make sense in what you say. You and Guido stay put in Luzerne. We will skin the cat another way. We will be in touch. Love to Marie."

Tocco felt the tension slowly slip from his limbs. Marie had fallen asleep. There was only the ticking of the bedroom clock breaking the uneasy silence. Where was this all going? Tocco was thinking. How far would Bocca push the gambling issue? This blindness to present-day reality on Bocca's part baffled Tocco. More importantly, how could he and Guido extract themselves safely from Bocca's grip?

He thought of Stark. Where and when would Bocca decide to finish him off? He lifted his wife up and slid her beneath the blankets and shut off the reading light. "I'll sleep on it," he told himself. But sleep wouldn't come. He was too caught up in his own irresolvable dilemma.

11. NAP TIME

Doctor Blake, with his customary punctuality, arrived to pick up Flint at the Sheraton at precisely ten minutes before two. And Flint, with his equally habitual manner of being on time, came right out of the hotel's back entrance to meet Blake. As they drove off to meet with the Gibsons, Blake handed Flint an envelope.

"I haven't submitted a bill yet," Flint told Blake.

"Oh, that's not money, Mike, it's a memo I got from Duffy two days ago. Funny, Duffy never mentioned it at our meeting. Perhaps it slipped his mind. At any rate, I found it quite interesting. Maybe even intriguing."

It was a three-page, double-spaced typed message, presumably created on Duffy's ancient Underwood typewriter, the machine Flint had once seen at Duffy's home. It read,

Dear Arnold:

As an addicted Saratoga history buff of long standing, I have researched myriad things on the Spa, not the least of which is folklore stemming from the region's earliest days, dating back to when the Mohawk Indians were its sole inhabitants. I recall reading that the Mohawks introduced William Johnson to Saratoga by way of its healing springs. This Johnson, an Irish fellow, was real tight with the Mohawks. Later married the daughter of their most celebrated leader, Joseph Brant. Brant's Indian name was Thayendanegea. Smart fellow this Brant. Became a Christian and was a missionary among the Mohawks. Also got educated at Eleazer Wheelock Academy in Lebanon, Connecticut. Certainly not your average Iroquois for that time, I'd say. One of the few early warriors to survive that bloody period. Ended up doing his missionary work in Canada. Died, I believe, in 1807, at age sixty-five. Anyway, Johnson damn near died from a bad wound following a big battle with the French.

Well, the sacred springs must have worked their magic on Johnson, for he recovered. The British Crown appointed him Superintendent of Indian Affairs in North America. He had a good ride until the Revolutionary War came along. When it was over, he and his family took everything they could carry and hightailed it to Canada. He's got descendants up there to this day. Quite understandably, the Mohawks considered this region special. A unique place of healing waters and uplifting spirits. A hallowed place of Indian worship. Come to think of it, a place we should all have in our lives, but don't. The true historical fact of the matter is that Saratoga, and many such Indian places of worship, were stolen from the tribes.

I could cite chapter and verse on the many ways the great white fathers – meaning us – snatched up Indian land over a 300-year period in grand fashion. The treaties written back then were every bit as vague as some of today's ambiguous New York State Legislature bills. Some worse. "Worthless words on bark," as one Mohawk chief described them.

Well, Arnold, history has a way of repeating itself, doesn't it? Take, for example, the recent inroads Indian tribes are making into the gambling business across the country. They've practically reinvented the gaming business; and on their own land and own terms. Seems like some of those worthless agreements on bark are coming back to haunt us white men after all. I find the key word to be "Sovereign."

That's a really big word in the context of today's gambling environment. Lots of little nations inside the 50 states. Just think of it. We shoved them into these small pieces of supposed wasteland called reservations, only to find out that they're turning them into gold mines. It's all legal. Good for the Indians. High time they came out of the abject poverty. A poverty, I might add, we white chieftains imposed on the nations from New York to California. Our forked tongue came back to stick us in the financial ear. We deserve it.

So I wasn't surprised to get a call from one Professor Halfmoon of Union College in Schenectady who sounded very concerned about the proposed Saratoga gambling issue. He heads up Union's anthropology department. Says he's a full-blooded Mohawk, with ancestral ties to the same tribe that inhabited Saratoga as far back as 1600. I can honestly say, that two subjects of little interest to me are math and anthropology. Neither of which, I might also add, make banner headlines at The Star. At least not on my watch. Nevertheless, Arnold, it poses a new twist to the gambling wrinkle.

Naturally, at the paper we keep abreast of the many new Indian casinos popping up around the country. Two that come to mind are Foxwood in Connecticut and, more recently, Turning Stone near Utica. Both seem to be doing just fine. It would seem a way out for all tribes with the nerve and knowledge to pursue starting up a gaming complex. Professor Halfmoon, however, gave me the impression he was leaning in the other direction.

From what he told me, several of his fellow Mohawks – he didn't state any numbers – were dead set against gambling. Especially any gambling slated for Mohawk ancestral land. He was quite adamant on this point. The professor qualified his call by saying he was not speaking for every member of his tribe, pointing out that there is division among the Mohawks on the gambling controversy. Confidentially, I believe he is worried that some of the more radical, younger

tribe members were even capable of defending ances-
tral lands and ideals at any cost. Which brings me to
speculate, though Martha thinks I'm reading too much
into all this, that a talk by our group with Professor
Halfmoon at some convenient date would be beneficial
to all. Let's have your thoughts on this.
Regards,
Duffy

* * *

They had pulled up in front of Judge
Gibson's Circular Street home, a white, turn-
of-the-century Greek revival structure that Flint
noticed was badly in need of painting. Blake,
as instructed by Beatrice Gibson, drove in under the portico.

Flint, still holding Duffy's message in his
right hand, turned to Blake. "That's it. Duffy
nailed it down."

"Nailed what down?" Blake asked.

"The third party I talked about at our meeting," Flint told him. "Other interests. It was right
before our eyes. Totally obvious, yet we didn't
see it."

"The Mohawks?" Blake asked.

"Certainly," Flint said, "Professor Halfmoon
laid his cards on the table. The Mohawks fit
perfectly. Think of what happened to Jake
Palermo. The Mohawks dealt very severe pun-

ishments to their captives years ago. Didn't someone say Palermo's death appeared ritualistic in nature? When last, if ever, did you see a body so stripped and mutilated? It may not be the Mohawks, but we have to factor them in at this juncture. At least we can get together with Professor Halfmoon and prove otherwise."

Blake cupped his hands over his forehead. "Poor Saratoga. We're back to *Drums Along The Mohawk.*"

"Is that a prediction?" Flint asked.

"Perhaps," replied Blake. "Actually it's the title of an historical novel of the region by Walter D. Edmonds. Quite old. Written in the '30s. Recently saw Henry Fonda in an old re-run of *Drums* on TV. Strange thing about Duffy's memo. Professor Halfmoon contacted me a few days ago, which tells me just one thing – he must have Duffy and I connected. Maybe even Nealy and Farrell. How, I can't say, but it's a disturbing thought."

"More disturbing if he's got my name connected to all of you," Flint agreed. "We'll definitely have to check him out. I'd say real soon." Flint was moving out of the car. He and Blake went to the front of the house and headed up the carpeted stairs to the wide, dark, oak doors. Blake proceeded to ring the bell, but the doors suddenly opened and a small, gray-haired lady, dressed in a faded pink full-length dress, peered at them from behind wire-rimmed glasses and invited them inside.

"Welcome, Doctor Blake, I'm Beatrice Gibson. And, who might this be?" she inquired when Flint followed Blake inside.

"Mike Flint, a close associate," Blake said. From over the tops of her glasses, two blue eyes gazed at Flint as she stepped closer. "I'm not familiar with Doctor Flint. Are you new in Saratoga?" Flint glanced at Blake and shrugged his shoulders.

"Mr. Flint is not a doctor, Mrs. Gibson. He is, however, a professional advisor of sorts to doctors, when called for. Isn't that right, Mr. Flint?"

"Yes, yes. I wear many hats," Flint admitted.

Her small hands gave a push on the heavy doors, which slammed shut with bang.

"The Judge has been sleeping, but that should wake him up," she assured them with a smirk on her narrow, rose-colored lips. "He's upstairs. Stays up there most of the time. Has trouble with his legs of late. Circulation's bad. A terrible affliction on a man who was a long-distance runner in college. Graduated from Yale, you know? Yale Law School. Did his undergraduate studies at Fordham. But he's a local boy. A true Saratogian. Class of 1929 at Saratoga High. We met in high school. Mind you, he won't let you get a word in edgewise once he gets talking. It's been going on for days.

"As I said, Doctor, his mind is trapped in the early '50s. That's all he talks about. Endless, repetitive tirades of those terrible days during the Kefauver investigations. Later, Dewey and his crowd. You'll see for yourself."

They ascended the wide staircase slowly. Flint noted it was a staircase designed for Rhett Butler, and just about as wide and long. There were dust balls visible on the red-carpeted steps, and there was soil from years of use and lack of cleaning. Flint imagined that in earlier days, when the Gibsons were in their prime and riding the pinnacle of Saratoga's judicial helm, the home was a showplace of social grace and envy. It was obvious now, since the Judge went down in disgrace some forty-odd years ago, there was little Beatrice Gibson could do but persevere, to live out her remaining days with reserved dignity, no matter how tedious her present existence. Flint walked slowly at her side as they approached the judge's upstairs study. Suddenly down the hallway, Flint and Blake simultaneously caught sight of a female.

She appeared for just a moment. They didn't see her face as her head was turned away and the hallway light was too dim. But before she disappeared into a far room and closed the door behind her, they caught a glimpse of wavy reddish hair and a long white gown. Or was it a white robe? Flint really wasn't sure. Beatrice Gibson pretended not to notice her. Neither did she acknowledge her presence, nor explain to Flint and Blake who the woman was. It was as if Beatrice Gibson, like he and Blake, was caught completely off-guard by her brief appearance.

Mrs. Gibson held up her hands, then went quickly into the judge's sitting room. They could hear her talking to the judge. Subsequently the judge's deep, nasal voice came back to her with a blistering salvo. Shortly, Ellen Gibson came back out and motioned Blake and Flint to enter.

The judge was seated in a highback, cushioned chair, his back to the door, his eyes staring straight ahead at a dark, empty fireplace. Each time he let out a yell, it echoed off the sandy brick face. Blake went in and stood directly in front of him. Flint stayed back near the door with Mrs. Gibson. Blake didn't say anything. Judge Gibson was blasting away, hyperventilating between sentences. The words poured out. He talked in a rapid, staccato pattern, unintelligible at first because he was mumbling. Suddenly aware that others were in the room, the mumbling ceased and he began to speak clearly, though loudly.

A quick glance around the dimly lit room revealed a period of time stopped in place. Velvet curtains were drawn almost closed at windows on opposite sides of the room. A matted and frayed Oriental rug was badly in need of repair. A large, solid, cherry desk, situated in one corner, was strewn with newspapers yellowed from age. Ceiling-high bookshelves, stuffed to capacity with law books and case studies, apparently taken out and shoved back haphazardly, had a fine spray of dust on all.

The rancid smell of stale cigarettes permeated the room. The judge, clad in a black bathrobe and wearing tattered slippers, was bearded and his thick, gray hair curled up where it met his shoulders. The old man could use a shearing, Flint mused. Clutching a burned-out cigarette in his right hand, he addressed Blake.

"Who the hell are you?"

"A friend of the family," Blake said.

"I have no friends," Gibon admonished him.

"I'm the local pariah. All my so-called friends stay clear of this house. Haven't you heard?"

"Apparently that's an assumption on your part, Judge. I don't know if it's true."

The Judge put the cigarette in his mouth, and quickly took it out. "Stand aside," he shouted at Blake. "I have to spit." Blake moved just in time. The Judge, moving his head backward then leaning forward, sent forth a disgusting spit ball directly into the darkened fire place.

Then, letting out a loud cough, he screamed, "It was that rotten district attorney, Tom Clare, that caused all the problems. Always poking his nose into affairs that didn't concern him. Probing. Probing. Always probing. Well, we showed him, didn't we? Jake Palermo did him in proper. Knifed him amid the whole congregation. Tom got what he deserved. He went out horizontal, in a pine box, like many others who stuck their damn faces where they weren't welcomed or belonged."

Then looking directly ahead at Blake, he asked, "I suppose you're here to talk about the investigation? If so, it won't do you any good. No one in this town is doing anything wrong. Oh, they've come to me so many times to indict this or that one. It's all an exercise in futility. No one beats me in my court. I'll match wits any day with Tom Dewey. I've forgotten more about jurisprudence than he'll ever know. My stance is clear on this whole issue. Without positive proof of wrongdoing, I'm allowing no indictments."

Flint moved around to the judge's right side so he could hear every word. Blake remained motionless, arms folded over his chest, saying nothing. For the moment he was content to let Gibson rant, though he fully intended to revive the Judge's memory later on the point he made about Tom Clare's murder. Clare's death, Blake recalled, was never solved. How strange that four decades later, in one delirious sentence, the mystery should be solved. If the Judge didn't say another thing, this one point was worth coming here for, Blake quietly told himself. Of course Flint, not knowing this history, never picked up on the judge's revelation.

On the other hand, Blake thought, if Nealy had been present, he'd probably suffer a heart attack. The trick now was to keep the judge talking. To take this little session as an opportunity to resurrect a piece of Saratoga's past that few men alive were capable of revealing. In the rush of the day, Blake forgot to bring his tape recorder. An oversight he knew he'd later regret. A unique time and place when a tape recorder would be invaluable. Across the room, Flint was staring back at him, a soft smile on his face. The session was, for all its frankness and weirdness, both serious and amusing. Flint shot another glance at Blake lifting, as he did, a small metal object from his right coat pocket.

He laid it on the table next to Judge Gibson. Blake immediately recognized Flint's miniature recorder. Was it mental telepathy? Had Flint been reading his mind? Blake was doubly glad he invited him on this call. No doubt, Blake reasoned, Flint has telepathic skills. How else could he have survived so long in such a dangerous profession? This was turning out to be an extraordinary day indeed.

Blake's attention was drawn once more to the judge.

"Can't count the money fast enough, can they?" The judge blurted out. "Dumb bunch of clucks, none of which can count past ten. Just imagine bringing in several sacks of cash each night and tossing it all on one big table to be counted? Every conceivable size bill in circulation – thousands of dollars. And a row of dummies to try and count it. It's no wonder we have trouble keeping the account straight. Chris Harris, you remember him? You know that fat, no-good cop. We made him a sergeant. Piping Rock Harris we nicknamed him. He couldn't count past ten, either, but he had nerve and could be trusted. You couldn't give a man a sack of cold cash, say ten or twenty thousand dollars, unless you could trust him.

"Oh, we have a few who try to go south with our cash. They don't get far. One call to

Meyer Lansky and the word is out. Smart guy, this Lansky. Knows figures. Can add and subtract faster than anyone I know. Handles millions, you know. Keeps most of the accounts in his head. Yes, the mob will get you. Better that the cops get you first. The mob's justice is deadly and swift," he laughed. "Usually a one-man jury, The Don. One thing I've learned, you can't rob a crook. It is real bad to steal from the mob. Money is their God. The sun comes up and sets on their money. Shame on the man who tries to rob them. The mob can rob. That's considered fair game. But you don't dare rob them. They have their own code. It worked damn well in this town for years, until Dewey and Kefauver stuck their noses in. So what does that prove? The game goes on, Dewey or no Dewey. If not in New York, somewhere else. Lots of my friends are running to Florida. Not a bad place to be if you want to evade New York's high taxes. They say it's too damn hot in Florida for Dewey. Good. Keep him out. He's already loused up New York. Don't get me wrong. Dewey's a basically honest guy. Likes crusades. That's why he was so successful busting criminals in New York City.

"But this is different. No one's breaking any laws in Saratoga. We enjoy our gaming places. The public enjoys them. Otherwise the Piping

Rock and Riley's wouldn't be so popular, don't you agree?"

"Most certainly," agreed Blake, getting a word in for the first time since entering the room.

"Know who started it all, don't you?"

"Dewey, from what you've been saying."

"Guess again."

"Kefauver?"

"Try again."

"Not the slightest idea."

More spit shot toward the fireplace. Gibson cleared his throat. "Housewives. Just imagine. A bunch of housewives brought a motion to close down gambling because their husbands lost a few bucks. It took corage for a state Supreme Court Justice to deny their motion. He tossed out their temporary injunction, just like I would have done. Like any sensible judge would have done. You know why? I'll tell you. Their complaints failed to state the cause of action. And also because the housewives had the only complaint in town against gaming. So now Dewey and Kefauver are using them as a springboard for their investigation. I tell you, they're on a fishing expedition. Isn't it all nice and tidy?"

Blake eyed Flint and shook his head. "Tell me, Judge. What year is it?"

The gray hair fell across the judge's face as he pondered Blake's question.

"Why, Doctor, you know damn well what year it is. Why ask?"

"No," Blake insisted, "I don't. You tell me."

Gibson shifted and stared at Blake. "No head games with me, Blake."

"What year is it?" Blake again soberly asked. The judge reached for his cigarettes. "I mark my calendar each day," he replied. "It's March 23, 1951. It's Thursday. My day off at the court. I'm due in on Friday. They want me to draw a grand jury. Well, they can wait. We've got more important matters pending right now."

"Go on," Blake said. "Tell us more."

"Joseph Brant. You know Brant, don't you? Everyone in Saratoga knows Brant. Brant runs all my errands. He's been a courthouse fixture for forty years. He's got more horse sense than most lawyers I know. If Brant tells me something, I can bet the farm on it. Same goes for his uncanny knowledge of law. Brant never read a law text. But he knows the law. I trust his judgment implicitly." Gibson stuck his index finger out at Blake.

"Right to the point. Brant's always right to the point. Tells me, and I believe him, that no grand jury will convict a living soul here in Saratoga on gambling related charges. You know why? I'll tell you. No one's got the heart for jailing those who participate. Dewey and his gang are chasing moonbeams, Brant says. All the charges flying around are as thin as the hot air Dewey and Kefauver are blowing. I'll toss out any and all of the charges that come into my court. That bunch in Albany can't take this town from us. Not while I'm on the bench."

Blake pulled up a chair and sat directly in front of Gibson. "That's all well and good, Judge. But you haven't told us anything. I get the impression you don't know all you claim to know about casino gambling."

Gibson jumped up. The eyes narrowed and he poked his finger once again at Blake. "That's what you say, Doc. Let me tell you, I've got my arms around the whole gaming thing. Have had for years. Played with the big boys, too. Just like my great uncle Ed did when Canfield Casino was going full blast back in 1870."

Gibson's unruly, uncombed hair stuck out at all points, almost as if he'd been given an electric shock. His glasses, sitting on the end of his nose, drew attention to his large, round, penetrating dark eyes – eyes almost too big for his narrow, bone-thin face. He waved his right hand back and forth in a sweeping gesture, and continued with his monologue.

"Brant keeps tabs on the money runners.

When the casinos fill up with cash, Brant sends over the nearest patrol car and brings the money to town. I've already told you, it's counted a dozen times over. So much so, we even check the serial numbers on any bill over a hundred. They're all recorded. Let me see. We average two pickups a night at around eight thousand dollars each. Times six, that's forty-eight thousand dollars. Mind you, it's all cash. Seven nights a week, times forty-eight thousand dollars, hauls in over three hundred thousand dollars weekly. And that's only what goes over the tables. The private gaming money for the big hitters is kept in a separate account. Oh, it all ends up in the same pot. A pot that is split many ways. Brant's a whiz at distribution.

"Let me tell you where much of it goes, right into the hands of people in town that need it most. The poor working stiffs. If Dewey were to shut down gaming, half of the locals would be unemployed. A minor point missed among all the investigative rhetoric. Who's going to feed these workers if Dewey gets his way? Has he got jobs for them in Albany? I doubt it. It's all a very moral, high-minded crusade. A flag-waving politician's do-gooder dream. Stamp out gaming and save souls. How noble. How noble and stupid. No, thank you. Things work pretty well here. Gaming has hurt no one. It's helped many. See where I'm coming from?"

Blake shifted and wiped his forehead. "Sounds like you've got it locked down, Judge."

"You bet I do," said Gibson stiffly.

"Meyer Lansky, where does he fit in?" Blake quickly asked.

Gibson's hand raised once more. He drew an imaginary line in front of Blake's eyes. "Right about in the middle, I'd say. Yes. Right in the middle. Fifty-fifty. Meyer's not greedy. He's a businessman. After all, it was their seed money that made it all possible to begin with. He, Lucky Luciano and Don Cira. They took the risks. We merely provided the vehicle by which it could all function smoothly. It's a sweet arrangement. Something in it for everyone. Just last week Dewey and his crew hauled Lansky off to the Ballston Spa jail, calling him a common gambler. They nailed a friend of his, Joe Starcher. Charged Starcher ten grand. You know what? Starcher will come through my courtroom, and I'll tell you right now he won't serve a day behind bars. I'll give him a one-year suspended sentence. Dewey and Kefauver can eat crow on this one.

"As for Lansky, that's another story. To save the mob some embarrassment, and some further probing by Kefauver, Meyer pleaded guilty. So what, he won't get more than ninety days.

Imagine. Lansky's gambled all over the country, from Florida to Las Vegas, and they trump up this gambling charge in Saratoga to make an example of him. I tell you, he created more jobs in Saratoga than the Chamber of Commerce ever did. I think he's a hero. He's got lots of friends in this town. The IRS has been stalking him for months. Income tax evasion.

"Who the hell do they think they are? Can they possibly believe he's as stupid as Big Al Capone? Lansky's smart enough to run the IRS. He's got a better bookkeeping system than the Feds. No, this witch-hunt has nothing to do with gambling. It's all about politics. Republicans and Democrats. Dewey's eyeing the White House. If he really wants to shut down Saratoga gambling, why not start with the Race Course in August?

"There's a considerable number of poorer widows and orphans because of the track than the casinos. Dewey doesn't address this during his investigations, does he? Let's see, to my recollection, the taxes received by New York State two years ago – 1949 – averaged twenty thousand dollars. That's two hundred thousand dollars over the last ten years. I see no difference between an oval race track and a roulette wheel, except the track's revenues are greater. It's all a matter of simple math isn't it, Doc?"

Gibson stopped to catch his breath. His quivering fingers fumbled to tighten the bathrobe string around his waist. He then sat back down. By now, Flint had moved to Blake's side and was facing Gibson.

"Your friend, Brant. You didn't finish telling us about him," Flint interjected before Gibson could resume his rambling tale.

"Ah yes, Brant. Remarkably self-sufficient. Totally reliable. A man who knows how to get things done without anyone telling him. A rare human commodity these days, I might add.

"Such individuals are in short supply. But we make the most of Casey's talents. He's handsomely rewarded for his efforts. Deserves it. Earns it. Lansky calls him a wizard. You see, the gaming establishments deposit more money a week in the local National Bank than most corporations. It's all neatly accounted for by Brant. Every nickel and dime." A broad smile crossed Gibson's face. "Not much from Dewey and Kefauver about the National Bank's involvement, is there?"

Blake nodded his head. "You're right on that point, Judge."

"All legal," Gibson insisted. "All legal and fine. There's no gambling at National. Just money from gambling flowing through the bank's coffers." The white hair fell back over

185

his shoulders as he tossed his head. "Old Tom Dewey knows lots of bankers. Guess this Kefauver has a few banking buddies, too. See no evil; tell no lies. Take the money and run. Some morality play on the men in their pinstriped, Brooks Brothers suits, wouldn't you say? Lansky's in the pokey and the bankers glide by. Who's really breaking the law here?"

Blake interrupted Gibson. "This Joseph Brant you talk about. Why does his name ring a bell with me, even though I don't recall ever meeting him in Saratoga?"

The wily eyes of Gibson opened wide and he smiled. "It's a famous name in these parts. Has been for over two hundred years. He claims family ties to Joseph Brant, the Mohawk Chief. He's as true a Mohawk you'll ever hope to find.

"Whether he is or isn't directly related to Joseph Brant, is not my concern. His ancestors, however, were in Saratoga long before the white man came here. In a way, you can say we're trespassing." Gibson let out a soft laugh.

"Brant's always saying that his ancestors' ghosts will one day appear to destroy us all. I believe him. Anyway, he's my right arm in court. Mohawk or no Mohawk."

Blake and Flint exchanged glances, and the image of tomahawk-wielding Mohawks flashed before Flint's eyes. Flint was sure that Blake, with his unique sensory channels, was seeing the same images. Flint's mind then turned to the sequence of events leading up to Jake Palermo's ghastly demise. His brutal death, the way he was virtually hacked apart, beyond description.

Could it be, Flint thought, the work of latter-day Mohawks come back to avenge past wrongs? The very possibility of it sent a shudder down Flint's back. Yet, the Joseph Brant of which the rambling judge spoke most likely was long dead himself. If there were Mohawks involved in Palermo's death, might they not be Brant's descendents? Mrs. Gibson came forward.

"It's getting past the judge's nap time," she suggested. Then she took Blake by the arm, walked him to the side of the room and whispered, "Was I right, doctor? Has my husband reached a point that requires he be committed?"

Blake held her cold and slightly trembling hands. "No," he assured her. "But I do recommend we put the judge on some medications that will ease things a bit. I'm sure we can help him back to some normalcy. I'm certain we can." The wistful stare in Mrs. Gibson's eyes suddenly disappeared. The toughness lifted from her face and she grinned widely at Blake. "You really think so, Doctor?"

"Yes. I do."

Flint came to them. "I think we've heard enough for one day. At least I have."

Blake nodded, then turned to face the judge.

"We'll be leaving now, Judge. It was a pleasure meeting and talking with you. We'll have to do it again."

Gibson started to rise, then sat back down. "You haven't heard the half of it."

"I'm sure we haven't," said Blake, "but it's late now. I'll come by again. We will continue our conversation about Dewey and Kefauver."

"Yes," replied Gibson. "Those damn rascals."

Outside on the porch, Blake and Flint halted momentarily to say one more good-bye to Mrs. Gibson, and waited as she slammed the huge front door tightly. Before entering Blake's car, Flint eyed the house once more. Suddenly, in an upper window, silhouetted against a dim light, the female figure they had seen earlier appeared for a split second. Blake saw her, too.

"Who the hell is she?" Flint asked.

"Take your pick," said Blake.

"Take what pick?"

Blake rubbed his hands together against a chill wind. "Well, Flint," Blake said with a touch of doubt in his speech, "some say it's Gibson's living daughter. Others say it's her ghost. It's a sordid story. A tragedy. Like so many things in Saratoga, it borders on the macabre. I've been told that their daughter, Eileen, a promising young attorney in 1951 who was to be married to an attorney, went to pieces when her father became entangled in the gambling investigations. Her engagement fell apart and she went into seclusion. Subsequently she left Saratoga in disgrace. A few years later, or so I was told, she began drinking and eventually committed suicide somewhere on the West Coast. According to the reports there was no local funeral.

"All arrangements were handled on the coast. It was also reported that the suicide was a cover-up for her actually being placed in a mental ward – possibly near San Francisco. It's a murky report at best. So some say she finally came back to Saratoga and has been secluded in this mansion ever since. For all my curiosity, I'm not sure I want to know the truth."

Blake slapped Flint on the shoulder as they moved to the car. "But knowing you, I expect you won't rest till you know who really was in that window a minute ago. Am I right?"

"Probably," answered Flint, still gazing at the window, now dark.

As they drove over Spring Street toward Broadway, Flint couldn't help but ponder Gibson's words about Joseph Brant. Were the

Mohawks on a modern-day warpath? Was there a link between them and Palermo's bizarre death? And if so, what was it all about?

"Penny for your thoughts, Flint," Blake said.

"Not sure they're worth a penny at this point," Flint said. "Not even a plug nickel. My mind is working on two items: the Brant angle and our mysterious Gibson girl, so to speak. In order of priority, I think we should take a serious look at the Brant thing. My gut feeling tells me we have several players in this game. Deadly, serious players. If what I think is going on continues, we're in for a bloodbath before it's played out."

12. TENNIS ANYONE?

Don Bocca had been doing a slow boil ever since speaking to his nephew. Perhaps, Bocca reasoned, his lawyer nephew was becoming too smart for his own good. Too high and mighty. Too ingrained in his dream world of professional neatness and comfort. Was his nephew short-sighted? Wasn't it the family who made him what he is? Hadn't they put him through college and law school? Investing thousands in the process, while other family members carried out the work of providing for the family, carrying out often dangerous assignments not required of Tocco or his cousin?

Sitting at his desk, Bocca thought about it. In fact, it was the first time he could remember anyone in the family presenting such a test of will. Inside, Bocca chided himself for letting his nephew so cleverly talk himself out of this most urgent request. Bocca decided there would be another time, another request for Tocco. One that he would not be allowed to turn down.

Everyone in the family had to pay his dues. There would be no exceptions. But for now, he would let it slide.

A deck of cards was on his desk. Actually, six decks, comprising three hundred and twelve cards. Keepsakes of a long-ago trip he took to Monte Carlo where he was first introduced to Chemin de Fer, the intriguing, high stakes European card game. It was, in time, to become Bocca's favorite game. It served him well in his casino rounds and taught him a valuable lesson in all of his dealings with people. For Chemin de Fer was one of the few games where you bet one another, not the house. He'd played Blackjack and Baccarat, the American version of Chemin de Fer. The lesson he learned best from Chemin de Fer was secrecy. No one ever sees your cards. All options are left open. Such as with the family business. You kept everything secret, even your thoughts, at times, and you used the options to your advantage. It would be this way when next he moved on Saratoga.

His options, as he viewed them, had narrowed to one. Bocca stared at the overturned card, the Jack of Hearts. "Yes, yes," he sighed. "Tom Bochard. The dominant male holdout on the Saratoga City Council."

It was Bochard who most certainly influenced Molly O'Neill and John Stark on their negative gambling vote. Bocca was sure of this. His most trusted informants had told him such. Bocca had followed Bochard's actions all the way on this one. He considered Bochard the poison political pill against the family's wishes. Not that Bocca had exempted Molly O'Neill or John Stark from his hit list.

When, in good time, the heat was dropped from the bungled O'Neill attempt, Bocca would again deal with her. And Stark would be eliminated, too. Right now it was Bochard's turn. No bungling this time. The hit would be deadly and swift. Bocca's retribution would put the fear of God into all opposition. The statement would be so strong, that even Chief Nealy would shiver in his sleep.

Bocca checked his desk calendar. Already mid-March. Time was flying by, he thought. Precious time he needed to set up his Saratoga organization, once things were going his way.

This O'Neill debacle, though both disturbing and embarrassing, was not the end. No, Bocca had faced many similar roadblocks in his career. He'd forge ahead with the Bochard issue and then proceed from there. Tempering, as he always did, his future moves based on the reaction from Chief Nealy and his group once Bochard was out of the picture. It would be

one step at a time. A grinding, methodical process of elimination designed to break all resistance to the family's ultimate return to Saratoga
gaming. There was no other way around it.
Brute force would be used. All of Bocca's attempts at intimidation, bribery and political
arm-twisting had, in his estimation, been exhausted.

Bocca gave the matter a few minutes'
thought, glanced once again at his calendar and
let out a weary yawn. His index finger touched
a small white button beneath the desk. He then
waited. Seconds later his office door opened
and Rocky Steadman, a long-time trusted family capo, entered. Bocca looked up at Steadman.
"It's time, Rocky."

Steadman leaned over the desk and smiled
at Bocca. "Tell me when and where. It's as good
as done, Don Bocca."

Bocca drew him closer and rested his two
hands over Steadman's. "You have never failed
me in the past. But this is no ordinary request.
I have experienced disappointments lately. Jake
Palermo was good at these things, but he failed.
So we cannot always say that things will go
smoothly. Still, for a job of this importance, I
have chosen you. This Bochard must go. I must
have your word that you will not fail me. Can I
count on you?"

Steadman felt Bocca's hands press on his. They were firm, but cold. "Well, Rocky, can you handle Bochard?"

"It will be done," Steadman assured him. "It will be done to avenge the honor of Jake Palermo."

Bocca's face drew tight and he gave Steadman an icy stare. "No, no," he insisted. "Just take care of Bochard. Leave sentiment about Jake Palermo out. Death is final. There is no reason to mourn Palermo. I want to be clear on this. Concentrate on your task. Sentimental thoughts lead to distraction. Do you follow me?"

"Yes, Don Bocca." Steadman said.

"Good then," Bocca said, releasing Steadman's hands. "Bochard likes tennis. Indoor tennis. Vigorous exercise makes one thirsty. Bochard always carries a water bottle with him while playing tennis. I want him to drink plenty. Make sure his water bottle is ready and waiting," Bocca grinned. "It will no doubt be his last drink."

Steadman felt a dryness in his own throat as he weighed Bocca's words. He managed a forced smile, then left the office.

The following morning, Steadman drove to the Catskill Racquet Club and picked up a stunning, tall, blonde ex-tennis star who accompanied him to Saratoga. Not yet thirty, Peggy

Hoag was considered a hot, go-for-broke, aggressive tennis player who, when not found on a court, loved to sniff cocaine. It became such a habit that she'd do anything for her supply of the white powder. Rocky Steadman, knowing Tom Bochard's penchant for beautiful women, figured Hoag would have no difficulty getting Bochard to play a set or two with her. Somewhere between points, Hoag would switch water bottles.

It would be that simple. Bochard, according to Steadman's calculations, would have time to finish his match, take a shower and drive halfway home before dying.

Steadman, very much aware of Peggy's trim body seated next to him in a smart-looking, blue and white sweat suit, maneuvered the Buick Riviera out of Catskill and onto I-87, headed north. At one point along the way, Peggy brushed a lock of hair from her forehead and turned to face Steadman. "I'm dry for two days now. No chance of slipping me a little booster in advance, is there?"

"No my darling, Peggy. We have a job to do. You'll have to be patient."

"Not even one hit?"

"Not one. After Saratoga you can splurge. It's a promise."

She looked crestfallen. She slumped back

and curled her hands in her lap.

"Cheer up," he said. "This time tomorrow, it'll be all over."

He realized his remarks in no way raised her spirits. Also thinking that if things didn't go well on this assignment, Don Bocca would hand them both their heads. He glanced at Peggy again, but she was asleep. Her head resting against the window. "Oh," he said quietly, "what a gorgeous junkie."

By the time they had reached the outskirts of Albany, Peggy was awake. She gazed over at the towering office buildings of Albany's skyline, then to the right at the frozen Hudson River.

"How much farther?" she asked.

Steadman checked his watch. "About a half hour. Why, are you getting antsy?"

She squirmed in her seat, tucking her legs beneath her body. "I need a hit, damn it! I need a hit!"

"Don't flake out on me now," Steadman demanded. "Let's get to Saratoga, do our thing and get out. You'll be rewarded, as promised." She reached over and touched his right arm.

"I'm not sure I can wait that long. I'm telling you, I'm starting to crash. I need that hit." He sensed she was beginning to panic. Through his suit jacket he could feel her nails digging into his forearm. Her grip tightened as Steadman steered the car north toward Saratoga. Five minutes later, with Peggy still clinging to his arm, Steadman had a frightening thought. What if this girl falls apart before they could pull off the hit? He wasn't sure if he could trust her at this point not to come unglued. His experience with junkies was not all that good. He heard other family members talk about cocaine and crack users, how they'd be flying high one minute and collapsing the next. If this were to happen at the Saratoga Racquet Club, right in the middle of getting to Councilman Bochard, how would he ever explain it to Don Bocca? He knew he had to make a decision – either scrap the hit right now, or let shaky Peggy have her cocaine to settle her down. Perhaps half a hit, just to calm her nerves. Once on the tennis court, she'd be fine. He shook his arm and she let go, sinking back against the car door.

"We'll make a quick stop before Saratoga," he said. "I'll give you half a snort, no more. When we're done with Tommy boy, you can have all the coke you want. Is it a deal?"

"You can be a lovely man when you want to be, Rocky," she murmured feebly.

He sneered back at her, inwardly cursing himself for having given in to her demand. His lips drew tight against his teeth. "Lovely. Lovely, you say. Not quite. You put me in a precarious position. Consider this favor nothing more than the lesser of two evils. Purely expedience. Sweet words don't work with me. Get my point?"

Halfway between Saratoga and Albany, Steadman got off I-87, drove a quarter mile, and pulled into the parking lot of a McDonald's.

"I'm going in for coffee," he said. "Take this and do what you have to do. I'll be back in five minutes." He handed her a small plastic bottle, which she slipped quickly into her pants pocket. He hesitated outside the car and watched her. But she didn't move. When he went inside for coffee, he glanced once out the window, but he couldn't see her clearly. He was wondering just what state of mind she'd be in when he returned? He was worried that the cocaine might impair her judgment and performance at the racquet club. Maybe she'd forget which water bottle was which. He drank his coffee black and hot, suddenly realizing that he was also hungry. So he ordered a cheeseburger. Sitting once more, he began eating his cheeseburger.

"You always dine alone?" she asked.

He looked up. "It's all I can afford."

"Well, I'll eat half of it," she said.

"I'm not that broke," he replied. " I'll buy you one."

"I'll buy my own," she insisted.

As she moved toward the counter, he noticed for the first time that she was actually taller than he. He was exactly five feet, 10 inches. He figured she was at least an inch taller. Her slim, long legs made her look taller still. She came back and sat across from him. In the car she was wearing sunglasses, so he never saw her eyes. She wore none now as she stared straight at him.

Her face was perfectly formed. Deep set blue eyes, with evenly shaped waxed eyebrows, high cheekbones, and a wide mouth with narrow lips that hinted of a smile but never really attained one. No doubt about it, Peggy had a dynamite presence. Steadman knew Bochard would flip for her. Her attitude had improved.

How long the junk would hold her, he didn't know. But if she could keep looking this good and appear as calm as she was at this moment, Steadman felt he could pull this hit off without a problem. His doubts of a half hour earlier left him. Once done eating, they left McDonalds and continued to Saratoga.

"You look fine," he said. "How do you feel?"

She reached out and touched his arm. This time it was a soft grip.

"Try some cocaine and you'll find out for yourself how good I feel."

"I'm fine without any," he assured her. "To each his own. You enjoy it."

"Steadman," she said aloud. "Who's this dude we're after anyway?"

"It doesn't matter, my sweet Peggy. Just do as I ask." He pointed toward the tennis club. "Shall we proceed?"

* * *

Nealy was one of the first to learn that Flint, having arrived earlier in the day at the racquet club, had disappeared mysteriously. Without hesitation, Nealy placed an afternoon call to Sandy at the Sheraton Inn, catching her in the middle of nap. She faintly heard the phone ringing, and slowly got up from the bed and answered it.

"Is that you, Sandy?"

She immediately recognized Nealy's voice. She detected an alarming urgency.

"Yes, it's me. Can I help you, Chief?"

"Is Mike with you?"

His tone further frightened her.

"No. He told me he was going out to check on a few things. He didn't say where."

"Was he attending a meeting of some

201

kind?"

Sandy paused to think. "Not that he mentioned. Why do you ask?"

"Something's come up, Sandy. I don't have all the details. It may or may not involve Mike. I'll have to call you back. Stay put for now. I'm not trying to alarm you, but we can't be too careful. Please try and understand."

She felt a sudden rush of blood to her temples, and her right hand, holding the receiver, began to shake. "Has Flint been hurt?" she instinctively asked Nealy.

"I don't know. I'm not even certain he's involved. We had a call from the Saratoga Tennis Club. There was an altercation there a short time ago. We do know that a local Councilman, Tom Bochard, and some unknown people were in a fracas of some sort. A third party might have been in the middle of whatever it was. I have two detectives on the scene as we talk. My information is vague. Keep your door locked. I'm sending a cop over to the hotel to keep an eye on your suite. Let no one in. Unless, of course, Flint shows up. When I call you back, let the phone ring. Don't answer it. Then call me back at my office. You have the number?"

"Yes, I have it."

She glanced at the small black notebook

on the desk to make certain she did, her nervous fingers flipping through the pages. Then, on the next-to-last page, her eyes were drawn to Flint's unmistakable scribble. He had written down Tom Bochard's name with the notation "Tennis Club" next to it. Her whole body shook.

"Are you still with me?" she heard Nealy say.

She began gasping. "My God, Chief," she blurted. "Flint must be there. Bochard's name, and that of the tennis club is written on his note pad."

There was a sudden knock at the door. Sandy froze in place. She held the phone away from her ear and stared at the door.

"What's wrong, Sandy?" Nealy said. "Is someone there with you?"

"No. I heard a knock at the door."

"Don't answer it." Nealy warned her. "Let me verify something first."

She heard a second knock. It sent shivers through her body. It seemed like endless moments went by. Then she was aware of Nealy's voice again.

"Relax," he assured her. "It's my man out in the hallway. I just made cell phone contact with him. His name is Terrance Kelly. He'll remain in the hall. As added precaution, I'm sending

Kelly a backup. We're not taking any chances at this point."

Her body stopped shaking, but large goose bumps appeared on her arms. What of Flint, she thought? What was he involved in at the tennis club? She was thinking the worst, but tried to wipe it from her mind. Flint could take care of himself. Hadn't he proved that a thousand times in his life? Yes, Flint was fine. He'd be calling her soon to say he was OK. He always did.

Aware that Nealy was still on line, she told him. "I won't hold you any longer, Chief. I know you have work to do. Please keep me posted as soon as you find out anything. That's all I ask." She went and sat down on the bed. Across the room she saw her herself in the mirror. As if she was staring at another human being, the face she saw looked haggard and full of worry. It scared her to think she was in such a state of mind. Then she tried to piece together Flint's movements up to the time he had left that afternoon.

She recalled he had gone to the local library where, with a phone call from Doctor Blake to Genny Sands, the librarian, he was given permission to use the Saratoga Room. He had told Sandy that he wanted to do some research on Joseph Brant and that the Saratoga

Room had just about the best records of that earlier period in American/Saratoga history. Then Sandy remembered Flint mentioning a possible luncheon with Thomas Drake, the current director of the Thoroughbred Racing Museum on Union Avenue. Drake and Flint had drummed up a friendship during Flint's last assignment in Saratoga. Besides, Drake was generally knowledgeable about most Saratoga happenings, past and present. Flint said on many occasions that Drake was a valuable, ready source of information. She thought of calling Nealy back to tell him of the pending lunch date with Drake, but decided she'd call Drake instead. If they had had lunch, Drake might be able to shed some light on Flint's next move.

On phoning the museum a young girl's voice answered. Sandy hesitated, then spoke.

"Is this the Racing Museum?"

"Yes, it is. May I help you?"

"I'm trying to reach Thomas Drake."

"He's here," the girl said. "I'll see if I can locate him."

"This is Drake," said a man firmly.

Sandy clutched the back of her neck where suddenly there was a sharp pain. "Oh, Mr. Drake, my name is Sandy Blair. Perhaps Mike Flint has mentioned me? He said you were to have lunch today. Did you?" The pain crept further up her neck and was now turning into a slow, persistent headache, one she knew would turn to a full fledged migraine before it was done.

"Yes, Mike has mentioned you on several occasions. About lunch, we never made it. Flint called and said he had to go to the tennis club.

"We decided to do dinner some evening. Flint said he wanted to meet with Tom Bochard, the councilman. I know Bochard plays tennis three afternoons a week. Actually, Flint invited me to go along, but I'm not a fan of Bochard's.

"We've had our little political differences. In fact, the man infuriated me at a recent city council meeting. I'm not an official member, but I do attend meetings when I think the issues at hand are important. I'd suggest you call the tennis club. He's probably still out there."

She clenched the receiver and held it away from her ear. Then softly replied, "Thank you, Mr. Drake. I'll call the club. Thank you."

"Good," said Drake. "Tell Flint not to forget our dinner date. And it's high time I meet you in person. Make sure he brings you. I insist."

"I will Mr. Drake. Thank you. I'm looking forward to it."

With the phone call ended, Sandy stood in

silence, shaken to the core. Chief Nealy's call was not a casual inquiry. In this lonely moment, she feared the worst and was terribly worried for Flint. If anything serious were to happen to him, she knew she'd come apart at the seams. In the past three years their interdependence had become so strong, so magnetic, and their love so enrapturing, the very thought of separation of any kind would, she knew, be impossible to handle.

It was a romance of complete opposites from the start. Forget the twenty-eight-year age difference. Even their closest friends, and that included the Saratoga ones, found it difficult to believe that she could be so wrapped up in a hard-crusted private investigator like Mike Flint.

But what these friends didn't know was that it was she who pursued the relationship. Flint, knowing full well the negatives of such a courtship, tried to back off. But she wouldn't let him. Now their bond was fully cemented and growing stronger each day. She was thinking these thoughts and picturing Flint in her mind when someone knocked on the suite door. Slowly she moved to the door and looked through the peephole.

She spotted Nealy's police officer leaning against the far wall. Who was knocking? She saw no one else. Following Nealy's words, she dared not open the lock. Then, to her surprise, Dr. Blake's face came into full view. She unlocked the bolt and threw open the door, falling forward as she did right into Blake's arms.

"My God, Doctor. I'm so happy to see you," She exclaimed. "I've been sick thinking about Flint. Is he all right?"

Blake turned to Officer Kelly. "You have a backup coming, don't you?"

"Yes," said Kelly. "He'll be here momentarily."

"Good," said Blake. "Position him near the elevator. Don't let a soul come near this suite." Kelly stepped forward, smiling. "It's not a he, doctor. It's a she. Officer Ryeback will be assisting me. Gail Ryeback. She's one of our best cops."

Blake shot a questioning glance at Sandy. "I hope she's the very best. Before this is over, we're going to need all the good people we can muster."

With that, Blake ushered Sandy inside the suite and shut the door. He shed his blue overcoat and flung it over a chair. His face was flush from the cold and his eyes, which Sandy had always remembered as steady and reassuring, stared at her with the utmost concentration and worry. The message he was about to tell her was written all over his drawn, pale face. It was a look she had seen many times while working for this noted psychiatrist, but one she saw on the frail faces of his patients, never his.

Her hands covered her ears. She was anticipating his words and didn't want to hear them. He waited a minute for her to get her composure. Then gently, taking her hands in his, he sat her down on the lounge chair and remained silent until he was sure her emotions had stabilized. Her bowed head slowly lifted, and her eyes met his once more. He let her speak.

"Tell me straight, doctor. Is Flint dead?"

He drew a long breath and sat back. "No, not that we know of. But he is missing. Where, we don't have a clue. There was a struggle outside in the parking lot of the Saratoga Racquet Club this afternoon. There were witnesses, but there was so much confusion, no one seems to know what really happened, or who was involved, aside from Flint. Unfortunately, there are two deaths related to the incident, one male, one female. Nealy and the state police are checking their identities as we speak. We do know that Flint went to talk to Tom Bochard, who was playing tennis at the time. The manager remembers chatting with Flint just before he went into the court area to see Bochard.

The manager also said he believed the dead

man and woman were friends, or acquaintances, of Bochard. At least they implied that to the manager. Based on that, he gave them guest privileges and permission to use a court. We learned he never checked with Bochard first.

The manager said he saw Bochard engrossed in conversation with the two. Shortly after, the girl, a tall, stunning blonde, according to the manger's description, played a single set with Bochard while her partner sat it out. From what we have pieced together, some strangers entered the court from a side entrance, unannounced, and confronted the blonde and her friend. It must have taken place at just about the same time Flint was making his entrance. The next thing the manager knew, all were in the parking lot scuffling. Except that Bochard was not there. He was later found in the men's locker room passed out on the floor. The Saratoga fire department's EMT team was called in. They couldn't revive him immediately, so he was rushed to Saratoga Hospital. That's how we became aware of the whole incident."

Sandy slumped forward and Blake caught her by the right arm and assisted her back. Her face was ashen.

"Let me get you some water," Blake insisted. She drank one gulp and buried her face in her hands. "Go on. I don't want to hear it,

210

but I must. I have to face this thing."

"You need a stronger stimulant," said Blake. "Do you have some whiskey handy?"

She pointed to the service bar. "Flint's got a bottle. You're right. I need a drink."

Blake fetched the whiskey. It was Jamison's, one of Flint's favorites. "Irish firewater," he recalled Flint describing it.

Sandy sipped the whiskey and washed it down with water. She felt its immediate warmth in her stomach and limbs.

Blake patted her on the arm, and continued. "We now feel Bochard was poisoned. He had all the symptoms, though he'll recover. The EMT's quick work can be credited here. Bochard's so-called acquaintances weren't that lucky. There wasn't a mark on their bodies. So we can only assume they were poisoned, too. Clad only in their tennis garb, they were found half-frozen at the far end of the parking lot. The man, whoever he was, had his ears slit. Not deep. So this wasn't the cause of death. But a damn strange thing to see. Distinctive, criss-crossing slits. Nealy said someone was making a statement. Much like they did when old Jake Palermo was found a few weeks back."

Blake looked again at Sandy. His eyes squinting as he labored to form his next words.

"Flint, we fear, has been abducted. By whom

and for what reason, we don't know. A victim of circumstance? Perhaps. Might he have known the assailants? Also a possibility."

For the first time since his arrival, Sandy detected a break in Blake's voice. She expected him to cry. The mood was so somber, they were both on the verge of tears when they were interrupted by another knock on the door.

This time it was Nealy, appearing disheveled, with his coat unevenly buttoned and a haggard look on his face. The deep frowns on his forehead made him appear ten years older than his seventy years. And it was apparent that the cold air was affecting his acute asthma. He reached in his pocket, took out an inhaler and put it to his lips.

"Sit down, Chief, and take a long breath." Blake told him. "You're pushing too hard."

Nealy coughed once and then took off his jacket. He faced Sandy. "I'm sorry this whole mess is laid in your lap," he said apologetically. "Lousy luck. Lousy timing. We shouldn't have let Flint go it alone. If I had only known he was going out to see Tom Bochard, I would have personally tailed behind. Who would have expected this in broad daylight? Who would have expected this at all? Didn't Don Bocca and his gang get the message last time around?"

"You can't blame yourself, Tom." Blake said.

"We all know that Mike is a man who keeps his own counsel. He does what he feels he has to do as things come his way. None of us in the room would have it any other way." Blake looked at Sandy. "Let's not write Flint off this early. Let's assume he's exactly where he wants to be. Right on the heels of the bad guys. It's Flint's resiliency that we count on, don't we?"

Each one in turn had his or her say. In the end, they all talked themselves out. It was a baffling, disturbing turn of events. Sandy had all she could do to keep her composure. Finally, Blake suggested they all go home and tackle it tomorrow when, as he put it, "We can collect our wits and approach this dilemma with clearer heads."

Nealy, always fearful that the worst was yet to come, had a third cop posted in the hotel to protect Sandy. As short as Nealy was on manpower, he felt he owned it to both Flint and Sandy. Wherever this nightmarish situation would lead them all was anybody's guess.

After saying good-bye to Blake and Nealy, she instinctively glanced down the hallway, wistfully hoping that Flint might appear. No such luck. Only Nealy's trusted cops. She knew in her heart it was to be a long, sleepless night. "My God," she groaned, "Where is he?"

13. WHERE'S FLINT?

Doctor Blake made a late night phone call to Harry Waite's home in Tarrytown, the place, Flint had told him, where Harry found refuge from the Big Apple. He used the code number Flint had given him on his last assignment, hoping that it was still good. In the whirlwind of events, and the apprehension that now hung like a dark cloud since Flint's disappearance, Blake was mindful of the delicate nature of calling Waite, especially at home.

Waite's special police force operated with top secrecy. If through incompetence, or merely mistake, certain political and criminal forces were to uncover Waite's operation, many persons within the organization might be put at immediate risk. Still, Blake felt he had to call.

He knew Harry was the only one who could really help. Blake listened as the phone rang five or six times. Then the line was silent. Blake figured he'd lost the connection. Or worst yet, the line was no longer in use. He pressed the receiver closer to his right ear. He detected a faint humming sound, low but too garbled to distinguish. Then the line went silent a second time, and Blake, in uncharacteristic frustration, shook the phone, shouting as he did, "Harry, are you there?"

Then the gravel voice that Blake clearly discerned answered. "I retire early if you don't mind. Who the hell is this?"

"Arnold Blake. Doctor Arnold Blake. Mike Flint's Saratoga friend."

"Flint gave you my coded home number? How sweet of him. No, how very uncustomary of him. Where is he? I want to chew him out personally."

"I'm sorry, Harry, but that's my reason for calling. We don't know where Flint is. He's disappeared."

"Oh, hell," Waite tried to reassure him, "that's Flint for you. He's been known to disappear for days on end. You'll get used to it, Doc. Now let me get some sleep. And, if you'd don't mind, don't call this number again. It's too sensitive. In fact, I've been meaning to get it changed. I'll do that tomorrow."

Blake, afraid Waite would terminate the call, jumped in, declaring, "Wrong, Harry. Two people were killed in Saratoga today. Flint was there when it happened. He's not been seen nor heard from since. We all think he's been abducted. Chief Nealy says it all points in that direction."

Blake waited for Harry's response, but it was slow in coming. "Who got killed?" Harry finally asked.

"They've not been identified," Blake said. "A man and a woman. Nealy thinks they were a hit team sent by Don Bocca. A tall, athletic fellow with a mustache, and a blonde gal, also the athletic type. A tennis player. The whole thing took place at the Saratoga Racquet Club. Sandy says Flint went to talk to one of our councilmen, Tom Bochard. Bochard is a member. He plays tennis once or twice a week at the club.

"Whatever happened started on the courts and quickly moved outside to the parking lot. The man and woman were found in the lot. It was not a pretty sight, I've been told."

He heard Harry cough and then draw a deep breath. "Did anyone see all this?"

"Only the club attendant was on hand. A dumpy, older guy, I'd say in his early sixties who wasn't, in my opinion, very alert. Said he heard nothing and saw nothing. We've drawn a blank trying to figure it out at this end."

"How strange," Harry said. "There had to be others. Who the hell was playing tennis with

Bochard? And if Flint is missing, where's his vehicle?"

"To answer the last part of your question, Flint's rented car was found near the front of the club, keys in it and the motor still running. The attendant said Bochard was scheduled to play with a lawyer from Lake Luzerne. I believe his name is Tocco. Apparently Tocco never showed. Our two dead friends came by and the attendant said they talked for a time with Bochard. The last he knew, Bochard and the blonde were hitting practice balls. The blonde's partner, whoever he was, didn't play.

The attendant said he went back to folding towels in the outer office and paid no further attention to the group. He doesn't remember ever seeing Flint, or anyone resembling Flint's description, on the premises. The state police are involved in the investigation. They're working closely with Nealy. Sandy's staying in the suite she and Flint rented at the downtown Sheraton Inn. Nealy sent three cops to guard her room. She's pretty worked up over this. We all are. We need your help, Harry."

Another long pause, with Harry's heavy breathing on the phone. "Doc, if Flint is really in a jam, I'll do anything I can to help him. That said, wanting to help and being able to help has its inherent complications. As you well know, my unit officially doesn't exist outside of New York City. In fact, in most of our operations, we're acting illegally within the city limits. It's the nature of the beast, so to speak. We can't expose ourselves without risking disclosure to certain other law enforcement bodies, and to some criminal elements for that matter, that would just love to air our dirty laundry. It's that touchy, that secretive. And without trying to sound too callous, Central can't, and won't, acknowledge any of its operatives, in-house personnel or freelance types. The pay is high, and the risks are equally as high."

Harry paused again and Blake, feeling a tinge of abandonment, tried to think of a more convincing way to articulate his urgency on behalf of Flint, but couldn't. Blake perfectly understood Harry's predicament and the delicate position of Central's operations, but it did little to ease Blake's own mounting fear for Flint's situation. Callous was too mild a word, Blake reasoned. If Harry could not come to Flint's aid at this time, it would be pure desertion. Blake waited for Harry to continue, which he did.

"This is a rough, unforgiving game at times, Doc. Mike never tackles these assignments knowing any different," Harry droned on. "I also can assure you Mike has been in the lion's den before. He's been bitten, beat up, scarred, shot, knifed, torched and left frozen in a meat cooler, but he's a survivor. So let's give this some more time and see if he, as he's proven in the past, shows up. That's not to say he's not in danger or … " and for the first time in the conversation, Blake detected a break in Harry's voice, "possibly killed. But I'm opting for the former."

"We all are," Blake assured him.

"Sure. I know you are," Harry shouted. "Look, Doc. We better address Sandy's precarious position now. Guards or no guards, she's in a fishbowl at the Sheraton Inn. I'd get her to safer quarters, pronto. Might even consider talking her into going to stay with Monica in California. She'll probably resist you, but I see no other option right now. Monica gave her comfort and reassurance when Flint was nearly killed in Canada three years ago by St. Jacques and his mob, if you recall. Aside from Sandy, no one knows Flint better than Monica. God knows, she's probably the one female most responsible for Flint being alive today. Romantically, the thing between Flint and Monica was a shallow relationship compared to his love for Sandy, but I've always admired Monica's firmness and resolve in tough situations. I guess that's the only way a middle-aged actress can survive in tinsel town. I really haven't figured out where Sandy and Monica stand concerning Flint. Knowing the dynamics, I'd say it's a classic hate-love relationship, tempered by a mutual understanding. But at least they can console one another during this new crisis. What do you think?"

"I agree, Harry. You're absolutely right. I'll get to her right after this call. Perhaps you can contact Monica and fill her in. I'm certain Nealy will arrange protection for Sandy to the coast. We should be able to get her a flight out of Albany Airport. She'd have a stopover in Chicago. Anyhow, Nealy's in tight with officials from American Airlines. He'll be able to bag a flight, hopefully no later than tomorrow. If not, we'll drive her to Kennedy and fly her out nonstop. I assume you can handle this flight, if need be?"

"No problem," said Harry.

"Now back to Flint," Blake went on. "Isn't there anyone you can send up to help out?"

"Not one I'd trust operating outside the city. The men and women I have filtered around the city are too urban in their thinking and ways. They'd screw up any rural assignment. No, we need someone who can fit into the scene without being too conspicuous. The nearest free agent I have in New York that comes even remotely close to that description can't find his way around Central Park."

"Look," Blake insisted, "the worst of your agents have to be better than Chief Nealy's locals. I don't think we can let this drag another day, Harry. Send up the best one you can think of. We'll take our chances. If you're on a tight operating budget, don't worry. I'll personally pick up the tab."

"That's not necessary, Doc. I have a dozen operatives that would go to bat for Flint for no pay. Forget the money. As I say, it's really a matter of sending the right person. As I see it, the core of all your problems in Saratoga is Don Bocca. That old bat is living in the dark ages. Still, he's very dangerous and very unpredictable. Smart in many respects, but he comes at you like a viper. He's probably bordering on senility, and that makes him even more dangerous. His organization still packs muscle and is backed by plenty of money. But he operates on old mob parameters.

His younger lieutenants would like to retire him to Florida. It won't happen soon. In the meantime, he can be downright scary. The man I have in mind is not known to Bocca or any New York mob people. Nor does Flint know him. If he'll take the job, he'd be our best bet. Fearless, cunning, experienced and a tenacious, stalking investigator once he's got his compass set in the right direction. Much like Flint, when I think about it. If anyone is capable of sniffing out culprits, it's him."

"You've got my full attention," said Blake. "Now who is he?"

"A good man," replied Harry. "That's all I'm going to tell you about him right now. Except he comes from Vermont, and goes by the initials E.N. Vermont's not one of our more heavily crime infested states, though it does get its share of hard criminals."

"Fine, Harry. Do what you can and get back to me. I want to check with Nealy and the rest right now. I won't say a word about this talk unless, of course, you don't mind."

Harry hesitated, then answered. "I don't mind if you tell Nealy. We've got to keep him in the loop. After all, Saratoga is his turf. If E.N. decides to take the assignment, I'll let you know. But as I said earlier, Doc, Flint's a survivor. Three-to-one says he'll show up. You can go to the bank on that prediction."

"I pray you're right, Harry."

Doctor Blake stood for several moments dangling the phone in his right hand once Harry had hung up. The soft, amber-colored glow from a corner table lamp in his mahogany-paneled study cast an eerie presence over the room. The moment was reminiscent of what Blake experienced the first time the old Spa was facing a crisis and he, acting on behalf of the others, was making identical phone calls for help. It wasn't a task he appreciated or enjoyed. And there was also the dread that one of these times, perhaps now, he was going to the well once too often. He decided he'd call Sandy. It was almost 11 o'clock and a sudden, nasty rain mixed with strong wind gusts was pounding Saratoga. Certainly not ideal flying weather, Blake mused, but better than snow. If successful in coaching Sandy to go to Monica's, there wouldn't be much time to make flight arrangements. He pondered the option of calling her or going to the Sheraton to convey Harry's suggestion. He finally settled on calling her to say he was coming over for a drink to discuss the latest findings. Getting her to leave Saratoga while Flint was missing would not be easy. He knew Sandy Blair much too well for that.

Given a choice between leaving or staying was, as Blake knew, no choice at all. Somehow he'd have to convince Sandy that going to California was something Flint himself would insist on.

On the short drive across town to the red-bricked Sheraton Inn, with the pelting rain drumming on his car and the glare of headlights making him squint, Blake silently rehearsed his opening lines. "Mike would be the first to tell you to go. It's the safe thing to do..." Then, realizing that line would be too weak, too mushy, he erased it from his head. No, the approach would have to be based on reason. Sandy was a reasonable woman, wasn't she? He recalled that she always was level-headed when she worked for him at his clinic. Practical, even-tempered and able to reason. Three years within the erratic, dangerous lifestyle of Mike Flint, however, might have changed her. But Blake still felt she'd listen to him. After all, wasn't the doctor always right?

He swung the car into the Sheraton parking lot just as a big rush of rain swept up along Broadway, making it difficult to pick out a parking space. The walk from the parking lot to the lobby, though only a distance of twenty yards, proved a wet one. A two-inch-high stream of run-off water soaked his shoes. All the way through the lobby, along the hallways and up to the fourth floor by elevator, his soaking shoes left a footprint trail. His feet were still uncomfortably wet when Sandy opened the suite door, welcoming Blake and waving to Nealy's watchdogs still on guard duty. Inside she took his dripping trench coat and, noticing his shoes, insisted he take them off. She brought him a towel and a pair of Flint's red slippers.

"Doc," she surprised him by saying, "you're a damn dripping mess."

"Oh, a little Saratoga spring water won't hurt anyone," he joked.

"Not till you come down with a barking cough or head cold. It's March, not August." He sat in a large, cushioned lounge chair near the suite's oval-shaped window that faced Broadway. The blowing rain and wind lashed at the large, dark pane. Sandy mixed him a bourbon on the rocks and poured herself a glass of sherry. She raised her glass to his.

"We'll toast Mike Flint. We'll pray he comes through that door tonight. If not tonight, tomorrow. He will come back to me, I know that in the depth of my heart."

Blake watched her face as she spoke. Two fine lines drew tight at the corner of her eyes and her chin, with its classic, Grecian features, protruded forward, as her lips parted ever so slightly to sip the wine. He observed more closely as her eyes shut momentarily, then blinked open. She stared at Blake.

"This is the most severe time of my life, Doc. I can't cry another tear, and I can't smile either. I'm like one of those mannequins you see at Macy's. I'm fixed in place. Petrified on the outside and terrified inside. As a doctor, what's your professional diagnosis of my present state?"

Blake drank some bourbon, before speaking. He knew she wanted a truthful answer. After another sip he managed to giver her one.

"Professionally, I'd say it's acute anxiety. At times like this, it's not uncommon to live in an emotional straitjacket. It tightens most severely around you because of your attachment to Mike. We're all affected by it, but you're taking the brunt of this emotional trauma."

She came and sat next to Blake. "I can't weaken, do you understand that. I can't weaken or break down now. I don't have Flint at my side, but I feel his strength and his presence. If he's given me anything worthwhile these past three years, it's the will to be strong when I need to be. I had no confidence till he came into my life. Mike showed me how to be strong. He is so filled with inner strength it radiates to others. I'm energized by his strength. Does this make sense?"

Blake stared down at his empty glass, running his fingers over the rim. He shifted sideways to face her. "I've never heard it put more elegantly, Sandy. That's exactly what Flint is all about...strength. We're all weak-kneed babes next to him. You've described Flint in a way we never could. Nealy refers to Mike as hard, tough, wiry, crafty. You've discovered differently.

Strength is the right word."

Sandy went to pour him a refill. He waved her off. "Just one more. I think you need it."

"No, I've had my limit, thanks."

"Well then," she said, "let me hear where this investigation stands at the moment."

Blake's rehearsed line about going to Monica's crept into his consciousness, and he just as quickly dismissed it again. As she poured herself another wine, he was groping for the right words. Nothing seemed to fit, so he simply told her what Harry Waite had said. He labored to get the sentence out. As expected, Sandy was not pleased. In fact, she was very upset at the very idea of leaving Saratoga, and furious with Harry for even suggesting it.

"Has Harry's job become so hard and impersonal, so very mundane, that he'd make a statement like that?" she questioned Blake with a bold look.

Blake rubbed his forehead. "Probably. Men in Harry's position become hard-boiled after a time. Though in this instance, I know he was trying to help."

"Help, hell," Sandy snapped back. "Walk out on Flint? How does that help?"

Blake moved from his lounge chair to the window. "I think he was honestly thinking of your safety," Blake whispered. He paused for her reaction.

"My safety? How about Flint's?" she said, quite agitated.

"I'm sure he was thinking of Mike when he suggested you go to Monica's. Harry may be hardened to the core, but he and Mike were..." Blake caught himself, "...are good friends. Harry's even offered to send one of his trusted investigators over from Vermont to help find Mike. I have no idea who this guy is, but I'm certain he's very competent. We need all the help we can get."

Sandy began walking slowly around the room, stopping once near Blake to peer out the window. It had stopped raining, yet the wind was still strong. She heard it rustling the barren maple trees near the hotel's perimeter. Across Saratoga's Broadway, she could make out the lights of the former Firehouse Restaurant, though the image was not clear through the water-streaked window.

"Everything changes in time, doesn't it?" She remarked in a soft, almost distant voice.

"How's that?" said Blake.

She walked quietly over to the built-in wet bar and grabbed the wine bottle. "Oh, everything. We change. Towns change. Our attitudes and beliefs about things change." She pointed to the window. "See the Firehouse over there?

It's closed. For years you could walk into that restaurant most weekend evenings and be entertained by Ruth at the piano. It was a certain. You wanted to hear her play so you went there. Single or with someone. It didn't really matter because there were always others there for the same reason. Now you can't."

"Can't what?" asked Blake.

"Ruthy. You can't hear Ruthy. She doesn't play there anymore. Like everything else, since the Firehouse closed. It's just one of many changes I've noticed since Mike and I returned."

"Perhaps she'll play elsewhere."

Sandy looked at him with glazed eyes. "Sure, she may. But would it be the same as the Firehouse? No, it wouldn't. That's what I mean about change. Like Flint and me. We're a pair. We've been almost inseparable since we met. His not being here is the worst change of all. This dank, wet night doesn't help things, either."

Blake could feel Sandy's tension from across the room. She was nearing her breaking point, so he braced himself for it. When it came, it came out in one big, sorrowful sob, followed by tears that dampened not only her face, but the light-blue blouse she was wearing. He let her cry for several moments before going to comfort her. This great flood of emotion, which she courageously had been holding back, had to come forth. Her whole body shook. She buried her face in her hands and cried some more. He then went and held her tight, waiting several moments until the worst of it was over.

When she finally stopped crying, he sat her on the lounge and went to get her some more wine. She drank it in silence, her head bent.

Blake said nothing. He knew she needed these few minutes to adjust. He poured himself another drink and waited for her to come around. He tried to use professional detachment as a mechanism for not being overwhelmed himself by Sandy's suffering, but found it didn't work. His own friendship with Flint was impairing his doctor's ability to stay unemotional. He had to fight back the urge to cry. Sandy's longing for Flint and the sadness of the moment were contagious, compounded by the fact that neither knew where Flint was, nor if he was dead. It was one of the most perplexing, frightening experiences Blake could ever remember. And that included the trauma experienced by some of his more severe mental patients at the clinic.

As Blake and Sandy sat across from each other, their emotions nearly spent, Blake realized his mission was doomed unless he could pull himself, and Sandy, out of their sudden, spontaneous depression. He reached over and turned on the nearby TV, catching a variety show in progress and cranked up the sound in an attempt to jolt Sandy out of her deep mood. It worked to a point. She slowly came back to her normal self, a faint blush returning to her cheeks.

"You feeling better?" he said.

"Somewhat. As fine as I can feel, I guess." Blake knew he was overstaying his welcome. Sandy was tired and drained. Convincing Sandy that going to Monica's was in her and everyone else's best interest wasn't going to be easy. Also, he thought, if he failed to talk her into going and something were to happen to her, he'd never forgive himself. Besides, if some harm did come to her, how would he ever explain it to Flint? No, Blake felt a strong duty to convince Sandy to go. So he made another attempt to persuade her. For this, Blake opted for some sound reasoning. Straight, matter-of-fact dialogue Sandy could relate to.

"Was it, or was it not, Flint's near brush with death three years ago which forced you to go live with Monica?" he said.

The question seemed to catch her off guard, and she spun around to face him. "You know damn well it was. Why ask?"

"I ask it for a good reason," he assured her.

"And that is, plainly speaking, that there wasn't any alternative under the circumstances. We had a killer lurking about Saratoga who had your number, and keeping you here was tantamount to committing suicide. Isn't that right?"

She listened intently to Blake as she slowly moved about the room. "Well, Doc, it wasn't exactly as you say. Yes, we hypothesized there were still killers in Saratoga. How many, we didn't know. We knew for sure that at least one of them was dead. Flint saw to that. Thought this didn't rule out others. Of course, no one knew that Harry's man, Georgio, was one of he bad guys until the end. But, come to think of it, I didn't just trek off to Monica's out of fear. I went because Mike was also in California, re-covering from his beating in Montreal at the hands of St. Jacques. Don't forget that. If Mike had been laid up in Saratoga, I would have stayed right here, just like I'm doing now. You have to know where I'm coming from. You have to know that I wouldn't leave Mike for any rea-son, even if my life depended on it. I'll stay put till we solve this. He'll come back, I know it. If not today, tomorrow. He's not dead..." Her words broke off and she sat down once more.

Blake simply nodded and fell silent. He looked at the time. It was almost midnight. Too late now to call and make flight arrangements anyway. Harry's caution about the Sheraton Inn being a fishbowl was still fresh in his ears. If Sandy wouldn't budge from Saratoga, at least she had to vacate the hotel. The presence of Nealy's cops in the hallway was reason enough to draw undue attention her suite. The cops couldn't stay on guard indefinitely, for Nealy was short of manpower as it was. Harry was right. Sandy was not safe here.

He approached Sandy, gently resting his hands on her shoulders. "No one can deny your reason for staying. Least of all me. But if you insist on being in Saratoga while the investigation goes on, you'll have to hole up in a more secure location. Can we agree on this?"

Her eyelids lowered, then lifted, so that her large, round dark eyes went straight to his.

"Look, Arnold, I've been ungrateful, I know. Maybe even stubborn to a fault. I know all of you mean to help and I appreciate your concerns. If you feel I'd be safer someplace else, that's fine by me. But where?"

For the first time in the evening's conversation, Blake felt relief. Perhaps once she's out of the Sheraton, he could then talk her into visiting Monica. One step at a time, he thought. In Sandy's state of mind, it could be done no other way. She and Flint came to Saratoga with little baggage, so the move would be easy once a safe house had been agreed upon.

"You know Martha Duffy, don't you?" Blake inquired.

"Certainly." She said. " Why do you ask?"

"I was thinking, Duffy's house would be as safe as any right now. Would you mind staying with them till we can work out other quarters?"

"That's fine by me, Doc, as long as it won't put too much burden on Martha. She's no spring chicken, and neither is Duffy. But if they'll have me, I'd enjoy their company. The Duffys were very gracious to Mike and me when we were last here. I was worried sick when we thought Duffy had drowned in that river up near Lake Placid. For a newspaperman his age – what is he now, seventy-six? – he's as crusty and tough as a mountain goat. Martha is a dear person. I hope they can put up with one very frustrated, worried ex-nurse."

"I'm sure they will." Blake said.

Blake called the Duffys and got their permission. Within the hour Sandy had packed all of the clothes, shoes and small extra things she and Flint had, and Blake took her to Duffy's Circular Street home. Blake cleared the move with Nealy before leaving. Nealy, always leery of making moves that might be detected, decided to leave one of his cops at the hotel. He did it, he said, for two reasons. If Don Boca's henchmen did have a fix on Flint and Sandy's Sheraton Inn suite, then the guard could act as a decoy, making Bocca's men believe Sandy was still there. Nealy's second reason for keeping his man at the Sheraton was for Flint's sake.

If Flint were to suddenly show up, someone would have to fill him in on Sandy's whereabouts. The fact that Flint was still missing also presented Nealy and Blake with the dreaded thought that should Flint ever be found dead, Sandy would be alone in the world. They didn't want her staying by herself if this scenario became reality. If that day ever arrived, at least she'd have comfort with the Duffys. As each hour passed since the tennis club fiasco, hopes of finding Flint alive appeared less likely, though no one among the group dared express that thought openly.

It had been a trying time for everyone. The cold, wet, Saratoga night seemed to linger forever, and more than one participant caught up in Flint's mysterious disappearance, including Sandy, spent sleepless hours wondering how it would turn out.

And although April was fast approaching with its hope of warmer weather, the stark reality of what might be facing Saratoga in the coming days prolonged the winter's chill.

14. WHO'S MOVING IN?

The search for Flint intensified once Sandy was settled in with the Duffys. Nealy called it the most systematic reverse dragnet for one man in Saratoga's history. Every news organization in the region would have been covering it. But Nealy had the delicate task of keeping Flint's name out of the headlines. It was also a matter of keeping Don Bocca off balance. If, indeed, Flint was in Bocca's hands, Nealy wanted to proceed cautiously, yet firmly. He'd let Harry Waite comb Bocca's Catskill hideaways for Flint, kowing that Harry would leave no leaf unturned. Nealy, unaware that Blake had already made contact with Harry about Flint's plight, contacted Waite himself. Nowhere in Harry's conversation with Nealy did Harry mention Blake's previous call. As was his practice in most of his dealings, Harry's unwritten policy was not to reveal anything unless asked.

"We've hit a brick wall, Harry," Nealy admitted. "Not a trace of Flint since he was last seen entering the tennis club. I just got a make on the man and woman. Definitely mob assassins. The type Bocca hires for special hits."

"I'm familiar with both of them," Harry interrupted.

"Am I correct?" said Nealy.

"Almost," said Harry.

"I don't understand."

"They've both worked for the mob, but neither were what you'd call totally professional killers. Can't figure out why Bocca would use them. Then again, it could be the desperation of an old Don seeking revenge. The body beautiful tennis player, I'm told, had a long, seductive history. Let me ask you this. Was your councilman a lady's man?"

"He chased every skirt in Saratoga," said Nealy. "By the way, who filled you in on the blonde?"

"A little birdie in Central Park. He knows all the cute, tan, blonde female tennis players in these parts, dead or alive."

"Well," Nealy said, "Bochard warmed right up to her, I guess."

"That's what I thought," Harry laughed. "It wasn't her tennis game he was admiring. She probably had him drooling from the first volley."

"No doubt," Nealy agreed. " But where did

her buddy come in? According to the attendant, her partner wasn't dressed for tennis."

"Exactly," said Harry. "It was a double hit. She attracted while he attacked."

"I don't understand," Nealy said, puzzled.

"Councilman Bochard wasn't shot, not knifed, not beaten."

"Then he's alive?" Harry asked.

"Most certainly. Quite sick, but alive."

"What do you mean, sick?"

Nealy had to think about it. "Really haven't checked with Saratoga Hospital, but I know they had to induce vomiting. Did hear one of the EMTs on the scene say he thought Bochard had swallowed something. The EMTs claim he had bluish blotches under both eyes when found. He was lying face down in the men's locker room, dressed in his tennis garb."

"Well, it's easy to figure out, then," said Harry. "While Blondie was giving him an eyeful, her friend was filling his water bottle with whatever it is they use these days to poison someone. Find his water bottle, have it analyzed, and that part of this investigation will be done. I'd say they used arsenic, but that's only a guess. You never know. Perhaps strychnine. Take your pick."

As he listened to Harry, Nealy was trying desperately to remember if the forensic people had secured Bochard's bottle. Hell, they must have. If not, he'd make damn sure someone did the minute he was off the line with Harry.

"You still with me?" Harry shouted.

"Yes, Harry. Just trying to recall if we got Bochard's water bottle or not. Things were pretty hectic out there when this all went down. Besides, everyone was searching around for Flint. He vanished, simply vanished. What do you make of it?"

"I have no more idea than you, Tom. You said Flint's vehicle was still there, running?"

"That's correct."

"The hit team is dead. The attendant saw others but can't identify who they were or how many there were. Flint's disappeared. We have to ascertain whether Mike was taken or if he found a way to tag along with the intruders."

"What do you mean, tag along?" Nealy asked.

"Just that Flint's resilient. Depending on what type of wheels the strangers were driving, be it cars or maybe even trucks, he might have jumped aboard undetected and gone along with then."

Nealy looked strangely at the phone.

"Come on, Harry, you're comparing Mike to James Bond, aren't you?"

"Maybe. I'm simply saying that Mike has

done some extraordinary things in the past, and he's lived to talk about them. If the intruders killed the hit team and left them in the parking lot, why not Mike? As wild as it sounds, I'd say Flint found a way to outsmart them. How, where, and in what shape he's in at this very moment, I don't know. I'm a hunch player. My hunch says he's surviving whatever ordeal he's now facing. I'd bet on it."

"Sounds good," Nealy added, "but let's be realistic. Let's say Mike doesn't make it, what then? We'll be stuck with the same problem we faced from the beginning. Who knows where Bocca will strike again? I don't have the right men or resources to sort this out. We all were depending on Flint to solve it. I can't bear the thought that he's possibly been killed. Without Flint, who's going to combat Bocca? Sandy will be devastated. We all will."

"Get off the negative," Harry told him. "Give Flint more credit than that. Hey, I'm not saying he couldn't be in trouble, but I don't buy this dead talk. Furthermore, I don't believe you've covered all bases leading up to the tennis club meeting anyway. Have your teams stay out there and question everyone over and over again. The trail's always hottest at its source. I know the club is somewhat isolated, but there had to be people in the vicinity. After all, it was broad daylight, wasn't it?"

"Yes," Nealy sighed. "That's what makes it so damn frustrating. All that action taking place in the middle of the afternoon. I wouldn't believe the mob would stage such a stunt at that time of day."

"You're right," Harry agreed. "It's not their style, but these days who can say? Besides, they probably had no choice. They had to move on Bochard when opportunity presented itself. The fact that the club is in a remote place made it feasible. And if I'm right about the poison, it makes even more sense. No guns, no noise. Looking at this, I'm not as concerned about the time of day as I am about the number of players involved. I'd say someone upset Bocca's plans, making this a real triangle. Look, didn't the same thing happen to Jake Palermo? He came to Saratoga to take out Molly O'Neill, and wound up dead at the hands of unknowns. True?"

Nealy scratched his head. Harry Waite was spelling out the obvious. Why hadn't he thought of it? "I'll buy that, too," Nealy conceded.

"Question," Harry said. "Where did these intruders pop in from? Is it Canadian mob muscling in? Perhaps even the Boston mobsters? Maybe some we haven't thought of yet? Any number of possibilities. Rule nothing out at this point."

"I'm trying to keep a focus on Flint's disappearance. It's all I can do with my limited manpower, Harry," Nealy replied, realizing Waite was giving him a mild lecture on police procedure, a chastising he felt he didn't deserve. "I'm also hamstrung by the fact that in protecting Flint's identity, I can't use the New York State Police's help.

"Oh, they're already investigating the tennis club deaths and so on, but they don't know about Flint. Fortunately for us, Flint never gave the court attendant his name, so they haven't linked him to the fracas. Unless someone slips up and says something, Flint will remain out of the investigation. Good in one way, bad in the other. Without state police assistance, my investigative powers are limited. It's not fair to Mike. He put himself on the line here, and he didn't have to. I'm afraid we need Central's help more than ever."

Contrary to his dictate of not revealing conversations with others, Harry let Nealy know he'd already discussed the situation with Blake and had promised to send over a special Central agent from Vermont. Though Nealy inquired who he was, Harry, as he did with Blake, would not say.

"He's wiry, tough, tenacious, and familiar with Saratoga," is all Harry would tell him. Harry decided his man would operate totally incognito, reporting only to Harry with any information relating to Flint. Finding Flint would be his main concentration. Harry said he'd be on a single mission, and that was to find Flint. The broader investigation of who was behind the Saratoga murder attempts on Molly O'Neill and Tom Bochard would not be addressed.

"My guy is a seasoned tracker," said Harry. "If Flint left a trail, he'll find it. Once Mike is found, his job is done. Agreed?"

Nealy observed a change in Harry's attitude with this last statement. He had the sneaking suspicion that Harry was telling him, ever so subtlety, that Central's generosity was reaching its limit as far as Saratoga's problems were concerned. There was also a detectable irritation in Harry's tone, perhaps a feeling that Flint's services had, in many respects, been over-extended in Saratoga.

Nealy elected to say no more, except to thank him for soliciting the aid of his nameless Vermont agent. Surprisingly to Nealy, Harry never once mentioned Sandy in their talk. A point Nealy found odd. Perhaps, Nealy reasoned, Harry already discussed Sandy's situation with Blake.

At the end of the conversation, Nealy poured himself a beer and drank it in silence. He thought of calling Blake and comparing notes on Harry's position, but decided not to.

15. SANDY BLAIR

Sandy Blair was growing more restless with each passing day at the Duffys. Oh, Martha and Frank did their very best to make her feel at ease, and Duffy himself kept her thoroughly informed on the investigation, as difficult as it was. As Duffy tried to explain to Sandy, "We have more investigative personnel roaming around Saratoga than we have actual residents.

"There's the state police, federal agencies, Nealy's men and, last I counted, a host of county enforcement officers. How the Feds got involved, I'll never know. I'd say Nealy has sole jurisdiction, but they say otherwise. That's the problem these days. Too many layers of law enforcement; one climbing over the other. Except for Nealy's men, not a one is looking for Mike. The very nature of Flint's assignment has proved a hindrance in locating his whereabouts."

Sandy bowed her head in her hands and pressed her fingers to her forehead. Martha offered her coffee, but she waved her away. She could feel the rage creeping over her body, so much so that she developed a wicked neck pain. She'd listened to the same words for a week now, trying to be calm and composed, but it was straining every nerve in her body.

She wanted out. She wanted to be with Flint. Anyplace far away from Saratoga would do. The beach at Waikiki, a yacht in the West Indies, looking into his deep-set blue eyes and sipping sherry in Harry's Paris Bar. She wanted to hold him tight and tell him how much she loved him. How wonderful the world was when he was with her. How terrible it was when he wasn't. To smell that cologne that drove her crazy after he had showered. Windsurfing off Palos Verdes Cove. Her mind raced on.

Her hands trembled and she pulled on her hair, now wet from sweat. The Duffys could do little more than exchange sympathetic glances across the room. It was as if, Duffy thought, she was exorcising a demon. After a time, Sandy's ashen face regained some color and she sat up straight and looked at them with wide open, yet swollen eyes. Duffy had seen this stare on many bewildered faces over his sixty-year career as a journalist. The look that told you life wasn't worth living. All the hurt, frustration and anger was coming forth. He'd seen it before, but because of his fondness for Flint and

Sandy, had never felt its deepness so profoundly. The stark reality of it scared him, as it did Martha. Sandy's mood created a foreboding sense of loss in them all. The unspoken, help-less atmosphere in the room was stifling. More solemn than any Requiem Mass Duffy had ever attended. He knew if he didn't do something to break Sandy's dark mood, they'd all succumb to its ugly spell.

"Damned if I don't need another stiff drink," Duffy shouted, bursting from his chair and head-ing for the kitchen. "I think we all need a stiff one, don't you agree?"

"Speak for yourself," said Martha.

"No, he's right," Sandy startled them by agreeing. "That's what Mike would do. He'd have himself a double scotch. So, why not? You can pour me a tall glass of scotch on the rocks, Duffy."

"Might just as well make that two," said Martha.

"No," said Duffy. "I'll make that three double scotches. Lord knows we need it."

Within an hour's time they had managed three rounds of double scotches, though Martha cheated by sneaking off to the kitchen once or twice to water down her drinks. Still, considering what little drinking she had done in recent years, she held her own. Duffy and

Sandy were feeling their drinks, with Sandy getting giddy and Duffy slurring his words – always a signal to Martha that he'd had a few too many.

Billy Farrell was the real drinker in the crowd. You never knew when he was tipsy. As Duffy used to say about Farrell's drinking prowess, "There wasn't a bar in Saratoga County that Farrell couldn't drink dry."

Duffy knew in his heart that none of this nonsense was doing Flint much good, but it certainly loosened up Sandy, if only temporarily.

"You know something, Duffy?" she said. "You pour a real fine drink."

"I've had lots of experience," he assured her.

"If he hadn't gone into the newspaper business, he'd have made a great bartender," said Martha. A point Sandy seconded by raising her glass, as they all laughed, though Duffy wasn't sure if Sandy was laughing or crying. He watched her closely. She suddenly put her drink down and stared morbidly at the door. Her eyes glazed over and she fell back into the soft living room sofa, as if exhausted. In a minute she was sound asleep.

"There," exclaimed Duffy to Martha. " She'll get a good night's rest after all."

Martha, half asleep herself, with her head resting in the crook of her right arm, nodded her head and sighed. "The poor girl."

"You know something," Duffy said, "maybe it's the drink in me, or maybe I'm just damn tired. But I had a premonition a moment ago that Flint will come out of this fine." Then he hesitated, as if puzzled by his thoughts, adding, "Wouldn't it be great if I was right?"

Martha slowly lifted herself to a standing position. "I say we poor old dogs had better go to bed. What do you think, Duffy?"

He looked at Martha, then down at Sandy. "I hate to disturb her peace."

"Then don't," Martha commanded. "She'll be fine right there."

Well past midnight, while the Duffys were enjoying a deep slumber, Sandy awoke and went to the kitchen and made some coffee. She definitely had a royal scotch hangover, but otherwise felt quite stimulated.

"My nerves working overtime," she told herself. She drank her coffee at the kitchen table while listening to the Duffys snoring upstairs. She loved the Duffys dearly. Two more gracious people never existed as far as she was concerned. No doubt Sandy could stay here indefinitely, or at least till Flint's ordeal was over one way or the other. However, sitting back and taking a passive role was not what she had in mind. No, she'd already convinced herself that it was time to act. To go out and find Flint on her own, if necessary. How and where to start, she didn't know. Would she work through Nealy and the others, or try and establish a new route of investigation? If so, who would help her? Who could help her? She pondered her own questions over three cups of coffee until she was so wide awake, her hands began to shake. Then it dawned on her who could help. The only person probably willing to come and help: Monica.

Together they could muster the will to search for Flint, no matter how difficult or how long it took them. If not her and Monica, then who else? With all due respect to Chief Nealy, Sandy knew that the power to rescue Flint was in herself.

16. E.N.

Bobby Maxwell, the Saratoga Racquet Club court attendant who was on duty the day Flint disappeared, scarcely heard the sliding glass door of the courts' inner locker room open, but he felt the sudden, cold draft of air that sent a shiver down his spine. Maxwell, startled by the intrusion, spun around to face a short, bearded man dressed in hiking boots, jeans, a jean jacket and, as Maxwell further observed, smoking a mahogany-colored pipe that appeared too big for the stranger's mouth. Certainly not your average tennis buff, Maxwell reckoned.

"Can I help you, sir?" Maxwell said.

"Yes, you can," the man replied.

"Here to play tennis?"

The stranger smiled. "Afraid not."

"Friends playing today?"

"Nope."

Maxwell, still shook up from his earlier experiences at the club, eyed the man with suspicion and some caution. It was a slow, quiet,

Tuesday morning and only four club members were courtside. Maxwell remembered it was like that the day the man and woman came by. Now, in his mind's eye, he could plainly picture them entering the club, the blonde girl so strikingly beautiful and lively, while her male companion appeared reserved and said very little. Coincidentally, they had come through the same sliding door and announced themselves. The similarity of the entrance, with its abruptness, put Maxwell's nerves on edge.

Since the killings and the subsequent intensive police investigation, Maxwell dreaded opening the club by himself in the morning, or being the last to leave in the evening. He avoided the very place in the parking lot where the two were found dead. If he had had another job to go to, he'd have vacated the club long ago. His attendant job was only tolerated out of pure necessity. The incident also had taken a toll on the club's membership and general attendance. It had become hauntingly eerie around the place.

"You must be Maxwell?" the man said, resting one elbow on the reception counter and shifting his pipe from one side of the mouth to the other as he spoke.

"Yes, that's me."

The stranger jangled his car keys on the

counter in an annoying fashion. "Been on this job long?" he asked.

"No, not long"

"How long?"

"About three months. No, make that four months. Yes, exactly four months come this Thursday. Time flies."

"You bet it does," The man agreed. "That's the problem with time. It can work for you, or against you, depending."

Maxwell didn't understand. "Depending on what?"

"For instance, your job. If you're busy, time goes fast. Slow times, like these, and it seems like an eternity, right?"

"Guess so," said Maxwell.

The man moved closer. "The incident that took place here a few days ago, was that a busy or slow time for you?"

Maxwell fidgeted with his thin-rimmed, metal glasses, and tried to remember. The man's eyes were frozen on Maxwell, and that in itself made him nervous. "Well, I guess it was slow, now that I come to think of it. Though I don't understand what you're getting at."

The stranger cracked his knuckles and stepped back a foot or so, as if observing the room around him. "My reason for asking is simple. A man came in here just before the incident took place. Is that correct?"

"Could have," said Maxwell.

"Do you recall his name or what he looked like?"

Maxwell's brow furled into a concentrated series of wrinkles. "I try not to think of that day. It was a very bad scene. I told the cops everything I could remember. One man, two men, maybe three. It's hard to recall now. I only really remember the blonde lady. The cops said she came with a man, but I didn't remember. Except she was found dead with a man, so I suppose they were correct. There was so much confusion that day, I just can't piece it all together. If that's the man you're talking about, then the cops have all the facts."

"Another man. I'm talking about a third man. He probably came in on his own. You don't recall that?"

Maxwell's face drew tight again. "No, I don't recall. That's all I can tell you."

"I believe you," the stranger said, removing the pipe from his lips. "How much do you recall of the blonde and her friend?" he paused.

"Oh, that's right, you weren't certain she was with anyone. Is that true?"

"Not exactly. She could have come with a guy, but with all the uproar, I can't place them as being together. No more so than I can recall another guy coming in here. You have to realize, I sign people in who play tennis, but I also have other duties in between, and it's difficult keeping track of everyone coming and going. Mostly club members come here, but guests are allowed."

The stranger swaggered across the room and peered out at the tennis courts, now empty. Maxwell watched and observed his moves, curious to who he was and why he was asking so many questions. He noticed the stranger's casual style of dress.

Maxwell, never good at guessing one's age, figured the man was in his mid-fifties, only because his hair, thick and dark in the middle, was silver gray from his sideburns through his beard. Whoever he was, Maxwell felt his strong presence and inwardly feared him. The man's every gesture told Maxwell he was an authority figure, regardless of his attire.

Maxwell watched as the man shifted from one foot to the other, as if doing a small dance. When he was finished looking over the tennis courts, he turned once more to Maxwell and smiled. "This Bochard, they say he came to meet someone. Do you know that person he was meeting?"

"No," said Maxwell. "I never met him. Can't recall that he ever showed up. I have his name on the call sheet, though. Councilman Bochard called me earlier that morning and said he was to meet a Mr. Tocco. He asked me to tell Mr. Tocco to wait in case Bochard was late. Bochard has a habit of being late. I know this, because I've had to hold a court for him on more than one occasion. Got living hell from some members for delaying their starts as a result. We've got a hard and fast rule here at the club of starting play on time when courts are reserved. Generally we release the court to any waiting players if the reserved party is more than ten minutes late." He glanced up at the wall clock.

"Bochard was often late a half hour or more. I personally never play favorites. If they're late, I give the court away. But Bochard has political clout. Management makes exceptions in his case."

"High on the pecking order, was he?" the man remarked.

"Something like that," said Maxwell.

"About this Tocco fella," the stranger inquired. "Any idea who he might be? Perhaps a resident of Saratoga?"

"I haven't the slightest. As I say, I never met him. Never heard his name until Bochard mentioned it."

The stranger came back to the chest-high counter and leaned both elbows on it, placing his chin in his hands. "Tocco's name ever come up during the investigation?"

"Not that I know of," Maxwell assured him. "I never thought to tell the cops. Actually didn't give it a thought among all that confusion. It was a hectic time. Had all I could do from coming unglued in the process." He looked nervously at the stranger. "I hope you can understand where my mind was during all the ruckus."

"Can well imagine," the stranger nodded. "Yet I'm sure if you dig a bit, you'll remember something. It takes a while, sometimes."

They stared at each other for a time, the stranger, still with his chin in his hands, and Maxwell, leaning uncomfortably against the back wall, every nerve in his body dancing about.

"Well?" asked the stranger once more. "Think of anything worthwhile?"

The muscles in Maxwell's face suddenly relaxed and he half smiled. "Might have something," he said excitedly. He turned and went out through a white door to a rear room, as the stranger watched. When he returned, he was carrying another copy of the club's registration book. "Yeah. As I said, we may have just what you're looking for in here."

The stranger's chin lifted from his hands and his eyes brightened. "What you got there,

Maxwell?"

Maxwell shoved the book beneath the stranger's nose, flipping open the pages. "This is Jim Stedman's log book. You see, I wasn't working the day before..." he looked sheepishly about the room, as if afraid of being heard. "I took the call from Councilman Bochard the day all hell broke loose, but Stedman was on duty when the court was reserved, and that was the day before. Yes, Tuesday. Stedman was working Tuesday. Let's have a look."

"Who are we looking for?"

"Why, Tocco. The guy who called and reserved the court to play with Bochard."

Maxwell's fingers brushed aside each page till he found it. "There, you see," he said, holding the book up for the stranger. "It's right there in old Joe's handwriting. Lamar Tocco. How about that?"

"Right on the money, Maxwell. I knew you'd find something."

"I can go one better," Maxwell assured him. "I can tell you where he called from."

The man pulled at his beard and tilted up on his toes. "No. You can?"

"Sure," said a jubilant Maxwell. "We have caller ID. We list every incoming phone number. The membership doesn't know we have caller ID. Not even sure Mr. Stark, the club's general manager knows. Stedman and I have been using it for over a month now. Isn't high-tech great?"

"I'd say it is," the man said, while in a motion so quick Maxwell hardly noticed it, he took out a pen and scratched the number down on a small note pad.

Maxwell's jubilation quickly left him, as he cautioned the stranger, "Wouldn't want it known we have caller ID here, if you don't mind."

The man popped a fifty dollar bill on the counter. "They'll never hear it from me." He pushed the crisp bill at Maxwell who, upon seeing it, looked momentarily dumbfounded.

"No club policy against accepting tips, is there?"

"Not that I know of," replied Maxwell. "But it is quite generous. Overly so, I'd say."

The stranger drew out some more bills, but held onto to them. "Tell you what, Maxwell. If you can ever recall anything about this other man, Mr. Mike Flint, the whole wad is yours. Is that a deal?"

"Damn. That's a lot of money you're holding," said Maxwell. " How much is it?"

The man put it back in his pocket. "You'll only find out if you can come up with anything on Flint. I mean anything I feel is important. Did you see him talk to Bochard? Did he go

261

out of the building on his own, or was he with the blonde and her friend? Any recollection of the others who came in? Let's call them the bad bunch. You know what I mean? Think hard. Try and draw on that subconscious of yours. If not now, maybe tomorrow. Sleep on it. Go back over the day, step by step. In your mind, re-trace your moves. From the time you arrived at work till the cops came. I know there's a miss-ing piece of memory you're capable of recap-turing if you try. I'll contact you again. I keep my promises. The wad is yours if you can cough up anything."

A car pulled into the lot outside the office. Two couples got out and started walking to-ward the clubhouse. "Well, we've got members coming in," said Maxwell.

The stranger twirled around, took one quick look and headed for the far door. He stopped just short of the door and called back to Max-well. "We have a deal, Maxwell. Remember that."

Maxwell motioned him to stop, shouting. "Do you have a name?"

"Certainly," came the man's reply. "E.N. Easy to remember."

"What's that stand for?"

The stranger lingered in the doorway a mo-ment and whispered. "Eternally Nasty."

Just then the four club members, who Maxwell didn't readily recognize, came in. Maxwell looked at them and then back to E.N., but he was gone. It then dawned on Maxwell that his mysterious E.N. apparently didn't come by car. Otherwise, he would have been parked in the lot. If not by car, then how did he come? Maxwell patted his pants pocket where he had safely deposited the fifty.

At the same time his mind was churning over and over about Flint. Had he talked to a guy named Flint that fateful day? Not being able to recall it irked him to no end. He just couldn't remember. And that big wad of bills just waiting to be had. He then was aware that the club members were waiting to sign in. He went through the motions of entering their names and assigning them courts, but his real concentration was on the wad. He really needed that wad.

Afterward, thinking about his encounter with E.N., it became apparent to Maxwell that the tennis court murders were only the beginning of a tangled, complicated mess that somehow would show its ugly side again. Where did E.N. fit in? Maxwell could only guess. One thing Maxwell knew, he personally didn't want further involvement in it. He'd decided he'd say nothing about meeting E.N. to anyone.

17. MONICA WHITE

The statuesque woman with long, flaming red hair descended from the American Airlines jet at Albany International Airport. On the tarmac, her spiked heels clicked so loudly they could be heard over the engines' dying drone as she quickly made her way to the main terminal. People stopped and heads turned as Monica White, dressed in a purple pants suit and a short, off-the-shoulder tan leather jacket, ignored a stiff April breeze as she strutted inside the terminal to meet Sandy.

There were about sixty people waiting inside to meet the flight and Monica White's appearance had them all buzzing. She walked as she had been trained to walk, with command. Shoulders square, chin forward, eyes hidden behind large-rimmed dark glasses. Her hair was meticulously brushed back, with one falling lock ending just over her right eyebrow. She had tan leather gloves that matched her jacket. Monica was the stuff the real Hollywood leading ladies were made of, with a firm yet graceful presence that radiated like platinum.

Sandy, standing away from the crowd, couldn't help but admire Monica's entrance and was amused at the crowd's reaction as she came forward, arms outstretched, to hug Sandy. There was no denying it was Monica, except for the red hair that had replaced the blonde hair she had the last time Sandy had seen her in L.A.

"Sweetie, you're the best thing I've seen all day," Monica complimented her, while placing a soft kiss on Sandy's cheek.

Sandy drew back a step to look Monica over. "Well, you never change, though I was almost fooled by the new hair color."

Monica let out a hearty laugh. "You know how it is when you're a silver screen maven. We switch hair colors almost as often as we switch scenes." She twirled around and shook her head. "I've decided, red is me. No more blonde."

"I love it," said Sandy. "Wait till Mike sees it.." The very mention of his name sent a chill through both of them. "Oh, Monica," she cried, "How could I have said that?"

"I understand," Monica assured her, putting her finger to her lips. "It just came out. Besides, you're right. Flint will have an opinion on my hair when he sees it. We will find him. He will be with us soon. Trust me."

Once they were in the car, Sandy began to fill her in.

"These past two weeks have been hell," Sandy said. "Blake and his friends wanted me to go to your place at first. Can you imagine that? Deserting Mike at a time like this? I told them flat out, no deal. So they more or less sequestered me with Frank and Martha Duffy. He's the senior editor of the *Saratoga Star*. I believe I've mentioned them to you before when Mike finished his last assignment in Saratoga. Anyway, against Martha's well-intentioned advice, I borrowed Duffy's car to pick you up. Of course they have no idea why I borrowed it. I'm certain Nealy, Blake and the rest would have a fit if they knew I was out of Duffy's place. The Duffys promised they'd say nothing about it. Let's hope now Blake doesn't visit Duffy and find me gone. So far he's stayed away. Blake and Nealy are afraid the same people who got Mike might have targeted me. They felt the Sheraton was not safe. The Duffys seemed like the best choice. But who really knows in a town the size of Saratoga?

"Worst of all, they don't have a clue as to who these people are. Nealy keeps harping on Don Bocca, this mob kingpin down in the Catskill Mountains. He's supposedly angling to get back to Saratoga with casino gambling, which some locals say will happen. Mike told me this Bocca will front his operations with legitimate managers, but that Bocca will eventually skim each casino once they're in place."

"So if not Bocca, who?" Monica interrupted her.

"Any number of operators. At least that's what Mike mentioned several times. Nealy and his bunch are amateurs when it comes to things like this. Nice cops, but not very swift when dealing with hard-core criminal types. They don't have the personnel or resources to do an adequate investigation. At best, they lean on the New York State Police to do the real digging."

Monica, tired from her flight, slumped in the passenger seat, though still awake. "You said Mike mentioned several things. What were they?"

"Yes," said Sandy. "Let me see. He was fond of making the observation that the obvious in any investigation was too obvious. And the not so obvious seemed to most people to be the obvious. Don't know if I can properly interpret that statement, but he also said he always looked for the third and fourth equation to solve most crimes. He said criminals are very smart. He has great respect for their talents, bad as they are. Once told me that for every preventive move cops come up with to thwart criminals, the crooks have two solutions. Mike said crooks spend their entire lives figuring out how to outsmart the law. It's the only way some of them can survive.

"The day before he left for a luncheon meeting, Mike was working on several possible scenarios to Saratoga's most recent problems. He was sure there was that third or fourth equation lurking out there. In a sense, he ruled Don Bocca out of it. Mike was certain Bocca tried to have local councilwoman Molly O'Neill killed. After all, his henchman Palermo later showed up dead in Saratoga. But, Mike also surmised that another interested party was interceding on O'Neill's behalf, for reasons he hadn't determined as yet. Three days before he disappeared, Mike woke in the middle of the night, saying that he'd envisioned another group's involvement. He had a series of dreams about this. As you probably know, Monica, Mike's uncanny sensory perceptions can be scary at times." Sandy consciously kept his name in the present tense.

Monica shook her head up and down. "I once called him an Irish Witch Doctor when he went off on one of those speculative tantrums. We'd be sitting poolside, or at a restaurant with friends and suddenly, Mike would think of some angle to a case he was on, and the rest of the day would be a wash. I can well sympathize where you're coming from."

Sandy had been driving on cruise control, but dropped her foot on the gas pedal to pass a slowing truck. The jerking action brought Monica erect in her seat.

"He had the feeling ever since we arrived that the gambling issue in Saratoga stirred so many divergent interests that sifting it all out was not going to be easy," Sandy said. "Told me he wouldn't be surprised if some of the old gambling gentry were involved."

"What did he mean by old gentry?"

Sandy maneuvered past another car and Monica could feel the force on her shoulders and lower back. She had not the slightest idea how far they were from Saratoga, but hoped they'd arrive in one piece. Out of friendship, however, she didn't comment on Sandy's driving. They crossed over the Mohawk River into Saratoga County. Monica, not familiar with the area, figured it was the Hudson River she'd heard so much about.

"Oh, Mike's alluding to old gentry," Sandy said, answering Monica's previous question. "He feels there's still some of the old gambling guard that wants to get back into the action. If not the original operators they tossed out in the

'50s, perhaps their heirs. Nealy told us some of these former casino owners stashed millions away before Gov. Dewey busted it open. Their mob partners left with millions, too. I know Mike was checking out real estate holdings in Saratoga. He and Nealy had some local real estate appraiser working up a computer analysis on all key properties that might be ideal for future casino sites. Mike said once he knew who owned the prime locations, it'd be easy to pinpoint the players."

Monica shifted sideways and tossed her falling hair to one side. "I remember when they did that in Vegas years ago. Of course the mob put the pressure on all the Nevada farmers in those days. They'd bring in some dumbo local from Reno or Texas and put his name on the deeds so the Feds couldn't track 'em. No matter, it all came down to money. The big bucks ate up the choice real estate. Hell, it happened right in tinsel town. It's still going on. Super bucks buying up everyone in sight. If I had made the right investments back then, I wouldn't have to bust my hump today." Monica thought about it, adding, "Timing is everything, isn't it?"

"That's something Flint would say," said Sandy.

"I probably picked it up from him," Monica

confessed. "By the way, where are we?"

"Five minutes from Saratoga," said Sandy. "I've got you a room at a small bed and breakfast on the east side of town. Would have put you up at the Gideon, or some other fancy spot, but didn't what to take the chance you'd be recognized."

"In Saratoga?" Monica quipped.

"They do have cinemas," Sandy laughed.

"Anything you say," Monica said. "As for being recognized, I'm a master at disguise. I gave Flint lessons on disguise. Just ask him."

Sandy looked over at her. "My God, I wish I could. I wish we both could."

"I'm sorry, Sandy. It just slipped out."

"I know. It's just that I keep doing it. I talk as if he will be waiting for us. I can't imagine it any other way. The thought of not seeing him again is tearing me apart."

Monica reached over and touched Sandy's arm. "I didn't come all the way from L.A. for nothing. We're going to find Flint. I'm personally going to rip Saratoga to pieces, brick by brick, 'til I do. And you're going to be with me every step of the way. And if Harry, Nealy and the rest get in our way, we'll deal with them pronto. If it's that Don Bocca guy who's got Flint, then he'd better watch out, too. This is no time for sentimentality. I'm glad you called me, Sandy. I'd have been terribly disappointed if you hadn't. I'll always have a soft spot in my heart for Flint. You know that. He's not a guy one forgets in a hurry, if ever. But I'm here for both of you. We're a team on this one. Get me to the B&B so I can get a good night's sleep and tomorrow, bright and early, we'll begin. Bring along all of Flint's notes you have. Names, dates, addresses – you know how he scribbled down all sorts of things. I used to watch him do it. Seemed mostly like a lot of garble at times, but pieced together, it always made lots of sense. He's a damn thorough investigator. I know you agree."

Sandy let out of sigh of relief as she slowed the car to make a right turn off I-87 at exit 14, and headed west toward Saratoga past the entrance to Yaddo Park. An eighth of a mile further, they both were treated to the spectacular sight of the April afternoon sun reflecting off the gray-slate roof of the famous racecourse.

"Don't tell me," Monica said. "That's Flint's favorite track?"

18. HALFMOON

When Frank Duffy arrived at *The Saratoga Star* to start his day's work, receptionist Mary Park gave him the high-sign as he came through the office door, pointing to a small, mustached man in a wide-brimmed tan hat, sitting in the visitor's foyer.

Duffy ducked backward, then peered around the corner to see who Park was pointing to. He didn't recognize the man. Park leaned across her desk and whispered,

"Says he has to see you. I wasn't sure you'd be receptive to visitors this early."

"Well," Duffy told her, "unless I climb in through a window, I don't see how I can avoid meeting him. Did he tell you his name?"

"Yes. Says he's Professor Halfmoon from Union College in Schenectady. "I've never heard of him."

"Look," said Duffy, "I'll go down to the press room. You call Professor Halfmoon over and occupy him for a few minutes. I'll sneak up to my office from the other side. I want time to make one phone call. I'll buzz you when I'm done. If he hasn't lost his patience by then and left, please escort him to my office. I think I know why he's here. I'm just not sure I want to hear what he has to say. If that sounds redundant, it is. You're a peach for helping me out."

Duffy left Mary Park with a worried, puzzled frown on her face. She glanced suspiciously at Professor Halfmoon, who sat poker-faced staring straight ahead, while she waited apprehensively for Duffy's buzz.

Duffy made his way back to his office by a side door unobserved by Professor Halfmoon. Halfmoon's arms were folded across his chest, his head erect and his eyes staring straight ahead. To Park's amazement, he'd been sitting in that rigid pose for a good half hour. If patience is a virtue, this guy has it, Park was thinking.

The first thing Duffy did was place a phone call to Chief Nealy's house. Knowing Nealy's daily routine, it was unlikely he'd be out of bed yet. But Duffy wanted to check with him before talking to Halfmoon. Somewhere, either in a passing conversation with Nealy, or perhaps even at one of the group meetings, Duffy remembered Halfmoon's name mentioned. Duffy just couldn't place the reason or the connection. He figured Nealy might know.

As expected, he roused a sleepy Nealy.
"Sorry to disturb you Tom," Duffy apologized.
"I need to know if you have had contact with
Professor Halfmoon from Union College?"

"Not directly, that I can recall," Nealy mut-
tered.

"But you're familiar with him?"

"The name sounds vaguely familiar, that's
all I can tell you."

"Why did I think you knew him?"

"Can't say."

"That's baffling," Duffy exclaimed. "I heard
him mentioned some place. I thought he had
talked to you, isn't that funny?"

"I'll check it out when I get to headquarters. I may have some details on him there. If I
did have any contact with him, I'm sure it's sitting there on top of my desk with the hundred
or so other notes I haven't been able to file
properly. Then again, maybe officer Galea can
help me. I'll have to call you, Duffy. Afraid you
got me too early. You caught me in the middle
of a good dream, though at the moment I can't
remember what it was all about. Age does that
to us."

"Well, I suppose I'll meet with him and see
what it's all about."

"Yes. Do that and fill me in later."

"One other item, Tom. Have you and Blake discussed Sandy's situation further? I mean, will she be staying on here or going to California? Mind you, she's no bother to me and Martha. In fact, she's a delight to be around, considering the seriousness of everything."

"Blake still thinks she's safer in California, but he realizes she's not about to go, no matter how much we insist. Just keep a good eye on her and don't let her go wandering about Saratoga. In my opinion, she's only safe as long as she's inside your home. She'll be getting itchy soon. Try and convince her it's all for her own good."

Duffy looked at the car keys he'd just dropped on his desk, and cringed when he thought of Sandy borrowing his car the day before. He dared not tell Nealy. Then the unsettling thought occurred to him that if Don Bocca's people were to make a move on Sandy at his home, how on earth would Sandy and his aging Martha ever defend themselves? The scope of his responsibility finally sunk in. Had he bitten off too much by accepting Sandy into his home? Had he really given the gravity of it any real consideration when he said yes to Nealy and Blake? Had any of them weighed just how dangerous and precarious Sandy's presence on Circular Street was? How would he confront her if she asked to borrow the car again? So many ifs, it disturbed him. Yet, he also thought of Mike Flint, perhaps fighting for his life somewhere, if, in fact, Flint still had a life to fight for. Yes, Duffy told himself, he'd done the right thing. Admittedly the risks were great, the outcome uncertain. His experiences, both in service and in newspaper work, taught him that lesson long ago. You do what you have to do, no matter how unpleasant.

Mary Park heard Duffy's buzz and looked out once again at the stoic, statue-like Professor Halfmoon in the foyer, his eyes fixed on the far wall. How strange, she noticed, he doesn't ever blink. She went to him. "Mr. Duffy will see you now."

He stood immediately up, as if stretching. The first time since he arrived, his eyes blinked, as he politely responded, "Fine. Thank you."

"Second door to the left," she directed him, and watched as he adjusted his hat, straightened his tie, and walked into Duffy's office.

Duffy was typing away on his desktop terminal when Professor Halfmoon entered. He'd come in so silently, Duffy wasn't aware he was there till he looked up. Duffy hadn't heard his office door open or close. Now this was an original, old, heavy wooden and glass door that normally made considerable noise when used. Either my hearing is going or someone's fixed the door, Duffy thought. He was still thinking about it while he reached to shake Halfmoon's hand.

"Welcome, professor. Forgive the delay."

Halfmoon was still standing, so Duffy offered him a seat.

"I tried to contact you a while back," said Halfmoon, removing his hat, which left a distinctive mark across his forehead. "I'll be direct in what I have to say. It concerns the killings in Saratoga. I may be able to help you solve them."

Duffy's blood pressure went up another notch, as he fought to compose his reaction, and tried to convey the calm, pragmatic demeanor of a senior editor. In two weeks of drawing blanks on the investigation, here was a man saying he may be able to solve the mystery. Duffy observed Halfmoon's smooth, olive-colored round face, particularly taking note of his jet-black hair, braided in the back, a point Duffy hadn't noticed when the professor was wearing his fedora.

"You're a native American?" said Duffy.

"That's right. My parents were full-blooded Onondaga. Or, if you like, I'm Iroquois."

Duffy sat back in his swivel chair, and rubbed his hands together. "You're also a resident professor at Union? Anthropology?"

"I'm department head. I've taught at Union for twenty years. I'm originally from Grand River, near Branford, Ontario. My former home is known as the Six Nations."

"How's that?" Duffy asked.

"Most of the tribes in the Iroquois confederacy live at Six Nations. It's a long story. Briefly, they went to Six Nations after the American Revolution. The Iroquois confederacy began in 1450. That's a long time ago." Halfmoon, as if visualizing some far distant ancestral place, lowered his eyes to the floor and paused momentarily.

"We once lived all over New York State. Our lands were taken away from us, including Saratoga. My tribe ceded most of its land to New York in 1788 through the Treaty of Fort Schuyler. There were a series of subsequent treaties, too. Senecas negotiated a treaty in 1797, so their four communities could live on protected reservations at Buffalo Creek, Cattaraugus, Allegheny and Tonawanda. Then, more land was sold and this was all skewed until a compromise treaty of 1842 returned some of the land. I could spend a year going over the good and bad parts of all these treaties. Let's just say, it was not a happy time for Iroquois."

Again his face drew tight and he lowered

his eyes, adding, "It's been a tragic story of dislocation. One also of continuing fraudulent practice on the Iroquois people. More recently there have been a few rays of light shining on the Iroquois. My brothers, the Oneidas, are doing quite well with their Turning Stone casino near Utica. But who controls the Six Nations leadership now, is anybody's guess. My Onondagas are the only tribe officially still operating as a functioning local unit, or government, if you will. I don't want to bore you with a history lesson, however, I'm driving toward my main point, your current problems in Saratoga."

"Don't tell me the confederacy is involved here," Duffy said.

"No," Halfmoon assured him, "not the confederacy, but I wouldn't rule out some Iroquois factions."

Duffy moved from his desk and came around to face the professor. "You'll have to be more clear than that, sir," he demanded. "Who are these factions?"

"The same ones that have fought, argued and have been trodden on for the past three hundred years; the tribes of the Six Nations. In case you're not familiar with each of them, and most people aren't, let me name what I often describe to students as the real lost generation." Halfmoon lifted his eyes to meet Duffy's. "And excuse me if my voice quivers, I find it painful to talk about this historic tragedy."

"I understand," Duffy said. "Name the tribes for me."

"Mohawks. The Oneidas, Onondagas, Cayugas, Senecas and, some two hundred years later, the Tuscaroras."

"I'd forgotten," Duffy confessed. "I knew all those names when I was in grade school. Dare say, few teachers today are interested in the confederacy's history. Same goes for newspapers, we're too busy covering national scandals."

"I'm fortunate to have caught a sympathetic ear," Halfmoon said.

Duffy sat back down. "When humanity is involved, I always listen. Not that I have the power to right things, because I've found in most cases, I don't. As an educator, you can appreciate that, I'm sure."

"I find there is more intellect about than wisdom; more apathy than concern. We live in a very indifferent society. Perhaps it was like that when the Iroquois confederacy was formed. The age-old quest for understanding is not easily obtained."

Duffy looked at his desk clock. They'd been talking for over twenty minutes and Duffy had some copy to edit and three phone calls to return. Besides, he hadn't even checked UPI and

AP for national wire stories yet. He'd be facing deadline on some issues soon. So rather than let Professor Halfmoon go, he phoned out to the editorial room and designated the work to his capable assistant, Christina Peterson. Duffy was well aware that in the board room of a large newspaper and television conglomerate, plans were already in the making to acquire the aging *Saratoga Star*, a highly confidential piece of information he wasn't at liberty to discuss with his present staff. Another one of those bothersome cloak and dagger decisions that Duffy surmised would mean an ultimate downsizing at a paper that was already understaffed.

Consolidation was becoming more important than good journalism. Forget that *The Star* was built on local reporting. Why worry? You can always produce pages with filler copy, even if it's not what local readers want. Who are they to say, anyway? Big daddy knows best.

Christina, dressed in a pale blue pants suit, her dark hair neatly combed back, appeared outside his glass office door and waved her appreciation. Duffy smiled back, hoping in his heart, that she'd be able to avoid the unemployment ax that was certain to fall once *The Star*'s acquisition was cemented. He snapped back to the moment.

"Now where were we?" Duffy addressed

Halfmoon again, resuming the conversation.

"I was about to tell you my theory on the recent killings. I have no direct proof, nor do I pretend to be an amateur sleuth. Nevertheless, based on what I do know of the situation, I'd dare say some Native Americans are involved."

"Iroquois?" Duffy asked excitedly.

"Perhaps. I've not been able to identify them. You must realize, as in the old days, there are different factions among the tribes. We have some members still very much interested in making progress peacefully. Others have never given up their bent of military prowess. The union we've all wished for since the time of Hiawatha is seriously splintered to this day. Two Iroquois traditions exist that separate the two sides. Tobacco is dropped on council fires to symbolize peace. Conversely, the warmongers drop white lake shells on the ground. The ones I speak of prefer white lake shells. I hear of a renegade band in a makeshift camp not far from the Auriesville Shrine near Amsterdam. They have constructed long houses they cover with plastic wraps and heat them with wood stoves instead of the traditional hearths. I hear of all-night council fires burning and talk of revenge for past wrongs."

"Auriesville?" Duffy questioned. "Where could there possibly be land enough in that area for such a layout?"

Halfmoon drew his hands over his head and stretched them out, bringing them to his side in one sweeping motion. "Down river. There's a snaking turn in the Mohawk above Auriesville, beyond sight of the shrine, where the land to the east dips behind two rolling hills. It's hidden from the Thruway that parallels the river, and also from a small road that runs on the east side. It's thickly wooded and difficult to approach. You can't get there by conventional vehicle. I expect they use ATVs. There's a series of narrow, shallow streams in that area that they may navigate by canoe. Still, it's hellish, rough country. The hills are so tightly bunched together, helicopters would have difficulty maneuvering among them. If it comes to a showdown and the renegades have to be flushed out, it would take a full-fledged ground assault."

"But why would they want to be near the very place that defies war and mayhem of any kind? It makes no sense they'd want to camp anywhere near the sacred grounds of the North American martyrs," asked Duffy.

"Well, that's depends on whose sacred grounds you delineate, Iroquois or the Catholic Church's. To some Iroquois, Auriesville is their ancestral sacred grounds. Same goes for

Saratoga. The power play revolving about Saratoga, put in modern day terms, is about gambling, or no gambling. Am I correct?"

"Suppose so," Duffy admitted.

"That's my point," insisted Halfmoon. "Power, political and financial. Greed, position, all the assorted conniving that goes with it. Pure avarice, reminiscent of the thirties when Saratoga's casinos were humming. I'm afraid what we're facing here is a spirited Iroquois attempt by one faction to sabotage the return of gambling on what they deem as hallowed ancestral land, with the renegade faction supporting the pro-gambling element. If so, it's a very complex tribal struggle that won't go away soon."

Duffy listened in disbelief to Halfmoon's hypothesis. "If the renegades are for gambling, who's the other faction?" he asked.

"I'm not sure. Perhaps some of my people, but that's only a wild guess. If I was to base my theory strictly on history, I'd say it's Mohawks. Where they're from and to what band they belong, I don't know. If they are Mohawks, they're probably from the group that is more akin to those early members of the confederacy that revered Iroquois traditions. In short, they worship Saratoga and resent gambling and its connected vices, though they have managed to tolerate thoroughbred racing. Beyond racing, any additional abuse of their sacred place, is not accepted."

"I appreciate this information," said Duffy, shifting nervously in his chair. "I hadn't contemplated this angle, but you may have pinpointed an area we've obviously overlooked. If it's true, how can we unravel and defuse the situation before more innocent people get killed?"

Halfmoon, tired of sitting, was up and moving slowly about the office. He twirled his hat between two fingers and fanned himself with it. Duffy, noticing it was getting a bit stuffy in the office, leaned back and opened a window. A fresh scent of warm spring air filled the room. Halfmoon drew in a deep, long breath.

"In answer to your question, I must reply in two parts. First of all, and most importantly, the desire here is for peace. I mean peace between the two waring factions. It's no different than it was three hundred years ago. The confederacy was born of peaceful principle. Reason must take precedent over mayhem. How do I suppose you go about this? That's the second part of my answer. You make contact with both factions, either directly, or through some intermediary." Halfmoon smiled. "Perhaps myself. Am I brave to volunteer? No.

288

Actually, I'm a coward. I suggest it only because I'm Iroquois. My blood ties will give me an advantage you don't have. What do you think, Mr. Duffy?"

Duffy was listening, but his eyes were drawn to a faded, historical map on the wall, ironically depicting early explorers to New York state greeting two Mohawk tribesmen on the bank of an unknown stream. The images conveyed a warm, friendly greeting. He turned to Halfmoon. "Your offer is very kind, yet the danger, as I view it, far exceeds the risk. Isn't this better left to the professionals?"

"So far, the professionals haven't handled it too well, wouldn't you say?"

Duffy bristled. "It's only been two weeks."

"Two weeks since the last incident," Halfmoon reminded him. "The issue I speak about has been festering for over two hundred years."

"Clarify that," Duffy demanded.

Halfmoon took delight in answering. "Saratoga is a sacred Iroquois landmark!"

Duffy glanced up. "If you bring religion into it, old or new, that'll just muck up already dirty waters."

"It is what it is," Halfmoon said. "It's more than religion, it's tradition, a whole culture trying to reassert itself. Crying out to their forefa-

289

thers from a haunted past."

"I follow your train of thought," Duffy said earnestly. "I question if it's relevant in this day and age. The past wrongs are past wrongs. Trying to reconcile them in the twenty-first century poses a tall order."

"No, on the contrary. It might be the best time to address them," said Halfmoon, trying now to carefully choose his words for Duffy, whose eyes followed the professor around the room with intense interest. "It's never too late to correct past wrongs," Halfmoon persisted.

"What we're talking about here is rights. Rights not only of the natural order, but those rights guaranteed by treaties. Dozens of treaties that have been tossed out or simply not honored. Written on bark or carved into stone, they remain legal documents nevertheless. This is a resurgence of native Americans exercising their legal rights, nothing more. The unfortunate part is these renegade factions going about it in their own way. I have a plan that may or may not work. I want to go to the Six Nations and discuss it with the chiefs. I'll ask for their help to see if they know anything about this group near Auriesville. If necessary, I'll go directly to the renegades and see if I can't broker something. Mr. Duffy, this is no indictment on my part against the Iroquois who are united, or for that matter, the renegade bunch. I have no raw data to support that either faction is involved in Saratoga's problems. I have heard rumbles that many Iroquois, especially the Mohawks, are dead set against casino gambling in Saratoga. Just how far they'd go to prevent its return is questionable.

"As for the renegades, no one knows exactly who drives their agenda. I do know that few of them have steady employment, so some person, or some organization, has to be financing them. If we could determine the money source, it would give us some idea what we're really up against. Now, I've heard also that the mob bosses from downstate have designs on reestablishing their influence in Saratoga gaming. I'll leave it up to the law to figure that one out. I'm only interested in what the early confederacy's constitution was all about, and that was peace.

"Peace is what the Hiawatha Belt, the original one, or Wampum Belt of the Confederation, signified. I've always adhered to its principles. Most Iroquois today still do. I feel I have a moral obligation to be a peacemaker. We, that is the tribes, have been mourning the lost peace we all deserve for too long."

A big truck was moving down Maple Avenue, and as it passed by the open window to

Duffy's office, it let off a loud backfire. Duffy, startled by it, spun around to take a look. The truck, a pale yellow box-shaped vehicle with no identifying lettering on it, hesitated, then moved forward in one quick jerk, turning left up Lake Avenue toward Broadway.

"Damned if it didn't sound like a cannon going off," Duffy announced to Halfmoon as the truck disappeared from view. Duffy slammed the window shut and twirled around to Halfmoon.

In that instant, the color left Duffy's aging, wrinkled face, for slumped against the office door, his torso leaning to one side, sat Halfmoon, the top of his head literally half blown off. Nausea crept over Duffy. Blood was splattered in every direction, with drops of bright red dripping from the ceiling. It gushed up like an oil well from Halfmoon's head, pouring forth till it trickled down his face, neck and soaked into his clothes. Duffy was frozen in terror. The ghastly sight in from of him numbed his body. He was paralyzed in his chair, while outside his office door he could see reporters and editors moving about, quite unaware of the tragedy. Then Duffy heard a thud that made him jump up. Halfmoon had fallen over on his side and now lay full-length on the floor. Wrapped about Halfmoon's neck was his neatly tied braid, the ends soaking up some fresh blood that ran out from beneath his contorted arms. Duffy dropped back into his chair. It took him what he deemed were several minutes, but he managed to dial the front desk.

The woman who answered sounded as if she'd just come off the tail end of a good joke, for she was half answering and half laughing.

"Who is this?" said Duffy, weak-voiced.

"Millie. I'm filling in for Betty."

"Millie," Duffy said, in whispered desperation, "call 911."

"Anything wrong?" Millie asked.

"Call 911," Duffy gasped before he passed out at his desk.

19. THE GANG'S ALL HERE

The first things Duffy saw when he awoke were three smiling female faces. Martha, Sandy, and a nurse he couldn't identify, stood over his hospital bed. Martha held one hand tightly. Behind Martha, Duffy made out the brooding, worried face of Chief Nealy, and behind Nealy, Billy Farrell. To Farrell's right stood Doctor Blake. Duffy wasn't sure if it was a dream or he was actually seeing all of them. The nightmarish happening in his office suddenly flashed across his memory, and he closed his eyes. Opening them again, he looked up and forced a smile.

"My, what a reunion," Duffy said.

"The gang's all here," Martha assured him.

Farrell, coming forth, grasped Duffy's free hand. "You're still a tough old bull, Duff," Farrell exclaimed.

Sandy leaned over and kissed his forehead. "And it was me you were worried about."

Tom Nealy had his say. "I have to hand it to you, Duffy. You never live a dull day, do you?"

Dr. Blake appeared more somber, touching Duffy lightly on the shoulder, saying, "That retirement you've talked about - perhaps it's time you really thought about it."

"I'll second that," Martha intoned.

Duffy's thoughts leaped back to Halfmoon. "The professor, is he dead?"

The room went silent. Nealy faked a cough and Martha squeezed Duffy's hand.

Blake finally answered him. "Yes, he's quite dead. He died instantly. Thank God you weren't harmed."

"The truck. The truck..." Duffy said.

"What truck?" Blake asked.

"I remember. It was hot in my office. I opened a window, the one facing Maple Avenue. We were talking, the professor and I. There was a loud bang. I thought a passing truck had backfired. I looked out and saw this dirty yellow truck. Then it was gone. I believe someone in that truck killed Halfmoon."

Nealy leaned over Duffy. "So that's it. We couldn't figure out how it happened. Your office was a bloody mess and the professor lying there made no sense. Sergeant Galea said the lab boys were going nuts wondering what happened. At first they thought it was a letter bomb. What other explanation was there?"

Duffy was not physically injured, yet he felt

a weird pressure in his neck, as if he had been hit by something. He told them so.

The young nurse, who introduced herself as Karen, took his pulse and temperature.

"What are you doing?" Duffy said. "Checking for ear wax?"

"No, your temperature."

He grinned at her and the others. "Well, it's a big departure from the way they used to take temperatures. Right Billy?"

"And quicker, too," said Farrell.

The gravity of Halfmoon's killing had escaped no one, though they did their best in Duffy's company to keep the mood light. Only Nealy showed obvious strain, and couldn't even force a smile. He'd had a hectic day, first fending off questions from every city official lucky enough to make contact with him. He used his timeworn trick of referring each questioner to someone else, or telling them he'd be back to them soon, or that he had two phones waiting.

The New York State Police wanted a piece of the action, too. Nealy had to diplomatically tiptoe around this one. He just couldn't brush them off, even though his Saratoga police had jurisdiction. After all, Nealy had relied heavily on the state police in prior investigations and always felt they had treated his department with respect.

What Nealy had not expected, though on second thought he realized he should have, was the onslaught of questions from Duffy's staff. A barrage of questions like he'd never experienced before. Frightened, bewildered young reporters demanded to know how such a thing could take place at *The Star.* Many of them were so damn scared after the killing, they refused to stay in the building. It was a day as disruptive and unsettling as Nealy could remember. So here in Duffy's hospital room, with the editor looking a bit peaked but otherwise unharmed, Nealy just went along with the rest in trying to keep Duffy amused. While the others made small talk with Duffy, Nealy, with his notebook in hand, pulled Blake to the side of the room and gave him a brief report of the incident.

Halfmoon's killing happened around 9 A.M. and by the time the first Emergency Medical Technician arrived at *The Star,* he had been dead for approximately thirty minutes. Upon first entering the office from a side door, they immediately discovered Halfmoon on the floor, his body blocking the main office door, and Duffy, with his head on his desk. The first EMT, Todd Fisher, ran to Halfmoon and checked for life signs. Sam Hazelton, an EMT trainee, attended to Duffy. Fisher motioned to Hazelton that

Halfmoon was dead. Hazelton expected Duffy was dead also, but when he got a pulse, both he and Fisher immediately called the emergency hot line at Saratoga Hospital. The report, as far as Nealy could remember, was that while they were on the phone, Duffy, though still groggy, sat up and said something to the effect of, "Get a doctor."

"Duffy was then rushed over here," said Nealy. "Fisher and Hazelton deserve a medal. That office could have been booby-trapped. We were all baffled. If Duffy hadn't told us about opening that window, I'd be doing handstands trying to pin this down. Duffy's probably correct, Halfmoon was shot." Nealy scratched his head. " But you know something, Blake? We don't have the bullet. My ballistics people went over that office at least five times. Figure it out. If a high-powered rifle was used, capable of taking most of Halfmoon's head off, why didn't the bullet continue right out into the editorial room? Neither the glass door nor windows in Duffy's office were shattered."

"Maybe it wasn't a bullet," Blake theorized.

"Had to be," said Duffy.

"That's your department, Tom. If it was a bullet, it's there someplace."

"I'll have my people scour that office again. They'll be doing the autopsy on Halfmoon in the morning. The pathology report may help us determine what caliber was used. I'd much rather have the bullet so we could trace the weapon. Let's hope we get lucky."

At bedside, Duffy, now more alert, was becoming his old talkative self. Nealy had hoped to debrief Duffy about his talk with Halfmoon, but this was not the time or proper setting. An hour later Duffy was given a thorough examination and told he could go home, with recommended bed rest for at least forty-eight hours. It suited Nealy and Blake, for they wanted him home safe and sound, as they did Sandy. Her presence at the hospital made Nealy jumpy. His gut feeling ever since Flint's disappearance was that Sandy was a prime target. The nagging question in the minds of Nealy and the others was, "Who are the stalkers?"

Once clear of the hospital, Nealy personally drove the Duffys and Sandy home, while Blake followed. As a precaution, Nealy put two men on watch near Duffy's house.

They used their own cars and dressed in plain clothes. Naturally they'd get special pay for their efforts. Where the money would come from was another matter Nealy had to worry about. His budget was squeezed to the quick. "Oh, well, I'll find it someplace," he told himself.

When the Duffys had retired, Sandy called Monica and filled her in on the day's proceedings, much of which Monica was aware of from the local TV news. Halfway into their conversation, as if reading each other's mind, the thought occurred to them that Halfmoon's ugly slaying, for whatever reason, could be Flint's fate too. Sandy, in speaking, almost broke down crying in fear it many have already taken place. To which Monica, definitely the stronger of the two at this point, told Sandy to wash the thought from her mind.

"Remember," Monica said, "we made a pact to bring Flint home. We will keep our promise. Now I want you to get some rest. Call tomorrow and we'll start mapping out our strategy."

"Yes, you're right. I need some sleep. One thing, though. In Duffy's hospital room, I overheard Nealy telling Dr. Blake the sordid details about the EMTs discovering the dead professor from Union College at *The Star*. Did the evening news elaborate on the professor's background?"

"Let me see," Monica said. "Guess he was a big muckety-muck at the college. He'd been there for quite a few years. Oh, and I found this strange; they said he was a full-blooded Iroquois. What relevance that has I don't know. Why in hell was he with Duffy? Did Nealy say anything to Blake on this?"

Sandy, thinking she'd heard a noise in the kitchen, cupped her hand over the receiver and listened. Now she heard nothing.

"Are you OK, Sandy?" Monica asked.

Sandy looked in the direction of the kitchen again, still heard nothing, and resumed her conversation with Monica. "I'm fine. Thought someone was in the kitchen. I guess it's nothing. Where were we?"

"Nealy. I was wondering why he thought the professor was there? Has Duffy said anything?"

"No. Not that I know of," Sandy said. "Nealy told Blake he wanted to debrief Duffy, but that was all. Obviously he didn't want to talk with Duffy with all of us in the room. Now you have me wondering what Halfmoon was doing with Duffy. It's almost too much to take."

"Halfmoon. What's with Halfmoon?"

"The professor," exclaimed Sandy. "His name was Halfmoon. It all makes sense, especially that he was an Iroquois."

"I must have missed the name on TV," Monica said.

"Funny," Sandy informed her. "On the way into the house tonight, Martha said she vaguely remembers a call from professor Halfmoon. She couldn't remember when it was, or what he wanted, other than he wanted to talk to Duffy. She mentioned it in passing to Duffy, but he fluffed her off. Understandable, considering the shock of his experience. He wasn't very talkative once we left the hospital. Perhaps the gravity of it all was sinking in. They're both sleeping now."

"Well," Monica said, her voice lowering, "you're right near the source. I'd tactfully prod Duffy a little and see if he'll tell you. He may open up more in the morning when he's fresh. I'd work Martha into the conversation, she may get him to loosen up. Unless, of course, Nealy's got the muzzle on him until he's debriefed. They're your close friends, honey, so use your own judgment. I'm groping for any clues at this point, no matter how absurd or trivial. We've got to start thinking and acting as Mike would. Taking any tidbit, piece by piece, till we can get our teeth into something. Intuition says this Halfmoon had lots to say to Duffy. Let's find out what we can."

"I'll do my best," Sandy agreed. "I'll call you mid-day. I probably can get Duffy's car again, but I don't want to motor around in broad daylight. I'll try to come by tomorrow night. Thanks for all your support, Monica."

"Forget the thanks," Monica said. "Thank me when it's all over. That'll be some celebration. Just imagine all the champagne."

Sandy sat quietly for a minute in the vestibule after Monica hung up. She was deep in thought about Flint. She wanted to reach out and touch the scrubby whiskers he sometimes avoided shaving, and press against his strong, muscular shoulders. She wasn't sure how much longer she'd be able to stand this separation from him. The uncertainty of not knowing his fate. The wrenching, terrifying possibility he might be dead.

She lifted herself up and slowly started toward the stairs. She felt a migraine coming on and cursed herself for not having any Advil. Sleep would not come easy.

Just then, something dropped on the kitchen floor. Sandy heard it bounce on the hard tile surface. Her heart began to pound. She froze at the stairs and stared in the direction of the kitchen. A pencil-thin streak of light glared from the partially closed door. She gulped, trying not to make a sound. Feet were shuffling back and forth over the tile. Someone coughed.

Her heart was beating so fast she had trouble breathing. "A burglar" she thought. No, "a stalker." They'd found her. What could she do? Make a dash for her bedroom and lock the door? No. That would leave the slumbering Duffys vulnerable to attack. Go out the front door and scream for help? Unlikely she'd find anyone at this hour. Another object hit the floor, and her heart rhythm increased. She knew her options were limited and dicey at best. She looked toward the fireplace and spotted a brass poker. It's my only hope, she reasoned. If I have to go down, I'll go down fighting. She took three long strides and picked up the heavy poker. Flint had personally instructed her in close-combat hand-to-hand assault tactics. She told herself, as Flint had taught her, if he comes at you, grip both hands tightly on the poker, thrust it forward, bayonet style, and go for his gut or breastbone. Once you've stunned the opponent, then concentrate on finishing him off with blows to the vital parts, the groin or head. The first moment of attack was crucial, Flint had always told her. Surprising one's opponent is the secret. With Flint's words clearly ringing in her ears, Sandy went and stood just outside the door. When she was pretty certain the intruder was somewhere mid-kitchen, she forced one shoulder against the door, pushed it open, and charged in screaming at the top of her voice, poker held tight and forward.

"God almighty, what are you doing?" she heard Duffy yell, as he let loose a bowl of strawberries and milk that spilled all over the tile floor.

Sandy's momentum carried her to within one foot of the startled old man. He stood in slippered feet, amazed and half-frightened to death. Two spontaneous upheavals within twelve hours were too much to take.

She pulled back and fell against the wall. "Oh, Duffy, it's you!"

"Who did you think it was, Count Dracula?"

She shrugged her shoulders and shook her head. "I thought you were upstairs sleeping. I had no idea who was out here. When did you come down?"

"I was sleeping, but I woke up and couldn't get back to sleep. I came down the back stairs."

Spontaneously she went over and hugged Duffy. "You nearly gave me heart failure. I thought someone had broken in," she told him.

"Well, now that we're here, let me clean up the mess and then we'll have some coffee," said Duffy. "Or, would you prefer a stiff drink?"

She smiled. "Coffee is just fine."

When the coffee was ready, Duffy dug into Martha's round-tin pan and came up with some chocolate chip cookies. "Here, try one of these," he said, handing one to Sandy.

They sat at the kitchen table and munched on their cookies, with Duffy dunking his into his cup like a school kid. The urge to ask Duffy outright about Halfmoon was overwhelming, but Sandy held back. She didn't want to rush him. Besides, she wasn't sure how he would react. It was well past midnight and both were fully awake.

After a time, it was Duffy who voluntarily began to discuss the day's tragic scene at *The Star*. Almost, Sandy guessed, as if it were a weight on his shoulders that had to be lifted.

The whole story just started pouring out. He told her of Halfmoon waiting to see him. Of his call to Nealy before actually seeing Halfmoon. How, for some strange reason, he felt Professor Halfmoon's visit was connected to the recent killings even before Halfmoon told him of his theory.

He explained Halfmoon's desire to visit the Six Nations and to seek their help. Also of the renegade bunch near Auriesville. Without asking one question, Sandy was getting the full, detailed account, including the moment the pale yellow truck backfired and Duffy, after watching it, turned to face the horror in front of him.

"I pray I never have to be witness to a sight like that again," Duffy lamented. "It was sickening."

Sandy shivered listening to him. "The part about Six Nations," she asked quietly. "Do you think he was serious about the chiefs helping?"

Duffy's eyes narrowed behind his glasses and he stared over at Sandy. "Perhaps. Being an Iroquois himself, I'd say he had hopes they would. What I really thought he was angling at, and probably would have told me if he hadn't been cut down, was, and I can only speculate now, is that the chiefs might have some insight into the renegades' motives."

"What kind of motives?"

"Don't know. Perhaps motives is the wrong word. He probably meant involvement."

"In the killings?" said Sandy.

"Yes, if I understood him right."

Sandy placed her hands palms down on the table. "How many fingers do I have Duffy?"

"The same as me," he quipped. "If I've still got 'em all."

"We both know I have ten, correct?"

"Correct."

"Of the ten, which one would you say is the most important?"

"I'd say the index finger."

"Any particular reason for singling out the index finger?"

"Yes, it's used for more purposes."

Now she locked her fingers together in a fist. "I still have ten fingers, right?"

"If you say so."

"Well, I do. Only I'm using them in a different configuration. They're all attached to the same body and they spread and contract when my mind wills it."

"OK, Sandy," he said, eyeing her with questionable skepticism at this point. "What are you driving at?"

She unclasped her hands, and her slender, white fingers had red blotches from being squeezed so tightly. "The Six Nations!" she said frankly. "Don't you see? They're one body, but they're also all different. I believe that was Halfmoon's message."

Duffy toyed with his empty coffee cup. "You're right. Yes, he said it in so many words. We talked briefly of this division between tribe members on the merits and drawbacks of casino gambling. Halfmoon said Saratoga was sacred ground to many Iroquois and any attempt to bring casinos back to Saratoga might meet with determined resistance. By the same token, the professor felt some council members condoned gambling here."

Sandy looked puzzled. "When you say council, are you talking about the former Iroquois confederacy?"

"It's still a confederacy, though somewhat diminished from its former self, from what Halfmoon said. Like all institutions, he said it changed over the years. Halfmoon said there are two co-existing councils. One's made up of elected members, the other of hereditary chiefs. Many of the rituals are still maintained. He didn't go into all the tribal details. His mission was to help in any way he could in solving our problems in Saratoga. He truly seemed like a man of peace and harmony. Just before he was shot, he told me he wasn't a brave man. He might have believed that, but I'd argue otherwise on his behalf."

Duffy paused to pour more coffee, continuing. "The professor appeared meek on the surface, but underneath I detected a hidden reservoir of strength. I had the feeling all the while we were talking that he really hadn't fully opened up. Too bad it ended so tragically. When I feel up to it, I want to go to Union College and talk to some of his peers. Maybe even some of his students. I'd even like to attend his funeral which, I've been told, takes place in two days. Nealy advised against this. He thinks it's too risky."

Sandy could feel Duffy's sadness. "You know something, Duffy?"

"What's that?"

"That's what Mike would do. He'd go to the funeral. You know why?"

"He'd feel obligated!"

"Yes. He'd feel obligated. Loyalty is one of his strengths. He'd also go to see who else attended. He'd be watching every face that passed by. No one would escape his scrutiny..." Mentioning his name made her choke up.

Duffy took notice, saying, "We'd better turn in now, Sandy. Be assured Nealy will be over tomorrow and I'll have to go through a whole litany of questions all over again. I've had my say and I'm glad you were here to bear it with me. Though I won't mention our little talk to Nealy. It's our secret."

"My lips are sealed, too," she told Duffy, as they both made their way upstairs. From the far bedroom at the end of the upper landing, Sandy could hear Martha's soft, syncopated snoring. Before Sandy retired, Duffy's snoring had blended with Martha's.

Sandy made a mental note to call Monica first thing in the morning. For whatever it was worth, Sandy would ask Monica to go to Halfmoon's funeral. Not that she'd expect Monica to recognize anyone. Rather, as Flint often did during his investigations, Monica could eavesdrop on casual conversations. Surely some of Halfmoon's brethren would attend. To go one better, Sandy would try to get Monica to attend the professor's wake. That way, she could observe names on the bereavement book,

311

another trick Mike had taught her.

Sandy began dreaming a half hour into a deep sleep. On the banks of a dark, winding river, she observed a great Iroquois chief in full headdress. He was dressed in exquisite deer-skin garments and carrying a wide Wampum Belt with a pine tree design woven in its middle. She called to the chief but he didn't respond. Instead he stepped into a canoe and floated away. On the far shore, a young brave came forward holding a scroll in his hands. He was reciting *The Song of Hiawatha,* Henry Wadsworth Longfellow's poem she knew so well from her childhood days. When he'd completed reading the famous lines, he folded the scroll and, in that instant, Sandy, screaming, suddenly woke. Duffy, awakened by her scream, rushed to her room.

"My God, child, what's happened?"

She sat up in bed, wringing wet with per-spiration. "I saw Flint's face."

Duffy took her hands in his. "Where, when?"

"On the bank of the river."

"You've had a bad dream," Duffy said, trying to console her.

She pulled on his arm. "No, it wasn't a dream. It was too real. It was a premonition. Yes, that's what it was, a premonition. Mike's alive. I know this now. He's telepathically trying to reach me. I feel his energy around me at this moment. Can't you feel it, Duffy?"

Duffy glanced about the bedroom, directing his eyes to the ceiling. When he lowered them he beheld Sandy's beleaguered face. Patting her on one shoulder, he leaned over and kissed her forehead.

"Yes, Sandy, I feel his presence, too."

He waited until Sandy went to sleep, then Duffy returned to his room. Duffy crept to the front window and pulled aside the drawn curtain and looked out on a pitch black Circular Street, save for the far corner street light shedding an eerie glow. Parked a few feet from the light were Nealy's trusted watchmen.

"What a terrible way to live," Duffy thought, "having to be guarded in your own house."

20. LAKE LUZERNE

On a rather quiet, uneventful Wednesday morning at his headquarters in New York City, Harry Waite received a coded message from his Green Mountain boy which, in effect, said he'd done some snooping about in a little hamlet about twenty miles north of Saratoga, called Lake Luzerne. E.N.'s message said he was in Luzerne to check out Lamar Tocco. He informed Harry that he got Tocco's name on his visit to the Saratoga Racquet Club two days earlier. E.N.'s message was fairly routine and had, as far as Harry could determine, no sense of urgency.

Nevertheless, E.N. did ask Harry to run a background check on Tocco. E.N. said he'd be holed up at the Roaring Brook Dude Ranch, a few miles further north of Luzerne on Route 9N. If Harry had anything, E.N. said he could be reached on his beeper. E.N.'s message said he'd do nothing more than a preliminary investigation on Tocco, along with some other names he'd picked up in Saratoga, including that of Al

Guido. E.N. signed off with a touch of home-spun humor, telling Harry, "This region is not Vermont, but it will do." This triggered Harry's memory about an old saying he'd once heard: Vermonters are to be appreciated, not under-stood.

Waite wasted no time tapping into his data base. The name Guido stuck out like a sore thumb. Guido, as a mob name, was a fixture in New York. That fact in itself didn't necessarily mean that the Guido E.N. mentioned was con-nected to the New York City crime family. Nevertheless, it was worth checking out. As for Lamar Tocco, it was a name Harry thought he vaguely remembered, but couldn't place. Still, like Guido, it was worth a look. Harry de-cided also to make an inquiry on Lake Luzerne. Not that he expected to find any earth shatter-ing information, for he doubted any serious mob influence would be found there.

Harry's faith in E.N.'s ability to sniff out crooks in the most remote places had never wavered. In Harry's estimation, only Mike Flint topped E.N. for uncovering the unlikely. If E.N. was on to something in Luzerne, especially any-thing that may lead to Flint's whereabouts, it had Harry's full support. Every cop in Harry's unit was feeling depressed over Flint's disap-pearance. Many volunteered to go upstate and look for him. A few suggested confronting Don Bocca himself about Flint.

Harry, more upset than most, avoided any impulsive moves. If Flint was still alive, and Bocca was holding him, any sudden attempt to free him, might spell death. Harry knew the old mob adage, "Dead men tell no tales" and, through his tenure as mob kingpin, Bocca had left a string of dead bodies to back up his words.

So Harry ordered all his unit people not to mess with this investigation on their own. The strategy was to let Bocca come out in the open. Let E.N. piece together what he could in and around Saratoga, while Harry worked on his New York pipeline. Or, as Harry had told others, perhaps Flint is neither captive nor dead, but tracking the killers. He might not surface for days if this were the case. He'd been subject to long investigations before, sometimes gone for two to three weeks without checking in with anyone. Was it that way now? Harry hoped so. Though, with each passing day the prospects of Flint's return appeared gloomier.

While waiting for the data on Guido and Tocco, Harry went out for a cup of coffee. A cool breeze was blowing in off the Hudson River near Harry's Battery Park office. The building that housed his special police unit was chosen for its location. Near enough to everything in

Manhattan, yet comfortably removed from view, which avoided attracting curiosity seekers. The rent was reasonable, parking adequate and, if needed, there was room for expansion. Harry walked a block east of his office to a street corner coffee vender. It was a daily ritual Harry had formed, just to get some time out of the office. A way of shedding the minute-to-minute pressure that came at him from all sides with endless ferocity. He called Central the ultimate pressure cooker. The job of running such a complex operation was made even tougher because of budget restraints. With crime on a steady upward curve, drug dealing becoming so pervasive no one knew how to combat it, and Central being asked to investigate a broader range of crimes, Harry wondered if he'd be able to hack it much longer. He finished his coffee and started back toward Central. Fifty feet from his building, a short, stocky man sprung from a nearby alley and called his name. Harry pretended not to hear the man, though he did glance over to see who was calling.

"Hey, it's Freddy The Street. Don't you recognize me?" the man called out in a squeaky, nasal voice.

It was like hearing a ghost from the past, Harry thought. "Where in hell did you come from?" Harry shouted back, finally stopping.

"Mount McGregor," Freddy told him.

"Mount what?"

"Mount McGregor. The minimum security joint near Saratoga. I just got out, Harry."

Freddy came closer and held out one hand. Harry reluctantly shook it.

"It's my second day back in the Apple," said Freddy. "Been upstate at McGregor the past five years. Much different than here. Now that I am back, I find New York City is creepy. Damn bad place. I rode the Long Island Railroad earlier today, and you know what? Some punk kid tried to push me out of my seat. Imagine, pushing me out of my seat in broad daylight. Can't afford to get arrested for fighting on my second day in the city. So, when we got off the train, I slid in behind the punk and drove my heel into his right calf while he was walking away. He went down crying like a baby. Yeah, Freddy The Street can still handle himself."

"The old dog still has bite," Harry agreed.

"Yeah, something like that."

"Well," said Harry cagily, "I suppose you're looking for a good meal?"

Freddy pushed back his black, woolen cap and wiped his brow. "No, I've got money. Enough to hold me for a few days. But I do need a favor. In fact, I need two favors."

319

"What's that?"

"In the old days when I used to supply information to Central, I was treated with respect. And as far as I know, my information was always reliable, right?"

"Yes, for the most part."

"That's what I want. I want that respect again. I lost it when I did a bad thing and they carted me off to Mount McGregor. Secondly, I need a job. A real job. I'm fifty-six years old, no kid anymore. I can't make a living in the streets now, especially here in New York. There's no code among thieves these days. Drugs have ruined it all. They'd kill you for a nickel. So, there you have it. The streets are no longer mine. The creeps have taken the streets over."

"About the job," Harry told him. "Let me make a few phone calls. If memory serves me correctly, you were always good with numbers. Wally Fields, an old friend of mine, is looking for an inventory clerk down on the docks. They import tea and such from the Orient. Might include some night work, but the pay is decent."

Freddy's ruddy face beamed with this news. "Numbers. Can I do numbers? Any kind of numbers. No problem. They call me the walking calculator," he boasted.

Harry knew Freddy had the natural math-

ematical ability of a bookie. There wasn't anyone faster at adding, subtracting and multiply-
ing than Freddy.

"You're a gem, Harry. I knew you'd come
through for me."

"Don't count your first paycheck just yet,"
Harry warned him. "I said I'd call, that's all."

"Thanks," said Freddy. "I won't mess this
up. Get me that job and I'll make you proud of
me."

"It may take a day or two," Harry said. "I'll
give you a number. When you call, tell the op-
erator Mr. Jones is calling. Remember, Mr. Jones.
She'll reach me."

Freddy's lips pursed up and he broke into a
broad smile. "Just like it used to be, Harry. Very
secret. Your work is very secret."

"Let's just say it's private."

"Oh, I know what you mean. Private it is."

Harry looked Freddy over for a minute.
"That Mount McGregor, Freddy," asked Harry.
"Much drug action taking place inside while
you were there?"

"Mainstream," Freddy admitted. "A real cake
walk."

"More than in Dannemora, or Sing Sing?"

Freddy tucked his hands in his front coat
pockets and stuck out his belly. "A man can
make a nice living in that place."

"Who are the big suppliers?" Harry asked. He got back a blank stare from Freddy.

"Well, Freddy, who?"

"You're pretty sure I might get that job, aren't you?" Freddy asked.

"That depends."

"You mean, that depends on what I tell you?"

"Could be."

They stood on the sidewalk eyeing one another. "Source. You wanted to know the source of the drugs at McGregor. Personally I never had contact with the suppliers. I never really played in that arena. It's never been my bag. I believe you know that. Theft, lots of petty stuff, and a few things necessary to keep me going, fine. Drugs, no. I see it, I follow the action, but I don't participate. As for Mount McGregor, most of the drugs were supplied by Indians. Some ragtag group who, as I understand it, come from Lake Luzerne, a small town somewhere south of Lake George."

"Lake Luzerne?" Harry yelled.

"Yeah, Lake Luzerne," a startled Freddy replied. "You familiar with it?"

"Until today, I wasn't," admitted Harry.

Freddy leaned over to Harry and whispered. "I spent a week at Luzerne on a work detail. McGregor is famous for its work details. Most of the inmates are not hard-core. So they use

322

them on various jobs around the area. I got that detail. We drove back and forth every day. Nice little town. One of the druggies told me he'd heard some lawyer in Luzerne was supplying the Indians. A guy with super bucks, I was told."

Harry grabbed Freddy's shoulders and squeezed him tightly. "Does this lawyer have a name?"

"I really need that job," Freddy insisted.

"Give me the name and the job is yours," Harry said, his large hands still gripping Freddy's shoulders.

"Tocco. Lamar Tocco."

Freddy couldn't recall when he'd seen a man Harry's size run so fast. He was out of sight in a matter of seconds, leaving a befuddled Freddy standing with his mouth open, wondering what had triggered Waite's sudden departure. "Oh, well," Freddy told himself. "I wangled a job from Harry Waite."

Harry tore through Central's main office like a rhino on a rampage, going directly to the operations room, or "Nervous Center" as some of his staff referred to it. Once there, he ordered the code clerk to send an urgent message to E.N. It read: Cease investigation at once. Contact me immediately. He then had the clerk repeat the message. Harry then called E.N.'s beeper number and put in the digits 4444, which was Harry's SOS code to all special agents. With Freddy's words still ringing in his ears, Harry sat down and waited anxiously for E.N. to make contact. Glen Stewart, Central's Manhattan bureau chief, saw Harry sitting by himself and went into the operations room. "You look like a man who lost his best friend, Harry."

Harry moved slowly around in his chair. "As strange as it seems, Glen, I might be on the verge of losing two good friends. First Flint is missing and now I find out that E.N., my man from Vermont, may have walked into a hornet's nest. I don't even want to think of the possibility."

"We've all been following Flint's disappearance," Stewart said. "I didn't know E.N. was working for us these days."

The worried look on Harry's face became graver. He rubbed his eyes.

"E.N. was in semi-retirement. Still investigating small stuff in Vermont, but retired from serious work. He came back out for Flint. Maybe I pushed too hard. But, E.N. knows Saratoga. I felt he could find him."

"So what's happened?"

"This mess in Saratoga is far more complex than we originally thought," Harry admitted, his voice dropping. "I believe we're caught in a triangle. We went in on the premise that Don

Bocca was pulling a power play for casino gambling, and concentrated solely on Bocca. Flint soon discovered there were other power brokers. Flint must have gotten too close to whoever these brokers are. The gig at the Saratoga Racquet Club drew a real blank. We don't have a clue what really took place. So E.N. went sniffing around the club and came up with Tocco's name. Apparently Tocco had a tennis date with the Saratoga Councilman Bochard who was poisoned. Two goons showed up that day at the club looking for Peggy Hoag, a former tennis star turned druggie, and Rocky Steadman, one of Bocca's family members. As you probably know, they both were killed that day. Hoag, with her sexy looks, was bait for Bochard, an apparent womanizer."

"I've seen the position reports of those two," said Stewart. "Haven't seen anything on this Tocco character. What's his story?"

"Until five minutes ago I didn't know what Tocco's connection was. I think I do now, and it scares me. Our old snitch, Freddy The Street, mentioned Tocco's name. So did E.N. in his last contact. E.N. knows only that Tocco is a lawyer in Lake Luzerne, a small town near Saratoga. Freddy, who was doing time at Mount McGregor, says Tocco is supplying a local Indian group with drugs, which are then sold to the inmates at McGregor. As we speak, E.N. is in Luzerne checking out Tocco. If I look upset, I have reason to be. I just tried to reach E.N. to warn him about Tocco. He hasn't replied. I have the worst gut feeling that Tocco may be our missing link to Flint. We're in a helluva dilemma."

"Who else do we have up there to back up E.N?"

Harry threw his hands up in the air. " No one."

"Then I'll go," Stewart volunteered.

"No." Harry pounded the desk in frustration. "I've already put two agents in jeopardy. If anyone goes, it will be me." He rolled his eyes to the ceiling. "This damn, dirty business gets worse every day. Sending Flint to Saratoga for the third time in a row goes against my own dictates. I've always told people never to do anything in threes. It's bad luck. Flint's friends up there said they desperately needed his help. I really didn't want him to go. Nevertheless, I interrupted Flint and Sandy's Hawaiian vacation. Now look where we are. I won't be able to look Sandy straight in the face."

Stewart was listening intently to Harry. He was known at Central for being a unique problem solver, analyzing situations others couldn't begin to assess.

"Harry," he declared, " I have an idea."

"I'm glad you do, I'm racking my brain for one."

Stewart moved to the center of the room. "Freddy The Street may have given us a way of finding Flint."

"How's that?"

"Well," Stewart suggested, "if the Indians are pushing drugs into McGregor, why not go to McGregor and nab one in the act?"

Harry pondered Stewart's idea, then snapped back. "Too obvious. You can't do the obvious. Come to think of it, that's one of Flint's credos. If it looks and sounds simple, forget it."

"I beg to differ," Stewart insisted. "Let's beat 'em at their own game. Grab one dealer at a time and make them disappear. We'll hit this Tocco right in the pocketbook. We'll also cause him to think his problems are internal. We'll plant the seed of doubt and let him squirm a bit. It won't be long before he'll be pointing the finger at his own men. If he's holding Flint, it may throw him off balance and buy us some time."

"But what if Flint is already dead?" Harry said, his words barely audible. "Then it's all the more reason we squeeze him."

It wasn't often that Harry found himself indecisive and unable to take charge in a pressing situation. He'd always been the dominant, commanding force when the going got rough. Just how to proceed from here had him stymied. He made one more trip to the code clerk. When he came back, Stewart could read the answer on his face. E.N. still had not checked in. Without hesitation, he turned to Stewart. "You may be right. We'll have to play hardball with Tocco. I want you to go find Freddy. He wanted a job, I'll give him one. He may not like it, but money is money."

"Freddy? Where does he fit in?"

"Oh, he doesn't" Harry quipped. "That's why I need him. Like it or not, Freddy may have to do another stint at Mount McGregor. He can be our inside spotter. We'll decoy Freddy to set up the grab on Tocco's boys. I'm on my way north if E.N. doesn't make contact by midnight." He gave Stewart a high sign. "If you want to go along, I can use your help. Maybe we'll need additional help. I'd say no less than six of Central's best people. Include Sara Lee, that new woman from Brooklyn that just came aboard. I hear she's an excellent marksman and knows the martial arts as well as anyone in this department. If things get really rough in Saratoga, I want Lee at Sandy's side at all times. It's the least I can do for Flint."

There were twenty important investigation

files sitting on top of Harry's desk when he returned to his office. Each one needed his attention. He thumbed through them quickly, trying to decide how best Central could handle them, based on budget, available manpower and time. This laborious task took up the remainder of the day and continued well into the night. At five minutes to midnight, Harry was disturbed from his work by the night-shift code clerk.

"Hello, Harry. You left a note to call if E.N. didn't check in."

"That's right," said Harry. "I did. I hadn't realized it was this late, I've been reviewing files."

"No word from E.N., I'm afraid," the clerk apologized.

"Thank you," replied Harry, his entire body feeling the strain and fatigue of the long day and evening. "Do me a favor. Call Stewart and tell him to pack his Saratoga duds. He'll know what I mean."

21. HURRY UP AND WAITE

Harry Waite's hurried trip to Saratoga caught Nealy off guard. In one respect, Nealy welcomed Harry's involvement. However, he was highly concerned that demands on his own time during this critical stage of the investigation would not allow him ample opportunity to guide Harry through all the intricacies surrounding the investigative parties now combing through Saratoga in pursuit of Bocca's connection. Besides, Nealy was fearful the state police might find out about Central's meddling, which Nealy knew was illegal. Central didn't exist, no more than Flint or E.N. existed, at least not legally. As much as Nealy wanted to acknowledge Central's contributions in solving past problems in Saratoga, he couldn't.

Harry's operation had no investigative authority outside of New York City. That Harry elected to send his agents into forbidden territory still didn't give him the right to do so. Working him into this arena now would require a magic trick on Nealy's part. But Nealy had to take the risk for Flint's sake. Nealy had mixed feelings about all this as he made a quick visit to Dr. Blake's office to discuss Harry's unofficial, secret visit.

Dr. Blake had just finished with his last patient for the afternoon when Nealy arrived. He spotted Nealy coming up the long slate walk, his hat off and his white, unruly hair blowing about his face. He met Nealy at the door, remarking, "You look a bit disheveled, chief. Can I fix you a drink?"

"No, thanks, Arnold, it's still a tad early."

"Well maybe a cup of coffee?"

"Now you're talking," said Nealy.

Blake led him toward the small room at the rear of his office that served as his kitchen. "It's not Compton's Diner," Blake said. "Our menu is limited to coffee and sweet rolls. Just enough to keep a psychiatrist from starving when he's seeing too many patients and can't go out to eat."

"Sounds like police headquarters, except we hoard donuts," Nealy laughed.

They drank their coffee from paper cups, black with no sugar. Blake suggested they sit in his office to talk. The large, red leather chairs that faced Blake's highly polished mahogany desk were favorites of Nealy's. He'd sat in them many times before. He chose the chair nearest the outside wall, the larger of the two. With its firm padding and wide arm rest, Nealy's six-foot, three-inch frame was supported comfortably as he sat back and admired the richness of Blake's workplace. No matter how many times he'd seen the office, it always impressed him.

Though it was still early afternoon, the office drapes were closed. Blake hit a button and the drapes automatically peeled back, letting in a bright ray of sunlight. It transformed the room's appearance, enhancing its decorative wallpaper, textured white ceiling and, most noticeably, illuminating the hue of the Oriental rug.

"Arnold," Nealy's tone turned serious, "Harry Waite will be in Saratoga in about six hours. The question is, what do we do with him?"

"Treat him like a guest," Blake said.

Nealy tossed his hat nervously from one hand to the other. "It's a tough call, Arnold. The man feels guilty about Flint. He told me so. He'll be with another guy from Central, I didn't get his name. My concern is that Harry, from what little Flint told us about him, is a take charge person."

"Anyone in that position, yourself included, has to be assertive."

"That's the problem," Nealy sighed. "Can Harry and I work together?"

Blake slowly drank some coffee and thought about it. "Given the fact that Central's not supposed to be in Saratoga in any capacity, I'd say you can't work with him. That said, we both know you have to. I view it this way. Harry might give your department some relief by allowing you to focus on the O'Neill and Bochard murder attempts, while he concentrates on finding Flint."

"And, now this E.N. character from Vermont," Nealy added.

"E.N.'s missing?" asked Blake.

"Guess he hasn't heard from E.N. since early yesterday. He didn't give me many details, but did say he feared that E.N. may have overextended himself. That's all he said. That and the fact that he'll be here tonight." Don't even know what E.N. looks like, do you?"

Blake poured the last of the coffee into their cups. "Where's Harry staying?"

"He asked me to find him an out-of-the-way spot."

"That's no problem," said Blake. "I still have that little cottage on the south end of Lake Lonely. I've only used it twice all winter, but it's heated, has two bedrooms and now that the snow is gone, the road's in fair shape. It's got a phone, too. That should give him all the privacy he wants. It will make a good meeting place should we have to get together."

"Fine by me," Nealy said, checking his watch. "I have to run, Arnold. I think we'd better touch base tomorrow." On his way out of Dr. Blake's office, he suddenly stopped. "Come to think of it, we best get everyone together tomorrow and have a sit down with Harry. I'll call Duffy, Farrell and Sandy. Would 2 P.M. be a good time for you?"

"I have some appointments," said Blake, looking over his desk calendar. " Make it 4 P.M. Do you want to meet here or at the cottage?"

Nealy shrugged his shoulders. "That's your call."

"The cottage it is," said Blake. "Now, let me give you the keys to the cottage. Tell Harry the light to the detached garage is just inside the kitchen door. The damn pine trees out there are always shedding cones and dripping sap, so I'd suggest he keep whatever car he's driving in the garage. Aside from that, I don't think Harry and his friend will see much activity in that area. A few locals ice fish the lake, but their season is over."

"Isn't it strange how that lake has all but died?" Nealy remarked. "Not like the old days when Riley's and the other casinos were open.

Surprised you kept a cottage out there."

"It's the only reason I kept it," Blake told him. "I thrive on the solitude it offers me."

On the way to his car, Nealy was trying his best to figure out the philosophical reason that Blake, of all people, would want to sequester himself at such a lackluster place as Lake Lonely. Solitude or no solitude, why not Saratoga Lake? Or, for that matter, Lake George? For a man who could well afford the luxurious life, Blake certainly lived on the conservative side.

22. RUNNING SWIFT

The memorial service for Professor Halfmoon at Union College in Schenectady was, to Monica's surprise, a formal Christian rite, and had nothing to do with his ancestral heritage. Because Sandy was not able to get Duffy's car the day before, Monica missed Halfmoon's wake. She was told he was waked at the Daly Funeral Home on McClellan Street in Schenectady, and all arrangements were handled by Daly at the bequest of the college's Anthropology Honor Society, which Halfmoon held in high regard and had served well for most of his years at Union.

The service was held in Union's main chapel at 11 A.M., with a full complement of Halfmoon's peers and students in attendance. To Monica's further surprise, upon inquiring, she learned that Halfmoon had no immediate family and had, to the consternation of some native Americans, converted to Christianity some twenty years earlier after a visit to the Shrine of the

North American Martyrs at Auriesville. Monica, asking a man seated next to her what the Auriesville shrine stood for, was told it was a shrine dating back to pre-Revolutionary days. It was a present day holy place for Christians primarily of the Catholic faith, though individuals such as Halfmoon, himself a convert to the Episcopal Church, made occasional visits. He especially, because of his tribe's historical ties with the area.

The minister gave a moving eulogy, saying Halfmoon was a man who was a highly thought of specialist in anthropological perspective, who always was striving to close the gap between conflicts of all natures. In the half-hour eulogy, however, there was but one mention of Halfmoon's Onondaga heritage. All references centered on his academic career and his accomplishments while teaching at Union. No sweeping words to identify how this Native American had spent his childhood on a reservation and ultimately overcame many hardships to become a full professor in the hallowed halls of Union. No, the preacher eulogized Halfmoon as one among equals at the college. Halfmoon's historical identity was all but omitted, a biographical omission that Monica found startling, considering what Sandy said he'd told Duffy. I should have one of my script writers along for this, she was thinking, amazed how, in death, one man could be so isolated from his own roots.

Monica, wearing a black woolen hat and matching lace face veil, had seated herself in a pew about halfway up the aisle. All during the ceremony she kept an eye on as many attendees as possible. If Halfmoon had kept in touch with any tribe members, it certainly wasn't reflected in this mostly white, waspish gathering of academicians. In the confines of the chapel it became quite warm. Monica, trying not to appear irreverent, discretely fanned herself with the ceremonial program. She also felt a sudden pulsation in her brain, the kind that usually preceded one of her classic fainting spells. "Don't let me pass out now," she told herself, while continuing the fanning.

When the proceedings reached a point where she didn't believe she could stay conscious a minute longer, the ceremony ended. At the chapel's entrance she managed to slip past a slow-moving elderly couple and was able to make her way outside just in time to catch a fresh April breeze blowing across Union's campus. Supporting herself on the chapel's railing while watching the crowd come out, her eyes were suddenly drawn to a man standing some fifty feet away. He was dressed in an unusual, light tan garment that she first thought was a faded suit, but then realized he was in Indian dress. A plain deerskin coat and leggings, that showed some wear. It was a similar garment to the ones she had seen a hundred times on movie sets.

The man apparently went unnoticed by others or, as Monica surmised, was probably mistaken for a jogger. She started walking slowly in his direction. Once she reached him, she wasn't sure what she'd say. Inwardly she was already resenting the female sleuth role Sandy had talked her into. It might work for Flint, but she saw no progress thus far on her part. She was now within fifteen feet of the man and feeling nervous. From this distance he appeared quite young, perhaps in his mid-twenties.

He turned his head in her direction as she approached. It was then she noticed his right eye patch. A black patch, tied with a thin string behind his head. He had long, black hair that fell below his collar line and rested on his back in one single braid. Monica noticed he was carrying a string of beads in his left hand. As she stepped closer, she was tying to decide how to open up a conversation, but she didn't have to.

The man spoke first, asking. "Were you inside for the memorial?"

His frankness caught her off balance. "Why,

yes. It was ... a wonderful tribute," she replied, taking further notice of his deep-set eyes and noble facial features.

"I would have gone," he said slowly, "but I wasn't invited."

He faced the chapel and spoke a few words she couldn't understand, then quickly reverted back to speaking English. "Perhaps my dress bothered some. They may have felt I wasn't presentable."

"Who would they be?" she asked.

He gave her a distant look and shook his head. "The elitists," he said wistfully.

"Which elitists?" she demanded.

He raised his arm and pointed at the crowd. "See for yourself. They are not his people. He walked and worked among them, and they used his fine mind, but they never had his heart. It was always with us; always with his tribe."

Monica's heartbeat quickened. With the mourners still leaving the chapel, some walking, others getting into their cars, Monica reveled in talking to this extraordinary personality.

"What tribe are you referring to?"

"Halfmoon's tribe, the Onondagas."

"But he lived in Schenectady. He didn't live with the tribe."

He looked at her triumphantly. "As I said,

his heart and spirit was always with us."

"Have you come to take Halfmoon home?" she said meditatively.

"No. He'll stay here where he has taught for the last twenty years. They will inter his remains someplace in Schenectady." He paused and gave her a slight smile. "I will return his spirit. They can never have that." Then he spoke again in his native tongue. This time holding the beads in the palm of both hands. She waited patiently until he was finished.

She approached him. "I'm curious. Were you praying?"

"If you want to call it praying," he acknowledged. "I was calling his spirit back to the Six Nations. I besieged the big waters of Lake Erie and Lake Ontario to calm themselves so that Halfmoon's canoe can pass safely to the far shores so he can meet with those that have gone before him. I called the Iroquois tribes, the Mohawks, Oneidas, Cayugas, Senecas, Tuscaroras, and Onondagas, to accept him back and to make his journey peaceful."

He held the string of wampum beads in front of her eyes. "This wampum stands for peace. Peace of the soul and mind. It has powers that can recall past deeds, good and bad. I spoke to our ancestors to recall only the good things in Halfmoon's life. There was a time when

wampum was used as payment to atone for killings. In accordance with our ancient customs,
a man's life is worth ten strings. I have ten
strings, you see. As the lone tribe member here
today, I am condoling Halfmoon. Around the
campfires at home, and in reservation dwellings, other Onondagas will chant his name. He
will be remembered."

Monica, always a sentimentalist at heart,
was caught up in the melancholy of the moment. She couldn't recall ever seeing anything
so touching, so real. A passing couple stopped
to watch, stared curiously at the Onondaga,
seemingly amused at what they saw, and went
on their way. He bowed his head and concluded
the short ritual.

"I'm sure the spirits heard your plea," said
Monica.

"Thank you," he replied.

She looked at him approvingly. "It took
courage to come here, didn't it?"

"Not courage, dedication," he said.

"Well, I know Halfmoon would approve."

"Again, I thank you," he said, putting the
wampum into a small leather pouch.

"I didn't get your name," Monica remarked.

"My name is Running Swift. I'm a full-
blooded Onondaga. I'm of the same tribe as
Halfmoon. We never met, but I knew about him

for years. He was much talked about in our council circles. They referred to him as the one who has learned much. We were informed of his death just yesterday. The tribe members elected me to come to this memorial. I drove down in the middle of the night and slept in my car. I had no place to bathe or change into more presentable attire. I don't always dress like this. I do so now to fulfill the ritual. No matter though, what I came to do I have done."

"My name is Monica," she offered. "I didn't know Halfmoon. Some friends of mine did. I came on their behalf. The circumstances surrounding his death have left my friends very puzzled. Do you know why Halfmoon was killed?"

Running Swift's eyes opened wide, and his tan, deeply lined face drew taught. His lips began to form a word, then he held back. Monica watched and waited for his answer, which he seemed to be choosing carefully. Finally, he found the right words. "There has been much unrest in the council of late over issues not easily resolved. Drugs is one issue. Like most of society, we are cursed by this drug demon. It has crept into every corner of our world. Some of our people have been lured away by the easy money drugs generate. We know Halfmoon was opposed to drugs of any kind. He wrote and spoke of the evils many times during his teaching career. Of late, he was outspoken on casino gambling. He didn't approve of the Iroquois involvement in casino gambling, claiming the temporary rewards would bring long-term misery.

"He made many enemies by speaking his mind both within the Iroquois nations and from outside. But, Halfmoon was not alone in this thinking. Many in our council sided with him. In the end, two opposing camps were drawn. Those for gambling, and those against it. It was a division we Iroquois had not seen since the English and French went to war, and the confederacy was divided in its loyalty to one or the other. If you studied our history, you'd know that issue was settled when the confederacy decided not to support either the French or English. Even though the confederacy stayed neutral, certain factions took up arms and participated in the great wars of that earlier time. The chiefs could not control everyone.

"You ask me who killed Halfmoon. Specifically, I can't tell you because I don't know. I can speculate who killed him. I can say he was a victim of greed and malice and demented minds. Of men with wild dreams of grandeur. Desperate men who will go to any length to get what they want. Men who will destroy anything and anyone who stands in their way."

Running Swift paused to reflect on his reply, then continued. "That's who killed Halfmoon. I can't identify exact names and faces for you. There are so many of them now splintered off from the council, who's to say which one killed Halfmoon? I blame them all."

Monica stood awestruck listening to his words. "Are you saying his own people killed him?"

"I'm saying it might have been his own kind, but we have to qualify that. The story circulating in the council is that these misguided tribe members are being controlled by white men. Men with money and power who want to keep drugs flowing into the region and also support the return of casino gambling to Saratoga and other nearby towns. The forces of evil killed Halfmoon. They wanted him silenced."

Monica looked around. They were all alone now. The chapel doors were closed and all the people had left the grounds. The quiet of the surroundings was broken by the distant tolling of a Schenectady church bell. A solemn ending to a sad day indeed, Monica was thinking.

"This group you speak of, where do they live, if not with the Six Nations?" He suddenly knelt down and drew an oblong map in the dirt with one finger, and finished by making an X at either end. Then he divided the map by drawing a twisting line. He looked up at Monica with an expressionless stare. "The first X is Lake Luzerne, where I have heard some tribe members stay. The second X is the approximate second location of the group, not far from the Auriesville Shrine, which you can see from I-90, or the New York State Thruway. The curving line is the Mohawk River near Auriesville. The group located near Auriesville is camped due east of the shrine somewhere downriver. I'm almost certain the truth of who killed Halfmoon can be found at one of these two locations. I have not visited either site, though I have been tempted to go see for myself." He stood up and brushed some earth from his leggings.

Monica eyed him. "It would be very dangerous, would it not?"

"That depends if they knew I was coming," he remarked.

"Then you'd go spy on them?"

"Spying is an appropriate word," he agreed.

Monica's mind was now racing with ideas. "Would you be willing to take someone with you?"

"To which site?" he said.

"Both, if necessary," she told him.

He stared at her quizzically. "Who would that someone be?"

"Why, me," said Monica, her words forced out.

"I don't understand," he said. "For what reason? Didn't you just tell me five minutes ago that you hardly knew Halfmoon?"

"There's a man.. a good friend of mine. He's been missing for several days now. I...I mean we, my other female friend and I, suspect he's been taken by the very tribe members you describe. It happened in Saratoga shortly before Halfmoon's death. The group you talk about, I've heard bits and pieces that tie into what you've told me. This man I speak of reminds me very much of you. Not that I know anything about you, it's just what I feel about you. That you're honest, sincere, and searching for the truth. Am I correct?"

"You are very perceptive," he smiled.

"Then you will guide us?" she pleaded.

"I'm not sure," he replied. " If I go and get caught, it's one thing. I only have myself to account for. If I take you and your friend, and any harm were to come to you, I'd have great guilt. I don't think I want that responsibility."

"We'll go at our own risk," Monica assured him.

Running Swift squatted down, crossed his legs and covered his face with his hands. He remained in that position for nearly five minutes before finally looking once more at Monica. "I have asked he spirit of the great chief Hiawatha to help me decide," said Running Swift, his tan face showing his concern. "I will guide you and your friend. I must caution you, it could be a perilous trek. Those that would kill Halfmoon will kill anyone. If I take you, we must have an understanding."

"What is that?"

"That your reasons for wanting to go and mine are very different." He said. "You go to save your friend, and I find that admirable. Few women would dare such a thing. My motive for going is quite different. It is not one man I go to save, it's a whole nation. Yes, if I can get these few strays to reconcile their differences with the council, and renounce revenge, the peacemakers will smile down on me. Salvation for these warped minds is my sole mission."

"Then it's a pact," Monica said excitedly. "My friend, Sandy, and I will honor your wishes. I'll give you a number where we can be reached, day or night. The sooner we go the better. But I'll leave that up to you."

He took out his string of wampum beads and gently ran his fingers over them. "Let's pray there'll be no need for these in the future."

On her drive back to Saratoga, Monica's thoughts were on Running Swift and their brief, but consequential, meeting. Was it just by chance that she had met him or, as he had demonstrated in his ritual offerings, was it the majestic intercession of his ancestral spirits that had drawn them together at Halfmoon's memorial? In any event, it was the first ray of hope she'd encountered since her arrival. She couldn't wait to tell Sandy.

23. NOT A WOODCHUCK

One of the worst early April rain storms in memory pelted down on Saratoga as Chief Nealy, barely able to see the narrow road leading into Lake Lonely, drove Harry Waite and his associate, Glen Stewart, to Blake's cottage. It had been a dozen years since Nealy had last negotiated this excuse for a road. Even with fog lights, visibility was limited because of the storm. Waite and Stewart had arrived earlier in the evening by train from New York City. Nealy prearranged a meeting at the cottage with Blake, Duffy and Farrell. He was going to include Sandy, but rejected the idea. Nealy was afraid Sandy might become too emotional with Harry present. It was to be a no-holds-barred meeting, with Nealy and Blake laying all their cards on the table for Harry.

In return, they expected Harry would be up front with them. If he had some sensitive information about Bocca, they wanted to hear it. Hopefully, through an honest exchange of information, they'd be able to zero in on Flint's predicament. None of this, however, was discussed as they made their way along the twisting, one-lane road. Fortunately, Nealy had taken his own Jeep Cherokee. He slipped the vehicle into four-wheel drive and gingerly toed the pedal. He wanted to avoid going off the soft shoulders and into the thick, spring muck he knew was axle deep.

"Where in hell are we going?" Harry yelled. "On a safari?"

"Blake likes his solitude," replied Nealy.

"Tell him I live in the Big Apple," Harry said. "I'm not a woodchuck."

"Just a little farther, Harry," Nealy promised.

"At precisely that moment, Nealy felt the front wheels sinking and sliding to the right. He instinctively turned the steering wheel hard left and gunned the engine, and the jeep lunged forward and righted itself. Nealy had all he could do to see the road. Fifty feet farther, the road took a sharp right and became a steep incline. Harry and Stewart were thrown back against the seats, as the jeep's four wheels spun on the soft, slick surface, propelling the vehicle upward.

"What in hell was that?" Harry shouted to Nealy.

"Just one of the worst roads in the county."

Harry tapped him on the shoulder. "No, I don't mean the road. Who was that person we just passed?"

"I didn't see anyone," said Nealy.

"You damn near hit him," Harry exclaimed. "He was in your headlights for a full second. Then he disappeared. You must be losing your sight."

"I haven't the slightest," Nealy said. "Could it have been Blake?"

"Did you see someone walking in the road?" Harry said to Stewart.

"Yes, something was in the road. It looked like a man, but I couldn't tell."

Nealy braked the jeep to a halt. " I have my portable spotlight, let's have a look."

All three got out of the jeep. The rain, driven by a stiff wind, lashed at their faces. Nealy went behind the jeep and searched the road with his spotlight. "Nothing here," he called back.

"Well, there was something or somebody here a minute ago," Harry barked.

Stewart came around the jeep to Nealy's side. "Try scanning the brush to the right. I know I saw someone."

Harry joined them, trying to wipe rain water off his glasses, which now had fogged over. "Only a damn fool would be out in this torrent."

"We've got plenty of them in Saratoga," said Nealy, still moving his light from left to right.

"There," screamed Stewart, grabbing Nealy's light and shining it near a tree to the left. "Who is that?"

Nealy ran toward the tree. Suddenly a figure moved and darted across the road, stumbling as it went off the soft shoulder and into the thick bushes. Harry, his Smith and Wesson at the ready, caught up to Nealy. Stewart, with his gun also drawn, took a position to their right.

"Whoever you are, come out," Harry demanded.

The bushes moved, and a man's voice called out. "I'm not doing anything."

Harry took five paces and stopped. "Then you have nothing to fear from us, mister. Just make sure that when you show your face, your hands are raised above it. Way above it."

The man came crashing out of the brush, tripping again on the soft shoulder, and fell face down in the muddy, rain-soaked road. Nealy went over and pulled him to his feet, shining the light directly in the man's eyes. What he beheld was an aged man, stocky and nearly six feet tall. He wore a red woolen cap, a dark navy pea coat and baggy brown pants, with rubber knee-high boots. The man's face was heavily whiskered, and deep-set owlish eyes peered out from under thick, salt 'n pepper eyebrows.

"So, who are you?" Harry asked, sticking one hand under the man's chin and holding his head erect as he studied his face.

"Albert. They call me Albert. I come here to fish. I live nearby."

Nealy laughed. "Fish in Lake Lonely?"

"Yes," Albert replied. "I fish year-round here. Ask anybody."

Harry took Nealy's light and held it closer to Albert's face. "Even in weather like this?"

The deep eyes stared back at Harry. "Tonight's rain caught me off guard. It got too wet. I came earlier to fetch some bait in the small streams. I was walking home when you came along." He opened his jacket and showed them a transparent plastic bag hanging from his belt. The bag held a few minnows.

Stewart grilled him. "Why did you run?"

"I thought you were the kids."

"What kids?"

"Oh, the wild ones who occasionally use this road. They come here to party. Lots of drinking and hanky-panky...you know. They've tossed beer cans at me. Cursed me. Stole my fishing equipment. I'm an old man. I try to keep to myself."

"Are you familiar with Dr. Blake's place?" Harry asked.

"Not really," Albert said, still wiping splattered mud from his face. "There's only one or two camps on the lake. I have no idea who owns them. It doesn't interest me. I want to be left alone, that's all."

Harry was aware that Albert was looking at his gun. He put it away. Nealy did likewise. The rain was letting up somewhat, though the wind was still brisk. "Well, you go on your way, Albert," Harry said. "Forget we were here. Catch lots of fish."

They drove on for another quarter mile and finally came to Dr. Blake's place. Blake's car and Farrell's wagon were already there. They smelled smoke from the fireplace as they entered the front door. Blake, Duffy and Farrell were already having a drink, so Blake introduced Waite and Stewart and offered them a drink. When everyone was served, Blake took a large piece of grid paper and pinned it on the wall.

"Now that we're all here, I thought we'd do some brainstorming. We can begin with Tom's assessment of the investigation to date, and then go around the room for comments. Let it all fly. No detail, no matter how trivial it may seem, should be omitted. Duffy, I'll be calling on your editorial skills to keep track of this meeting, if that's okay with you."

"Fine by me," said Duffy.

Blake handed Duffy a pen and pad. Then, turning to Nealy, said, "You're on, Tom."

For the next few hours the five men focused on all the incidents, starting with Molly O'Neill, and hashing over every step of the weird and complex investigation. Nealy even added information he'd picked up from the State Police, though in the course of the evening, they all found out that much of the information was either too sketchy, or blatantly redundant. Toward the conclusion of their gathering, Duffy spent twenty minutes relating what Halfmoon had come to see him about. When Duffy was done, Nealy added a surprise by telling them that the bullet that killed Halfmoon wasn't a bullet at all, but a musket ball. He explained why Halfmoon's head was so gruesomely ripped apart.

"Yes," said Nealy. "They found the lead ball imbedded in Halfmoon's skull at the autopsy. My ballistics people went back and double-checked the area where Halfmoon had fallen. Wouldn't you know, right above the door, there was a dent in a metal casing. Apparently he didn't take a direct hit. The ball ricocheted off the casing and tore through Halfmoon's head at an acute angle. It was carrying enough velocity to take off one-third of his skull."

"The backfire," Duffy said. "It's the last thing I really remember. I never realized...never thought it was a muzzle blast. I don't understand why they used a flintlock. Why not a high-powered weapon with more accuracy?"

Nealy drew a big S on the grid. "Easy. They were making a statement. Firing a flintlock got our attention, didn't it?"

The final half hour was taken up by Harry who, with Stewart's help, brought everyone up-to-date on Bocca's influence in mob matters, with particular emphasis on Bocca's Saratoga gambling designs. Harry ended his critique by telling them of his meeting with Freddy The Street and his plan to use Freddy at Mount McGregor to trap some of the drug runners.

"If we can pull off the Mount McGregor trap, we'll bring maximum pressure on this operation," Harry boasted. "Glen's idea of snatching off the drug runners one-by-one has some merit. Of course we can't do it on New York State Prison property. All we need from Freddy is a signal that he's made contact with a runner. We can equip Freddy with two-way communications for this. We'll have to make our grab somewhere down McGregor's access road. It may be unorthodox, and completely illegal, Tom, but we'll need your help with these grabs. Not to mention a place to hold the runners for a short time. Glen has a contingency plan to ship them to the city if holding them here becomes too cumbersome, or if we take more time than expected implementing this plan. Any questions?"

"Who's to say the runners will lead us to bigger game?" Farrell asked.

"No one," said Harry. "It's only a plan. If you can think of another, I'm all ears."

Farrell could think of nothing. Harry's eyes went around the room. When no one volunteered a better alternative, Blake called an end to the meeting.

"I hope you two find my camp comfortable enough," said Blake. "The fridge is full of snacks, there's bottled drinking water and, if you search in the right place, a few choice cigars."

"When do the bears come around?" Harry quipped.

"They're still hibernating, Harry. Besides, you probably snore too loudly."

On the way out to his car, Nealy shouted to Duffy and Farrell to be careful driving the road. "We don't want to hit old Albert," he warned them.

"Albert who?" said Blake.

"Some old fisherman we damn near ran over on the way in. Said his name is Albert."

"You probably mean Sacca," Blake informed

him. "The name is Albert Sacca."

Harry, standing at the open door, grabbed Blake's arm. "That name, Sacca. I know that name. Where's he from?"

"He's been a fixture here for years," replied Blake. "Comes here every day. Ice fishes the lake all winter. Lives in a little shack just off Union Avenue, right on the fringe of Yaddo Park, a stone's throw from the main race course. Quite eccentric, but harmless."

Harry turned to Stewart. "Dig into that computer brain of yours. Sacca ... Albert Sacca. Why does that name ring a bell?"

Stewart closed his eyes and meditated for a minute. "I've got it. It's a name out of the past. I associate it with Bocca, Palermo, Cira ... yes, yes. Sacca. One of Cira's family members. Good God, he must be in his eighties by now. His name came up in a round-robin profile we did five years ago when Central was compiling a fifty-year mob tree. Do you think that old coot was really Sacca?"

"Dr. Blake just gave us his name, didn't he?"

"Sacca ... Smith ... Jones," said Stewart. "There's more than one Sacca in this world."

"His age," said Harry excitedly. "That fisherman was old. Yes, I'd say it's the same Sacca. If so, he's probably on the phone with Bocca this very minute. We're sitting ducks out here.

Where are Blake and Nealy?"

"I'm afraid they've already left, Harry. So have Duffy and Farrell. Let's rest on this, and discuss it with them in the morning."

"It won't wait," Harry said.

"There's no need for concern," Stewart insisted. "I can't tell you what Sacca is doing in these parts, if it is really the Sacca you refer to, but I can tell you he's had no position in the former Cira, or present day Bocca family, for years. I remember this from the profile. In fact, no one has seen or heard of him in mob circles. If it will make you rest easier, I'll personally check him out tomorrow."

"Maybe you're right," said Harry. "This whole mess has got me unnerved. I think I'll have one of Blake's cigars."

Inside the camp Harry poked through the kitchen cabinets and found the cigars. Once lighted, he puffed it until the smoke curled to the ceiling.

"Mind if I join you?" asked Stewart.

"By all means."

They smoked their cigars in silence, listening to the rhythmic rain on the camp's roof and the logs crackling in Blake's fireplace.

"You know something," said Stewart, flicking his cigar ashes in the fireplace. "If Flint and E.N. are dead, we're in one hell of a predicament, aren't we?"

"I can't bring myself to think it," Harry moaned. "Worse yet, if they are alive, how are we going to find them?"

Stewart yawned and stood up. "We can always hope for a miracle. I'm bushed. Let's sleep on it, Harry."

24. WHERE'S SANDY?

Martha Duffy was beside herself with worry. Sandy was missing. Martha had tea with Sandy after dinner on Tuesday and had chatted briefly with her again just before they both retired to bed at 10:30 P.M. When she went to wake Sandy for breakfast on Wednesday, her bedroom was empty. In fact, Sandy's bed had not been slept in as far as Martha could see.

Martha called Duffy at *The Star*. "Frank, is Sandy with you?" she asked.

"For what reason?"

"I mean did she have you drive her anyplace this morning?"

"No," Duffy replied. "Far be it for me to take Sandy out in broad daylight when we're trying our best to keep her out of sight."

"Well," said Martha in a cracking voice, "she's not here. We talked last night and she went to bed the same time I did. I'm scared to death."

Duffy was in the middle of entering an overdue editorial on his terminal and had the receiver tucked under his chin. "Let me finish this one thing I'm doing and I'll come right home. She probably just went for a short walk," he assured Martha.

"I'm sorry, Frank. Maybe I'm overreacting, but strangely enough, I have the impression she didn't sleep here last night. She didn't take your car out late, did she?"

"She wouldn't take it without my permission," he said angrily. "Besides, it was in the garage this morning just the way I left it last night. She couldn't remove it without the Genie door opener. Look, I have to finish this piece I'm writing. I'll be there shortly."

The forlorn look on Martha's face when Duffy finally arrived home made him wince. Her forehead was creased with worry. "I take it she's not back?" he said in a low voice.

She ignored his remark and looked at the clock.

He went to the kitchen table and sat down. "It's inconsiderate of her to go off like that." He sighed. "I guess we better call Nealy and Blake. If not, and she's really gone, they'll be raising hell with us."

"Maybe I'm nuts, or maybe it's just my intuition working on me, but I believe Sandy might have left Saratoga."

Duffy's face went white. "What do you mean, left?"

"The pressure was too great," said Martha. "All these days waiting for something to break in Flint's favor, and nothing has. All the talk from Nealy and Blake. How would anyone act? Ourselves included?"

Duffy picked up the kitchen phone and called Nealy. He wasn't in. So he called Blake, but was told the doctor was at the hospital on an urgent call and could not be reached until after 3 P.M.

"That's a damn fine kettle of fish," said Duffy, slamming the phone down. "You can't get a cop when you need one, and even the good doctor is indisposed."

Martha came around the table and put her arms around his shoulders and placed a kiss on his head. "Duffy," she said sadly, "I'm growing weak and weary from this mess. How can so many people just disappear?"

He patted her hands and gazed up at her, his eyes moistened. "It's like a wicked curse. I can't fathom it."

"The question is," Martha said, "where would Sandy go?"

Duffy raised one eyebrow. "Depends if she left on her own, or was she taken?"

Martha held him tight and shivered ever so

slightly. A minute later they received a call from Nealy.

"What's up, Duffy?" Nealy's voice boomed.

Duffy handed the phone to Martha. "You tell him."

The next five minutes was consumed with Martha's heart wrenching tale of Sandy's disappearance. Within the hour, Duffy's kitchen was filled with all the concerned parties, including Harry Waite and Glen Stewart. Bringing Harry over to Duffy's wasn't exactly what Nealy had in mind, but this twist of events seemed necessary in Nealy's opinion.

What made matters even more perplexing was that Sandy was able to leave Duffy's house undetected by the watchful eyes of Nealy's two men. A matter Nealy took up immediately and minced no words in questioning how she could have gotten by them.

It wasn't until everyone had finally left that Duffy, searching in the hallway closet for his missing fedora and trench coat, figured it out.

"My God," he murmured to Martha. "She used one of Flint's old disguises."

Martha stared at him grimly. "On her own, or forced to wear them?"

"I haven't the slightest," he said. "But if Nealy's men spotted a man coming out our front door, they'd more than likely not question it at all."

"Why not?" asked Martha.

"Easy. They'd probably think it was me."

"That might be so," Martha agreed. "Though they still might recall the time. We'd better call Nealy again." She wiped her brow.

Duffy, his hand shaking, made the second urgent call of the day to Nealy's office.

25. ALBERT SACCA

In the dimly lit Saratoga shack he called home, Albert Sacca was preparing for his trip to Catskill, replete with a neat-fitting dark wool worsted suit he hadn't tried on in years. His eyes watered as its mothball odor filled the room. He lifted a highly starched button down white shirt from a box under his bed and held it in front of the wall mirror. Now for a tie. He only had one, a wide, brown silk tie he'd worn so long ago, he couldn't remember when.

His only disappointment was his worn, cordovan-colored shoes that predated the suit by five years. His lone and risky decision to try to see Bocca was motivated by suspicion, his suspicion of the men who had confronted him at Lake Lonely. Men with drawn guns whom he figured were coming to search the lake's bottom for the long lost MacEntyre jewels. He spread open a purple satin cloth and stared down at the diamond necklace, the prize of the ill-fated MacEntyre heist. The heist Dellarocco described in all its gruesome detail years back.

Sacca's imagination was running wild, almost insane in its intensity. He fantasized about his pending journey and how Bocca would delight in receiving this necklace. How he'd no doubt take Sacca into his bosom and thank him. As Sacca boarded the Amtrak train in Saratoga, Glen Stewart, assisted by Tom Nealy, arrived at Sacca's shack near Yaddo. As he had promised Harry, Stewart wanted to verify if Sacca was indeed who Harry thought he was. Stewart went up to the dilapidated structure and rapped on the door. When he got no response, Nealy speculated that perhaps Sacca had already gone fishing. Both men decided they'd try again later in the day.

On his train trip south, Sacca's eyes were drawn to the sun rising east of Saratoga on a rim of purple-tinted mountain peaks. He turned to a nearby female passenger, asking, "What mountains are those?"

The young, dark-haired, elegantly dressed women leaned over and studied them for a moment. "The Green Mountains of Vermont. Pretty, aren't they?"

"Yes, far away and very impressive" said Sacca, watching until a row of trees blurred his view of them. "I've never been to Vermont."

26. CURRENT EVENTS

The rippling waters of the Mohawk River at Auriesville glittered beneath a bright spring moon as Running Swift silently paddled his sleek sixteen-foot canoe past the revered shrine. Sandy and Monica were riding with him in a daring approach toward the hidden renegade encampment. The river's ever-changing and tugging current made navigating the canoe difficult. One moment the canoe would move on a straight line, then just as quickly be forced off course so that Running Swift had to constantly shift his paddling from one side of he craft to the other, taxing his strength in the process.

Running Swift kept the canoe close to the left bank, trying to avoid a steady, persistent wind that came in a series of gusts. At Running Swift's insistence, Sandy and Monica were seated low in the canoe's center, their arms resting on the gunwales, their hands gripping tightly to the canoe's thwarts. Running Swift, seated in the bow seat, angled his paddle as needed and ferried the canoe across the speeding current. They paddled silently past the flickering lights of Auriesville and into the darkened portion of the river, Running Swift sitting rigid and using powerful arm strokes to move the craft along. "We must go easy at this point," he warned them. "The cross currents are treacherous here. We don't want to suddenly capsize."

"We better not," Monica warned him. "I can't swim a stroke."

As the canoe moved in nearly total darkness, Running Swift had to avoid several low-hanging tree limbs, and at one point the canoe almost got hung up on a sand bar. Two-foot waves swept against the up-tilted canoe, and some water come in over the bow. Running Swift turned the canoe at an angle and cut through the waves, while Sandy and Monica clung to the craft in fear. Now they reached a shallow portion that Running Swift called rock gardens. Here he was particularly careful to hold the canoe straight, not letting it broach and get caught up between the rocks. Sandy felt a sudden nudge on her rear as the canoe passed over a rock. A second later, Monica experienced the same thing. Running Swift, however, managed to get through this section without slamming against any sharp rocks.

About one mile further along in the pitch

dark, they veered west, crossed the river, and paddled around a wide, beach area. A bit farther on, the river cut inward and Running Swift whispered to them that they were nearing a section of palisades. The moon was back out now and they could see a portion of the majestic black rocks jutting out and up at a height of twenty to thirty feet overhead.

"It's scary," said Monica. "Damn scary. You'd almost think they'll fall on you."

Running Swift paddled harder. As the canoe passed beneath the largest rock formation, a giant bird sprang from the darkness, letting out a blood-curdling shriek of terror, and flying so close that Sandy was brushed by its wing. Monica, frightened by the sudden flurry, lifted herself up and turned toward Sandy.

"Down," Running Swift shouted too late, as the feathery light canoe capsized. The shock of ice-cold river water was all Sandy could feel as she went under and came up. The river's swift drag was carrying her toward shore, but she couldn't see or recognize it. Her ears ached and the pain went to her teeth and eventually to her jaw. Had it not been for Running Swift making them wear life jackets, she knew she surely would have drowned. Still, with her wet, heavy wool sweater, pants and hiking boots, it was a struggle making it to the safety of the riverbank.

Pulling herself ashore on all fours, she rolled on her back to catch her breath. Suddenly, to her right, she heard something move. She sat up, terrified. She listened closely, then realized it was labored breathing she was hearing. She crawled sideways and found Monica laying on her side, unconscious and shivering. From a short distance up river there came a scraping sound. A minute later, as the moon shown again, the shadowy figure of Running Swift appeared. He came forward and tossed a dry blanket to Sandy. He then knelt down and wrapped a blanket around Monica and dried her hair with part of it.

"I have let you both down," he said sadly. "It was my fault. I lost control of the canoe. It was too risky taking you here. I salvaged the waterproof bag with our belongings, but I'm afraid we lost the canoe. You must get into dry clothes. We must dress Monica, too. We don't dare light a fire; however, I have some Sterno cylinders and a mess kit. We can boil river water. We will survive this night, though it won't be pleasant."

Sandy held Monica's hands. "She's still shaking."

"That's not a good sign," said Running Swift. "Get her into some dry clothes before hypothermia takes over. I'm going to look for the canoe once more. It has to be here somewhere."

Running Swift was gone for an hour, a time in which Sandy was able to revive Monica and get her into dry clothing. They had now wrapped the blankets around themselves in a tent like fashion, placing the lit Sterno Running Swift had left them, near the opening. It gave off just enough heat to maintain their normal body temperatures. Monica, however, was very thirsty. They waited patiently for Running Swift's return. While they waited, a southeasterly breeze began to blow and with it, at least to Sandy's ears, there came the sound of men's voices, not talking but chanting. Faint and indistinguishable, but definitely men's voices. Then Monica heard it. No music, just a distant, faint chanting that carried on the wind.

"Do you hear it?" she asked Sandy.

"Yes. It's been going on for a good ten minutes. Where do you think it's coming from?"

Monica pulled the blanket from around her head and listened intently. "It's not coming from the river. I believe it's behind us. Back in those hills someplace."

"I wish Running Swift would come back," said Sandy worriedly.

Monica lifted the blanket once more around her head and closed her eyes. "You know something, Sandy?" she lamented.

"What's that?"

"I have a feeling we're not going to survive this night."

"Nonsense," said Sandy. "Running Swift will get us through it."

"I hope you're right," said Monica. "I'm having my doubts."

Sandy turned the Sterno cylinder so that its heat hit them more directly. "That chanting. It's got me spooked, too. I'm frightened to the bone. But I can't let fear hold me back. Not as long as Mike is being held up there. We have to do something."

"You're right," said Monica. "We've come this far, now we have to take our chances." She looked at Sandy. "I'm a damn flake for losing faith. But now that push comes to shove, and all the chips are on the table, I realize that your love for Mike far overshadows all my superficial longings. I wish I were capable of loving someone that deeply. It's a gift."

"You have," said Sandy. "You wouldn't be here if you didn't love deeply."

"Thanks," said Monica. "Perhaps we all give it differently."

They heard muffled footsteps. Sandy squeezed Monica's hand. "I have returned," said Running Swift. "I couldn't find the canoe. I did find a stream leading inland. Lots of foot tracks, too. I heard their chanting. They can't be far away."

"Yes," said Sandy, "we heard the chanting, too. Now what do we do?"

"Wait until morning," he suggested. "Right now we need a hot drink and something to eat. I have tea bags and Ritz crackers. It was all I had in the protected bag. Now if you don't mind drinking some questionable Mohawk River water we can eat what's here."

"Some dinner," Sandy sighed.

"It's a rotten shame I forgot to bring silverware," Monica remarked.

Sandy stood up and stretched. "You said we'd wait until morning. What then?" she asked.

"That depends on how brave you are," he said.

"Explain," said Monica.

He had filled his mess kit pail with river water, which he now held over the sterno. The glow reflected off his face, making his eyes look much larger. He stared at them pensively.

"The group you heard chanting is located in a narrow wedge between two mountains that run west and south. I want to cause a diversion up there. I want to go in back of that encampment and make them think there's a whole army crashing down on them. To do this, I need you to first draw them off. By making some of them run in your direction, we can spread them out. It may or may not work. If it doesn't, we'll all be killed. So I say again, how brave are you?"

"Not as brave as I was back in Saratoga," Monica admitted.

"I'm no braver," said Sandy. "But we've come this far and I'm not turning back."

He poured boiling water into three small tin cups and made tea using one bag for all three. Then he passed out the crackers. It took away their gnawing hunger. He watched them quietly while they drank their tea. When they were finished, he suggested they sit closer in a circle while letting the Sterno burn. The blankets were arranged so that they acted as a tent, which he left open at the top for the Sterno fumes to escape. He knew their body heat alone would keep them comfortable enough until daybreak.

"You must sit with your legs crossed and lean slightly forward." He cautioned them. "Otherwise, you will get cramps. Rest your elbows on your knees if necessary and your chin in your hands. It will relieve back stress. You can sleep in this position quite easily."

"I feel the stress already," Sandy informed him.

"Give it a few minutes. It takes getting used to."

"My God," exclaimed Monica, laughing. "They'll never buy this one in L.A."

"I will make strong Onondaga squaws of you," he said, smiling. "In fact, you'll be seasoned warriors by this time tomorrow, providing all goes our way."

"What are you planning on doing up there tomorrow?" Monica asked.

"Anything I can to confuse the renegades," he replied. "I didn't want to scare you, but I have twelve sticks of dynamite that also survived our dunking. If I can get positioned just above the encampment, near the high rock formation, I think I have enough dynamite to blow those rocks so they slide into the wedge. Maybe take some earth with it. The echo effect will sound like an army coming down around them. If Flint and E.N. are still alive, I may be able to take advantage of the ruckus to slip in and find them. It's a long shot, I know. I see no other way around it. On the other hand, we could go for help. The state police have a unit in Amsterdam or Fonda. Our problem with the police is their procedures. They may exert too much force all at once and lose the element of surprise. There is another option, if I want to use it."

"Tell us," begged Sandy.

He adjusted the blankets, pulling the ends

tight so that the cool, dampish mist now blowing in off the darkened Mohawk was kept out.

"Your option," Monica reminded him.

"Yes. My option, such as it is. To go and sit in council with the renegades. To see if I can reason with them. To do what Halfmoon would have done had he lived. Plead with them to call a truce. To see if I can get irrational men to act rational again. That's my option. Will it work? Who knows?"

"It'd be suicide," said Sandy. "After all that's happened, I'd say it won't work."

Monica hunched her shoulders and tried to relieve a back pain she'd suddenly acquired. "The lion's den," she said. "They'd eat you alive. You can't go in there and try to reason. These men our killers. That's all there is to it."

"I have told myself this," Running Swift agreed. "Fight or talk, either choice has its risks."

"As cowardly as I am at times, I'll take my chances fighting this crowd," Monica assured him. "How about you Sandy?"

"We'll do it together or not at all," said Sandy. "And if they've harmed Mike, I'll jam one of those dynamite sticks right down one of their throats."

"Then we go in the morning," Running Swift said. "Now, if possible, let's get some rest."

Running Swift was soon asleep. Monica, once her leg cramps were gone, slept also. Sandy could not sleep. The chanting had stopped. There was only the occasional cry of a night bird, and the whirl of the fast-moving river. She was thinking of morning and the uncertainty of their venture. After a time she finally dozed off, or half slept, and her thoughts were of Flint. Only Flint.

27. LOST GROUP

The frenzy surrounding Sandy's disappearance prompted Nealy to call a special afternoon meeting at his office. Nealy wanted to pin down all the facts he could and then make a decision to act. He'd kicked around several ideas of his own, but he wanted everyone's input before setting out. When they were all gathered, except for Harry Waite and Glen Stewart, Nealy went around the room handing out writing pads and pencils, and asked each member to write down as much detail as they could possibly remember since Molly O'Neill's close call.

"Anything you can think of," he demanded. "Consider nothing trivial. Big and small details alike. Don't hold back, just write." Once this was done, Nealy collected each paper and asked Duffy to read them slowly. To Duffy it was redundancy. A time-consuming exercise that would only rehash previously disclosed information. But if Nealy wanted to do it, Duffy decided he'd comply. He began by reading Sergeant Galea's account, then went to Billy Farrell's. He even read Nealy's paper. Martha's list was surprisingly concise and informative, which made Duffy blush with pride at her keenness. Nealy waited and watched as each paper was read, shifting nervously from side to side in his swivel chair. Seven people had contributed. Duffy, Nealy, Galea, Farrell, Martha, Blake and the two officers that had kept the vigil at Duffy's while Sandy was there.

After thirty minutes, Duffy, clearing his throat and stopping to drink some water, finally came to his paper. He'd composed his thoughts and remembrances in single sentences, much the way he took down notes during interviews. The rest he could compose in his head if the need to elaborate on any point was deemed necessary. His details pretty much coincided with Galea's, both having had the advantage of being closer to the story because of their professions.

For Harry's and Glen's sake, Nealy taped the meeting so he could play it back later at Blake's camp. Nealy wasn't sure whether or not all this eleventh hour brainstorming would produce any meaningful results. He only knew he had to try. If, by this meeting, they could unlock just one piece of information not thought of before, it would be worth their efforts, Nealy reasoned. So far, they weren't getting anywhere. Duffy read on. Just before he finished his own assessment, he looked up and laid his paper down.

"I just thought of something," he said. "Halfmoon told me he was on a mission to bring peace to his people. Said he was dedicated to accomplish this above all else. He told me the tribe members at Six Nations were at odds with some of their younger, more disruptive members. He felt also that he was somewhat of an outsider, having not lived with his people for many years, since obtaining his academic credentials. That was his reason for coming to see me. He felt the newspaper could help him reach out to the splinter group. He had made up his mind to go visit with the Six Nations chiefs and discuss the whole issue. He said warfare among the Six Nations has been outlawed for many decades. He said he always followed the genius and principles of Hiawatha, to make peace at all costs. If need be, Halfmoon was willing to go visit with the "lost group" as he called them. He wouldn't use the word "renegade," as some have done. He found the term demeaning and unwarranted. He said any Iroquois who failed to resolve problems among his people while the opportunity was there, would be eternally haunted by disquieted spirits in death. I now know why he avoided acrimonious statements.

"Anyway, he told me the group was camped at a hidden place not far from Auriesville, one of the Iroquois' most treasured camping grounds. It all had something to do with tribal rebirth and a renewal of sprit. Misdirected, as Halfmoon put it, but genuine in scope."

Duffy stared around the room with saddened eyes.

28. FREDDY THE STREET

Freddy The Street was very apprehensive when he was led into Mount McGregor minimum security prison by two overweight guards. He'd made his deal with Harry and now he had to live with it. One month. That was all he'd agreed to. If no contact is made with the renegades in thirty days, Harry would get him out. Then he'd go back to New York and take that job Harry had promised. He wasn't at all happy being back inside the gray, dull edifice. It held too many unpleasant memories for him. Besides, he'd made a few enemies during his prior McGregor stint, and he didn't wish to renew those acquaintances. Hopefully, all those creeps were gone.

Fortunately he was put into a single cell on the prison's south, sunny side. Harry, with the full cooperation of the authorities, equipped Freddy with a two-way radio and enough cash to make some quick buys once the renegades came around. The rest was up to Harry and Stewart.

As prearranged, Freddy was assigned to the Grant Cottage detail. A job considered to be a plum by many at McGregor. He and two other inmates would trim brush on the road leading to the famous general's historic dwelling. Once tourists started arriving to visit the site of Ulysses S. Grant's last days, Freddy's detail would be moved elsewhere. Freddy didn't give it a second thought. By tourist time he fully expected to be back in New York anyway.

In the privacy of his cell, he made his first call to Harry just to test the communications. To his consternation, he experienced static on the line. A blurred signal followed, and then more static. It worried him. He tried again and got the same interference. Just when he thought his equipment was faulty, he realized he hadn't opened the thin antenna. This time it rang through. He let it ring exactly five times, the OK signal he and Harry had worked out. He waited a few seconds and Harry called back. No talk, just short, beeping sounds. He then relaxed, knowing it was working.

Freddy slept quite well during his first full night at McGregor. He'd eaten a full meal of ham, potatoes and green beans and had washed the meal down with three glasses of ice tea. In the morning he went through the daily routine, eating breakfast and returning to his cell to wash and straighten up things before leaving for detail. He worked two hours at Grant's Cottage, then took a ten-minute break. Sitting on a large boulder just east of the cottage, he could view the flat plains far below and look even further still to the rolling mountains of Vermont.

"You ever been to Vermont?" one of his co-inmates asked.

"Can't say that I have," Freddy admitted, "but I'll get there one day."

Later, on his way back to the "Gray Ghost," as they called McGregor, a man came out of the woods and approached Freddy. Freddy immediately recognized him as one of the renegades he'd dealt with several weeks ago, the one called Hawk.

Hawk called, " Is that you, Freddy?" I heard you were long gone from McGregor. What brings you back?"

Freddy studied Hawk's leather-tan face and his shifting dark eyes. Dressed in jeans, with a dirty-blue jacket, Hawk walked with a limp. His jet-black, matted hair came to his shoulders and fell over one eye. Freddy could also smell the smoke from his clothes ten feet away. As expected, Hawk was selling a variety of drugs. "Take your pick," he told Freddy. "Pot, cocaine, crack. I have it all. All the good stuff. We're discounting it this week. Cash only."

"I'm interested," said Freddy. "When can you have it?"

Hawk's face displayed a wide smile. "You name the time and place."

"Okay," said Freddy. "This time tomorrow. I have the same detail. I'll be alone. I've got five thousand for starters. I only want cocaine. Break it out into small bags so I can distribute. I want one free bag for the guards."

Hawk's smile disappeared. "No free bags. We're discounting to begin with. No free bags."

Freddy stood with his legs apart and his hands on his hips. "No deal," he said flatly. He then waited for Hawk's reaction. The smile came back. "One bag. I'll give you one free bag." Hawk said.

"Good," said Freddy. "If for any reason I'm with anyone tomorrow, don't make contact. I'll probably be alone, but you never know."

In a wink, Hawk was gone from sight into the green, wooded thickness. Freddy hurried to his cell and radioed Harry. Freddy was happy. Things were developing quicker than he had expected. He pictured himself leaving McGregor in less than thirty days. Though Freddy wasn't sure just how many renegades Harry wanted to capture before the sting was over, a point he should have clarified with Harry before coming to McGregor, but didn't. As in all his past dealings with Harry, one never really got all the facts straight. Harry had a way of being cleverly vague, Freddy recalled. It's what he often didn't say that kept you guessing.

"I'll get out of here soon," Freddy mused.

29. CORDIAL, BUT DEADLY

Albert Sacca's reception at Don Bocca's was cordial and routine. He was first searched at the massive iron gate to the estate, searched again when he entered the mansion, and made to wait the customary half hour before being ushered into the Don's expansive office. Bocca always chose to meet visitors in the office because it was wired and equipped with hidden cameras. Sacca had already removed the diamond necklace at the Hudson rail station and put it on his own neck, along with the gold chain he'd worn for many years. How ironic, Sacca thought, that Bocca's men didn't notice it during their searches. He remembered the advice he'd once received from Lou Russo, a philosophical fellow mob member: "Put it in front of their eyes and they'll never see it."

When the time came for Sacca to go in, he momentarily hesitated, took a deep breath, brushed some white flecks off his suit with a trembling hand, and walked slowly to his historic reconciliation with the big man. When they first saw each other, the room seemed to crystallize. Dominant was their age. Both were aware they had grown into old men. Bocca seemed visibly upset by this revelation.

Bocca, clearing his throat, spoke first, asking, "And how have you been, Sacca? Have the years treated you well?"

Oh, he's already trying to provoke me, Sacca was thinking. Why else would he ask me how things have been when he knows they'd been lost, lonely years? I will not let him goad me into a like response. No, I will talk low, with respect, and give him the dignity he has never given me. I will kill him with kindness.

"Quite well, Don Bocca," Sacca lied. "Quite well. And you?"

The beady, deadly eyes stared at Sacca. "I must always be well, Sacca. If not, then the whole family grows ill. It has always been that way."

"Then I salute your good health," Sacca lied again.

Bocca offered Sacca a glass of wine. He accepted. Bocca motioned for him to sit. Sacca chose a large, red-leather chair that smelled vaguely of linseed oil. Bocca selected a smaller, wooden chair. He drew it to within four feet of Sacca. "We're drinking New York State Cherry

Valley wine, old friend. Vintage '68. Quite good, do you agree?"

Sacca sipped the wine and held up the glass to the light. "Choice. Choice nectar."

"Fine," said Bocca. "It is my understanding that you have something special to show me. Some relic of Saratoga's past that no one else has seen. Have you brought it with you?" His penetrating stare was still fixed on Sacca. It was the same disarming stare Sacca remembered from the old days, and in that moment, Sacca was weighing whether or not to show him the necklace.

Perhaps I'll tell him about it. Tell him it's still in Saratoga. That it was too valuable to tote here.

By delaying showing the necklace to Bocca, Sacca figured he'd buy more time while cementing his renewed relationship. But under Bocca's forceful gaze, Sacca thought better of it and decided to show him the gem. As calm as Bocca could appear on the surface, beneath that exterior dwelled the mind of a genuine psychopath.

I'll take my chances and show it to him now, Sacca decided.

"I need more light," Sacca said. "Can we go near the window?"

"By all means," said Bocca, rising. As he moved to the window, Bocca pushed a button on the wall and shut down the entire surveillance system. He wanted this conversation between him and Sacca to be strictly private.

Sacca's eyes widened when he saw the view of the Hudson from Bocca's drawing room window. The sweeping, verdant landscape stretched for miles, winding beneath mountain slopes and shear rock cliffs. Sacca felt the power and wealth of Bocca's position from this visage.

Sacca loosened his tie and undid the top three buttons of his shirt. Slowly he drew the necklace out for Bocca to see, pulling gently on the chain's gold ringlets until the diamond itself appeared.

Bocca, his face ablaze, reached out and clutched the diamond. "This stone, where did you get it?"

"From the depths of Lake Lonely."

Bocca's large hands yanked so hard on the necklace it cut into the back of Sacca's neck.

"I know this stone," Bocca said. "There could not be two of them. What other gems were found with it?"

Sacca had difficulty breathing. He pushed Bocca's hand away and stepped two paces back. Then hurriedly, unhitching the necklace, handed it to Bocca. "There were no others. If you must know, this came from a pike's belly I caugh ice fishing the lake."

Bocca looked at him in disbelief and took the necklace and held it under a lamp. "So, tell me more Sacca. This pike that ate the diamond, how big was he?"

Sacca recognized Bocca's sarcasm for what it was. Another humiliating remark to degrade him. He thought hard before answering. "Of average size, Don Bocca."

"What is average size these days for pikes?"

"Ten to fourteen inches."

Bocca flipped the diamond over and read the inscription. He studied it for several moments before looking up at Sacca. Sacca saw rage in Bocca's eyes. He was both shaken and disturbed by Bocca's reaction.

Then Bocca started repeating, "Catherine West. Catherine West. Catherine West."

"I don't understand," Sacca said, bewildered.

Bocca was now walking around the room, still repeating her name. He held the diamond to his chest and repeated her name several more times.

"Do you know this name?" Bocca said.

"No," said Sacca. "I have read its inscription, as you have, but I have no idea who she is, or was."

Bocca went and sat down, still holding the necklace in his hand. "I want you to tell me everything you know concerning this neck-

397

lace," Bocca demanded. "You can leave the pike out of it. Tell me where you really obtained it."

Sacca was beginning to sweat. He could feel his visit backfiring. He had not anticipated this ungrateful reception on Bocca's part. To the contrary, he'd envisioned Bocca would be ecstatic upon receiving such a gift. He could not figure out Bocca's negative mood after seeing the necklace. His instincts told him he'd have to choose his answers very carefully. The question was, should he make up some wild story about the necklace to satisfy Bocca, or simply relay the story as Belmonte had told it to him?

To hell with it, he finally decided. I'll tell it the way I heard it.

For the next half hour Bocca sat transfixed, clutching the necklace to his chest, as Sacca, laboriously at first, repeated Belmonte's story of the long-ago bungled MacEntyre jewel heist. At the point where Gaspary's stiletto pierced Catherine West's neck, Sacca saw Bocca wince and press the necklace tighter against this chest. It was, Sacca thought, as if I was describing the death of one of Bocca's close relatives.

The silence of the drawing room, save for Sacca's monologue, was frightening. Sacca finished his story, purposely omitting the part about catching the pike. Bocca was silent, motionless. Sacca felt the tension growing. Beads of sweat now trickled beneath his wool suit. Suddenly Bocca sprang at Sacca, grabbing him by the lapels and lifting him off his seat with a strength and force Sacca had not thought him capable of.

"You killed her, didn't you?" Bocca screamed, his face a snarling, raging mass.

Sacca now tried to twist away as Bocca's hands began to wrap around his neck. Bocca was spitting and hissing words that were incomprehensible. Sacca expected one of Bocca's men to come in at any second, but none appeared. The two were now locked in a death dance, Bocca trying to strangle Sacca, and Sacca, at first, trying only to defend himself.

Their tussling moved them from the drawing room through the large connecting door to Bocca's office. Sacca, on the verge of collapse and gasping for air, spun Bocca to one side, breaking his grip temporarily. Just when it seemed that Bocca was incapable of continuing his assault, he lunged again and caught Sacca's neck. This time Sacca fought back. Bringing his right knee between Bocca's legs in one swift move that sent Bocca tumbling backward. Bocca's feet caught on a small magazine rack near his desk, and in the next instant, Sacca saw him fall to one side. The weight of

Bocca's body came crashing down on his desk. He bounced back and stood for a moment, then fell to the floor. Sacca, panting, steadied himself against the wall. Seconds went by and Bocca didn't move. Sacca realized that the only sound in the office was his own labored breathing. He knelt down and put his finger on Bocca's throat.

The Don was dead, still holding Catherine West's necklace in his fist. Sacca plied open Bocca's fingers and pulled the necklace free. Sacca quickly snapped it back under his own gold neck chain.

Panic was now starting to set in. Sacca was dripping wet beneath his suit and his hands shook violently. It had all happened so suddenly, so violently.

"I'm as good as dead," he thought.

His brain just wouldn't function. In the old days he'd have taken this all in stride, Bocca or no Bocca. He knew, however, he must act. He lifted Bocca into his desk chair and propped him up, sticking the telephone in his right hand and bending the arm so it appeared Bocca was making a call. Bocca, in this position, appeared quite natural. Sacca wiped the perspiration from his own forehead and straightened out his suit and tie. Mustering up all the courage and poise he was capable of, Sacca walked to the closed office door, opened it and stepped out to the large hallway where two of Bocca's men waited.

With the two guards looking on, Sacca simply called over his shoulder, "Thank you, Don Bocca, I'll be in touch." Sacca then closed the office door. He continued to walk calmly toward the front entrance. One of Bocca's men opened the office door and peered in. When he saw Bocca on the phone, he closed it again.

The train from Hudson was on time. In fact, it was running five minutes ahead of schedule. A welcome relief for Sacca, who paced up and down within the small station, his body still damp and shaky from the day's deadly episode. It wasn't until Sacca's train had arrived at Rensselear and had departed for Saratoga that Bocca's men discovered the Don was dead. Tommy Testo, one of Bocca's lieutenants, made a call to New York City to inform the commission of Bocca's death. His next call was to Lamar Tocco in Lake Luzerne.

"The old bastard is dead," he told Tocco. "I've informed the commission. We can't figure what happened. Some old family member, Albert Sacca, was visiting with him. He appeared okay after Sacca left, but we later found him dead at his desk. Probably a heart attack. Anyway, good riddance. The commission will no doubt appoint a new Don, but we're going along with your plans. Keep in touch."

"The timing could not have been better," Tocco said. "It now looks as if the New York State Legislature will be pushing for legalized gambling in Saratoga. No need for the family to muscle its way into gaming. We've got enough political clout to get in legally once its passed. Bocca never accepted this premise. We do, however, have some problems. We've captured two private investigators up here. Neither is talking, but I'd say they work for Harry Waite's operation in New York. My renegades are holding them at their encampment right now. They'll be playing some special games up there. I hope Harry's two friends can run fast. My renegades have some unique ways of loosening up one's tongue. Ever try running over hot coals in bare feet? Or dashing naked past fifty or so club wielding renegades? Our two guests will talk soon. I can assure you that."

"How about Sacca?" Testa asked.

"Never mind," replied Tocco. "Let him go. Think of it, he did us a favor. Probably filled Bocca's heart with so much nostalgia, it broke."

"Will you be attending your uncle's funeral?" Testa asked.

"No," said Tocco. "I'd be apt to spit on his grave. Tell the members of the commission I'm indisposed. Tell them anything but the truth."

"The old casino in the park he always talked about? Will we ever get it?" Testa asked.

Tocco laughed. "I'd say it's a dream that died today with Bocca. It was only a dream. The Canfield Casino, the one he talked about, is no prize. The real prize we're seeking is not Saratoga's past glory, but its future gaming potential. Remember, Tommy, we don't have to shoot our way into the action. The men in Albany who write the laws are for sale. Money talks and B.S. walks. Hang tight, a new election is coming. We'll hire more lobbyists and fewer hit men."

On his way north, Albert Sacca, with only thirty dollars to his name, was trying to figure his next move. He knew he had a lot to worry about. First of all, he deemed Bocca's men would come looking for him. Secondly, the strange men at Lake Lonely would certainly be back. So he decided he couldn't return to his shack or Lake Lonely. Where else could he go? He was very despondent. As the train neared Saratoga, Albert looked out the window and beheld the Vermont mountains he'd seen on his departure. This time they appeared much darker, longer in length and perhaps farther away than before.

I'll go to Vermont, he told himself. Why not? Fewer people over there. More rural than urban. I can hide out in any number of Vermont locations. Thirty dollars won't last me long, but I'll latch onto something there.

He felt the necklace against his chest. The silliness of it all, he thought. The MacEntyre jewel of the century, worth a million or more, and not a prayer of fencing it. And he wondered what had brought so much outrage from Bocca upon seeing it? Who was Catherine West to Bocca? Why such emotion over a gem lost so long ago? The answer to these questions, like so many other unanswered questions in his life, would haunt him to the end of his days. Of that he was certain.

30. FEDS, TOO

Tom Nealy's hasty phone call to Eric Thomas touched off a chain of events that even Nealy had not thought possible. Instead of getting help from the state police, Nealy found himself dealing with a whole array of law enforcement units, including special agents from the FBI, the Immigration and Naturalization Service, and several personnel from the Department of the Interior and Indian Affairs. Supplementing these unwanted federal men, Nealy's call also prompted the governor to call out National Guard helicopter gunships stationed at Albany International Airport. Try as he may, Nealy could not stop all the involvement.

By the time he finally reached the governor's point man, Philip Roth, the helicopters, filled with combat-ready troops, were already on their way to the renegade encampment near Auriesville. A dozen or more state police cars were en route via the New York State Thruway and at least three state police boats were speeding west up the Mohawk River from

Schenectady, while another made its way east from Utica. To Nealy's amazement, the only group not headed to the potential battle scene was the news media. All communication had been transmitted by code, not radio, so the media were caught unaware. Nealy wasn't even sure if the Amsterdam Police Department had been alerted. He could just picture the jurisdictional uproar over this campaign.

Things might get so confused during the assault, they all might wind up fighting one another while the renegades run away, Nealy mused.

The chief was beside himself with worry as he, Blake, Duffy and Farrell raced over Route 29 from Saratoga westward toward Amsterdam, hoping to reach the area ahead of everyone else. Waite and Stewart were in a jeep, right on Nealy's tail. Earlier, Waite warned Nealy that any show of force would most certainly endanger Flint and E.N., if they were still alive. Nealy said he was well aware of this possibility and had notified Eric Thomas of it. But things had been put into motion before all parties could be properly told of Flint's and E.N.'s precarious position.

Another impediment, as Nealy saw it, was the fact that no one knew exactly where the renegades were holed up. Once located, would it be possible for gunships to maneuver there? Would the troops be able to negotiate the terrain effectively? On the bumpy, curvy drive to Amsterdam, each one had his say on how the situation should be resolved. Duffy said the best thing they could do at this point is say a prayer and hope for the best. As Nealy's car crossed the Amsterdam Bridge above the Mohawk River, Blake spotted the first three of ten helicopters in the sky to their right.

"Looks like we're a bit late, Tom," Blake said, keeping his eyes on the gunships.

"Hang on," shouted Nealy, as he raced right through the toll booth, past a startled toll collector, and headed west on the Thruway.

"What in hell are we doing on the Thruway?" Duffy demanded. "Didn't you say the camp was somewhere close to the river?"

"I did," acknowledged Nealy. "But there's no road over there. "I figured we'd get as near to the crossover point as possible and try to snare a boat ride."

Farrell leaned forward. "We don't have a location. So where is the cross over point?"

"Damned if I know," Nealy admitted. "I'm doing the best I can. By the time those gunships start firing away, there'll be a second Erie Canal dug in those hills. You got a better idea?"

"Yeah," said Farrell. "Let's commandeer one

of the state's canal launches. The next stop is Fonda. We'll lose some time, but I can't think of anything else."

Nealy reached for his car phone. "Maybe I can contact Thomas once more. If he'll suspend operations until we get into place, we might be able to negotiate with the renegades before the shooting starts."

Nealy heard two rings, a pause, then two more rings. Finally a man's voice came on the line. "Thomas here. Who's calling?"

"Tom Nealy. Is this you, Eric?"

"Yes," replied Thomas over the drone of the helicopter he was flying in.

"Don't commit to any action just now," Nealy warned. "We have a friendly person among those renegades. We'd like to see if we can get him out before the fireworks start."

"Not sure I can do anything about it now," said Thomas. "The lead ship is zeroing in on their positions as I speak. We've dropped off some assault troops at both ends of the valley. It just may be too late."

Nealy turned to Blake. "They're going in and there's really no way I can stop them."

Blake grabbed the phone. "Eric, this is Arnold Blake. I see no reason for a firefight at this time. Where in hell can they escape to? Once they know they're pinned down, they'll surrender. Get hold of that National Guard commander and tell him to cease operations."

Suddenly the transmission was lost. Blake handed the phone again to Nealy. "We've lost contact."

Nealy quickly dialed an alternate number. It rang through, but was jammed with noise on the receiving end. "Damn it to hell," Nealy said, "I can't hear a thing over the choppers."

"What did they say?" asked Duffy.

"Nothing," said Nealy. "I believe the fight is on. At least it's beginning. Flint is probably right in the middle of it."

They were almost at the bridge to Fonda. They could see the helicopters hovering in the distance, just south of the river. They couldn't tell if the guns were in use.

"Roll down the window," shouted Farrell. "I'll see if I can hear them firing."

Duffy cocked a hand to his right ear. "I can't hear anything. How about you, Billy?"

"No," said Farrell, his head halfway out the window. "Not a sound. Perhaps they're too far away. Christ, this is frustrating."

Once in Fonda, Nealy headed straight for the state boat facility. They had to argue their way into using one of the small blue and gold buoy tenders. And it wasn't until Nealy had made a call directly to the Governor's office in

Albany that they were able to board the boat. Blake estimated they'd lost a good half hour in the process.

Nealy ordered the boat attendant to go full throttle once underway. Twenty-five minutes later they arrived at a scene reminiscent of a small amphibious invasion. Troopers, National Guardsmen, an FBI swat team, and all the backup federal personnel were scrambling about on the shore. Flying in and out of the hills were the helicopter gunships.

Nealy found Eric Thomas's second in command, Todd Freeman, from Troop G Headquarters, and called him aside.

"Listen, Todd, we have to back off this assault immediately. I already called Eric and told him we may have a close associate trapped up there with the renegades. We have good reason to believe they captured him several days ago."

"Who would that be?" said Freeman.

Nealy shot a glance at Blake. "A close friend. That's all I can tell you right now."

"Not good enough," snapped Freeman, waving his arms as he directed some troopers to move inland. "My orders call for taking this ragtag bunch as quickly as possible. The choppers won't fire unless it's necessary. But I can tell you this, the ground for miles around will shake from those giant twirling blades. That's what we're counting on. Scare the fools right out of their wits. If that doesn't work, we may have to fire a few rounds or take the chance on them escaping. You got a better idea?"

"Yeah," Nealy said. "Let us go up first and see if we can talk them down."

Freeman looked at Nealy and smiled. "From what I know of this group's history, they'll use you for target practice. It's your hide, if you want to take the chance. I'll call Eric and see what he says."

"I'll talk to him myself," Nealy said.

He no sooner said it when two of the helicopters came screeching low around one of the hills at a forty-five degree angle. As they flew overhead, Nealy saw Eric Thomas's face appear in the co-pilot's side. He was waving at Nealy.

Freeman made contact with Thomas as the chopper dipped to one side and swiftly flew along the north bank of the Mohawk no more than ten feet above the treetops.

"Eric, can you hear me?"

"Barely," replied Thomas.

"Nealy wants to talk."

"So, it *was* Tom Nealy I spotted down there."

Nealy took the phone. "Look, Eric, I want to talk to the renegades before we use all this force. You've buzzed them sufficiently for now. They've gotten the message by now. From what I can see, they haven't elected to shoot at anyone. The FBI swat team is still in place here. I don't believe these government units want to take any action until you've exhausted your options. Give me one hour. If I can't get them to release my friend, you can do what you want with them. Is it a deal?"

"I'd say you'll be wasting your time, and maybe your life, by trying to talk to them, Tom. It's against my better judgment, but I'll hold off for thirty minutes. No longer."

"Thanks," Nealy said. "I may borrow three of your troopers for backup. Aside from that, I think we can handle it."

"I have three very qualified swat team members assigned to Freeman's detachment. Use them, but be damn careful, Tom. These guys are dug in and very well camouflaged. We've sighted their shacks, tents and what appears to be a long house, but we haven't seen a soul. They may be spread out and waiting to ambush. Who knows how heavily armed they are. Just go easy. We'll be right behind you if things backfire."

Nealy decided he and Blake would make the walk into the renegade camp carrying a white flag. The swat team would follow at a distance of fifty yards during the difficult climb. The aging Duffy and Farrell stayed reluctantly behind. Duffy complained it wasn't fair that he not participate, and told Nealy and Blake he could make the climb as well as anyone, provided he was allowed to set the pace. To which Farrell, remembering the last time he and Duffy had made a hike, remarked that Duffy's pace was one step per minute, and faulty at that. Nealy put them in charge of a two-way radio, with instructions not to speak unless he made contact with them first. A rising sun brightened the gray morning light as Nealy and Blake began their hike.

At Thomas's insistence, the helicopter squadron landed in a farm field some five miles away. All the other assembled assault teams waited at the ready in various locations near the river. It was now up to Nealy and Blake.

The two men made their way along a stream which, according to their topographical maps, apparently originated in the high country beyond the rocky wedge where the renegades were positioned. The land became gradually steeper and the brush thicker as they moved along. Eventually they crossed over the stream and began hiking in the direction of the tall, black rock cliff, which Nealy guessed was the beginning of the opening to the wedge.

Nealy instructed the three assisting troopers to stay back, and only come if he called for them. From the map, Nealy figured the wedge grew wider at the upper end, possibly closing again at some distant point that wasn't clearly defined on the map. Blake read the map and came to the same conclusion. Fifteen minutes into their hike, they stopped to listen.

A few bird calls were all they heard. Five minutes later they stopped again to listen. This time Blake thought he heard a waterfall. Nealy disagreed, saying he was sure it was a trick the wind played blowing through the wedge. Not certain who was right, they moved forward.

On the ridge of a small rise they had just climbed, Nealy looked up. From this vantage point he could see the big opening between the rock ledges. He called to Blake. "That's it. I believe that's it."

Blake came forward to have a look. "I think you're right. Do you think they can see our white flag way down here?"

"If not, we'll raise it," said Nealy. "Maybe even climb a tree and wave it."

Nealy started for a hard maple tree just ahead. As he stepped onto a lower branch, the earth beneath his feet suddenly trembled. Blake wheeled around just in time to see two large puffs of smoke rise between the wedge, followed by a deafening, ear-shattering explosion. Nealy ducked as flying pieces of rock ledge sailed past him. Blake took cover under a fallen elm.

"Saints save us," yelled Nealy. "I thought he was going to hold the choppers off. We'll all get killed now."

Blake crawled out from under the elm. "No, it wasn't the choppers. Sounded more like a giant firecracker. Besides, I don't see any choppers. Maybe we've been spotted. I hope they respect the truce flag."

A second explosion sent them both diving for cover. When it settled down, Nealy was the first to rise. "You're right, Arnold. Those aren't firecrackers, though. Someone's blasting rock up there. I'd say it's dynamite. I've been around enough road construction and mining operations in my time to know the difference. I bet the renegades are trying to close the trail through the wedge, at least on this side. If that's the case, then they must have an escape route east of here. If they're on the run, Thomas may have to use the choppers."

Nealy was just about to call Duffy when they heard a loud rumbling coming from the wedge. Blake climbed up on a boulder to have a look. At a distance of about one hundred and eighty yards, Blake saw what he believed to be several motorcycles or dirt bikes climbing a steep path. "They're high-tailing it south," he called to Nealy. "Have Duffy inform Thomas. We'll lose them all if they get out of the wedge and into the dense forest area."

"If they're running, I doubt they're taking Flint. This doesn't look good," said Nealy, trying desperately to contact Duffy.

"Let's get up there," Blake said.

They started out once more, Nealy leading the way. The terrain became more difficult with each step. Blake lost his footing and slipped backward, but luckily regained it by grabbing a small tree. They made their way over several rock fields and were almost to the lip of the wedge when four new explosions interrupted their climb. The noise pierced their ears with such vibration that Nealy fell down. Blake ducked behind a boulder. A spray of fine stones fell on them. Shortly after, they clearly heard the motor bikes revving up again. Nealy tried reaching Duffy once more. It gave one soft ring and shut off.

"Can't get through," he declared.

"Try changing the frequency," Blake said.

"Won't work. I'm locked on one radio band."

"Well," Blake sighed, "it appears we're too late."

They waited for more explosions, but none came. Nealy, again on his feet, started climbing slowly upward. Blake followed.

"Wait," Nealy called out. "Did you hear a woman's voice?"

"No. Nothing."

"I swear I heard it."

They stood motionless, listening. The droning motor bikes could be heard, though faintly. Nothing else.

Nealy cupped his ear with one hand. "I definitely heard a female voice."

"The wind plays tricks up here," said Blake.

"It wasn't the wind. I'm losing a lot of my senses lately, but my hearing is still acute. I know a female voice when I hear one."

Suddenly, from the trail just above them, Sandy and Monica appeared. Blake and Nealy were speechless as the two, dressed in dirt-covered camouflage suits, came directly at them. Nealy found himself climbing hurriedly toward the two. When Sandy and Monica saw Nealy and Blake, they let out a scream.

"Good God, where did you come from?" Sandy asked excitedly.

Blake, still not believing his eyes, replied, "Better question: Where did *you* come from?"

Sandy ran up to Blake. "There's no time to explain now. Let's get out of here first."

"But what about Flint?" snapped Nealy.

"Mike is fine. So is E.N. They're safe, that's

all I can tell you now."

"What about the renegades?" asked Nealy. "Have they left?"

Sandy gave Nealy a blank stare. "I don't know, and I don't care. We did what we came to do, and that was to free Mike." Sandy pointed to Monica. "That includes Monica. Neither of you has met Monica in person. I'll explain when we get to safer ground. Now let's move out."

The hike back down to the Mohawk proved tougher on Nealy and Blake, simply because they were wearing street shoes whereas Sandy and Monica had hiking boots. At one point, Nealy had to sit down and rest his legs. He also tried to make contact with Duffy, but still couldn't get through. Five minutes later, however, they all saw the helicopters flying to the south.

"I guess Thomas finally saw the renegades retreating," Nealy said cheerfully. "Maybe we haven't lost them yet."

"Where are we going?" said Monica.

Nealy turned around. "There's a command post on the Mohawk, just east of Auriesville. You name it, every law enforcement contingent east of the Rockies is there. They'll certainly want to know where you two came from."

"I'll gladly tell them," interrupted Sandy. "We were on a hike and ran into the renegades.

That's all I'll tell 'em. Not a word about Mike or E.N." She looked around. "None of us will, will we?"

A big grin appeared on Blake's face. "Never heard of Mike Flint or E.N. How about you, Tom?"

"Same here," replied Nealy.

A smothering white mist was rolling in off the Mohawk as the four finally reached the command post. A light rain began falling. Duffy, apparently bewildered and shocked at seeing Sandy, didn't know whether to hug her or scold her. It was only with Nealy's quick intervention that Duffy was pulled aside and told to say nothing about Flint in the mixed group. Duffy was baffled by Monica's presence, but avoided any inquiry as to her involvement, or who she actually was.

Nealy learned firsthand from Thomas the renegades had a secret tunnel escape route from the wedge that was never identified on any map, and that they were in hot pursuit of the group, all fleeing on an assortment of dirt bikes and all-terrain vehicles. The helicopters were following them, but weren't firing. It was, according to Thomas, a foregone conclusion that the renegades had nowhere to go. Reinforcements already had been brought in from elsewhere to intercept them in any direction. The Bureau of

Indian Affairs was in charge from now on.

Nealy and Blake took advantage of the post-assault confusion to vacate the area, taking Sandy and Monica with them on the buoy tender back to Fonda. A glaring afternoon sun lifted the earlier mist off the river. Everyone seemed content to say nothing and just let the trauma of the day dissipate. Duffy, with his editor's curiosity boiling over, was prompted to ask Sandy, "How did they ever snatch you from my house?" To which Sandy, in a sweet, yet firm, voice replied, "They took me out through the chimney."

Monica, her long, dark lashes streaked with dirt from the day's ordeal, came over to Duffy and introduced herself. "So this is the famous newspaperman I've heard so much about. It's my pleasure."

"Ah, yes. You're the Hollywood one, aren't you?" Duffy said. "The actress that helped nurse Flint back to good health after his beating in Quebec by St. Jacques." He looked over at Sandy. "On second thought, I have an old editor's gut feeling you weren't snatched from my house. Would it be fair to say that you two ladies took it upon yourselves to go find Mike Flint and E.N. on your own? Or perhaps had some help in doing so?"

"A rather perceptive observation on your

part, Duffy," Sandy said.

"And if someone helped you, who might that someone be?" he inquired.

Sandy put her finger to her lips. "A name not to be revealed. Like all mysteries, there must be a nameless figure. What really matters is that Mike and E.N. are safe. Who gets the credit is irrelevant and immaterial."

The buoy tender was about to dock, and they all moved forward. Duffy, still hanging onto Sandy's parting remarks, called over to her. "Perhaps one day you'll tell me?"

31. LUCKY FORAY

Running Swift's single handed foray into the renegade camp to free Flint and E.N. after carefully placing and setting off the dynamite sticks had been successful, due primarily to luck and happenstance. The explosions did cause sufficient confusion so that he was able to slip in behind the defenders to begin his search. It wasn't until he was inside the encampment for some five minutes that he realized the renegades, after first being disorganized, quickly regrouped and were aware of the explosions.

His two main concerns when this happened were for Sandy and Monica, who might get caught, and his inability to establish if Flint and E.N. were indeed in the camp. Time was working against him. The situation might have proven fatal had it not been for the appearance of the helicopters. Then, and only then, did the renegades begin to scatter in earnest, eventually leaving by any means they could to run for safety.

Running Swift made his way to several small shacks and tents, but found nothing.

When the renegades made their grand exodus on motor bikes and ATVs, Running Swift made a dash for the long house. He knifed his way through the tightly stretched polywrap cover, and straight into the arms of the lone, startled guard who jumped back, dropped his rifle, and ran for his life. If the guard called for help, Running Swift didn't hear him. Nor, for that matter, could anyone else hear him over the roar of the renegades, the choppers, and all the motor bikes.

It was obvious to Running Swift that whatever solidarity existed at the camp prior to his arrival had quickly turned into a case of every man for himself. Running Swift found Flint and E.N. in a corner with their hands and feet tied. Of the two, Flint looked the scrubbiest. He had only Sandy's brief description of Flint to go by, but Sandy had described him to a tee. Running Swift had no description of E.N., but it had to be him. Having been abused for several days by the renegades, both Flint and E.N. didn't know what to make of Running Swift's sudden appearance. They would later joke about his rescue, claiming he looked more renegade than the renegades.

Running Swift then guided the two out of

the camp, taking a circuitous route that provided ample cover from any stray fleeing renegades or the circling choppers. Flint, after being told by Running Swift of Sandy's and
Monica's involvement, was reluctant to go without them. It took all the powers of persuasion
Running Swift could muster to convince him
he had to go.

Otherwise, he'd compromise E.N's and
Running Swift's identity to the authorities at
the command post, not to mention his own.
The circling, rugged footpath Running Swift
led them over ended at a secluded dirt road
where a car was waiting. Neither Flint nor E.N.
questioned who the driver was, and Running
Swift, short on words, didn't tell them. Flint,
however, figured he was a fellow Onondaga
from the Six Nations.

They drove by way of back roads to
Saratoga, actually returning long before Nealy
and the rest arrived. Once in Saratoga, with a
chance to clean up at a home occupied by a
friend of Running Swift, the three went their
separate ways. Flint wisely avoided the
Sheraton Inn and went directly to Blake's home,
waiting in the doctor's garden gazebo. E.N.
asked that he be taken to the Saratoga bus station where, within the hour, he was safely on a
bus back to Vermont. By the time Nealy drove

into Saratoga, Running Swift and his anonymous driver were a good fifty miles north of Saratoga on their way home to the Six Nations.

Nealy, after dropping Farrell off, cut across town to Duffy's home, where he left off Sandy, Monica and Duffy. He then had a short talk with Dr. Blake before taking him home. There was no doubt in Nealy's mind that the heat would be turned up once the renegades were caught. What he and Blake discussed was the possibility that any one of the renegades, faced with a stiff jail sentence, might break down and confess who and what was taking place at their encampment. If this happened, the names of Flint and E.N. might be mentioned, which would leave Nealy in a very delicate position with the state police and federal agencies. It was, as he told Blake, a legal and political tap-dance he didn't want to perform.

"Well," Blake suggested. "You can always avoid it."

"How's that?" said Nealy.

"Easy. You can resign and enjoy the rest of your life, like you should have done at least five years ago."

"Sure," Nealy nodded. "Duffy can retire, too. Then we two, along with Farrell, can go fishing every day. Better yet, I'll retire when you do, Doc. We'll all go fishing. And speaking of fishing, I understand Glen Stewart wasn't able to speak again to that Albert Sacca. I have to check with Glen about him."

"It's been a long day, Tom. Let's meet sometime tomorrow."

Blake waited near the curb as Nealy drove away. The late afternoon sun peaked between the tree branches, casting a mixture of light and dark shadows on the mansion's early budding spring landscape. Blake decided he'd walk about the grounds before going inside. He made a mental note to have the front hedges trimmed and the side yard cherry trees pruned. The faded patch of grass on the lawn's south side also needed attention. He'd have to take a day off to get to these tasks. It was just a matter of when.

He strolled along the narrow rear walk leading to the back door, past the wooden rose garden trellises and then near the gazebo.

"Arnold, is that you?" Flint called out.

Blake spun around, completely surprised. "Mike! Where in hell did you come from?"

Flint emerged from the gazebo. "I make a habit out of hiding in gazebos."

"You can't know how relieved I am to see you," said Blake, putting his hands on Flint's shoulders while studying his scrubby, bearded face. "We just left Sandy and Monica. She said you were safe, but gave us no details."

Flint looked puzzled. "You were with her on the raid near Auriesville?"

"Kind of," replied Blake. " We…that is Nealy and I, were late arrivals. You know, you have one very brave woman for a companion and I'll have to give Monica her due, also. Those two went up that canyon pass to rescue you from the renegades. Imagine it, those two taking it upon themselves to go in there. We haven't the slightest idea how they got you out. Nealy and I met them on the trail just short of the camp. The renegades were scattering by that time. We heard explosions prior to meeting Sandy and Monica. We weren't expecting National Guard helicopters to take part in the rescue. Eric Thomas of the New York State Police precipitated that action. In retrospect, though, the choppers' presence was enough to scare them off. Come to think of it, how did you get out of there without being spotted by the chopper pilots?"

"I'd tell you if I could," said Flint. "But I can't. I hope you'll accept that answer."

Blake rubbed his hands together and nodded his head. "It's your business, Mike. Forget I asked. Can I bring you inside for a drink?"

"I'll take a rain check, Doc. I really want to see Sandy," Flint said. "I don't want to see her

at Duffy's. Can you fix us up with a more secluded place for a rendezvous?"

"Consider it done," Blake said.

"I'll need some transportation," Flint reminded him.

Blake jangled some keys in his pocket. "I
have two vehicles. Take your pick."

It took Blake a half hour to set Flint and
Sandy up at a friend's cottage across town.
There they could have all the privacy they de-
sired. Blake then called Duffy's house and told
Sandy he wanted to see her within the hour.
Then he remembered that Monica was still at
Duffy's.

"I want to see you alone," said Blake. "I
hope Monica won't be offended by not being
included?"

"No problem," said Sandy. "Besides, Monica
went over to her place ten minutes ago.

"Good then," Blake assured her. "I'll pick
you up shortly."

"Wait," Sandy said anxiously. "Is it news
about Mike?"

"Could be," replied Blake. "I'll tell you when
I get there. I'm not including the Duffys in this
either. They've already had too long a day for
people their age."

"I'll be discreet," she said. "Just toot and I'll
come out."

On the way across town in Blake's car, the conversation between him and Flint shifted back and forth between Flint's abduction, E.N.'s mysterious role in trying to find him, and varied and complex power plays by Bocca and other unknown factions, all with designs on renewing casino gambling in Saratoga.

There still seemed to be a preponderance of unanswered questions that neither could properly address.

"So where does it stand?" Blake asked.

"I'm not at all sure," Flint said. "If Bocca is still bent on coming back in, it could go on for a long time. But I think now that we've severed the link with his nephew lawyer in Lake Luzerne, he may have second thoughts. Bocca has no other route to take. He knew he'd never make a return to casino gaming here in the conventional mob pattern. Tocco was the key. He had the one thing Bocca needed most."

"What was that?"

"Legitimacy," answered Flint. "All the time I was being held at the encampment, I kept telling myself that if and when I got free - and it was always a big if - the first thing I'd do is find out how many Saratoga real estate transactions were being handled by Tocco. I'd bet a sawbuck on it now, that every strategic piece of property short of the race course itself is being purchased by mob money, with Tocco's office processing all the transactions. Bocca considered the fact that three councilmen sought to vote against gambling a temporary stumbling block. Of course he bungled it by trying to rub two of them out, which got us all caught up in the mess to begin with.

"From what little I know of Tocco, I believe he was at odds with his uncle on both the method and means. So now, with Tocco on the run along with his co-conspiring renegades, Bocca is, I'd say, quite stymied at this juncture. With the New York State Legislature being pressured to pass a gaming bill within the next year or two, Tocco's approach would have worked. The mob's money and political clout would have assured them a casino or two in Saratoga. I see it this way. The Indian-run casinos have bitten too deeply into state revenues. Turning Stone between Utica and Syracuse alone is the biggest single cash cow in those parts. The Governor wants to leap-frog from Albany to Washington in two years. If he can ram a gaming bill through the legislature, and put some money into those depressed upstate communities, it'll help his cause. Right now the only economic stimulus he's had to offer them is more prisons..."

"Hold it," said Blake. "I have a beeper message." He checked the number. "It's Nealy."

Blake picked up his cell phone and punched up Nealy.

Flint reached over and grabbed his wrist. "Don't mention I'm with you."

Nealy came on line.

"What's up, Tom?"

Blake's face tightened. "God, no! When did this happen?" He stared over at Flint and shook his head. "Are you certain it was Bocca? This will change things. Okay, Tom, I'll talk to you later."

"They've arrested Bocca?" inquired Flint.

"No," said Blake clipping the phone to dashboard holder. "Bocca is dead."

"Dead?"

"Yes. Nealy just got the news."

"Well," Flint speculated. "The circumstances of his demise are important now. If he was knocked off by rivals, then we know we're playing with more than one deck. If he died of natural causes, then we will be dealing with his successor, whoever that may be. Right now I need to be with Sandy. But I want to know as soon as possible how Bocca died."

"What are you going to do about Tocco?" Blake said.

"I think E.N.'s reports, whenever they catch up to Harry, will seal Tocco's fate. Though

Harry just may want to let Tocco operate for a while, so he can trace any loose ends that E.N. may have missed. But then again, one of the renegades may blow his cover during interrogation. In this game you never know where things will end up. That's what makes it exciting and so interesting. Look how it's kept me entertained all these years."

"Some fun," remarked Blake. "Speaking of entertainment, I wonder how old Judge Gibson is doing. I've had no phone calls from his wife. And the ghostly daughter...what can one make of her?"

"I'm not so sure she is a ghost," Flint thoughtfully reflected.

"Oh, then you have given her some thought since we made our visit to the Gibsons?"

"Only in an abstract way. "

"What do you mean?"

"From what I know about ghosts, you may possibly get a momentary glimpse of one here or there. But when they peek back down at you from a window, like when we were leaving Gibson's house, it made me wonder. Then I got to thinking. Who is the last remaining link from Saratoga's former gambling days?"

"Judge Gibson?" Blake guessed.

"Right. A trifle eccentric, perhaps even nuts. But still, Deweys' boys never accounted for the only old timer of any influence who had his pulse on all the money. Money even Meyer Lansky didn't know about, or forgot to grab, in his hasty flight from here in the fifties. It all ties in very well. Before I leave Saratoga, I want to visit the Gibsons once more. Two-to-one, says Gibson's ghost is in possession of those lost gaming revenue records. Not to mention the millions they represent. Isn't it about time you looked in on the judge's health again?"

"I'll make an appointment this week," said Blake. "Incidentally, who do you think the ghost is?"

"A bad 'guy'," said Flint.

Blake pulled off the road and into the driveway of his friend's cottage. "I'll drop you here, Mike. It shouldn't take me more than twenty minutes to get Sandy. The key's under the backdoor mat."

"Who can I thank for the hospitality?" Flint said.

"A couple who wish to remain nameless."

Flint grinned. "We're very secretive here in Saratoga, aren't we?"

"Mike, I'm still puzzled by a few things," said Blake. "One is the strange happenings when Molly O'Neill was saved from Jake Palermo. If we assume that Palermo was sent by Bocca to kill Molly, and the renegades were

working for Bocca's nephew, Tocco, then who
interceded on Molly's behalf and ultimately
killed old Jake? Wouldn't that point to a third
party no one has yet addressed?"

"You've been reading my thoughts," said
Flint. "I've been trying to put this jigsaw puzzle
together ever since being out-foxed at the tennis courts. Of course that was my own fault. I
see it this way. Bocca, Palermo, Steadman and
Hoag all tie in. So does Tocco and the renegades. We can piece together most of their
actions and motivations. The third party you
allude to – and I now agree there is a third
faction – entered the arena with different motivations. I've tried to figure out why, but there
are no easy answers. This is more up your alley, Doc. I'd like to hear what you have to say."

Blake was looking at his watch. "Remember, Flint, Sandy is waiting."

"So am I, Doc. Still, I'm stuck on this third
party involvement. What's the answer?"

"Good guys," said Blake. "Among all those
bad guys some do-gooders jumped into the fray.
People interested in holding the status quo.
Mind you, this is only an educated guess. I may
be all wrong. But it seems to me, under the cir-
cumstances we've seen so far, that some good
Samaritans had full intention of thwarting
Bocca's dream while protecting the lives of

those persons who had the power to control gaming in Saratoga, namely the city council members. Who are they? Anybody's guess, though I got the impression from Duffy's story that Professor Halfmoon could very well have been one of them. It sounds far fetched, I know, but if still waters run deep, Halfmoon definitely fits that profile. If Halfmoon had associates of similar thought, then they'd be apt to carry out such deeds, even if it meant murder." He looked at Flint. "You wouldn't know anyone fitting that description, would you?"

Flint smiled indulgently. "No, Doc."

"Funny," Blake said. "We were wondering how you got out of the camp?"

"Oh," exclaimed Flint. "I walked out on my own."

"Interesting," said Blake. "We were also trying to guess how Sandy and Monica wound up near the encampment. I suppose they found it all on their own?"

"Can't say, Doc," Flint said. " I haven't talked to her yet, remember?" While speaking, Flint was thinking of Running Swift and his partner. Quiet men, like Halfmoon, thoroughly capable of killing adversaries for a cause they deemed worthy of protecting. The more he thought of Running Swift, the more convinced Flint was that he was the third party Blake was referring to. Flint decided, however, he wouldn't try to prove it. What was the point?

Blake waited until Flint was inside the cottage before driving to get Sandy. He was also wondering how Eric Thomas was making out with the renegades. And what of E.N.'s whereabouts? Flint hadn't volunteered any information about E.N. Almost as if he didn't exist. Perhaps, Blake thought, that was the way it should be. Men like Flint and E.N. lived on the edge, not for fame, but simply because they played the dangerous hands dealt them. Their very survival depended on anonymity in many respects. Blake, always amazed and intrigued by their chancy occupations, couldn't help but admire them.

Back home after dropping off Sandy, Blake found several messages on his answering machine. Five of them hospital-related, three from private patients, and a final long message from Nealy. He skipped over the rest and went right to Nealy's call. As expected, Thomas' men caught all the renegades. At last count there were twenty-seven. Also as expected, some were carrying drugs. Nealy didn't elaborate which kinds. Anyway, Nealy's message said the Feds took control after drugs surfaced.

There was a legal standoff between the state police and the FBI on this issue, but the Feds won out. None of the renegades were talking, and no mention of Flint or E.N. was heard from any of them. So at least for the immediate future, Flint's and E.N.'s identities were safe. Nealy said he'd received a call from Harry and Glen and, as Nealy predicted, no move was made thus far on Tocco in Lake Luzerne. Tocco certainly would have word on the raid, but unless the renegades directly implicated him, his mob identity would go unnoticed for a time.

Harry told Nealy he hoped for a month-long window before Tocco was exposed to the Feds or the media. By that time, Harry was certain he could piece enough evidence together to nail Tocco for good. Nealy signed off by telling Blake that he was damn proud of Sandy and Monica and their attempt to rescue Flint, but still couldn't understand how they got there in the first place. As usual, Nealy wanted to have a mid-morning meeting to discuss it.

Blake chuckled to himself. He had no intention of going to the cottage to disturb Sandy's and Flint's blissful reunion. Of course, he mused, Nealy wouldn't comprehend it. Blake knew it was always business first with Nealy – right or wrong.

32. REUNION

Sandy held Flint's face between her hands and kissed him several times on the forehead, nose and lips. "You had me scared to death," she told him. "I thought I had lost you for good. I'll never let you out of my sight again. That's a promise."

He pressed tightly against her, feeling the passion radiating from her body, smelling the sweet fragrance of her hair and returning her kisses with equally savage hunger.

"It was you who kept me alive," Flint gasped. "When it looked the darkest and I thought they'd surely kill me, I thought of you...only you. I could feel your warmth all around me in that damp, cold long house. At night they'd light a small fire, but it never heated up and smoke filled the interior, making breathing near impossible. E.N. has asthma, and was particularly bothered by the smoke. If your friend Running Swift hadn't come when he did, E.N. would never have made it. Actually, the young guard Running Swift surprised was too scared to shoot us, though he had orders to do so. I didn't know what to make of the explosions. At first E.N. and I figured our captors were going to bury us under a landslide of rocks. Then we heard the helicopters. We knew a rescue was underway. We didn't count on being rescued by an Indian. How strange and bizarre it all was at the time. When Running Swift told us you and Monica were helping him, I felt incredibly humble." Flint kissed her once more and buried his head in her chest. "I never felt that loved before," he admitted.

"It was that way from the very start," she said. "Don't you know I'd follow you to earth's end if necessary? I love you."

Flint released her and held up her face in the palm of his right hand. "I behold the most beautiful face in creation," he whispered. "The most striking eyes and the most gorgeous, fairest skin of any woman living. And if that sounds pathetically mushy, I'll repeat it."

"OK, repeat it," she giggled.

* * *

The night was no longer young.

"Strange," Flint added. " I still have the feeling I overlooked one of the players. It's been gnawing at me for days. I'm having a difficult time sorting it out. Somewhere in this Spa City one of the bad guys is still on the loose. Probably having a big belly laugh at all our stupidity. Just sitting and waiting until this all blows over."

"Who would that be?" Sandy asked.

He cupped her hands in his and kissed her fingers. Staring into the fireplace, he asked her, "Do you believe in ghosts, my love?"

"Believe in what?" she said with a startled expression.

"Ghost. Spirits. The kind that haunt houses."

She touched the end of his nose with one finger. "Only if they're nice ghosts. I don't like the spooky variety."

"Well," said Flint rising to his feet. "I may have to visit a ghost over on Circular Street to satisfy my suspicions."

He felt Sandy's hand go cold in his. She also rose and walked to the other side of the room. "It's not over yet, Mike, is it?" she asked, her words coming in an icy tone.

"I really don't know," he said. "I honestly wish it were over, that we could pack it in and leave the cleanup to Nealy and the rest. But that ghost I mentioned...I have to see for myself if it's real or not."

She poured herself a drink and swallowed it down in one gulp. "This is new to me," she remarked. "It may take getting used to. I've had lots of rivals in my time, but never a ghost. In fact, I'm so intrigued, I want to go have a look. Where is this ghost?"

"In a house owned and occupied by a former Saratoga County Judge Gibson and his wife. I went there with Blake on a house call some-time back. The Gibsons are two old coots who used to be tied into gaming and the mob. The judge is losing his marbles and his wife called Blake. Anyway, we saw a female dressed in white in the upper hallway during our visit. Just a momentary glance before she disappeared into a room. Eileen Gibson never acknowledged her existence. I saw the figure again when we were leaving. It...or she...was staring down at us from behind a curtain. Spooky, wouldn't you say?"

She poked him in the ribs. " Stop it, you're scaring me."

"I'm telling the truth," he insisted.

"On second thought, I'm not going over there. Are you?"

"I have to. Here's the reason. Putting all the facts together, one thing didn't make sense to me. Bocca tried to have Molly O'Neill killed, right? Then Tom Bochard. How come he never made an attempt on the third councilman, John Stark? Stark was a no vote on gaming, along with O'Neill and Bochard. Seems only logical that Bocca would try to rub him out, but he didn't. It may be a wild card on my part, but I think Stark, being the savvy politician he is, figured gambling would come to Saratoga with or without his vote. So politically he did the expected, he voted no. However, behind the scenes, through his real estate firm, he was making deals with Tocco. Just before I was so rudely removed from the tennis club, I was doing some checking on choice Saratoga property transactions. I ran across several key locations handled by Stark's office. And wouldn't you know, they were all potential choice gaming sites."

He held out his glass for Sandy to pour him a drink, then continued. "Now the big kicker. All of the legal work was processed under Louis Gibson's name. The ranting, raving judge who Blake and I had difficulty carrying on a comprehensible conversation with was capable of handling all these legal transactions. Amazing.

"Actually, it's simple when you think about it. Tocco stays out of the limelight. Gibson, nutty as he may be, is still a practicing lawyer, with full knowledge of Saratoga's real estate scene. And, probably still sitting on a ton of old gambling money never collected by the Feds or New York State during the gambling investigations. Probably a lot of the money Meyer Lansky and mob left behind in their farewell to the Spa. They've had no problems laundering this nest egg through Stark's thriving real estate operations, Buying buildings and vacant land through a variety of surrogate operatives.

"Surprisingly, Bocca probably knew nothing of his nephew's double-cross. The Don's obsessive vendetta with enemies, real or imagined, and his myopic view of the present, were his downfall. So now, before we can call this quits, I need to pay one more visit to Gibson's home." He winked at Sandy. "If I'm wrong and Gibson's ghost turns out to be real, I'll probably have the double hex placed on me. Ghosts can do that, you know."

Flint was fully aware of Sandy's sudden mood change. She didn't have to speak. Her furrowed brow and lip-biting grin said it all. He tried to comfort her with a kiss, but she withdrew. She stood for several moments staring at him. Then, setting her glass down, she grabbed his arm and pulled him toward her. "I don't like this one bit," she said, standing so close that he could see his reflection in her luminous eyes. "But no ghost is going to upstage me. Not where you're concerned. So let's go tackle this ghost together."

The urge to make love to her was overpowering. He fumbled for the light switch and finally found it. They moved silently in the dark room, seeking the couch and stumbling into it. Flint's strong hands gently lifting her sweater and trailing down the soft contours of her smooth, firm back. Her fingers brushing back his hair and sliding down his neck, coming to rest on his muscular shoulders. There was nothing to stop their driving, pent-up passion as they melted into each other's arms. Suddenly, Flint was aware of someone knocking on the front door.

"Hell's bells," he whispered. "Who...What...I hope the ghost hasn't come to us."

Sandy, feeling her way across the darkened room, made her way to the bathroom, while Flint went to see who it was. To his surprise, Flint saw Blake standing on the cottage porch. Flint, tucking in his shirt, turned on the porch light and opened the door.

Blake, looking very grave, stepped briskly inside. "Sorry to disturb your blissful reunion," he apologized. "But there's a raging fire over on Circular Street. I picked up the police band on my scanner. It's the Gibsons' home. They say the flames can be seen all the way to the race track."

"The last roll of the dice," Flint said, rubbing his eyes. "There goes my ghost."

"Where's Sandy?" Blake said.

"Powdering her nose, where else?"

Blake blushed. "I'm really sorry, Mike. I thought you'd want to know."

"Let's get over there," said Flint. "I hope the Gibsons are safe. Better yet, I hope my ghost hasn't gone up in smoke." Flint called to Sandy behind the closed bathroom door. "I'm going with Blake. We'll be back shortly, love."

She called for them to wait, but they didn't hear her. By the time she came out Blake's car was pulling away. She slammed the front door shut, cursed them both for leaving her behind, and went into the kitchen and sat down, knowing full well that Flint's "shortly" could mean hours. She poured herself a stiff scotch and turned on the TV. So much for teamwork, she told herself.

She fumbled with the remote control, jumping from one channel to the other, finally realizing it was cable TV with twenty or so channels. Nothing interested her, so she continued to click. Then, as if watching a home video, she saw Flint's face, full and right up close. Right alongside of him was Blake. They were standing on a curb while a horrific fire consumed a large home across the street. She then realized she was watching local news from an Albany station. The excited on-the-scene newscaster said she was reporting live from Circular Street in Saratoga Springs. The camera held steady on both Flint and Blake for at least a half minute before switching to the fire itself. Good God, she thought, since when did Flint start chasing fires? The dreaded thought also crossed her mind that this TV exposure could be harmful to Flint if seen by the wrong people. It thoroughly frightened her, hardly for the first time in the past few days.

At the fire scene, Flint and Blake moved to within fifty feet of the burning mansion. So close, in fact, that hot cinders began falling around them. A nearby fireman called to them.

"Don't be stupid, that place may tumble down any minute." So they retreated back across the street and away from the scorching heat. Within minutes of the fireman's prediction, a loud explosion blew out the west wall of the home. It was followed by a big puff of dark smoke. The firefighters around the mansion all began running, and the building, still aflame, slowly collapsed inward, the roof and side-walls crashing down in a thunderous roar. Fire hoses were then directed to the adjacent homes, wetting them down so they wouldn't catch fire.

One older volunteer firefighter rushed up and gasped, "They never stood a chance. God rest their souls."

Flint tapped him on the shoulder. "The

Gibsons, are they still inside?"

"I'm afraid so," replied the man in heavy, rapid breaths. "Couldn't get to them in time. The old place fired up like kindling. There's lots of tinder boxes like this one in Saratoga. Damn old town, you know."

A short time later, a rescue squad member shouted to his fire chief that the charred bodies of three persons were uncovered. There was a frenzy of activity among the standby TV crews and newspaper photographers for close-up shots. A situation that had Nealy scrambling back and forth in his attempt to keep it as orderly and dignified as possible. None of the dead was identifiable. But three bodies were definitely found. The county medical examiner had all three bodies removed to Albany Medical Center.

Two hours later, with the wet mansion's smoldering remains giving off a dank, eye-watering smell, Flint and Blake, also accompanied by Nealy, waited while some of Nealy's men rummaged through the charred timbers in search of Gibson's safe. The final depository, Flint figured, that would hold the real truth of Gibson's and Stark's real estate dealings. And, as was rumored for years, Gibson's safe no doubt held the long, unaccounted fortune the infamous Meyer Lansky had left behind. It was all Flint could do to keep calm, thinking about what secrets – past and present – the safe might reveal.

All that money, so long ago squandered at the poker tables and roulette wheels by a thousand and one Saratoga revelers, weaving their way from casino to casino in their never-ending quest for sudden riches. How ironic, Flint thought, that it should all come down to this. A lost safe of dreams, buried somewhere beneath a once idolized Spa mansion. He was amazed at his own morbid curiosity in trying to find the safe. It was the same feeling he got the first time he visited a morgue. He had to see the reality of it.

"We can't find a thing," he heard Nealy say. "If it's in this heap, it's buried deep."

Blake came over to Flint. "You'd best make a choice, Mike, the safe or Sandy."

"You're right," Flint said, checking the time. "We need heavy equipment to sift through all this. Let's get a backhoe here in the morning. Besides, I'll feel more comfortable with the media gone."

When Blake finally dropped Flint back at the cottage, Flint invited him in for a drink. Blake gracefully declined the offer.

"Okay," said Flint, leaving Blake's car with the strong smell of smoke on his clothes. "Meet me tomorrow about eight. I hope we can find the safe and settle this matter once and for all."

"Tomorrow it is," said Blake.

On his way up the walk, Flint was trying to think of an appropriate opening line, but couldn't. As he neared the porch, Sandy came down the steps and straight to him. She was holding a drink out for him. "They tell me firemen get very thirsty on the job. Is that so?"

"How did you know?"

"I watch lots of TV."

He took the drink from her. "Okay, okay, so they had it on the news."

"Better than that," she replied. " They had you on the tube."

He eyed her with a smile. "How did I look?"

"To be honest, you looked pretty good. Too damn good, I'd say. I'm not sure showing your puss on TV, local or not, was in your best interest. After all, aren't you supposed to be a secret agent. The kind people hear about but never see?"

He raised an eyebrow and laughed. "Foolish of me, I'll admit," he said. "But who knew they'd be aiming the camera on me and Blake?"

She put one arm over his right shoulder and sipped some of his drink. "You know something, Mr. Flint?" she murmured.

"What is that," he toyed with her.

"We have unfinished business. I hate unfinished business, don't you? Now go take a shower and wash away that terrible smoke, and we'll discuss that unfinished business without interruption this time."

33. SO MUCH FOR GHOSTS

The distinctive bellowing of diesel engines greeted Flint and Blake the next morning upon their arrival at the Gibson home or, as Blake more aptly put it, "The hole that once was the Gibson home."

Nealy and his men had been on site since 7 A.M. blocking off all unauthorized traffic so the backhoe and bulldozer could go to work digging and clearing away the charred remains. Yellow, plastic tape was strung around the home's perimeter. Only people who lived on the block could enter. And even it they did live nearby, they weren't allowed to venture near the fire scene. Nealy had given strict orders regarding site security and a zero tolerance policy was imposed on all would-be trespassers. Disregard the yellow tape, and you'd be arrested. It was that simple. Nealy's insistence in getting the job done was to avoid the scrutiny of any insurance investigators he knew would be prowling about shortly. If the alleged safe was found, Nealy wanted to avoid any complications, legal or otherwise. Opening it was illegal. Impounding it was full of legal uncertainties. So the thought crossed Nealy's mind that should the safe be unearthed, he'd have the backhoe give it one hard whack on the spot where they'd be able to look over its contents before anyone knew what was happening. All very unethical for a police chief, but very necessary, in his opinion; a view shared by Blake and Flint who waited none too patiently for its recovery.

By mid-day, with an ominous looking sky threatening a downpour, the backhoe cleared out the last remaining timbers from the mansion's cellar. The bulldozer pushed the tangled heap of materials to one side and its driver skillfully spread out the pile evenly with the machine's blade. No safe. Not even the traces of a safe. Nealy looked baffled and frustrated. Blake walked over to the hole and peered in. Flint actually jumped down into the hole and poked around with a stick.

"I'm stymied," admitted Nealy, waving the bulldozer driver off.

"Where the hell is it?" said Blake. "It's unlikely we could lose a vintage four-thousand pound Mosler cast iron safe."

"You sure it was that big?" asked Flint, coming back out of the hole.

454

"Quite sure," said Blake. "Didn't you see it in his office during our visit?"

"I saw it all right," said Flint. "I made a mental note of almost everything in that office. But to tell the truth, I didn't think it was still in use. Mosler. Hell, they made those babies in the 1800s, didn't they?"

"It probably outdates the Adelphi Hotel," said Nealy. "This town is full of relics of one nature or another."

Flint paced around the empty foundation trying to figure it out. He stopped on the far side and poked again with his stick. "If the safe dropped, it had to be about here," he suggested, pointing to an area where, as he explained to everyone, Gibson's second-floor office had been located. "Yes," he continued. "I can visualize the four thousand-pound iron box coming right through the floor boards. It had to hit the basement with the force of a meteorite."

"Maybe it's still going," Blake quipped, coming over to where Flint stood. "Very strange, isn't it?"

Flint poked around some more. Then, turning to Blake, he smiled. "I'm afraid we won't find it," he speculated.

"What do you mean by that?"

"I just have a hunch someone's already beat us to it."

455

Blake looked puzzled. "Sure, Mike, they just snatched it up under their arm and walked away with it."

"Something like that," Flint said.

"And who might they be?" asked Blake, shaking his head.

Flint smiled. "Why, the ghost, who else?"

Blake was walking over to Nealy as Flint answered. "You see, Tom, Mike has solved our missing safe mystery for us. He's of the opinion that Gibson's Casper lit off with the safe. Isn't that right, Mike?"

Flint called back across the hollow foundation, " Almost. Almost. Maybe our ghost had a little help, but all the same, the big iron box is gone. I'd say gone for good."

"It's unbelievable," Nealy grumbled. "How'd they get it out?"

"I don't know," replied Flint, "but it wasn't easy. Now we'll never know exactly what took place in this old firetrap. All the past and present secrets went with Gibson's great black vault." Blake kicked up some dark ash with his right foot, and watched pensively as the vapor-like cloud settled back down. The stink of burned timbers, roofing tar and charred paint filled their nostrils.

"Perhaps it's best we don't know," said Blake. "I believe we've had too much mayhem of late. I say let it rest. Racing season will be here in less than three months. Word out of Albany says the legislature has tabled the gambling issue for at least two more years. So we will be spared the agony of fencing off the mob and other hopefuls for now. I hope I'll be happily retired and out of here by the time this whole gambling issue raises its ugly head again." He pointed a finger at Nealy. "And I'm sure you agree with my sentiments, Tom."

"Right on," snapped Nealy.

Flint looked over at Blake. "They'll be back," he said. "Neither the mob nor the politicians are going to let the Indians make all those millions. You'll see casinos open again in the Catskills, and then spread up this way. Saratoga is a natural, we all know that. It may disturb the moralists in 'Toga, but money talks, it always has. Whoever has Gibson's safe will certainly be able to plunk down a sizable chunk of cash on a future gambling venture, wherever that may be." He blinked his eyes and smiled. "No pun intended, but any bets on where that might be?"

Nealy wiped his dry lips. "I've had enough of this. I'm buying drinks if anyone cares to join me. I say we call Duffy and Farrell, too." He reached to his lapel and took off his chief's badge. "There, I'm officially off duty."

"Good idea," said Flint. "I'll fetch Sandy, we'll make it a sextet. Name the place."

"Sperry's," Nealy suggested. "Where else?"

On the way to his cruiser, Nealy heard the phone ring. They waited while he answered it. Nealy nodded his head and sighed. "You don't say. Oh, that's too bad. I'll pass it along." He hung up and paused a moment.

"What is it, Tom?" Blake asked.

"Albany Medical Center has identified the third body." He murmured. "You were right, Mike. It was Stark. Definitely Stark. Of course the judge and his wife were also positively identified." He leaned back on the cruiser and stared at the sky. "Who would have thought it? What a strange partnership."

Blake chuckled. "So much for ghosts."

EPILOGUE

In the twilight of a cool Vermont evening, E.N. stepped off the Amtrak train in Essex Junction. He stood for a full minute breathing in the rarefied air of his adopted state, thankful that he had survived his Auriesville ordeal with Flint and was once more back on less treacherous soil. He wondered if all the Saratoga villains had been caught. He hoped so. He hadn't had a chance to talk to Harry about it, but that would come in time. Right now he was looking forward to a much neglected few days' rest at his cabin overlooking the Winooski River. He'd taken a quick glance at a *New York Daily News* someone had left on the train chronicling Bocca's death. Certainly a big surprise. The timing of it, however, amused E.N.

He was thinking about all the possible consequences of Bocca's passing as he walked along the train platform. At the entrance to the station, a ruddy appearing man in a drab, smelly trench coat brushed by him. The stranger, slightly bent over at the shoulders, turned momentarily to face E.N. Clutched in his right hand was a folded up fishing pole. E.N. stared back at the beady-eyed old man trying to recognize him. The man spun around and walked away, disappearing into a group of high school kids entering the station from the rear door.

E.N. was sure he'd seen the man before, or at least someone who resembled him. He just couldn't place the face with a time and location. One thing was certain, E.N. told himself, the stranger was no Vermonter.